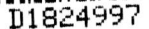

CREATURES
OF THE
STORM

Book One of the Rain Triptych

Brad Munson

A PERMUTED PRESS BOOK

ISBN (trade paperback): 978-1-61868-605-3
ISBN (eBook): 978-1-61868-606-0

CREATURES OF THE STORM
The Rain Triptych Book 1
© 2015 by Brad Munson
All Rights Reserved
For news, new releases, bonus material and more, visit www.bradmunson.com.

Cover art by Christian Bentulan

PERMUTED
PRESS

Permuted Press
109 International Drive, Suite 300
Franklin, TN 37067
http://permutedpress.com

For Alice & Lily

WHAT COMES NEXT

Ken Mackie stood over the body and thought about the last two days.

None of it seemed possible. None of it made sense.

Two days ago he was digging in his dying garden, terrified at the thought of a ringing phone.

Yesterday he was running for his life, escaping from a building as big as a football field, trying to stay alive a little longer as a newborn lake rose around him.

And now he was standing in the driving rain, looking down at a corpse with a hole as big as a dinner plate in its chest, made by a monster that simply hadn't existed hours before.

He fell to his knees as rainwater filled the hollowed body. She had been alive just moments before, grinning, triumphant, ready to go, *go* …

He barely saw the dripping shadow standing over him.

"What do we do now?"

He looked back across the roiling lake of mud at the ruined house he had loved so much. Years of work, shattered now. Sinking.

Rain poured out of the black desert sky, blood-warm and so dense it made him choke on his own breath. He couldn't feel single droplets anymore; it flowed off his head in tiny rivers and disappeared into the darkness.

It will never end, he told himself, and he believed it. *Never.*

They could go north. There was a small chance – a *small* one – that they could avoid the bone spiders and scumbles and needleseeds, all the eyeless and endlessly sharp creatures of the storm. Someone must have escaped from the drowning town in the last three days. Somebody *must* have.

Or they could go south, towards the source of the evil – towards the *thing* that was trying so hard to kill them all.

The sky cracked open and thunder fell like a bludgeon on his shoulders. He cringed under the power of it, still staring at the body as the water rose to cover it forever.

"Please," the looming shadow said again. "Tell me: what are we going to do?"

Ken looked up with empty eyes.

He had no idea.

None at all.

THE FIRST DAY

"Swift as a shadow; short of any dream; brief as the
lightning in the coiled night."

—William Shakespeare,
A Midsummer Night's Dream

ONE

Ken Mackie would always remember where it began: in his failing desert garden under a hazy blanket of spring heat. He had spent more than a year trying to coax something, *anything*, out of that sad patch of dirt behind his sprawling *hacienda*. He had churned a hundred bags of fertilizer into the crumbling soil, he had sown every seed that Dos Hermanos Feed and Grain could find. Hundreds of gallons of water had disappeared into the dust without so much as a stain, like spit on a sponge. And in all the hours he'd spent outdoors, painted in sweat and raising blisters, never once had it actually rained.

Not until today.

It started when he was scratching at the chalky, pale grit and trying to think only of what he was doing at that precise moment: the tool in his hand, the dirt under his nails, the sudden turn of his wrist. The sickly green plant in front of him – what was that, a watermelon vine? A tomato? – looked half-dead now, flattened against the parched earth as if it had been stepped on by a desert boot.

How did I let this happen? he asked himself. He wasn't thinking only of his tiny, ill-advised garden. He meant everything: the stupid contract that had brought him to the ass-end of nowhere, his headlong flight from Los Angeles and his daughter and his wife (all right, his *ex*-wife), his –

The cell phone at his hip played the opening bar of "What'll I Do?", and Ken jumped in surprise. He plucked it off his belt and peered at the screen.

Great, he told himself as he tapped it. *Just what I needed*

"Hello, Marty," he said. He was already tired of the conversation and it hadn't even begun.

"Where is it, Ken?"

"It's not ready."

He could almost hear his nervous little boss scowling and twitching on the other end. Ken had promised Marty, VP of Product Development at VeriSil International, a prototype of "Everybody's Assistant" no later than March first. It was going to be great, a personal assistant/organizer that was everything Siri wanted to be and wasn't, a true artificial intelligence, as smart and responsive as any human being. Effortless voice recognition, flawless human-sounding vocal synthesis – not that tinny *waka-waka* the Apple product made – high conversational functionality, continuing self-actualized upgrades, background RF satellite uplinks for high-level "fuzzy" queries, he had promised *all* of it. He had convinced the big guys at VeriSil that EA was going to be *it,* the first killer app of the year, maybe the decade, a nearly seamless and individualized 'personality' for the masses.

That deadline had passed almost two months ago. Ken Mackie was late. *Very* late.

"I don't have to tell you what a mess this is," Marty said, painful and annoying as a fly stuck in his ear.

Ken sighed. "No, you don't."

"You have handed me one total, rolling, six-by-six-foot fuck-up, you know that."

Ken stood up straight, knees popping, and gazed blindly into the crater valley below his rented home. The sad little town of Dos Hermanos, California looked like a set of worn-out building blocks tumbled on the desert floor below him. *I'm king of the butterflies! He quoted only to himself. King of the air! Ah, me! What a throne! What a wonderful chair!*

"Give me one more week, Marty," he said aloud, knowing it was a lie even as he said it.

"Kenny, come *on!*" Marty sounded ready to cry. "I got a whole development team here screaming at me!"

"One more week. Then I'll deliver the full package – working model, code, everything." *I'm Yertle the Turtle! Oh, marvelous me! For I am the ruler of all that I –*

A drop of rain as big as a Concord grape plopped onto the top of Ken's head.

He looked up in dumb surprise. *Rain?* he thought. *Here?* It hadn't rained in Dos Hermanos in more than four years. This was the most arid spot in North—

Another drop hit him right in the center of his upturned forehead. Almost involuntarily, he backed up and put himself under the wide eaves of the *hacienda,* shoulder blades bumping against the soft adobe bricks. It made him feel oddly trapped, even out in the open.

More drops fell. And more. Suddenly the rain was thumping against the ground, a dull drumming that grew louder and more insistent every second. A roll of thunder grumbled out of the north, and Ken felt a chill when he looked downhill again. The town had been replaced by a strange, colorless mist. Dos Bros was nothing more than a smudged blur now.

"Come in for a meeting," Marty said. "Tomorrow, ten a.m."

"Jesus, Marty, you want me to get this done, or you want to waste time with–"

"*Tomorrow,*" Marty said flatly. It was the first time he'd sounded certain about anything in the entire conversation. "*Ten a.m.* The boss – the *big* boss, Mr. Josephson himself – is gonna be here. You have to show him what you have. And it has to be something *real* this time, Kenny. Something we can stand on."

Ken put a hand over his eyes and squeezed. *Oh, Christ,* he thought. *I am in so much trouble.* When he took the hand away, he could see that the ground was mottled now, uneven and discolored like blistering skin. Droplets gusted onto his cheeks, warm as blood.

"Look," he said, desperate to end the call, "I have to go. My daughter's about to get here and–"

"Your *daughter*? Oh, *man,* that's *great!*"

Ken closed his eyes and took a deep breath. "No, it's not," he said. "But it won't get in the way. I promise. I just have to go, that's all."

"All right, Ken. But–"

"I have to go. I'll talk to you later."

"Tomorrow," Marty repeated.

"Ten a.m., Marty. I heard you."

Ken tapped the phone off and looked back at the half-dead plants in his garden. "Chow down, you poor bastards," he said, then edged his way along the side of the house until he came to the sliding glass doors that opened into his study. Another roll of thunder rose up out of the ground as he slipped inside.

The study was beautiful and serene, all teakwood and leather-bound books bought by the pound. His desk was ominously clean, only a computer monitor with the keyboard hidden in a flat drawer.

"Maggie," he said, "what is *that* all about?"

Maggie answered in a mellow, slightly amused voice. "Which *that* is that?" she asked.

"The rain, damn it," he said. He ran his fingers through his hair. They came away wet and gritty, a mixture of sweat and dirt and rain water.

The monitor on his desk flickered, and an enhanced satellite map appeared: a perfect brown oval surrounded by flat desert yellow. The oval was the meteor crater they called the Valle de Los Hermanos; the irregular blue blotch inside it was the town, neatly labeled DOS HERMANOS, CA, 14:15 PDT. A thin red line, twisted as a capillary and marked as CA HWY 181, connected DH to Barstow, almost 150 miles away. As Ken watched in silence, a swarm of gray-blue blots scuttled along the top of the screen.

"An unusually wet cell, part of a distant tropical storm series in the northern Gulf of California, is backing up against the Piedras Blancas Range," Maggie told him, "causing the formation of thunderheads. There will be some heat lightning, possibly resulting in brush fires in the foothills. However, the cell is expected to pass at least thirty miles to the north of us. It will dissipate entirely by midnight tonight. Chance for local precipitation is negligible."

Ken smiled and shook his head. "You know," he said, "Fifty years ago, I would have grunted, 'Gonna rain?', and my faithful Gal Friday – that would be *you*, Maggie – would have stuck a pencil in her bun and said, 'Don't think so, Boss.'"

"You asked."

He sighed. "Yes, I did. It's my own damn fault."

He looked down at the single photograph on his nearly vacant desk: Ken, Lisa, and Rose, taken more than two years ago. He loved that picture. It captured perfectly what they had been, *who* they had been: Lisa's reluctant smile, Rose's mouth open in happy astonishment, his own wide grin as he threw his arms around them both.

What had happened to that girl in the picture, he wondered. *That* Rose had been a sarcastic fourteen-year-old fascinated by politics; an intense twelve-year-old who was dedicating her life to veterinary medicine; a serious nine-year-old obsessed with PlayStation. He couldn't make any connection between *that* Rose and the one who was about to arrive – the hollow-cheeked teenager, white as typing paper, last seen lying on the gurney in the St. Johns Hospital ER. The one in the smeared, stolen makeup, with a witch's brew of cocaine, meth, and something they never identified swirling through her veins, who had awakened, taken a single look at him, and said "*Fuck you,*" in a sandpaper whisper he never would have recognized…just before she passed out for a week.

"Boss…" Maggie said, almost gently.

"*What?*"

"They're at the front gate. I'm letting them in."

It was like a bucket of cold water in the face. "Shit," he said. He looked around the study as if there was somewhere else to go. Then he took a deep breath and started down the long hallway to the front of the house.

A flash of blue-white light exploded over his head as he opened the front door. Thunder rolled through him like the roar of a passing train.

"Maggie," he said, "I think we need to redefine the concept of 'negligible precipitation'."

"Nobody's perfect," she told him. Her voice was tinny and distant a few feet onto the porch.

There was the car, rising up over the first ridge, half a mile away on the edge of the property. He could see the gray silhouettes of two figures in the front seat, and the jittering aura of raindrops jumping like popcorn off the hood and roof.

Silently, suddenly, a bright red ATV, a squat little bug-shape, nothing more than a curved and shining cowling with huge cartoon-sized tires, shot over the low ridge ahead of Lisa's BMW and *slammed* into the road right in front of the car.

The BMW swerved and plunged into the muddy ditch at the side of the road, rear wheels spinning madly. In a heartbeat it shot completely off the road and tipped forward, then lurched downhill at high speed. Ken watched helplessly as two things happened at once: the ATV threw out a rooster-tail of muddy water, surged up the steep incline on the far side of the road and disappeared…and the BMW slammed grille-first into a granite boulder as big as a steamer trunk.

He shouted into the storm as the car went up on its nose, back wheels spraying mud and water. The BMW teetered there, balanced on its headlights, and for one horrible, endless moment he could see his ex-wife and his daughter through the windows. Lisa had one hand braced on the wheel, the other thrown in front of Rose; Rose herself was pushed back in the passenger seat, as far away from the windshield as she could get. Then the sky cracked open in a burning white flash –

– and the car fell onto its roof with a thundering *SLAM*, wheels in the air. The windshield shattered into white crystals, doors flying open, roof collapsing.

"Maggie! *Maggie! Call 911!*"

He didn't wait to find out if he'd been heard. He jumped off the porch and ran down the quarter-mile of road, sandy mud shifting under him.

"ROSE! LISA!"

He slipped and slid down the incline to the side of the car. The rain roared and gurgled all around him.

"*ROSE!*"

He knew they were dead. He *knew* it. First there was Pat, then the divorce, then hiding in the desert and now *this*.

Now he had lost everything.

TWO

Lucy Armbruster looked deeply into the blank young faces staring up at her and seriously considered mass murder.

You little bastards. I come all the way down here in your hour of need, and the best you can do is gape at me like a bunch of sheep.

It was obvious that the combined second through eighth grade classes of the Dos Hermanos Public School were just as bored as she was. They had sat and squirmed through her forty-five minute presentation on "The Living Desert" only because their teachers were lined up at the back of the Cafetorium like vultures on a power line, waiting for somebody to make trouble.

This is what I get for being nice, she told herself, staring down at them from the stage. *Another line drive to the tits.* She scrubbed at her short russet hair in a habitual gesture of annoyance and self-control. This was all Frannie's fault, she decided. She was simply trying to do what Frannie would have wanted, trying to help this pathetic little town through its current crisis. *And what do I get? Cattle. Worse: **pre-teen** cattle.*

"Okay," she said. "Enough. I'm only going to share one more thing with you, and then I'll let you go."

There were a few faint, sarcastic cheers from the back of the house. *You and me both*, she thought. She reached down under the podium, dug her hand into the box she had brought with her, and held up a loose fist, leaking dirt and rocks.

"What's this?" she asked them.

A little boy in the first row – one of the precocious ones she hated, the kind who always had the answer hiding in his mouth – piped up with "Dirt!"

Ass-kissing dolt. "This guy here said 'dirt,'" she said aloud. "And he's partly right. Soil, stones, bits of plant matter. I picked this up right here from your playground, so it's nothing special…but there's something hiding in it, right now. You know what?"

Nothing again, though this time they actually seemed to be paying attention. "Seeds," she said, and she let the dirt pour out right onto the podium. It made a sandy, hollow thump-bump-hiss sound as it fell.

The kids oohed in spite of themselves. *Nothing like messing up school property to get their attention. I should have opened by kicking the podium to pieces. Then they'd love me.*

"In this one handful of local soil, there are thousands of seeds," she said as the last of the dirt fell to the floor. "In a cubic meter of Dos Hermanos soil – think of a box about this big, by this wide, by this tall – there are over one hundred thousand seeds. Flowers, plants, cacti, all of them in seed form. They're not dead; they're not alive. They're what's called *dormant.*"

"What's that mean?" said one dark-skinned little girl from the third row. Lucy recognized her type. In fact, she recognized herself in that suspicious, challenging glare. *Hang on, darlin',* she thought. *You're in for a bumpy ride.* "What's your name?"

"Kerrianne," the girl said.

"Okay," Lucy said, wondering why she'd ask. "It means sleeping…and waiting, um, Kerrianne. Kind of a combination of the two. And there's only one thing that will make these seeds come to life." To the whole group again: "Anybody know what that one thing is?"

Now half a dozen of them from all over the room said it at the same time: "Water!"

"Right!" She knocked on the podium of emphasis. "Water. These seeds are all examples of xerophytic adaptation – a big phrase, don't bother writing it down. It means they've all adapted themselves to really, really dry climates. They can wait for months or years or even many years for the water to show up. Desert Sand Verbena – you know, that wide-leafed plant with the little purple flowers that's out in front of the school?" Lots of nodding heads now. "That's one of them. Its seeds can go dormant for years, until the right combination of rain and temperature comes along. So can the desert paintbrush, and the ocotillo. Some desert animals can do the same thing – snakes and mammals and even fish, who live only in hot water pools in the middle of the desert. If those pools dry up, though, the fish don't die; they go dormant. They wait."

She looked down at them, silent again for a moment. Then the memory of Frannie made her say, "You know…you guys can be like that, too. You could be waiting for the right breaks at the right time, and then you could turn into something completely…unexpected."

Christ. Who am I supposed to be, Deepak fucking Chopra?

She straightened up and slammed her palm against the podium – a sharp fast *whack!* – and everyone jumped again. "Okay!" she barked. "Lecture's over! Mr. Pratt...?"

"Thank you, Dr. Armbruster." The school principal, a short, narrow-shouldered, flat-headed fellow with a well-groomed mustache and a self-satisfied expression, ducked into the mike as Lucy stepped aside. "Children, let's thank the doctor for taking the time to speak to us today …"

The applause was louder than she expected. She waved at them halfheartedly. "Yeah, yeah," she said under her breath. "Whatever."

"All right," Mr. Pratt said, "It's three-oh-five now, and your rides home have started to arrive. Remember to tell your parents again about tonight's Security Meeting, 7:00 in the Martin Luther King Conference Center Main Ballroom. Now, when I say so, you children can go out the back doors..." There was a great clattering stir as the kids snagged backpacks and lunchboxes –

"WHEN I SAY SO!" he bellowed into the mike.

Everybody froze. The students stood suspended for a long, long moment, while Pratt glared down at them.

Finally, slowly, he said: "Class…dismissed," and they all jumped back into action, surging for the doors as fast as they could move.

In that instant, Lucy Armbruster put Douglas Pratt on her long list of People Worth Hating, even as he put out a large, flat-fingered hand to be shaken. "Thank you, Dr. Armbruster," he said. "Most informative." He glanced distastefully at the floor. "Although we'll have to get Flaco out here to clean up your mess, of course."

Lucy let his hand hang there. "Then I guess it's good I didn't let loose the scorpion and tarantula displays," she said innocently. "Imagine that mess."

For one instant Douglas Pratt looked absolutely appalled. Then his face folded into something like a smile.

Okay, Frannie. That's it. I have done my bit for humanity. Now where the hell did I park my car?

Principal Pratt took a small walkie-talkie from his belt and whispered into it.

"Well," she said, feeling more awkward than ever, "I'm glad I could help out, given the, um, circumstances. It was good for the children to have some distraction during the questioning. Frankly, I don't think anyone, including the police, was taking this very seriously until… you know, until now. I get it," Lucy said. "I mean, one missing girl is a runaway, but two? In a town this size? In a week? That's something else."

Everyone had heard the stories. The rumors about The Little Girls were the hottest topic in town. Little Jennifer Toombs, age eleven, was the first to disappear, but by all accounts she was a hateful little brat who many were glad to see gone. No one knew very much about the second girl, and the local cops… well, no one expected much of anything from them.

"We've cancelled regular classes," Principal Pratt said, "but we do need to do something while the, um, interviews are taking place."

In other words, Lucy translated, *we needed someone to keep the kids occupied while the cops ask a lot of hard questions. And here I am, Straw Woman Number One.*

"It would be nice if they could crack the case," she said, eying the exit with something like desperation. "I guess it's not that easy, though."

"Never is," said a new voice. They both looked up at Sheriff Donald Peck sidling onto the stage.

Peck really did look like a TV-movie version of a smart cop: broad-shouldered, strong-jawed, steely-eyed. "Not that I would mind cracking the case," he said. "I always wanted to solve one like that Columbo guy."

They all chuckled politely. The cell phone clipped to the Sheriff's belt warbled. He held up an apologetic finger and turned away, looking for a little privacy, as he said, "Peck," but there was something taut and hard in his voice that made Lucy want to eavesdrop.

"When?" he asked. "Where are they taking them? Okay, I'll meet them at the Clinic, and – no, don't let her talk to anyone. No, god–"

He looked up and caught Lucy watching him… and for one moment she saw something hard and dangerous in Donald Peck's eyes, something that scared the hell out of her. "Just do what I told you to," he said into the phone, his eyes still on her. He clicked it shut and switched on his warm, comforting smile, only for her.

"Sorry," he said to her. "When it rains it pours."

Lucy made herself smile. "Sure does," she said. She swallowed hard.

It took a long, long moment for him to release her, like a cat releasing its prey. "I'm afraid I'll have to excuse myself," he said. "There's been a fairly serious car accident up–"

"Mrs. Greenaway?" Pratt said, talking past Lucy's shoulder to a woman in the center of the Cafetorium. "What is it?"

Sharon Greenaway was standing in the doorway to the parking lot. Lucy knew her; Sharon and her husband Jeff owned the only organic market in town, and Frannie had gotten her addicted to decent cooking, so she was a regular customer there.

Normally Sharon was a sunny, pleasantly plump woman; now she looked as if someone had punched a hole in her. Her eyes were three times their proper size. Her skin looked like warm tallow, moist and yellowish as she crossed the multipurpose room to the Sheriff and the knot of teachers.

"She didn't come out," Sharon said. Her voice was trembling. "I've been waiting."

"Oh my God," Lucy said.

Sharon was having trouble breathing. "All of her friends–" gulp "—came out fifteen minutes ago." Gulp. "But…"

Sheriff Peck took charge in an instant. He pulled out his phone again, barely took a pause, and began to hiss into it. "Jimmy?" he said into the phone "Get up here. Now. No, let Bo follow up at the Clinic; I'll meet him there. I need you– *no*, goddamn it, don't argue, *get here!*" Lucy could see the anger in him. If he could have slammed the phone down or thrown it across the room he would have.

He pointed to a group of teachers off to one side and began to bark orders. Then he turned to the stricken, trembling woman beside him who was staring wordlessly at him. "We're going to find her, Mrs. Greenaway. Hang tight." He didn't wait for a reply; he went back to snapping into his cell phone and his shoulder-mounted police-band radio at the same time.

No we won't, Lucy said to herself. She knew it, even as she heard the little girl's name being called across the campus. *We just...won't.*

"I think I'll make myself scarce," she mumbled to no one in particular. She moved quickly across the room and pushed open the double doors –

– to be hit in the face by a sheet of warm, slimy water.

"Gah!" She staggered back a step, thinking some adolescent prankster had planted a full bucket over the entrance. When her eyes cleared she looked outside for the first time in hours.

It was pouring rain.

Pouring.

Lucy stared at the sky, at the ground, then at the water already choking the gutters. The hand-painted signs about the Security Meeting were running and unreadable, like badly applied mascara.

Oh, Jesus, she thought as she stared into the iron sky. *Oh, jumping Jesus in a handcart.*

Lucy Armbruster had made herself into the country's single greatest authority on this particular desert's microclimate. She had almost singlehandedly built a research station on the crater's north ridge to study it up close. She knew the origin and meaning of every breeze, every flower bloom, every cloud in the sky. And all she could do was stare at the swelling rain rushing across the schoolyard and try to not scream.

"This is bad," she said aloud. "This is very bad."

THREE

Rose Mackie sat by her mother's bed and tried not to scream.

They had been fighting, as usual, when the accident happened. Neither one of them seemed to able to stop themselves.

"Look," her mother had said. "It's not my fault you're here." Rose hated it when she started the conversation with "Look," that way. It was bitchy and hard and said, *I know more than you do about whatever it is we're talking about.* "Look, I didn't make you take that shit into your body. I didn't force you to break your probation and go to that party and get arrested *again.* That wasn't me."

Rose had smiled bitterly. "You're right, Mom," she said very quietly. "You're right. I'm all alone in this. I know that. I figured that out a long fucking time ago."

The rain was rattling and sizzling all around the car, turning everything distant and soggy and gray as they forced their way into Dos Hermanos. Of course they got completely lost. They even had to stop and ask directions from a total stranger so they could get pointed the right way. It felt like hours before they finally came to a set of twin pedestals made from river stone that supported a wrought-iron archway.

With the car paused in front of the gate, her Mom turned in her seat and said, "We're here."

"No kidding," Rose muttered.

Her mom steered through a deep dip in the road, the water thundering around them, and started talking again, as if the gate gave her some kind of permission. God, *why* did she have to *talk* all the time?

"You be good to your father," she said as she drove up a second hill and into a new wave of rain.

"Oh, *sure,*" Rose had snorted.

"Rose, you need to give him a chance." They surged downhill again and splashed into a rushing puddle.

"Why?" Rose said. "*You* didn't."

The BMW roared up the third rise and there it was: the huge dark hulk of his ridiculous mini-mansion, hunched on the ridge line like a fat, sleepy snake. "It's not about me," Lisa told her.

"Of course it is," her daughter said.

"It's not–"

"*Don't!*"

"Rose, please listen to–"

"*Stop it!*"

A streak of red flew in from the left, a motorcycle or golf-cart or *something,* and slammed into the road right in front of her. Lisa jerked the wheel to the side, flinching away from the collision without thinking. Mud sprayed across the windshield.

Rose had screamed. She remembered that much, at least. Then there was nothing under the front tires, and they were tipping, plunging, roaring down the hillside, sliding to the side, falling faster and faster. Lisa screamed and threw her arm in front of Rose and an instant later they rammed into a solid block of stone.

Stop, Rose had been screaming. *Stop stop stop…*

And now she wasn't even moving. She wasn't even *moving*. Rose leaned forward, forcing the tears back, sorry about what she said, sorry about being here, sorry about everything…

And Lisa Corman Mackie opened her eyes.

* * *

Rose knew she looked awful. Her makeup had washed away long ago; her hair had dried into a mad black tangle. She didn't care.

Her mother had opened her eyes. She didn't look sleepy or confused at all. She looked right at her daughter, *into* her daughter, tears sliding down her temples from the corner of her eyes.

"I am so sorry," her mother said, and Rose knew she wasn't apologizing for the car accident, or the argument, or the stupid decision to come to Dos Hermanos in the first place. She was saying she was sorry for everything, from the minute it had started to go bad, and maybe even more.

Her mom's arms came up and Rose bent down. They hugged, awkwardly and not without pain. Rose's back was sprung, though she sure as hell wasn't going to tell the doctors that, and Lisa had needles in her arm and a bandage wrapped around one wrist. Still, they embraced as they hadn't in years.

"You're okay," Lisa said, and they both knew what that meant, too.

"I am. I am. It will be different now."

"I know. I mean it, I *know*."

They stopped talking for a while and cried together.

* * *

Ken let it go on for as long as it needed to. He didn't interrupt. He wasn't sure he could have if he'd wanted to. Finally the two of them disentangled, laughing at the confusion of tubes and twisted sheets. Lisa rubbed the heel of her hand across her cheeks to wipe the tears away before she looked at him directly.

"Hi," she said. "I'm okay, really."

"I know you are," he said thickly. "I mean, the doctors said… I talked…" Ken put his hands over his eyes to hide his own tears, but he couldn't stop them. "Christ, Lisa. *Christ*…"

Rose, standing close beside him, put a hand on his chest and made small circles, an oddly intimate, comforting gesture, like rubbing a baby's back. "It's okay, Daddy," she said quietly. "She's alive, and so am I, in spite of my best efforts."

He sniffed and wiped his eyes. "In spite of your best efforts," he repeated, almost laughing. "How old are you again?"

"I'm a hundred and twelve in dog years," she said, "and you made me that way. Come on. Sit down here." She pulled a second chair close to the bed, and Ken hovered over it, unsure what to do.

He and Lisa hadn't exchanged more than twenty words in a row since the day he'd left. All he knew about what she was going through was what Lisa told him, and that only came in dribs and drabs. He knew about her realtor business, of course, and he had a sense of how bad things were. *Why won't you take any money?* He wanted to ask. *Why not let me* –

Lisa pressed her lips together and scowled. "Don't be an ass," she said and gestured at the chair. "Sit down." Lisa caught a glimpse of a khaki uniform moving in the hallway.

"Is that a policeman at the door?" she asked.

"Yeah," Ken told her. "He's been guarding you since we got here."

The officer stirred as if he knew they were talking about him. He turned and stuck his head in the door, a handsome, dark-haired head with thick black brows and piercing eyes.

"You're awake!" he said, smiling.

"Yup," Lisa said, pushing her hair back. She hated the feel of the IV in her wrist.

"I'll get the doc, then. By the way, I'm Bo Cameron, Deputy Sheriff. We wanted to make sure you were okay." He flashed a smile and ducked away.

"What is that about?" Lisa asked.

"They want to get your statement about the accident as quickly as they can, I think," he said, glancing at the empty doorway. "About that ATV."

Lisa let her eyes fall shut. She was already tired. "I didn't see much," she said. "You probably know more than I do."

"Yeah, I told the EMTs what I saw on the way here. Guess they passed it along to the Sheriff."

"Sheriff? God, this *is* a one-horse town."

"Actually, we're saving up to buy our horse. Give it another couple of years."

Ken couldn't stop looking at her. He felt like a starving man in front of a three-course meal. He wanted to her to look at him, *him,* so he could tell her about dragging them from the wreck while it was still steaming in the downpour, about the wild ride to the Borrego Clinic in the '57 Chevy ambulance, about the argument in the ER when he refused to leave them. But he couldn't open his mouth. He couldn't even bring himself to take her hand.

God, he thought. *I'm an idiot. I'm such a fucking idiot.*

Lisa turned her head and opened her eyes, looking with great concern at her daughter. "What about you? Any injuries?"

"I'm fine," Rose assured her mother. "Clean bill of health, as if I'd let these guys touch me to find out."

The bizarre storm rumbled and hissed outside the hospital room's picture window. Lisa's eyes flickered to the glass, then back to Ken. "I thought you said it never rains here."

He would have sworn he heard something almost accusatory in her tone. "It doesn't," he said. "Usually. This whole thing seems to be some bizarre mountain-shadow effect. That's…"

He could see the flatness in her eyes. She didn't care. It didn't matter. The word died in his mouth.

This isn't what we should be talking about, he told himself. He knew they should be talking about important things: Rose's recovery, Ken's dead brother, his problems with the contract, or Lisa's own money troubles. But he couldn't get any of it out. He didn't even know where to start.

"Hey there," a new voice said from the doorway. They all turned towards it with palpable relief. Things had suddenly become very complicated. "Hey…."

He was far too young; in his late twenties, blond and handsome in a weary, unconscious way, with a very short haircut and an open, unguarded smile. He looked more like a frat boy than an ER physician. He took Lisa's free hand in his own.

"I'm Geoff Chamberlain," he said. "We've met before, but you were unconscious at the time."

"How many women have you swept off your feet with *that* line?" Lisa asked.

The doctor grinned. "Maybe I do need some fresh material," he said. "Anyway, I don't want you to worry. We did every test we could think of, and you passed 'em all. Looks like you've got a mild concussion, a dandy little contusion right above your hairline, and a badly strained right wrist." He looked up from his notes. "Let me guess, the Mommy Sweep?" He threw his right arm out to the side and kept it there, as if holding back an invisible attacker.

"Guilty," Lisa said, smiling at him. Rose had to admit it: he *was* cute.

"It defies all the laws of physics, you know," he said. "But I don't blame you one bit." He glanced at Rose who was standing to one side, arms folded, looking him up and down very skeptically. "I mean, look who you were trying to protect."

Ken gave him a killing look. "She's *sixteen*," he said.

Rose wanted to die.

Dr. Chamberlain held up a hand as he went back to his notes. "Just being understanding," he said, grinning again. "Part of the bedside manner." He looked back at Lisa, a little more seriously this time. "Head injuries can be tricky, Ms. Mackie…"

Rose could see her starting to correct him, to say "Corman," … but she let it go. *And what is* that *all about?* she asked herself.

"… and since we've got the space, like we usually do, I'd like to keep you here overnight for observation. Insurance will cover it. I already checked."

Lisa frowned. "Really, Doctor, I'd like to get out of here."

"I'm sure you would," Dr. Chamberlain said gently. "So would I. I'm off duty in about half an hour, and under normal circumstances, I'd be happy to take you all out for a drin…" he looked at the pretty sixteen-year-old again, then at her glowering father. "…for dinner. At Denny's. The one with the kids menus." Then, back to Lisa: "But seriously: let's not mess with it. You got a pretty mean bump, and there's no reason not to get a good night's sleep right here. We'll release you in the morning, and then none of us have to worry."

Lisa looked at Ken and Rose. They both nodded severely. "Okay," she relented. "One night."

There was a knock at the door and they all looked up to see an impressive-looking blond man in a crisp khaki uniform. He was standing inside the doorframe with his peaked hat in his hand. Bo Cameron was standing a respectful distance behind him with the oddest expression on his face: he looked wary, almost afraid.

"Ma'am?" the crew cut blond cop said, his voice a pleasant and carefully modulated bass. "I'm Sheriff Donald Peck. I was wondering if I could speak to you for a moment?"

"Only for a second, Sheriff, okay?" Dr. Chamberlain said. "She needs the rest."

Peck shot the doctor a hard look, a look that Lisa read as *Who the hell do you think YOU are, boy.* It was hidden by a smile in an instant. "Of course," the Sheriff said. "Only a minute or two."

He stood at the end of the bed and asked her a series of questions about the crash. How fast had she been going? How bad was the rain? What made her turn like that? Lisa described what had happened, Ken and Rose filled in with their own observations, and Peck took it all in without comment or a change in his serious, thoughtful expression. He didn't take notes; he obviously didn't need to.

He was particularly interested in the red ATV and the person driving it. "So," he said, talking to them all now, "no look at the face. Just a black helmet, black leather jacket… nothing else? No second person riding behind? No large bundles or boxes attached?"

They looked at each other and agreed, no, nothing like that, and only one person.

"I wish like hell I could give you more," Ken said.

Peck smiled tightly. "Not a problem," he said. "I have a couple of ideas already. It's not that big a town, after all." He put on his hat and shook hands all around. "I'll be getting back to you soon as I can," he said.

Thunder rumbled outside. It made the picture window's glass buzz like an angry bee.

"Sheriff, what's going on?" Ken asked. "I mean, this is a normal hit and run, isn't it? What's with the police protection?"

Peck smiled again, thinner than ever. "It's nothing like that, Mr. Mackie. Things are a little tense around here right now. You know about the missing girls?"

Ken nodded. "Sure, I've heard."

"Another one today. So anything out of the ordinary, we're looking at pretty hard. And believe it or not, speeding ATVs running people off the road, that's out of the ordinary."

"Got it."

"The officer," he shot another look at Bo, who almost flinched, "will be going with me now. Plenty of other things to do with the storm and all." He looked closely at Ken as he shook his hand. "Your daughter staying with you at the house up on West Ridge?"

Ken glanced at his daughter who made an unhappy face. He nodded. "Yes, she'll be with me. And her Mom will be here at the clinic overnight."

"Good. Good all around." He made his goodbyes, gave the doctor one last *don't you screw with me, asshole* look, and stepped out. When he left, a pretty young nurse came in with a cup of pills for Lisa. She swallowed them without objection.

"Lovely fellow," Ken said. "Can't imagine how I've avoided him for a whole year."

"Cream of the Gestapo," the doctor muttered. He checked his watch. "Oops, look at that, I have to get out of here."

"Big date?"

He shrugged. "Worse. Birthday party. *Mine*."

"Congratulations," Lisa said.

"Please. It's my thirtieth, and I begged my roomies to leave it alone. No such luck." He leaned forward as if telling a secret. "I hear there's going to be a girl jumping out of a cake and everything."

"Unsanitary, maybe," Lisa said, "but fun."

He frowned. "We'll see. Anyway, I'll check with you in the morning, Ms. Mackie."

"Lisa," she said.

"Lisa." He shook hands with Ken. "Are you okay with this?" he asked.

Ken nodded. "Thanks. I appreciate everything."

"All part of the service." He put his hand out to Rose, who accepted it with grown-up, serious grace. He smiled at her. "If that back *really* starts to bother you, let me know, okay?"

Rose gaped.

He grinned. "See you tomorrow," he said. He shot one last line over his shoulder as he left: "And let the lady get some sleep soon, okay?"

They stayed with Lisa for another twenty minutes, but there was less and less that needed to be said, and the new round of medications were starting to affect her. Ken put a hand on his daughter's shoulder. "I think I'll take her to dinner," he told Lisa, "then go up to the house."

"Stop at the mall for something to wear, too," Lisa said sleepily. Rose started to groan. "Oh, come on, now. All your clothes were in the car; I'm sure they're ruined."

Ken nodded. "Will do. And if you need anything…"

"I have a phone right here," she said, nodding at her bedside table. "I'm sure it will be fine."

"Yes, but if you need *any* –"

"*Kenny*," she said, a hint of the old edginess creeping back into her voice. "I've been taking care of myself for quite a while now. Don't get carried away."

He looked away. "Got it," he said. Then, with a false heartiness; "Okay, Rosie, let's go."

Five minutes later, she was alone. Ten minutes later, she was drifting into sleep.

FOUR

The careful truce between Ken and his daughter that had held firm in Lisa's hospital room began to fray the moment they hit the elevator. As Rose and Ken stood side-by-side, staring at the inside of the sliding door, Ken had a nearly irresistible urge to reach out and take his daughter's hand, but something stopped him.

"She looks pretty good," he said, not looking at her.

"Oh, yeah," Rose agreed. "Nearly perfect for somebody who's been slammed headfirst into a stone wall."

Ken scowled. "I mean it could have been a whole lot worse, Rosie. She–"

"I know what you meant," she said. "And please don't call me that. Please."

The elevator doors opened on a damp concrete cavern filled with dimly lit cars. Water was dripping from the overhead pipes, and cascading down the upslope to the street like the spillway off an aqueduct. It had only been raining for a few hours, and the water had already overwhelmed Dos Hermanos' rudimentary drainage system.

"Do you at least remember where you left the car?" she asked.

"God, Rose," he said quietly, "will you give it a rest?" She was right, of course. At that particular moment, Ken had no idea where he had parked the Range Rover. He let his hand steal into his pocket, where his fingertips found the rubber-and-plastic key ring. *Thank God I remember where I put* that, he thought, and pinched it with a vicious cut of his thumbnail. There was a sudden *blip* of a horn and a flash of lights off to their right. "There," he said. "That way."

Rose snorted. "Saved by the car alarm," she said. "Again."

He power-walked to the Range Rover with Rose close behind. A moment later they were inside and on their way.

* * *

The rain, gray and violent as ever, slapped at the windshield the instant they emerged from the parking garage. A moment later when he turned north, Ken's phone sang at his waist. He glanced at the screen: it was Maggie. He used the no-hands connection in the car, pointedly ignoring Rose's roll of the eyes.

"Hey there," he said. "We're just leaving the Clinic."

"We?" came the mellow, amused voice.

"Rose and me," he said, and glanced over at his daughter. She was staring at him with a mixture of disgust and dismay. He chose to ignore it. "Lisa's staying overnight for observation."

"Is that necessary?" Rose asked.

"Understood," Maggie said. "Alberto's Towing and Repo Center left with the remains of the BMW ten minutes ago. They managed to salvage Rose' purse from the front seat, but that's about all."

Ken passed the information along to Rose, half-shouting to be heard above the rattle of the rainfall on the Range Rover's roof.

"Oh, *bitchin'*," Rose said with false shallowness. "As long as I have my ATM card and my lip gloss, I am good to go!"

Ken ignored her. "We're going to do some shopping." he said into the phone. "Then we'll get something to eat. We'll be home later on."

"*Home,*" Rose echoed, sounding vaguely revolted by the concept. "My *god.*"

Ken shut the phone and put it away.

"You're sick," Rose said.

"What are you talking about?"

"You. You and that…it's *sick,* Daddy."

He set his jaw. "Okay," he said. "Fine." He was not going to get into it.

"And I don't want to go to the mall," Rose said.

"So you don't plan on changing your clothes for the next couple of days? Why the hell not?"

"You have a washing machine, don't you? Shit, you've probably got a live-in maid. So get Consuelo or whomever to do my dainties and I'll be fine."

"Her name is Lupe, she's a housekeeper who comes once a week and she doesn't do laundry." His jaw ached from being clenched so tightly.

"Fine! Fucking fine! But don't make it such a fucking *big deal,* will you? I only need one other pair of fucking blue jeans and a fucking T-shirt that I can wear when I'm washing *this* pair of fucking blue jeans. It's not like we're *going* anywhere or anything."

"Well, shit, *Rosie,* I thought this was the fucking *perfect* time to buy you a fucking *prom* dress."

"Oh, that's funny, Daddy. That is *so* fucking– LOOK OUT!"

Ken jerked to stop at the intersection. He had already seen the man in the black pea coat crossing the street against the light, but her screech made him slam on the brakes anyway.

The man didn't even look up. He clamped a hand onto his shapeless black hat, hunched deeper into the rising wind, and made for the far curb.

Ken stayed motionless in the intersection long after he was gone.

"You know," he said, "Driving in this shit would be a whole lot easier if you weren't alternating between insulting me and *screaming in my fucking ear."*

"You were going to hit him!"

"I was *not!"*

"How was *I* supposed to know that? *I'm* not the one who's driving!"

"Right! You aren't! So leave it to me and *stop screaming in my fucking ear!!"*

Rose stared out the window. Ken didn't continue the conversation, either. He let it go, distantly surprised at how shrill and unsteady his own voice sounded, and how white his knuckles were against the black webbing of the steering wheel.

This is going to be a very long weekend, he told himself. *Very fucking long.*

* * *

The trip to the Dos Hermanos Emporium, the one and only shopping mall in town, was short and unpleasant, and the storm grew steadily worse. They parked near the entrance and dashed inside. Rose wouldn't even let Ken go into the department store to shop; he was forced to wander on the outskirts, staring into the windows of the random, gaudy shops until she reappeared with a flat plastic bag filled with a very few items of clothing. She looked red-faced and upset.

"Are you okay?" he said.

"Don't ask," she snapped. "Let's just go."

They went. Less than half an hour after they emerged from the hospital's underground parking, they were crawling across town towards the business district and a decent meal.

Ken tapped on the Range Rover's brakes at an intersection that should have been buzzing with activity, as buzzy as any intersection in DH ever got. But it was strangely deserted, even though the car's clock read 4:28.

Rose didn't speak. She hadn't said ten words since they'd left the Emporium.

Ken took a deep breath and watched a trash can roll across the intersection, pushed by the wind-driven rain. A moment later a wave of economy-sized plastic bags, each a foot square, swarmed past them like a flock of transparent bats, whipping and twisting through the storm.

Somebody lost a year's supply of ZipLocs, he told himself, *while I'm sitting here losing my mind.*

He cleared his throat. "Sorry about yelling before," he said quietly, barely audible above the chatter of the rain on the metal roof. "Guess I'm still a little stressed out."

She didn't say anything at first. Then: "Me, too."

"Okay. So. Let's—"

"Let's eat, okay? Nothing else. I … I can't …" Her voice started to crumble.

"I got it. Off we go." Ken pointed the Rover towards the downtown district and did battle with the storm.

* * *

On any normal day in Dos Hermanos, it would have been an easy five-minute walk from the Clinic to the only decent restaurant in town. Today it required a fifteen-minute drive through blinding rain. The only good part for Ken was finding a parking space directly in front of the entrance to O'Meara's.

Ken and Rose lurched to a halt inside the doors, shedding rain and almost giggling. It took a moment for Rose to take the place in.

Ken barely recognized the slate-gray landscape. To one side, the Conference Center rose up like an outcropping of waterlogged granite; he could barely read the illuminated letters in its ten-foot sign, reminding passersby of tonight's town meeting about the missing girls. Behind it, the water tower rose on three massive metal legs, looking more ominous than ever with rain clouds hanging inches above its domed roof. Across from the brick staircase of the Center, the long sheet-glass storefront of O'Meara's looked incongruously warm and inviting. And right in front of it was the rarest phenomenon of all: an open parking space.

This time they made it from car to doorway without getting thoroughly soaked, and Ken was glad to see that the storm had not yet penetrated his favorite place to eat.

O'Meara's was a long, narrow room filled with round tables along the floor-to-ceiling windows and leatherette booths along the back wall. It sported fresh flowers at each station, real cloth tablecloths, and pretty young waitresses all in their twenties. It was a favorite of local businessmen and politicians; it even had a back room used for the weekly meetings of the Chamber of Commerce. Ken used it for the face-to-face meetings he had to have with VeriSil, whenever he could pry them out of their corporate headquarters at the south end of the Valle.

Tony O'Meara was the owner. He was a square-jawed, square-shouldered man in his forties with tightly curled hair and a superficial resemblance to Cajun cook Emeril Lagasse – a resemblance he liked to cultivate, as if it gave the establishment some subliminal sense of style. He came over to greet Ken as he swept raindrops from his shoulders, and Rose shook herself like a poodle one more time.

"You're lookin' good!" he said, pumping Ken's hand. "This your secretary who's always makin' the reservations? Finally givin' her an afternoon off?" Even after twenty years in the desert, Tony clung to a mild but noticeable Brooklyn accent.

Ken grinned. "My daughter, actually. Rose."

He wasn't the least bit fazed. "Ah! Should'a known! Look at you two!" He put out a cordial hand, and Rose surprised him by taking it, and even allowing Tony to bow over it and put it to his lips. "Those eyes!" he said, looking up at her. "Please tell me you're not wearing contacts."

"Not a chance," she said, smiling.

"Ah! You made my day!"

He escorted them to a table against the front window. Two tables down and across the way, Ken recognized the only other patron in the place, that scientist woman from the Ag Station, the one shaped like a sack of bowling balls. She looked up as they approached and scratched her head – a busy little gesture, like an otter scrubbing its pelt – and sketched a smile. Ken smiles and nodded back to her. No reason to have an actual conversation; the nod was enough for both of them. *Hi, I see you, you see me, have a good meal, don't bother me.*

Tony held the chair for Rose. She looked amused by the whole process.

O'Meara's was built right at street level. On a good day you could sit for hours in its industrial-strength air-conditioning and admire the pretty young professionals on their lunch. Today there were no pedestrians, and the perennially crystal-clear windows were marred with droplets and streaks. The Convention Center – a serious gray brick hulk that covered most of the opposite block – was scarcely visible across the four lanes of Central Avenue, a blurry slate-colored ghost of itself that seemed to be hunkering down, bracing against the rain.

The street itself had become a river, a single southbound torrent that filled the entire four lanes from curb to curb at least six inches deep. It was even beginning to develop its own chop and eddies underneath the constant pelting of new rain, more rain, *endless* rain.

"You know the menu already, so I won't bore you," Tony said. "Genelle is your waitress. Don't eat the salmon." Rose looked surprised. He put up a hand. "No, really," he said. "Don't." He nodded briskly and moved away. A moment later a dark-eyed blonde with slightly too much hair replaced him and took drink orders.

For a long minute, they were both fascinated with the view. From where they sat, the rain was not only heavy and dark, it was *right there*, a scant few inches from their faces but still impossibly remote, falling in dull silver sheets that simply would not stop. Ken put his fingertips against the glass; he could actually *feel* the rhythm of the rain as it pounded against the ground.

"Freaky," he said.

Rose didn't say anything.

Genelle came back again and they placed their orders: Caesar Salad for Rose, the World-Famous French Dip for Ken.

The silence grew longer and more uncomfortable. They both watched avidly as a middle-aged woman frog-walked down the sidewalk and almost threw herself in her car, covering her head with a flapping fragment of newsprint that offered no protection at all.

The food came. Ken selected a single French fry and steeled himself. Time for more conversation. "Pretty strange introduction to our quaint little town," he said with an entirely forced lightness.

Rose looked at him – *regarded* him with those wonderfully odd violet eyes. She wasn't simply ignoring him; it was more as if he hadn't spoken at all.

"I pretty much hate you right now, you know," she said.

The bottom dropped out of his stomach.

"I mean, you've been okay during this whole car wreck-rainstorm-hospital thing – better than okay, really, but…" She looked down and shook her head. "You were a complete shit two years ago, Dad. You were a great guy for my whole life, right up until then, and then Uncle Patrick died and you …*broke*."

He didn't say a word. He just kept looking at her, stone silent.

"You *left* us. Don't you –"

"I know what I did," Ken said. The food tasted like paste in his mouth.

Rose stopped talking and looked out the window again. The street-river had grown even deeper, rising past the level of the curb. Now it was an uninterrupted, roiling expanse that began outside the restaurant's glass wall and stretched to the Convention Center's brick staircase fifty feet away. Another step disappeared under the water while they sat in silence.

"Do you know how hard this has been on Mom?" she asked, trying to keep her voice low, but not entirely succeeding. "She's trying to get this real estate thing off the ground at the worst possible time in human history. She cleans fucking *apartments* to make the bills, do you know that?"

"I know that. She won't take any money from—"

"Of *course* she won't, and you know why! *You. Left. Us.*"

Ken pressed his lips together to keep the truth from pouring out. "Rosie, it's more complicated than—"

"Sure it is, Dad," she snapped, and glared at her meal, not at him. "Sure it is."

Neither of them said anything for a long time. Ken listened to the roaring hiss of the storm and let it fold around him.

"You know," she finally said, "I'm actually glad you're not trying to apologize." Her voice was very calm, very reasonable. She didn't sound hurt; she wasn't holding back tears or anger. She was *discussing* it, the way she might discuss a character in a movie or the problems of a distant friend. It was that distance that hurt him the most. "It wouldn't really mean anything if you did. It wouldn't matter."

A man in a black pea coat, shoulders hunched and head buried in a shapeless hat, trudged past them, outside the glass. He was so close it startled Ken when he slogged past, almost ankle-deep in water, sending up heavy sprays of brown water that nearly reached his knees. For a moment, Ken wondered if it was the same man they'd passed on the way to the restaurant, the one that Rose had screamed about. What the devil was that poor man doing out there?

He moved relentlessly north against the current, and an old pick-up truck passed him in the middle lane, going the other way. The water boiled around its slowly turning tires, the wavelets already touching the top of the hubcaps.

"I don't know what to say, Rose." It was the only honest thing he could come up with.

"Uh-huh."

"There was a lot going on. A lot you don't understand."

She gave him a bland and meaningless smile and put out her hands as if she was weighing something in each one. She let the left hand dip down. "Explaining yourself," she said, then let the right one dip, "Making excuses." Then she spread them into a shrug. "I've never been real good at telling those apart."

"I know," he said, and heard the anger in his own voice. "I *know*. It's just–"

There was a tremendous *thwack* on the glass above Rose's head. She said "Shit!" and flinched away, ducking down and covering her head. Ken jumped up and reared back, almost overturning his chair. He looked up to see a dirty white mass the size of a human head smashed against the glass. It held there for a moment, then slid down the entire length of the window and plunged into the brown water on the sidewalk with a thick, ugly splash.

"A bird," said a gruff voice. Ken spun around to see the scientist woman standing right behind him, frowning deeply at the streak of blood and mud on the window. "It was a bird."

"Yeah," he said. "I see that."

Genelle was hovering. "That's been happening all day," she fretted. "This rain is screwing up the poor things. Or maybe it's just the wind, I don't know."

"I'm not that hungry," Rose said. She pushed away the salad she had barely touched. "Can we go?"

Ken nodded, glanced at the check, and peeled a set of bills from his modest roll. "Same here," he said, with a glance at the scientist-woman. What as her name? Armstrong? Armitage? Arm…something. Why did she keep *staring* at him like that? "Let's go home."

Rose froze half out of her chair. "Uh," she said, and stood up much more slowly. "About that…"

"About what?"

"Home," she said, and grimaced. "At least, *your* home." She looked at him, then at their observers, and pitched her voice very low. There was more challenge and less certainty in it this time. "I really, *really* don't want to go up there with… with that…"

"Maggie," he said stonily. "You mean Maggie."

"Yeah. It's …it's *weird*, Dad. This whole thing creeps me out. So I was thinking I could just get a hotel room down here somewhere, in a nice part of town and everything, so you wouldn't have to worry. Nothing scummy, but –"

"That wasn't the deal." he said firmly. He felt as if he had swallowed a stone.

"I know," she said hastily. "I know." They were standing at the table now, but not moving toward the door. Genelle tried to give him change but he shook his head.

"Keep it," he said.

She thanked him and moved away fast. Rose was back to staring at the storm.

"You talk about me walking out on you," he said. "Abandoning you." He didn't care if the others were listening now or not. "Here's a chance to change that. But you won't even stay in the same house with me."

"It's not *you*," she said, but he didn't believe one word of it. "It's that – JESUS! What the hell *is* that?" She stepped to the window and put a hand against the glass.

A roughly cylindrical mass, as long as a man is tall, was rolling down the middle of the street, pushed along by the rising water. It looked like a bolt of tangled black cloth, or a log wrapped in fabric, or–

–or a human body, overwhelmed by the rush of water, rolling over and over in the surging current.

It was the same size, the same color, as the man in the pea coat who had walked past them a few minutes earlier.

"Is… is that a *person?*" Ken said, squinting through the rain.

"Oh my God. Oh my *God*." It was Genelle, standing behind them again. Ken turned to her and saw Tony O'Meara behind the waitress, and the scientist even farther back. He looked grim.

"We been seein' all kind of shi–ah, *stuff* all day," he said. "Maybe that's nothin'."

Rose pressed her hand flat against the glass. "Help him," she said. She turned to her father, outraged and desperate. "*Help* him!"

Ken moved towards the main entrance with Tony close behind.

"It's just somethin' got washed up in the rain," Tony said. "Come on, Ken, don't bring that crap in my place."

Ken didn't take his eyes off the turning black thing in the water. It was still rolling south. He was barely pacing it as he reached the door and tried to push it open.

The door didn't move. He looked away from the turning thing long enough to see that the wide glass door wasn't locked, so he pushed harder.

"*Wait* a second, for Christ's sake!" Tony said. He put a strong hand on Ken's arm. "Look at that water! You open that door, you'll flood the place!"

Ken looked down. At least eight inches of water was flowing past the door, holding it shut, and it would roll into the restaurant like a miniature tidal wave if the seal was broken.

"He's right," the scientist-woman said. "Maybe there's something else…we can…"

The turning thing had stopped for a moment, snagged on something under the water. Foam and mud was boiling around its trailing edge as it shifted, twenty feet away, right in front of them. There was a sudden flash of white – *What was that,* Ken thought. *A hand?* – that disappeared in an instant, then the thing came loose and started flowing south again, rolling and rolling.

"I'll help you clean it up," Ken said, and started to shove at the door as hard as he could.

Tony ripped him away from the glass, turned him around, and slammed his back against the opposite wall. "You leave that fuckin' thing alone," he said under his breath, holding him in place. His square face was bright red under his tan, sweating and slightly swollen. "*Leave* it. I don't want that shit in here."

The scientist didn't move to help. He didn't expect her to. "Tony. Come on. They could be hurt. Hell, it could be somebody you *know*."

Tony didn't let him go. "This is *my* place," he said. "*Mine*. And *that* is not my problem. I don't want it in here."

"But –"

"*I don't want it in here!*"

Ken tried to push him away and Tony shoved him back again, tight against the wall. "Don't," he said, and this time it wasn't a joke. "Just… *don't*."

They stood together, tight and motionless for a long beat… and one more. Then Ken nodded. "Okay," he said. "Your place."

Tony looked at him hard to make sure he wasn't bluffing. Then he let him loose.

Ken straightened up and looked into the street. The turning black thing was gone, swept south now, out of sight. Rose was standing at the edge of the waiting area, her hand on her mouth, her beautiful eyes huge and unblinking.

"I'm sorry," Ken said to her. He felt small and stupid and angry as hell.

"It's okay," she said. Her voice was almost trembling.

"I tried, I —"

"It's *okay.*"

Tony picked up their ridiculous tablecloth, neatly folded and ready to go. "We got the back entrance sand-bagged already," he said gruffly. "It's up a little higher back in the alley there. We'll help you to your car." He looked at the scientist with a mixture of rage and shame. "You, too, Doctor Armbruster."

That was the name, Ken thought distantly. *Armbruster.*

"Time to close," Tony told them.

Ken didn't say anything. He took the cloth and turned toward the kitchen. "Come on," he said to Rose.

Rose whispered "'Bye," as they plunged into the alley. The Range Rover was parked at the curb a few feet before the end of the block. They managed to get inside with only their shoes and cuffs soaked through.

Ken was still burning. "No motels," he said as the doors slammed shut and locked. "None of that shit. I know you're weirded out. I get that. But you're coming to stay at the *hacienda*, at least until your mother is out of the clinic, and that's it." He started the car without waiting for an answer.

Rose looked at her lap and nodded. "Okay," she said. The motel thing had been a bad idea all along, she knew that. And even though she hated that huge, stupid house on the West Ridge and the thought of everything that waited for her there, she was grateful that he had made the decision for her.

After all that had happened, after the wreck and the hospital and the restaurant, she didn't really want to be alone.

Not now. Maybe not ever again.

FIVE

I should just keep going, Lucy Armbruster told herself as the Civic grumbled north on Highway 181. *Just stay on the freeway, keep my head down and don't stop 'till I hit Barstow or Vegas or the friggin' Canadian border.*

She knew what was waiting if she stayed here. The satellite data at the station would confirm it, but the drive across town and a good, hard look at the clouds convinced her: it was a hundred-year event. Maybe a five hundred-year event. The old Dos Hermanos was as good as gone already, and if it didn't stop raining soon – by morning at the latest, there wouldn't be enough dry land left inside the crater valley to rebuild the town. Not ever.

A green and white highway sign passed on her right, whipping and trembling in the gusting wind like a living thing trying to pull itself free of the mud:

NORTH RIDGE EXIT 1 MI.
SCENIC VIEW
UC RIVERSIDE
AGRICULTURAL RESEARCH STATION

"Scenic view my ass," she muttered. The Civic plowed through the sheeting rain. On a good day there was a flat spot right near the off-ramp where you could see the entire Valle de Los Hermanos laid out like a piece of dirty burlap. This was most decidedly, most indisputably, most sure as shittedly not a good day.

Lucy was half-serious about the escape. She really could cruise right by and to hell with the consequences. Use the cell phone to call Cindy and Rebecca at the Station and tell them to go north, young women, go north. Hell, she would even leave a message for that cretin Steinberg to hit the road, not that he deserved it.

She sighed and wished Frannie would speak to her in some kind of soft-focus romance-movie moment, a scene where that wonderful alto of hers, smooth as single malt scotch, would echo out of nowhere and say something like *Nothing important is easy, my love*, or *The greatest good for greatest number, this is your shining moment, make the world your own*, blah blah blah. Or even *Shut up and get to the Station, you twit*. But there was nothing like that. In fact, it was getting harder and harder to remember what Frannie sounded like at all. Lucy had to concentrate now to remember that wonderful voice. It was drifting away, like everything did. *Drifting*, she thought bitterly.

The cell phone made the decision for her, bleeping from its holster on her hip where she wore it like a small-caliber pistol. It was a call from – oh, God, Cindy Bergstrom.

She tapped on the phone. "Yes?"

"Well, hey there, Dr. Armbruster!" Cindy chirped. It was the single most annoying voice on the planet. "Quite a little storm we're brewin' out there, eh?"

"Yeah," she said. "What is it you want, Cindy?"

"Oh, I was just checkin', y'know. Seein' how things were goin'?" The last word came out more like "goo-in'," and there was a charming little diphthong in there someplace. Cindy had been in Dos Bros more than seven years. She had come here with her husband and her sister when they both got jobs at VeriSil, but she still sounded like an apple-cheeked extra from a road company version of *Fargo*. At this particular moment, it was the last – the *very* last – voice that Lucy Armbruster wanted to hear.

Maybe it was the rain, or what Lucy knew the rain would bring. Maybe it was because Lucy really was scared and lonely and didn't want to admit it, or maybe it was simply because she was tired, but the sound of that relentlessly happy, insistently shallow, constantly demanding voice made some small but important restraint in Lucy Armbruster's head go *pop*.

For the first time in a long time, Lucy said what she really wanted to say. She said, "Cindy? How long have we known each other?"

That took Cindy back a bit. "Oh… five years now, Dr. A?"

"Six, actually, since you came to join our happy family. And in those six years, I've learned a lot about you. A lot. I've learned that your house in Lake Geneva is exactly the same color as your house in Dos Hermanos. *Exactly.* I've learned that your favorite yogurt flavor is pistachio, that you raise African violets as a hobby but not very well, and that your daughter Denise has a taste for her own fingernails. And I've learned that you always, *always* speak in code."

Cindy paused, as if she was swallowing. Hard. "In…code, Doctor?"

Lucy was going up the hill past the SCENIC VISTA. The single picnic table and drinking fountain in that bedraggled flat patch of land looked even more pathetic than usual in the iron gray light of the storm. Sunset would be coming soon. Then things would get even worse.

"Yep," she said. "CindyCode. Like, 'Gotta keep in touch with the family, y'know!' means, 'I'm about to make another long-distance personal telephone call on company time.' And 'Whew! Boy oh boy! Down in Mexico, it'd be siesta time right about now!' means, 'I don't intend to do any more work today,' whether it's morning or afternoon when you say it. And 'So how are things goooooin',' means, 'Can I go home early?'"

"But… I …"

Lucy was at the wide driveway to the Station. The modest wood-burnt sign on the left read,

TOMAS J. RIVERA
AGRICULTRUAL RESEARCH STATION
UNIVERSITY OF CALIFORNIA, RIVERSIDE
No. 312

She slowed to a crawl and turned in. Water was coursing down the gutter at least a foot deep. "I'll tell you what," she said into the no-hands phone as she turned, "Chances are you will get to go home early today. Hell, chances are you won't even be able to come in to work at all tomorrow, and isn't that good news? But you'll stay in that damn chair and answer the damn phone until I get back and damn well decide that. And you won't go any-damn-where *at all* until we've had a nice, long conversation about Cindy Code, and about that highly innovative 'come in late/leave early' employee benefit you've built for yourself, 'cause, damn, girl, I'd like to start trying that out myself!"

"But, Dr. Arm—"

"I'm here! I'll be inside in two minutes!"

She clicked off the phone with a single decisive punch of her thumb, wishing for the millionth time that it was possible to slam these things down the way you could a real phone. She pulled the Civic into its customary spot right next to the Station's red All-Terrain Vehicle.

She was halfway out of the car when she saw that the ATV was steaming. It stopped her cold.

For a long moment Lucy simply sat there, barely aware of the wind whipping around her, shielded from the brunt of the rain by the driver's side door. It was clear as day, even in the dimming light: wisps of steam were twisting off the plastic cowling, only to be lashed away by the driving rain moments later.

"Son of a bitch," she said into the open air. "Son of a bitch!" She climbed the rest of the way out of the car and slammed the door as hard as she could, and heard something crash and tinkle in the door.

She turned back for a moment, expecting to see a crack in the window or a broken mirror. It looked fine. She started to open the door again, and the pull-handle flopped uselessly in her hand. The door didn't budge. She would have to pop it open from the passenger side if she wanted to get in.

Oh, great, she thought. *Perfect. Now the goddamn door is broken.*

One more thing to worry about later. She sighed bitterly and turned her attention to the ATV, ducking down between the vehicles as the wind picked up.

She put her bare hand against the cowling. The body-temperature rain hadn't cooled it completely; it was still warm. And there was mud in a dark brown rill along the bottom of the chassis.

Lucy got down on her hands and knees, not giving a damn about dirtying her best pair of pants, and saw a thick layer of mud coating the undercarriage as well.

Not dirt or dust, sheltered from the rainfall, but *mud*, thick as a finger and still glistening.

The goddamn thing had been run out into the storm. That was clear as the new-potato-nose on Lucy Armbruster's face. It had been returned only moments before her own arrival, and there was only one person at the Station with access to the ATV's keys who was stupid and arrogant enough to break all the rules and go joyriding on a day like this.

One single, solitary, smart-ass son of a bitch.

She stalked to the entrance without conscious thought, the rain and all it meant momentarily forgotten. She swept open the glass double doors with a thump…then stopped in her tracks.

Cindy Bergstrom was sitting behind the reception desk, wide-eyed and wary as a whipped dog waiting for another whack. Lucy barely even remembered their conversation. Standing next to her – or rather, half-sprawled over the corner of the desk – was a tall, emaciated, gangling, hairy, patch-covered creature with granny glasses and a walrus mustache. Fender, their neighbor from across the highway. Lucy winced at the sight of him.

"Hey, Doc!" Fender said, showing a crooked double line of yellow teeth. "How about that weather, eh, man? I mean, man, you know? He used the heel of his hand to sweep his long graying hair back out of his face. "Man!"

Lucy looked dead-eyed at her receptionist, asking the clear and unmistakable question: *What in hell is HE doing here?*

Cindy understood perfectly. "Fender came by to make sure we were all right," she said breathlessly. "What with the storm and, and–"

"Is Steinberg in his office or his lab?"

Cindy blinked. This was clearly not the response she had been expecting. "Dr. Steinberg?"

Lucy clenched her teeth so hard it hurt. "Is Steinberg in his office or his lab?"

Cindy swallowed. She was a round, wide partridge of a woman with tightly curled hair and a face like an Oslo hausfrau. "Office," she said. "Last I knew."

Lucy pulled a tight left and pounded through the swinging doors towards the labs. She thought she head Fender say, "Wow, what–" before the closing door shut him off.

I'll get to him later, she told herself. *I'll get to the BOTH of them later.*

The Station was laid out in a huge "X" with the reception area and lobby at the intersection. One leg was administrative offices, one a series of small personal labs, and the other two hydroponic gardens and terraria, along with storage and server space. All of it had been built under the guiding vision and direct intervention of Dr. Lucy Armbruster. It was all her responsibility, her baby, her destiny.

And it was all about to come crashing down because of one semi-psychotic, egotistical idiot with a permanent hard-on instead of brains.

She would kill him. She would simply have to kill him, there was–

A beautiful young black woman came out of a side door marked COMMUNICATIONS and slammed directly into Lucy. Papers went flying; the woman tried to skitter back to keep her balance on her black patent high heels…and failed. Her shapely rump, wrapped in a nicely fitted black skirt, made a pleasantly meaty *thump* when it hit the cool green linoleum. More papers flew.

For one instant Lucy considered simply ignoring her and keeping on. Fortunately, good judgment prevailed, and she stopped to offer her hand.

"Jesus, Rebecca, what are you doing?"

The woman gratefully accepted the help and wobbled back to her feet. "Building up a really good workers' comp claim," she said a little breathlessly. "How do you like it so far?"

"You okay?"

"Fine, fine." Rebecca Falmouth-Hanson, her intern from UC Riverside, was twenty-two, brilliant, beautiful, and obviously in the wrong place. Her skin was a light mocha brown; her chestnut hair was loosely curled and cascaded down her back almost to her waist. She had hazel eyes that made everyone, man and woman, stop and stare. Narrow-shouldered, narrow-hipped, long-legged, and with a brilliant smile that revealed equally brilliant teeth, it had been obvious to Lucy from the day she interviewed her more than a year ago that Rebecca was hideously overqualified for this year-long gopher-and-grunt assignment. What was she supposed to have said to a PhD candidate with qualifications like this? 'Sorry, too pretty? Too good?' The Oversight Committee would have been on her like a bird on a bug if she did that, particularly given Lucy's well-known "gender issues."

What they didn't know was that Rebecca Falmouth-Hanson had "gender issues" of her own. For most of the last ten months she had suffered through a painful and painfully obvious crush on lumpy, gruff ol' Dr. Armbruster, twenty years her senior and of the same sex.

It made for a wonderfully ironic life, Lucy had noted on more than one occasion, but she really didn't have time for it. Not now.

"I have to go find that idiot Steinberg," she said.

"You'll want to see these first," Rebecca said, scooping up the escaped papers.

"It can wait," Lucy said.

"It's the satellite data on the storm. I know–"

"Rebecca, it can wait."

There was a sudden, deep, bone-rattling peal of thunder from above and beyond the station, an unavoidable reminder of how bad it was getting out there, and how quickly. It made Lucy pause.

Goddamn it, she thought. *I get myself all revved up for a good ass-chewing, and something always interferes.*

"Okay. You have a point," she admitted. "What's up?"

Rebecca handed her a photo from a high-altitude weather satellite, one that showed only the widest planetary view, from the North Pole nearly to the equator. There was the North American continent, there the tail of Florida, there the wide bulb of …

"Jesus," she said. There was a spiraling flower growing from the Gulf of Mexico, or was that the Gulf of California? Its arms spread out across half the print-out, beyond the edge of the image. "What are they calling this one?"

"Calliope," Rebecca said. "Pretty, isn't it?" She passed across another shot, this one much closer to home. "Biggest storm of the year so far, and the season's just begun. Winds topping one hundred twenty, centered north of Guadalupe Hidalgo."

Lucy had already moved on to a page of figures relating to the storm and the resulting weather in northern South America, the Isthmus, and southern North

America. This one was big, truly big, and it was being felt as far south as Brazil and as far north as, well, as far north as Dos Hermanos, California.

"The perfect storm," she muttered.

"What?" Rebecca asked.

"Nothing. Never mind."

It was a term she had admired at first. It came from a good book, and it was a nice metaphor in its own way, but she'd come to hate it more recently for its constant, inaccurate reuse. Besides, she'd realized long ago, there was nothing perfect about a storm. Perfection implied something beautiful, something flawless and even admirable. Weather wasn't like that at all, not really. It was the brutal collision of massive, often dangerous physical forces. It was messy and uneven; weather fronts were crooked and turbulent battle-lines of temperature and pressure that threw off swirls and currents, eddies and anomalies that defied not only mapping but real prediction of any kind. Hell, the entire field of chaos theory was created because of the great, huge, dark, hairy, damnable, impossible imperfection of the weather. It would never – it *could* never – be conquered or managed, let alone controlled.

Here was a perfect example of that. The high-altitude photography gave the event a smoothness, a beauty that simply wasn't real. In fact, this was really a huge, uneven landscape as messy as a close-up of bad skin, full of low-pressure pockmarks and high-pressure pimples. And the crater valley of Dos Hermanos was the biggest, nastiest lesion of them all.

Lucy didn't even have to hold out her hand before Rebecca slipped a new photo under her eyes – the tightest shot yet, and a perspective she had seen a million times before. It was 'her' half of the Anza Borrego Desert, as seen from only a few hundred miles up. El Valle de Los Hermanos and the surrounding desert for a hundred miles in every direction.

Sure enough, the swirling far edge of the massive hurricane with the pretty name thousands of miles to the south had set up a whole line of low-pressure systems and squall lines that defied geography and seasonal trends. One of those systems had snaked up from the southwest and wrapped itself around their little crater valley, a fat tentacle of supersaturated air pumping millions of gallons of water and God only knew how much energy into the upper atmosphere.

"And thus come the rains," she said more clearly this time. Rebecca nodded and popped another picture on top of the last. Lucy scowled. "You already showed me this one," she said. "I need to see some time lapses instead. Every hour, maybe? Every two?"

"This is it. Look at the time code."

Lucy opened her mouth to argue, then closed it again. "Shit," she said. "Do you have…?" Rebecca gave her the third in the series. And a moment later the fourth. Lucy swallowed. "Well," she said with false calm. "That's not moving at all, is it?"

The storm had created a stationery front, solid as stone, right over the Valle. They might as well have run a hose as wide as five football fields from the Gulf of Mexico to the Anza Borrego and opened the faucets all the way. Combine that with the data she'd already seen on monsoonal flow, and the mountain-shadow effects they saw around here all the time…

Damn. The cloud cover kept her from knowing for sure, but it was possible that it was bone-dry – or at least nothing more than humid – outside the crater, while inside it was raining like never before. So far, there was no end in sight.

She tore herself away from the printouts and looked directly into Rebecca's beautiful hazel eyes. "You were right," she said. "I'm glad you showed me these."

Rebecca's smile was like the summer sun, so bright and warm it made Lucy uncomfortable to look at it.

"So when are you leaving?" Lucy asked her.

The beaming stopped. "What?"

"Come on, you can read this as well as I can. This place is a disaster waiting to happen…except it's not waiting anymore. Your cute little house down by the VeriSil campus is going to be underwater in a matter of hours. You have to pack up and get out."

"Get out of that house, maybe, sure," Rebecca said defiantly, "but I'm not leaving the Valle. No way. This is a unique meteorological event, and I'm a meteorologist."

"Oh, for Christ's sake, you're Indiana Jones now?"

"This is high ground, Dr. Armbruster. It's got the most sophisticated technology available and a complete uplink to all the major weather satellite

systems and databases. It's a ringside seat, and it's a seat right next to the exit, too, if things do get hairy." Her grin was incandescent. "Heck no, I'm staying."

"No, you're not," Lucy said firmly.

"Yes, I am."

"No. You're. Not." Lucy dumped the papers back into Rebecca's hands. "I still have to talk to that idiot Steinberg, so we'll continue this later. After I've killed him."

She left Rebecca standing in the hall and fumbling with papers, her own mind whirling. There really wasn't much time. Lucy's own little condo was nearby; it would be one of the last to go underwater, worst-case. The rest of these people had something to worry about, and soon. She should let them all go right now. That might give them time to pack.

But first things first…

She reached the door marked LABORATORY #3 and knocked. It drifted open at her touch. She stuck her head inside and saw Michael Steinberg hunched over his computer terminal, busily punching and clicking. His narrow shoulders were high up and trembling.

He seemed to be laughing. Giggling, actually.

Behold the mad scientist in mid-cackle, she thought. She stepped fully inside. "Michael?"

It was as if she had set a firecracker off between his feet. He went "ACK!" and jumped – actually jumped – three feet to the right, clawing at a counter for balance as he spun to her. His eyes were huge and bulging under his limp, dirt-colored bangs. She was sure it took him a moment to recognize her.

"Dr. Armbruster," he said. "Ah. AH, Dr. Armbruster!"

"Michael, where did you take the ATV?"

"You've got to see this," he said, scrambling to the stainless-steel sink, knocking aside furniture and carts as he bulled through. It was as if he hadn't heard her.

"Michael, what did you do with the ATV?"

He waved it away without even turning around. "I had an errand. It doesn't matter. Look at these. Look."

He hauled up a steel tray filled with specimens, a wide collection of strange shapes, all twisted and stretched in different ways. They shared only one thing: an ash-white color somewhere between bone and chalk. "Don't even *think* of claiming this," he said. "I've got it all documented, locked up tight. This one is mine."

She almost laughed in his face. "Don't worry, Doctor. I'll leave it all to… what the hell is this supposed to be?" She reached out to pick up a long cylindrical item, roughly serrated along one side and hollowed completely through its long axis. Steinberg jerked the tray back before she could touch it, almost upsetting the entire affair. If he'd been able to, he would have slapped her hand away. "Careful!" he brayed. "They're very delicate!"

He fumbled with a pair of tweezers and picked up the cylinder, placing it on a nubby mat under a nearby magnifier. He snapped on the light and she bent over it.

"Notice the pitted anchor-points on the anterior. Have you ever seen anything like it? No, you haven't. Never. And this hollow center, obviously a conduit for nutrient or bodily fluids, but unlike anything we've seen in any other species, anywhere."

She frowned as she stared, rotating the mat this way and that, using a probe to gently prod and turn the object. Finally she looked up, her expression carefully blank.

"Well, of course I recognize this," she said blandly.

He looked devastated. "You…you do?"

"Of course. Species Fastfoodia. Genus Drinking Straw. But I can't tell, is it Mcdonaldiana or Jackintheboxia? Please," she slapped the magnifier back towards him. "Enlighten me, Doctor."

He goggled at her, uncomprehending at first. Then his expression curdled into rage. "Why, you … you bitch."

"Oh, for Christ's sake, Michael. A new species? We pick up crap like this off the desert floor every day. If it's not some bit of human detritus, then it's some skeletal fragment that's been warped by the wind or heat. You know that."

He jerked away from her and put the straw-thing back on his display tray. "It's nothing of the kind. Nothing like that. Look at this one." He used the tweezers to pull up a larger claw-like thing, straight as a ruler along the back, angling into a curve with an almost geometrical abruptness as it swooped into a circular arc, razor-sharp along the inside edge.

"Obviously avian," she said, dismissing it.

"Bullshit," he said. "You know goddamn well there's nothing in bird taxonomy that accounts for a claw like that. Not bird, not reptile, not mammal." He looked up to glare at her, and for the first time Lucy could clearly see the rage in his eyes.

What an ugly, ugly man, she thought. *How the hell did he ever get this far?*

"Have you checked?" she asked, carefully controlling her voice.

He gaped at her. "What?"

"Have you checked? If it's not a bird, at least not a local desert species, what about an exotic? What about some, I don't know, parrot or macaw that somebody bought over the internet from a pet store in the middle of Africa, then dumped in the desert when it croaked?"

"That's ridiculous," he blustered, busily putting the claw under the holding clamps on his microscope.

"What about simple birth defects of an indigenous species? Or malnutrition? Have you ruled that out? Or anomalous regrowth of an injury?"

"No," he said, staring fixedly into the eyepiece. "No, it's not possible. Look at the ligature marks here. It must be where the muscles, or something like muscles, linked to the framework. And here, the fine cross-hatching, it's as if a secondary element overlaid the substructure and–"

"And what, a whole new species is more likely than a stray bozo-bozo lizard from Macadamia or a bird with a busted wing? Come on, Michael. Think."

He slammed the countertop as hard as he could. Glass and steel containers bounced and rang the length of the laboratory. "You always do that to me!" he said, sounding like a petulant child. "Always! I come up with a new idea and you piss on it, without even trying to give it a chance!"

She stared at him. "Michael. Honey. That's because you're always wrong." For a moment she thought of putting a comforting hand on his shoulder, actually trying to talk to this asshole, to reason with him despite the wild gleam in his eye and his absolutely absurd proposal. "Look," she said, straining to be gentle,

"I don't know why you keep doing this. You have this schoolboy obsession with making The Big Discovery and becoming the Stephen Hawking of modern biology. But somewhere in there, Michael, you know the truth. Science isn't like that. It's hard work, and slogging, and incremental discoveries, not overnight fame and fortune." She gestured helplessly at the claw-thing. "This isn't going to do it, Michael. All you've got–"

"Just look at it," he said tightly.

"Michael. All you've got is some weathered speci—"

"LOOK AT IT, GODDAMN YOU!"

She stared at him for the longest time. She forced herself to count to ten. "Okay," she said, so quietly she could barely hear herself over the rush of water outside the window. "I'll make you a deal."

"What?"

"I'll examine the specimen…and you tell me where you took the goddamn ATV."

He glared at her. "I didn't take it anywhere."

"Oh, please."

"I didn't take it anywhere important. Just…out for a drive."

"Without permission."

He stared at her.

"After what happened last time."

Still nothing.

"When you know that another complaint or insurance claim will cause the liability coverage for the whole fucking installation to be withdrawn."

"It was nothing, Lucy. Really."

"No trespassing? No property destruction? No assault?"

"*No.* It was *nothing.* Now will you look?"

She put her hands up. "Fine. Fine." She bent over the microscope and looked through the eyepiece, adjusting it automatically. "You know I'm not going to see anything worth… wait a minute. Wait a minute."

She bent over more intensely and finely adjusted the focus. "Did you see the striations on the side here?"

"Where? Which ones?"

"These, these here. Complex. Delicate. Almost like…like writing. My God, Michael, look at this. It says "MADE … IN … JAPA–"

He shoved her away from the microscope and got in front of it, as if protecting his precious discoveries.

"You're a fucking moron," he said. "A fucking idiot. I give you the find of the fucking century, and you ridicule it like everything else."

Lucy wanted to rip his greasy little head right off his shoulders. Where was that celestial Frannie-voice now, she wondered. And would it say, *Walk away, walk away* or *do it do it DO IT!*

She clenched her fists so tightly she could feel her stubby nails digging into her palms. "I told you never to take the ATV again. I told you it was a terminatable offense. And not one week later, as soon as my back is turned–"

"Fine," he said. "Fine, fire me. You'll be the laughingstock of the field, of the *world* when I release this information, when everybody sees–"

Her cell phone rang. Michael stopped short and stared at it, offended that anything, even an inanimate object, would dare to interrupt him. He tried again.

"I mean it," he said. "I dare you to–"

It rang again.

She gave him a perfectly bland smile. "Pardon me," she said. "Important call." She plucked up the phone and clicked it on. "Yes?"

"Fair warning," Rebecca Falmouth-Hanson whispered in her ear. "The cops are here."

"Here?"

"Right outside. I saw the flashers."

"Is Fender still here?"

"Afraid so. At least it looks like just one guy, kind of big and handsome in an old sort of way."

Sheriff Peck. She'd bet a buck on it. "Thanks," she said, and turned back to the moist and arrogant scientist. "Well, congratulations, Michael. You've managed to bring the cops down on us again."

"What?" he said, still sounding offended. "Where?"

"In the lobby. Come on." She turned without waiting for a response and was halfway through the door before she turned back to look at him. She was secretly rather pleased with how he looked: like a small, hairless animal caught in a trap. "Oh, and before we go," she held out her hand, "the keys."

His hand went involuntarily to the pocket of his lab jacket; his jaw started to tighten.

"Don't argue about it, Michael. Just give me the keys to the ATV."

For one moment she didn't think he was going to do it. Then, almost in slow motion, he pulled the keys from his pocket and handed them over.

"Thank you. And Michael, please, *please* keep this in mind. If you give me one ounce of shit about this, ever, I will gladly have that police officer take you out back and shoot you into tiny little pieces. Are we clear?"

His back straightened at that. He stripped off his flesh-colored latex gloves and joined her in the hallway. They didn't speak a word to each other as they walked back to the lobby.

Sheriff Peck was already having a low, intense conversation with Cindy and Fender. Cindy was wringing her hands and ready to cry; Fender was goggling. Rebecca, meanwhile, stood well to one side, leaning in the doorway that led to the Admin wing and watching the cop with an expression made up of equal parts wariness and disdain. It was an expression that Lucy had seen before, and not only on Rebecca, but on black men and women of all ages, whenever there was a cop in sight.

"…meeting tonight?" Peck was saying to Cindy as they entered from the laboratory wing.

"Yes," she said. "You bet."

"'Cause you should," he told her, clearly not listening to her answer. "You really should."

"I have kids, Sheriff, I'll be there for sure."

"Terrible thing," Fender chimed in. "Totally sucks."

Peck's attention snapped to him. "What do you know about it, my friend?"

Fender's eyes got big and he took a step back. "Nothing, Sheriff. Not a thing, you know that."

Peck focused on him like a cougar fixing on a quail. "I don't know anything like that, Fender. But I know you're not coming to the meeting tonight, are you?"

Fender started shaking his head before the cop stopped talking. "Heck, no, Sheriff. No way."

"'Cause you have no kids, my friend. You have no family. You have your tacky little trailer way out here on the edge of forever, and you have no business bothering the decent people of this town. It's none of your concern."

Fender was almost pleading. "Shit, your honor, come on, you've rousted my place twice already and you didn't find a thing! You got no reason–"

The Sheriff was almost nose to crooked nose with the long-haired man. "Oh, I have reasons, my friend," he said, still staring him down. "I have good reasons. But I don't have to tell you about them, now do I?"

Apparently the phrase 'probable cause' hadn't made it into his vocabulary quite yet, Lucy mused. "Here we are, Sheriff Peck," she said loudly, stepping forward to pull the cop's attention away from her trembling neighbor. "What can we do for you?"

Peck took his time. When he did face her, his eyes had lost some of their hardness, and his smile was professionally bland. "Sorry to disturb you," he said, "but I had a few questions. For both of you, as it happens."

Lucy was surprised in spite of herself. "You two have met?" she said, looking at the Sheriff, then at Steinberg, then back at the Sheriff again.

"A couple of times," the Sheriff said mildly. "Nice friendly chats."

"Yes," Steinberg said, as if he had swallowed a turd. "Friendly."

Must have been about the last ATV incident, Lucy thought. She had been under the impression that it had never gone beyond a simple traffic ticket. Now... Steinberg had dealt with the Sheriff himself? And more than once? Yet again, and not for the first time that day, Lucy wondered how much she had missed while working all alone up in her lab, mourning for her lost love and generally hating the world.

"Okay," she said, recovering. "That's fine. I'm glad you're here in any event."

He raised a well-trimmed eyebrow at that. "Really?"

"Yes. You take care of your business first, then I have something important to talk to you about before you go."

"Oh... kay," he said, sounding strangely hesitant. Lucy thought maybe he wasn't used to talking to such decisive women, or maybe he couldn't imagine any business more important than his own. Either way, he seemed almost relieved to focus his attention on the other scientist in the room. "Dr. Steinberg," he said.

Michael regarded him, smirking.

"The ATV," he said.

Michael continued to smirk.

Peck sighed deeply. "All right, if that's the way you want to play it…" He pulled a small notebook from the breast pocket of his sharply ironed shirt and referred to it with a barely noticeable squint. Lucy wondered how he managed to keep that crisp crease in his clothing in the midst of a major storm. She also wondered how long it would be before the good Sheriff broke down and got himself some reading glasses. "At approximately 2:30 this afternoon, a silver BMW was forced off a private driveway connected to North Ridge Road. The driver subsequently lost control, rolled down an embankment at high speed, and collided with a rocky impediment causing serious injury to the driver and the destruction of the vehicle."

Lucy said, "Jesus Christ!" and turned to Steinberg. "Michael?"

Michael shrugged. "Impediment, Sheriff Peck? You gave your officers Word-A-Day calendars as Christmas gifts, didn't you? Admit it."

Peck didn't react. "Victims and witnesses identified a bright red off-road vehicle as the reason the BMW left the road in the first place."

"Astonishing," Michael said.

"To my knowledge, this facility has the only bright red ATV in town."

"Again, remarkable coincidence."

Peck sighed again and put the notebook away. "Look, son–"

Steinberg's expression twisted into an ugly new shape. "I am not your son," he said with all the venom he could muster.

Peck's eyes narrowed. His jaw tightened. "No," he said, "you're not. Because if you were *my* son, you little prick, you wouldn't talk to anybody like that unless you expected to get your head busted, and you sure as shit wouldn't talk to a police officer that way."

A cold blue current slithered down Lucy's back. She took a step forward. "Now, hold on, hold on, let's–"

Peck's hand came up fast, so fast that for a moment, Lucy wasn't sure if he had a gun in it. He didn't. All he had was a finger pointing straight up from a canted elbow in a "wait one moment, let me finish my point" gesture.

"I'll get to you in a minute, Doctor," Peck said without looking at her. "Let me finish with this one first." His eyes never left Steinberg, whose smirk was beginning to falter.

"Did you take the ATV out today?" he asked, very steadily.

Steinberg cleared his throat and darted a look at Cindy, then at Lucy. "No," he said, and looked away.

"You want to try that again?"

More boldly: "No," he said. "I've been working in the lab all afternoon. Since lunch. Which I ate in my office." He smirked again, a ghost of his original expression. "Chicken salad."

Peck's head swiveled to face Cindy Bergstrom. She seemed to jolt when he looked at her, as if he'd touched her with a live wire. "You agree, Cindy?"

Christ, Lucy thought, *does he know everybody here?* Okay, the Bergstroms had been in town a long time, and he'd been Sheriff for a thousand years, so, fine, he knew a lot of people, but still …

Cindy looked at her desk, at the floor, at the walls, everywhere but at Peck. "Yes. I mean, yes, sir. Um…"

"He was here all afternoon?"

"As far as I know."

"And the ATV stayed right where it is?"

"Yes."

"And you have no idea how it got all muddy and warm, just sitting there in the rain?"

Shit, Lucy thought. So she wasn't the only Junior G-Man in town.

Cindy's eyes got big as golf balls. Lucy could see white all the way around. "No," she said in the tiniest voice imaginable.

"I don't even have the keys," Steinberg said defensively. He managed to pull Peck's gaze away from the receptionist; Cindy almost collapsed the instant she was released. "Doctor Wonderful there keeps them on her ample person at all times."

This time Peck did look at her. Into her, with his head tipped forward, his high prominent brow shadowing ghostly blue eyes. He looked at her without a word, as if to say, *So now you're going to join this monkeyfuck?*

Shit, she said to herself. *Shit shit SHIT.* This was the last of it. This was the end. When the Oversight Committee heard of this – and they would – they were certain to pull the plug. Or worse yet, they'd leave the facility right where it was and get somebody else to run it, somebody who didn't let psycho employees run people over, somebody who hadn't spent seven years kissing ass and playing the game, and the last year pissing people off.

Great fucking choice, she told herself. Do the right thing – turn the little maniac over to the cops so he would finally get what was coming to him…and lose the facility. Or do the wrong thing and cover his pimply ass one more time, to save the Station. And, incidentally, herself.

Like it was even a contest.

She fished the keys out of her pocket. "Right here, Sheriff. Only one set, and I have 'em."

"And you've had them …?"

"All day. Since Monday, in fact. Maybe there's another red ATV in town after all. Tourists or visitors. Somebody who came over the ridge to raise hell."

He stared at her. And stared. And stared. Then he shook his head and turned away. "Frankly," he said, sounding truly disgusted, "I don't have time to deal with this right now. I'll be back when the storm breaks. You all stay in town 'till then, won't you?" He stopped and looked over his shoulder, straight at Michael Steinberg. "Won't you?"

Steinberg smirked one more time and added a shrug. "Where would I go?" he said. "After all, I work here, don't I?" he gave a sidelong glance at Lucy. She felt her stomach flop like a dying fish.

The Sheriff was already halfway to the door before Lucy realized he was leaving. She quick-stepped to follow him, moving as fast she could without actually breaking into a run. Damned if she was going to run after him like some eager schoolgirl.

She caught up with the sheriff inside the entrance. The sky outside had darkened even more as the hidden sun began to set. The rain was thick and dull as molten pewter, coming down harder than ever. Everything, including the palms and the succulents, even the carefully cultivated California poppies, looked ancient and lifeless in the dying light.

"Sheriff Peck?"

He turned on her with an expression that clearly said he had already taken about as much as he could stand. "What?"

"You have a town meeting tonight, correct?"

He did everything but tap his foot with impatience. "Yes. So?"

"I want you to urge everybody who shows up to leave town for a while. Immediately. At least until the storm breaks."

That stopped him. He shook his head as if to clear his ears. "I'm sorry, what did you say?"

"I know tonight's meeting is about the little girls who are missing, but look, we have data here that indicates it's going to continue to rain like this for at least the next two days, maybe longer."

He set his jaw. "Not a chance."

"No, it's not a chance, Sheriff, it's a fact. There's no way this town's drainage or emergency personnel can handle what's going to happen. What's already happening. You know that."

"When exactly did you become an expert on what my people can and can't handle?"

"Your people, Sheriff?"

"The people of this town are my people, yes."

They stared at each other for a long moment, sizing each other up, but Lucy wouldn't let it go. "You don't have to call it an evacuation if you don't want to. Just tell people it might be safer if they–"

"Oh, for …" He rubbed his eyes for a moment, clearly trying to control himself. "It's only been raining for three hours, Dr. Armbruster. And you're telling me I'm supposed to tell the whole town to up and go? And based on what, again? On the word of a scientist that nobody's ever heard of, who I met this afternoon? I don't think so."

"It's not about me, Sheriff. It's about the facts. I can show you."

"I have to go," he said, and fit his flat-brimmed hat back on his crew cut. "Let's talk tomorrow, if there's a reason to." He pulled open the glass door and almost threw himself out.

"Sheriff, come on!"

"Tomorrow!" he bellowed over his shoulder, and disappeared into the billowing darkness. Ten steps from the building, he faded into the mist like a bad dream.

Lucy stood in front of the glass doors for a long time, staring into the slate gray storm as the last of the daylight dissolved. Finally she turned around and faced the desk.

They were waiting for her. Looking at her. She didn't have a single clue what to say.

She spread her hands. "Go home if you want. Stay if you want. It's safer here on high ground no matter what happens. There are cots and bedding in storage, but…you know that. Of course you know that."

Cindy Bergstrom was gazing at her from under her cap of curls, still looking like a well-whipped dog. Rebecca Falmouth-Hanson was almost glowing with ready-to-serve sympathy. Fender, as usual, did not seem entirely clear on what had just happened. And Michael Steinberg was doing his best not to laugh out loud.

He was the first to break the silence. "I'll be in my lab if anyone needs to check up on me," he said. Then he turned on his heel and sauntered out of the room. The swinging door shut behind him with a flatulent *whuff*.

It was as if his exit caused an audible pop, and suddenly everybody was moving, looking busy, coming towards her, talking at once.

"What will we–"

"That cop was such a–"

"—got this rain gear from–"

"Stop it," she said, putting up her hands. Everyone kept talking and bustling around the room. "STOP IT!" she shouted… and they froze, all of them, and stared at her again.

She took a deep breath. "Give me one of the parkas," she said to Cindy. "I'm going to walk Fender back home."

Cindy held one out to her. It was yellow and shiny as a schoolgirl's slicker. "I'd be glad to do it, it's no–"

"No. Thank you. I could use the walk." Lucy nodded at Rebecca without looking her in the face. She couldn't bear to see the moist-eyed pity she knew was waiting there. *Big Boss gets ignored by the cop*, she thought. *Big Boss ain't so big after all.*

She motioned to the confused long-hair. "Come on, Fender," she said. "Let's go."

"'Kay," he said, and put his head through a cowhide poncho that made him look like a badly dressed Guernsey. "Comin' atcha." They pushed through the door together, and ducked against the wet wind that tried to push them back again.

The trip from the Station parking lot up the cement staircase to the highway was usually a quick and easy climb. Even Lucy could take two steps at a time on a regular day. Now, in the gathering darkness, with the wind and rain lashing at them from all sides, it was a slow and careful slog, one riser at a time with both hands gripping the cold, wet banisters fashioned from one-inch pipe.

They paused when they reached the yellowed gravel of the highway's shoulder, already weary.

"Totally insane!" Fender shouted into her ear. All Lucy could do was nod in agreement, and momentarily appreciate the smell of good dope and bad oral hygiene that came from him in a warm burst.

There was a sudden flash of blue-white light high and to the right. They both looked up as the first blast of thunder struck them like a fist. They staggered back, half in surprise, half from the actual force of it. They watched together, dumbfounded, as lightning struck the ridge to the north again. When the second thunder-roll hit, it struck again, a little farther to the south...and again...and again.

They stood in the pouring rain for five full minutes watching the lightning travel down the Valle in an almost straight north-to-south line, striking at rock outcroppings, trees, buildings, each strike a little farther from them than the last. The entire town was lit by a burst of sterile blue illumination with each arc. From where they stood, it looked like a slide show of stark black-and-white photographs, a serial portrait of a small American town in the midst of drowning. Lucy was distantly surprised that the Water Tower, Dos Bros' tallest structure – sheet steel filled with water, no less – was somehow spared a strike. She assumed it was well-insulated and equally well-grounded, but still.

They couldn't make themselves move. In spite of the wind and rain, they waited until the electrical storm finally collapsed in a web of lightning-strikes on the VeriSil campus, far to the south, half a mile from the bald, shadowy twin peaks of The Brothers. When the light flickered away and the thunder fell to an ominous grumble, Lucy forced herself forward. "Come on," she said. There were no car headlights in either direction when they crossed; they were alone on the northbound lanes of Highway 181.

"It was like… God walking, or something." Fender managed to sound reverent even while shouting over the storm. "It was… it was …"

She stopped when they reached the center median. "If you say 'far ouuut,' Fender, I swear to God I will leave you here to get hit by the next oncoming car."

He blinked at her from behind his speckled granny glasses. "Well," he said, "I was going to say 'awesome,' but… never mind."

"Good thinking," she said. They cross the southbound lanes without incident and walked down the off ramp to the wide, whitewashed gate with the overhead sign that read SUNMILL WINDFARMS. TOURS DAILY. Lucy knew, the last tour that Fender had given was in January, and even then the visitors had been lost and drunk.

They trudged shoulder-to-shoulder up the gravel driveway. Ankle-high grass stretched out on both sides of the road, dancing in the twisting breezes of the storm, hissing sharp and loud as the rain slashed down. The only illumination was from a set of forty-watt bulbs set at irregular intervals along a single power line that was strung between crooked poles running from the gate to Fender's trailer. The line was swinging back and forth, dancing up and down. Lucy half-expected it to loop-the-loop entirely, like a jump-rope twirling in the hands of giant invisible children.

The windmills that gave the farm its name and Fender enough cash to buy good dope were scarcely visible beyond the hillocks of grass. Lucy could see their naked steel legs shuddering in the wind, the rotor blades locked in place to avoid being damaged by the unpredictable winds. She knew he couldn't possibly afford any serious breakage here. Fender barely eked out a living as it was, selling his excess wattage to the local grid.

For all the eeriness of the scene, the storm seemed less harsh on this side of the highway. Lucy found she could actually hear something other than the splatter of the raindrops on her hood and the blackboard scratch of the wind whistling past her ears.

"Glad that crazy lightning didn't hit my mills," Fender said as they approached his trailer. "It'd blow 'em right out of the ground, I bet."

"I bet," she said. She wanted to keep the conversation to a minimum. Her plan was to get this poor creature into his home and get the hell out, so she could take her own sweet time getting back to the Station for another go-round. She longed to be alone for a while. It was no fault of Fender's; he was a braincase and a burnout, but not a bad neighbor. It was just too much to deal with his constant questions and comments right now, not to mention his entirely obvious crush on the totally clueless Rebecca Falmouth-Hanson. That was why he had come by as soon as the storm got serious, Lucy knew. He wanted to make sure his girl was okay. He was probably hoping to rescue her from some horrible storm-related crisis, so she would finally see him for the prince he was.

Poor Fender, she thought. *A knight in shining armor, smelling of pot and patchouli, in love with a gay-girl Guinevere.*

His trailer was a classic Airstream, a huge aluminum-colored slug as big as a train car, up on blocks at the dead center of his wide, gently rolling parcel of land. The well-worn patch of gravel directly in front of his wooden porch – a little platform slapped together from bits of cast-off lumber – was a puddle now, brown as chocolate milk and as churned-up as a ten-year-old's bathwater. It was a little too wide to step over. They paused at its edge to figure out their next move.

"Hope you got this thing anchored pretty well," Lucy said, squinting up at the Airstream. "You could end up floating away before morning."

Fender grinned at the thought. "That'd be kinda cool, wouldn't it? Wake up halfway to Hawaii."

There was a small movement at the edge of the puddle. They both looked down on what Lucy mistook for a cluster of seed pods or thistles. Some optical illusion of the churning foam made it look as if they had rolled out of the water under their own power. Of course they were just lying there, bumping against the tiny lake's tiny wavelets.

Fender crouched down next to the cluster. They were spherical and spiky, a little bigger than golf balls, a little smaller than tennis balls. "Now, what the heck are these here?" he asked. He reached forward and then stopped suddenly. "Hey!" he said. "Did you see…?" He scowled at the things, then shrugged and reached forward again, more carefully this time. He got a thumb and a forefinger on one spike and stood up, holding it out like a Christmas ornament on a string. "Weh-hell," he said wonderingly, "will you look at that, now?"

Lucy stepped forward and looked hard…and felt another cold blue current shudder down her back.

It was all spikes. Some were as thin and straight as needles from top to bottom; others were thick at the base, then sloped up like cactus-thorns or sea-urchin spines to a glistening point. There wasn't a curve anywhere on the thing, either. Each spike was made up of flat planes, three- or four-sided pyramids, even a few with eight or ten, each face like a facet of unpolished quartz, all meeting at a single tiny center-point you couldn't quite see. The thing seemed to have no real center at all. It was all thorns.

And they were moving. Growing, actually, or shrinking. Lucy resisted the urge to put her nose right up to the thing. She could see plainly from a foot away that some of the spikes were getting longer while others appeared to be falling back, becoming thinner and breaking away. The whole ball of thorns was in constant, almost organic motion, moving, reaching, retreating, like a living thing – a *breathing* thing, though it had no mouth, no lungs, no life. Even the spine that Fender held seemed to be growing longer, almost stretching, as if the weight of the sphere was causing that one spine to grow thicker and longer.

"That's not possible," she said.

"Wow," Fender said. "I mean… wow." He brought it close to his face.

A spike as thick as a darning needle shot out from the ball, straight for Fender's left eye. He flinched away at the last instant and the point of it dug into the side of his face instead, into the flesh below his cheekbone. Lucy gasped when she saw it pierce him deeply, at least a quarter inch, then rake through the skin and tissue as Fender's head turned. Blood sprayed as it sliced up and over, still going for the eye, still growing.

Fender yelped like a wounded beast and flung the thing away as fast as he could into the shadowed grass. "Shit," he said and cupped his cheek. His legs started to buckle. "Shit, shit, what was that?"

Lucy got an arm under him and held him up. She was surprised how light he was, and how muscular, like a man made out of twisted wire. "Wait a minute," she said. "Come on, now, wait a minute, let's get you inside." She turned and slogged through the puddle and got him up the porch. It wasn't until they were fumbling with the latch on the unlocked door that she realized there could have been a whole swarm of those things, those *needleseeds,* in the water she'd walked through. *Stupid,* she thought as the door screeched open, *but at least we made it inside.*

"Shit," Fender said, still doubled over and clutching his face. "Shit shit shit."

The inside of the trailer was cramped and precisely as messy as Lucy had expected, but there was one old steel-and-stuffed-vinyl kitchen chair that wasn't covered with stacks of paper or dirty clothes. She levered Fender into it and put a hand on his shoulder, comforting but firm. "Come on, Fender," she said. "Come on, look up here."

He didn't respond. She was still staring at the back of his trembling head. Lucy saw for the very first time that there were streaks of gray in his long blond hair, and a noticeably thin spot was starting to show right at the crown. *Even ageless hippies get old*, she thought with an unexpected tenderness. *Doesn't seem fair...*

"Come on, Fender," she said again. She put her other hand under his chin and slowly, steadily, forced him to look up.

He was crying freely. His glasses were crooked, almost falling off. She removed them and put them on the counter, then pried his hands away, still muttering meaningless, comforting things: "It'll be fine, let's just get a look. Come on, Fender, help me out here, man, let me look, you'll be fine."

"Shit," he keened. "Shit shit shit..."

It was worse than she thought. A gash over two inches long and a half an inch deep ran from the middle of his right cheek to within a quarter-inch of the corner of his eye. It was gushing blood, red and plentiful and, if anything, thinner and messier than she had expected. She had heard that head wounds were bad, that much she remembered that from her first aid classes. But this?

She looked around his tiny kitchenette and caught sight of a roll of paper towels. "Hang on a second, Fender, give me a second." She grabbed at it, tore off three sheets, and folded them rapidly into a thick pad. "Here. Hold this against your cheek, man. Tight, now, tight as you can. And no taking it off to look." She put the pad in his palm and pressed it hard again his face. *Apply pressure to the wound,* she told herself, *if only to keep the idiot from freaking out at all the blood.*

"Do you have a first aid kit?"

"Shiiiit," Fender said, groaning thinly as he held the pad to his cheek. He was starting to rock back and forth like an autistic child.

"Fender!" she said, and jerked him by the shoulder. "Join me, here, man! Do you have a first aid kit?"

He stopped groaning and shaking. After a moment he gulped in a mouth full of fresh air and said, "Kinda. Band-Aids and Bactine. Above the sink." He pressed down harder on his cheek and started to double over again. "Shit!"

She found it in the half-broken cupboard and brought it out. Just as directed: Bactine, Neosporin, a used athletic bandage, and three half-empty boxes of Band-Aids in different sizes, surrounding an unopened bottle of Tylenol.

"The best that modern medicine has to offer," she said. She pulled out the boxes, quickly locating the type of Band-Aid that was the large square pad usually used for scraped knees.

She turned back and pulled Fender's face up to her again. He didn't fight as hard this time. "What *was* that?" he asked, his eyes squeezed shut in pain.

At least that's better than 'shit shit shit', she thought. "I haven't got a clue," she said, "but the wind must have caught it and blown it into you."

"No way," he said. "It bit me, Lucy. That thing jumped on me, man! It *bit* me!"

"Okay," she said. The truth was, it had looked like that to her, too, but that wasn't possible. Seed pods generally didn't attack at will. At the moment, it didn't really matter. This guy had a serious facial wound, and they had to deal with that first.

"Never mind," she said, "We'll get this cleaned up and get you over to the Clinic."

"No way," he mumbled. "I hate those guys. Always thinking I'm OD'ing or something, even when I just got the flu."

She nodded in understanding. The Borrego Clinic wasn't exactly Cedars-Sinai, but it was all they had. This looked like it was going to need stitches and antibiotics at the very least. "We'll see," she said, then she reached out to gently pull the hand with the blood-soaked paper towel away from wound. She was braced to see the worst.

She saw a thick, scabby, almost dry line of blood no more than two inches long. That was it. No bubbling gash, no bright red gush, just a dark and crusty blot on his cheek. As if he'd barely bled at all.

"I'll be goddamned," she said to herself.

"What?" Fender asked in alarm. "What? Come on, it's already tingling like a son of a bitch, what's wrong?"

"Nothing, Fender. Christ, get hold of yourself." She wiped the blood away from it. He flinched, but didn't scream. Then she did it again.

The wound had closed up, though not in the way she'd expected. Not at all. A crust had formed over it, flakes of gray and white, like tiny chips of bone or rock that hadn't drawn the lips of the wound together but had filled the gash, like plaster troweled into a crack in a wall. It wasn't a scab, it couldn't have formed that quickly, and it wasn't the right color or texture. It was more like...like a *patch,* something you'd make in a concrete wall.

She took the water-soaked towel and wiped it over the wound again. It left behind a swath of moisture that glistened in the trailer's dim light…and then the crust along the cheek seemed to swell, to actually grow new chips along its edge as the water soaked in.

No, she decided. It didn't soak in. It was pulled in, *sucked* in, like a sponge.

For a brief moment, Lucy thought it was some bizarre infection caused by the needleseed itself. But it couldn't be infected – not this fast. This didn't look like the effects of any plant toxin she'd ever seen before, either, and she had seen plenty. There was no leakage, no pus, nothing. Only dry flakes, dry particles. *Dry.*

How can an infection be dry? she asked herself.

Fender was pulling himself together. His breath was slowing down and his wiry muscles were loosening, if only a little. "Shit," he said one last time. "Okay. Not so bad now. Whatever you did is helping."

Lucy hadn't done a thing. And as she watched, the last of the moisture from her towel, and the last of Fender's tears, were pulled across his drying skin and drawn swiftly into the wound.

"It's cool now," he said now, barely panting. "It's cool. Whew." He looked up at her and tried to smile. "Hey, can I have a glass of water?"

She stared at him. "What?"

He passed a hand over his cheek very tenderly. He didn't seem to notice the wound shifting under his fingertips.

"Water, please," he said. "Please. A nice, big glass, too."

SIX

She's a moron, Michael Steinberg thought. *She's a joke. She doesn't deserve what she got, and when the time comes I'll take it from her. ALL of it.*

This time he locked the door to the lab. No one would disturb him again, especially not that fat fuck with the Napoleon complex.

He was through being a target for her and her twisted kind. No more playing the role of the little white cake in the urinal that everybody pissed on. These specimens, this *evidence,* was going to change the whole fucking world, and put him on top. The very top.

He didn't bother with the latex gloves. He wanted to get the specimens back into their carefully made sponge-rubber pockets so he could work on the documentation a little bit more. Finishing touches. The last polish.

The New Taxonomy, he said to himself. It had a hell of a ring to it.

It didn't matter what *she* thought. It didn't matter what any of those smelly, squishy pus-pockets thought, if they thought anything at all. His paper was nearly done now, and in a matter of days, months at the outside, he'd be on the cover of everything from *Scientific American* to *USA Today,* and *she* would be begging for scraps.

He was still trembling with anger, still red-faced and muttering to himself about Lucy Armbruster and Jennie Sommerfield and that fucking cop, when he seized the microscope that held the claw-specimen. "Rank *bitch,* he snarled. "*Fire* me? Fire *ME*? What the fu—OUCH!"

The pain was like a spike in his palm. He jerked around, cursing, and his elbow hit the edge of the specimen tray. It skittered across the metal counter and slid into the sink with a splash.

He hadn't been paying attention. When he had tugged the claw-specimen from under the scope's clips, it had snagged on one side and turned in his hand and the wickedly sharp tip had dug deeply into his palm.

Michael hissed in a breath and raised his hand to his eyes, the claw still dangling from his palm. Runnels of blood were flowing through its channels and running down his wrist, turning his ragged shirt cuff a bright, almost theatrical red. The curved point of the specimen had doubled back; it was coming out of his palm a full inch from where it entered. Blood bubbled up from both cuts like water from an Artesian well.

While he watched, the bleeding just...*stopped.* Tiny white particles, oversized grains of sand, appeared from nowhere, and were welling up out of the cut or condensing right out of the air. He watched in fascination as they clustered around the base of the claw, building up in a heartbeat, layer on layer, sealing the specimen to the flesh. And as they accreted, the sharp, thin pain of the cut itself simply drained away.

Michael felt a mild tingle, almost a buzz, rising from his hand and filling his head. It was warm and soft-edged and *right,* like the pulsing in the storm had been right in his head a few hours earlier.

Still, it looked out of place, an alien claw, sharp as a bird's beak, sprouting from his palm? *No,* he told himself. "I don't want that *there,*" he said in a dumbfounded voice. "Not *there.*" Without even thinking about it, he wrapped two fingers around the vicious curvature of the claw and yanked it free, hard as he could. It ripped out of his hand with a thick and meaty squishing sound, but offered almost no resistance, spraying a fan of grayish blood and ash-colored particles as it pulled free. He barely heard the droplets and granules spatter against the window glass above the sink.

The sink. *The sink.* Oh, *god,* he thought as he plunged both hands into the water despite his cuts. *The specimens! The evidence! Holy Christ, they'll be ruined by the water!*

He hauled the tray out, careful to keep it straight, and peered through the water as it sheeted off, checking for each precious specimen, each carefully measured and photographed and recorded piece.

It was all there. All intact. Everything was fine, *fine*.

And everything was…

… *growing*.

"Look at that," he said, his voice a wondering whisper. "Look at *that*…"

The specimens were sprouting new limbs, building new layers. Needles were extending, legs were unfolding and struggling to bend. As yet, no eyes, no mouths that he could recognize as such, but…life. A strange, brittle, sharp-edge kind of life, far from human, but still, life in each of the pieces he had found.

In *his* specimens.

He could still feel tingling in the cuts on his hands. The same particles, the same growth that was changing the specimens was taking hold inside his body as well, he realized, drawing on the water, *building* with the water. The buzz in his head was still there, too, more than ever like the huge deep pulse he first felt in the rain today. Something that had never quite left him, that kept beating and *beating* and BEATING.

ACTION, it told him, exactly as before. *Take ACTION.*

There was a mind even greater than his own at work here. There were thoughts even deeper than his own thoughts. They echoed over him like thunder, surged around him like the roaring wind.

He wanted them inside him. *Inside* him. He wanted to be part of it completely.

Michael Steinberg looked down at the tray of specimens, wriggling and shuddering in an inch of standing water. As he watched, the water level sank by half as the creatures took it in and changed.

He reached into the tray and picked up one particular specimen, a squashed sphere with a bite taken out of it, no bigger than an apricot. Its surface had originally been covered with small pimples and warts. Now each of those bumps had growing into a short spike, a blunt needle of its own. Soon the specimen would be nothing *but* needles, nothing but *sharp*. He could see its final form in his mind's eye already.

He picked up the sphere and looked at it closely. He watched it grow and change as he held it between his fingers.

Then he opened his mouth very wide and laid the wriggling, bumpy sphere on his tongue. He could feel one of the needles jump at the sudden moisture in his mouth and grow thicker and sharper to take it all. He could feel an extrusion eagerly pierce his tongue, while another bit into his palate. He felt the curve of the sphere dissolve and flow down his throat like dry sand.

He closed his mouth and bit down. The brittle, papery taste of the thing surged briefly behind his teeth, then mixed with his blood and spittle.

It was the right thing to do. Michael Steinberg stood alone in his lab, staring at nothing, feeling the tingling buzz build and build and *build,* and he knew it:

It was the right thing to do.

SEVEN

It looked as if the entire town was melting. The buildings, the trees, even the unnaturally straight lines of curbs and power poles looked soft and pulpy in the dying light. Rose watched it pass, shivering, wet and cold, in the passenger seat of the Range Rover.

Rain isn't only about getting wet, she told herself. *It's about getting* weak. *There's nothing sweet or gentle about it, and there probably never was. We just weren't paying attention.*

After a while, the Rover's headlights revealed the hunched shoulders of the *hacienda* on the crest of the West Ridge at the end of the long dirt drive that led to it, really nothing more than a wide, lazy circle of decomposed granite on a base of pounded earth. The driveway sidled along the entire length of the two-story adobe, past an endless display of deeply set, small-paned windows. Lights burned in some of the rooms – fire-yellow, ember red, electric silver-blue. As they trundled by, Rose caught glimpses of an exercise room, an old-fashioned study, a parlor of some kind and a kitchen. Empty, she knew. All empty.

The turnabout made a three-hundred-and-sixty-degree circuit around a huge flat-topped boulder as big as a guest cottage, more than ten feet high and thirty feet across. It seemed to surge out of the ground like the base of a ruined tower. The detached garage was beyond it, and when they passed the rock, water hissing and glittering down its rough, piebald surface, the garage door in front of her eased upwards. Water sheeted off its sides in sprays so wide and thick it looked like a mouth opening under a dirty brown mustache.

The interior of the garage was immaculate and antiseptically illuminated by a bank of ceiling-mounted lights. Ken killed the engine and Rose climbed out of the Rover, very watchful and quiet as Ken opened the door to the covered walkway that connected the garage to the house.

The storm blew across their path in a tumble of mist and wind. "Everything's set everything up for you already," he called over the gale as they crossed the ten feet of covered walkway. Beyond him, Rose saw the lights in the kitchen pop on, and the outer door click open all by itself.

Rose stopped moving while Ken kept going.

"I have no idea what you like," Ken said, "so I got a little of everything. If there's some…"

He was halfway across the kitchen before he realized he was talking to himself. He stopped and turned to see Rose still standing in the doorway, wide-eyed and hesitant.

"Something wrong?" he asked.

"You ever watch *The Prisoner*?"

He blinked at the non-sequitur. "What, the old TV show?" he said. "Gad, Rose, that was way before you were born."

"They show it on BBC America all the time," she said, still not moving.

He frowned more deeply. "Okay…"

She looked at him like he was a complete idiot. "The lights," she said. "The door."

He blinked again. "What about them?"

She sighed bitterly. "Never mind." She ducked her head down, gripped the sides of the door and pulled herself into the house, only to stand inside the doorway, frozen in place, as if waiting for lightning to strike.

Nothing happened.

"Are you finished?" Ken asked her, truly annoyed now.

She scowled and walked carefully into the kitchen.

It was a great room. Expensive china and glassware gleamed on open shelves along two walls. There were plenty of counter space and wonderfully deep cabinets. Even the stove looked important, a brushed-steel professional-grade monstrosity with six burners and an oven large enough to cook two turkeys side-by-side. And everything was *clean. S*uperbly, impeccably, deep-down-scrubbed-to-see-your-reflection *clean.*

"Damn," she said, impressed in spite of herself. "This is bigger than our whole apartment back home."

Ken gave her a strange, quick smile. "I'd like to see your place sometime," he said, almost asking permission.

She chose to ignore him. Ken shrugged and led her into the dining room, with a table large enough to accommodate twenty, and then through a high arch into the front entrance's anteroom and a huge, high-ceilinged living room. The entire house was decorated in Desert Modern, from the nubby off-white area rugs on burnished hardwood to the chocolate-brown exposed beams. The far wall was dominated by a wide, low-stepped staircase that swept up to the second floor, looking as if it had been sculpted right out of the wall.

"Your room is upstairs," he said, "with all the other bedrooms, including mine. Third door on the left for you, last door on the right for me. Down this hall there's—"

"Is that where you keep it?" Rose demanded, sounding angry.

"Keep *it?*"

Rose looked disgusted. "Oh, for …" she said under her breath. She looked around wildly and swept open the door to the hall closet. There was nothing inside but an old windbreaker, a mop, and box of replacement light bulbs. "Not in here, anyway," she said and slammed it shut, then turned and stalked down the hall as if she knew exactly where she was going. Ken followed three paces behind. She found his study with no trouble.

It was just as he had left it, including the open drapes that looked out onto the small backyard and his dying garden. *Probably washed away now,* he thought as he crossed the threshold. Lightning cracked open the clouds above the ridge, and for an instant they could both see the rounded, hard-edged silhouettes of cloud banks behind the slashes of rain, sharp white against the carbon sky.

"Do you keep it in *here?*" she asked impatiently, and swept open the double-doors to the media center. There was nothing inside but a huge wall-mounted flat screen and a complicated remote with lots of fashionably unreadable black buttons and sliders.

She hopped to a dark wood filing cabinet Ken had put against the far wall. "What about in *here*?" She rolled open a drawer and peered comically inside.

"Rose–"

"Oh, don't tell me it shows up as a cartoon-face on your computer screen," she said. "How *eighties*." She started to punch keys at random on his onyx keyboard. "Hello, Siri. Greetings, Max Headroom. Open the pod bay doors, Hal. Come out, come out, wherever you–"

"*Hey!*" Ken snapped. "*Stop* it!"

She snatched her hands away from the keyboard and stood there, faced away from him, for a long moment. Ken saw that she was staring at the photograph of the three of them, but he couldn't see the expression on her face well enough to guess at what she was thinking.

After a long moment she turned to him, looking guilty and sullen at the same time.

He tried to pick his words carefully. "We thought it was probably a good idea if Maggie didn't, um, join in at–"

"*We* thought?" she echoed. "*She?* What, you sat around and discussed this like, like *buddies?*"

"Rosie, that's the whole point to Maggie. She's supposed to be an assistant, a colleague, a trusted friend."

"God! Dad! Listen to yourself! Didn't you see *Her?*"

"See what?"

"It's a fucking *computer,* it's not your *friend.*"

"She's designed to be both," he said very calmly. He looked nowhere in particular as he said, "Maggie, talk to her."

Silence.

Ken scowled. "Maggie, show her what I mean. Come on."

Silence. Only the rumble and spatter of the rain.

Rose cleared her throat. "Um…Daddy?"

"What? You think I made this whole thing up? Do you think I'm totally insane?"

Rose put up her hands and answered too quickly. "No no no, of course not. Maybe there's something wrong with the, the program."

"There's nothing wrong with the program," Maggie said.

Rose squeaked and jumped two feet into the air.

"I like to mess with him sometimes." As always, the AI sounded like a beautifully modulated adult female who seemed to be standing right beside you.

Rose clutched her chest like a heart attack victim. "Jesus," she said. "That scared the *shit* out of me."

"Boy," Maggie said, "one little disembodied voice in a strange house in the middle of an enormous rainstorm, and she gets all jumpy. What a wuss."

"A *what*?"

"Take it easy, Rose," Ken said, trying to sound soothing. "She's trying to put you at ease. Make you comfortable."

"*She*? Make *me*…? I'm gonna be sick."

"Come on, give her a–"

"No. Really. Seriously. I am going to be sick." She looked around for an exit.

"There's a half-bath through the door to your right," Maggie said, still sounding amused. "No tub, but a nice place to pu—"

"*SHUT UP!*" Rose shouted, and ran out of the room. Ken could hear the slap of her shoes on the hallway tiles, then on the stairs, then a distant *slam* echoing down from the second floor.

"Well, at least she found her room," Maggie said in a low voice.

Ken didn't move for a long time, just stared blankly at the empty doorway. Finally he said, "Well," and rubbed his eyes. "That didn't go well at all, did it?"

"Let her be for a while. Besides, you have a couple of other things to worry about."

"I do? Like what?"

"For one, the storm has caused some damage to the house. Nothing serious – yet – and I've taken care of most of the repairs already, but you should know about them."

He sighed deeply. "Okay," he said.

"And Marty Fein has called back four times since you left. I out-referenced that original cell phone call for voice stress analysis, and Ken, he's not kidding. If you don't show up with a *really good* presentation tomorrow, they really *will* cancel your contract and come rip the equipment, and the programming, right out of your system."

More sighing. "I know, I know."

"So what do you say we get to work and come up with a killer presentation? Convince them of what we can do?"

"We," he repeated.

"Hey," she said, and he could almost have sworn she was laughing. "Who knows the project better than me?"

* * *

Rose's room, the third on the right, just as she'd been told, was large and high-ceilinged. There was soft, warm lighting and exposed beams and a set of windows that looked over the circular driveway with its huge broken-tooth stone centerpiece. There was clean linen on the bed with a thick comforter folded at its foot, and even a clear glass vase of California poppies on the end table.

Rose hated every cleaned, vacuumed, polished, dusted, carefully prepared square inch of it.

It keeps pulling at me, she thought as she lowered herself onto the perfect bedspread. *It's like gravity. You can't escape it. It's always* there.

It would be so easy. There was sure to be liquor in that huge dining hall they passed. Good shit, too. There were probably pills in the medicine cabinet, and Rose would know the name of every one of 'em. She was a fucking encyclopedia of prescription medications and their off-label uses. Really *really* off-label.

"It's too much," she said out loud to the empty room, and then again, in her head. *It's too much. I hate this place, I hate that man, I hate my* life. *All I want to do is sleep. Float away. Get* away.

She fell on her side, into the pleasantly floral fragrance of the comforter, and did her very best not to cry.

She was remembering a corner in East L.A. She'd forgotten the names of the streets, if she'd ever known them, but she remembered that corner in painful, cutting detail. Every crack on the sidewalk where she'd laid her cheek, ever particle of grit ground into her knees and the heels of her hands.

That had been the very bottom of it. That morning, when she'd dragged herself up into the greasy morning light with a hangover so bad she couldn't speak. When that man, that *thing* that hobbled like a man, put his fist up her torn skirt and whispered something so wheezy and wet she couldn't even understand it, but she could smell it. In fact, she realized, God damn it all, she could *still* smell it. She would always smell it.

At that moment, she had raked him with her nails – the ones that hadn't broken off – and kicked him with her one remaining high heel. She had staggered away, and he had been too hurt to follow her. Some chick at the Beverly Center, a thousand miles away from that corner she couldn't forget, had let her borrow her phone. She'd never even thanked her. Her mom came and got her and she slept in a bed that night for the first time in month. She still remembered thinking, *no matter how bad it gets, or how shitty I feel from no drinking or smoking or shooting, it will never be as bad as waking up a broken wrist and a knife-cut on my taint and somebody else's vomit in my mouth on that corner in East L.A. Never as bad as that.*

She could feel the tears rising. She hadn't cried, actually *cried,* since that day. But now…

"I was wrong," she said to the empty, perfect, fucking beautiful room. "I was so wrong."

Because the gravity never let up. The pull never went away. It didn't get any better, she didn't get any happier, and all the really good reasons she'd had to run in the first place were still there, still cutting her, still working, especially her fucking father and his fucking toys and her fucking mother and her paper smile and… everything.

The world she was living in now, the one without all that wonderful stupid shit she had put into her body, was simply too hard. It was all sharp edges and hard landings, nothing but dead eyes that made her sick and angry. It was all …

Too much.

She turned her face and buried it in the double-thick pillows and *screamed.* She let it go on and on, and when she ran out of air, she turned her head, gasped in another breath, and did it again. When the second scream ran dry, she lifted her head up…and found that she actually felt a little better. A *little.*

There was a *clink* against the window above the bed. She looked up to see a twig – no, a whole tangle of twigs – pasted against the window screen. Some of the sticks were thin as a pencil; others thicker than a finger. They looked eerie, bony, illuminated by the spilled light of the bedroom and, for a pulsing instant, the flash of lightning far across the Valle.

As she stared, the pile of twigs seemed to shift in place – *twitch*, as if plucked at by the wind or…

There was a knock at the door and she jumped again…then forced herself to stop. *Too fucking much JUMPING going on here*, she thought. She was acting like a third-rate actress in *Halloween 14*.

The knock came again, short, soft, polite.

"Nobody home," she called out.

"Rose? It's Maggie."

Rose felt a sudden chill. She spun around and sat up on the bed, cross-legged. "How the *hell* are you *knocking on the door?*"

"Special effects," Maggie told her. Her voice seemed to be coming, quite convincingly, from the other side of the door. It was distant, muffled, slightly hollow. "You like?"

"Frankly," Rose said, "it creeps me out. *You* creep me out."

Maggie paused, almost as if she were taking a breath, choosing her words. "I only wanted to tell you that you have all the privacy you need in there."

There was a strange, metallic zipping sound behind her head. Rose looked over her shoulder and saw that the bundle of sticks – was it bigger now? – had actually cut its way through the window screen, driven hard against the window by the force of the wind.

"…not listening to what you're saying, and your Dad can't hear you either. Just so you know."

Rose had missed the first part, but she got the gist. "Okay," she said shortly. "Thanks."

There was a long, deep pause. "Okay," Maggie said. "If you need something, all you have to do is open the door and call out."

Rose didn't bother answering.

Another pause. "I'm gone, then," Maggie said.

"What, are you going to make tiny little footstep-sounds that get softer and softer?" she asked.

Maggie chuckled. Rose was sure she heard it, a *chuckle*. "No," she said, "I'll go. 'Bye."

Rose was alone. She could feel it. She glanced at the sticks jittering against the window as she fumbled for her purse and pulled out her cell phone. The twigs had worked their way even more deeply into the cut in the screen. And they were definitely bigger now. How was that possible?

She speed-dialed her mother's cell phone. It rang twice before a voice answered – a *male* voice.

"Um … Lisa Mackie's cell phone," the voice said. It was vaguely familiar to Rose, but she couldn't quite place it.

"Lisa Corman, actually," she said. "She changed it back. And who is this?"

"Rose? That you? It's Bryan Chamberlain. At the clinic."

Oh, right, the cute doctor-guy. "You normally answer your patient's phones?" she asked.

He laughed easily. "Hardly. I was checking on your mom and the phone went off. It was sitting on the end table, and I didn't want it to wake her so …"

"Oh," Rose said, disappointed. "She's asleep?" She didn't realize until that moment how much she'd wanted to talk to her mother, just to hear her voice. How embarrassing was *that*?

"Finally drifted off a few minutes ago. She was having a tough time of it. She got up and walked around with me a bit."

Skreek. The sharp shriek of metal on glass. Rose turned with the cell phone still in her hand and saw the sticks scrabbling against the window glass. They were bigger than her fist now, and it didn't look like the wind was pushing them; it looked like they were *moving*, all by themselves. Like fingers on a hand, but a hand with no palm, no wrist, no–

"Rose?" the doctor said. "You still there?"

"Yeah," she said distantly. "So… Mom's okay?" She stared at the sticks in fascination. What *were* they? She got up on her knees in front of the window and lifted one hand. There was another flicker of lightning outside, far across the Valle. It made her hand a black-etched shadow against the window for an instant. The sticks were a scrabbling, twitching blur.

They were reaching for her. She could feel it. *Reaching* for her.

"Rose? You okay?"

"Yeah," she said, fascinated. "Yeah, I'll…we'll talk tomorrow …" She dropped the phone and brought her hand up to touch the window right where the sticks–

They jumped at her, grabbed for her right through the glass. The cutting noise became a mad shrieking as they scrabbled frantically to get at her.

Skree-skree-skree–

"*Jee*-sus!" Rose snapped her hand back and jumped away, clear off the bed. The finger-sticks scrabbled and scratched and jerked to get at her now, the cutting-noise getting higher and sharper than ever.

Skree! Skreet-SKREE!

"Daddy?" she called out. "Daddy, can you–"

There was a voice at her shoulder, a deep, rich female voice, like Julie Andrews without the English accent.

"I'll take care of it, Rose," Maggie said.

SKREET! SKREET! SKREE—

There was a deep, grating VUMMMMM that came from nowhere. Blue and white sparks jumped from the window-screen to the sticks, an angry, blinding spit of light. The sticks jumped again, but this time it was more like a convulsion. The humming stopped for a moment, then came again, louder: VUMMMM. More sparks, and the sticks hopped off of the window, away from the screen, and were snatched away by the wind and rain.

Gone in an instant. All that was left was a ragged three-inch incision in the window screen, and a triangle of mesh that whipped around in the storm-driven gale like a waggling flap of skin.

"That's better," Maggie said. She sounded grimly satisfied.

Rose stared at the window. She swallowed hard. "What'd you do?"

"Electrical charge," Maggie said. "All the windows and doors are wired for it. Discourages break-ins when I activate it."

"You activate it much?"

"Actually," she said, "this was the first time."

The door flew open and Ken barreled in, tripping over his own feet. "Rose? You okay? Maggie said something was happen—"

Rose put up a hand and smiled. "I'm fine, Dad. It's cool. Something just … hit the window. From the storm. Made me jump." For some reason, she didn't want to tell her father about this, not yet. He had other things to think about, and they'd had enough weirdness for one day.

Ken looked suspicious. He frowned at her. "You sure? Maggie said–"

"Positive," she said. It occurred to her that Maggie was the ultimate multi-tasker: she had been talking to her Dad downstairs even as they'd had their conversation about privacy up here. "Just a jittery teenager, that's me. Probably withdrawal symptoms, y'know." She grinned wickedly.

Ken went pale, and she realized it wasn't yet a joke to him.

"Kidding," she said. "Jesus, Dad, really, come on. I was *kidding*."

"Sure," he said uncertainly. "I knew that."

"Anyway, Rosie the Robot here zapped the thing away, so–"

Something occurred to her. She turned from her father and addressed the empty air. "Hey," she said. "I thought you said you couldn't hear me unless I called out into the hall. I didn't even get near the door."

"Oh, that," Maggie said. "I lied."

Rose sighed.

EIGHT

Sheriff Donald Peck was having a particularly vicious fantasy about beating the living shit out of Doctor Daniel Fucking Steinberg, geekfart cocksucking pain in the ass that he was, when his smart phone *bleep-bleeped*.

He froze behind the wheel of his parked cruiser and clamped his teeth together.

The phone went *bleep bleep* again.

Only four people were supposed to have that number, and none of them were people he could afford to ignore.

Shit, shit, *shit*.

He pulled the phone free and looked at the Caller ID.

"What the fuck?" Without another thought he took the call. "Armbruster? Who the hell gave you this number?"

The dyke scientist's brassy voice was as clear and painful as a fucking French horn. "I work with computers all day, Sheriff," she said. "It was no big challenge."

"Never use this number," he ordered her. "This is for official business only."

"Sure," she said, dismissing him.

He closed his eyes and ground his teeth again. *Bitch. If you ever, EVER get on my side of the line, I will fuck you up SO bad.*

"I've got more information from the NWS and Earthwatch, not to mention our own sampling stations around the ridge line," she said. "Satellite data confirmed–"

"Don't tell me," he said, already bored. "Let me guess. It's *raining*."

Now *she* was the one giving a bitter sigh. "Brilliant, Sheriff. Really. The point is, it's not going to *stop* raining for at least forty-eight hours. Maybe longer. It's not even going to slack off."

"Or so you think." Peck massaged his temples with thumb and forefinger. Was this bitch never going to let him go? If she didn't already have the ear of everybody at the goddamn public school, and through them all the parents who were already hating his guts, he would cut her off right fucking *now*.

"This isn't opinion, Sheriff. It's fact. This little crater valley of yours is like a, a teacup that's already starting to fill up, and it's going to fill up completely in the next two days."

"You can't know that," he said.

"I can. I *do*. You have to start evacuation procedures immediately."

"*Evacuation?* Are you out of your fuc– are you –" He stopped himself, took a breath. "Doctor, do you have any idea how much money the city would–"

"There isn't a city, you ass! Not anymore! That's what I'm trying to tell you!"

"I'm supposed to take your word for it, and tell three thousand people to leave their homes? After less than, what, *six hours* of rain? What makes you think I could do that, even if I wanted to?"

"You've got that town meeting tonight. Do it then. Convince them. Get them to pack up and move out, if only for a little while."

He was already shaking his head. "No," he said. "No way." The storm closed in around the cruiser, as if on cue. He lost sight of the hood ornament not five feet away in a chattering wash of rain and debris.

"If I'm wrong, I'll take full responsibility," Lucy said.

"Oh, that would make all the difference," Peck laughed. "No one even knows who you are, Doctor. You're just another crackpot scientist to these people, like your crazy friend Steinberg."

"Goddamn it, Sheriff, if you don't mention it at tonight's town meeting, *I will*."

Even the thought of that made him go cold. "I'd advise against that, Doctor. I'd advise against you attending at all. You don't have any connection with the children, after all, do you? I mean, it's not like you're a parent..." *you pathetic old gone-to-seed bull dyke you.* "...and your interest in the children might be seen as…I don't know, unhealthy? Suspicious?" Peck could hear the shock in her voice.

"My…what? *What* did you say? "

"Why don't you sleep on it, Doctor?" he said smoothly. "We'll talk tomorrow…*if* there's anything to talk about." He tapped off the phone and stopped short of throwing it as hard as he could against the windshield.

"Son of a bitch," he said under his breath. "Son of a fucking *bit*—"

Something big and wet and glassy *splopped* against his windshield, and Peck jumped back in surprise.

"What the—"

It looked like a rain-soaked piece of plastic, wrinkled and soggy. It nearly covered the entire window. The wind made it ripple and twitch like it was moving on its own.

Peck grunted under his breath. *Can't drive with that fucking thing in my way.* He took a deep breath and popped open the door. The rain slapped him hard, a face full of wet towel. He levered himself out into the storm, cursing under his breath, and pawed at the thing that was blocking the–

"SHIT!" He snatched his hand back in surprise.

That fucking thing STUNG me, he thought, astonished. *No, it—it BIT me.* He squinted through the downpour at his finger and saw it was intact but swelling, as if he'd jammed it in a door. At least it hadn't broken the skin.

"What the fuck is–"

The thing flew off the windshield and came right at him. Peck dodged to the right, halfway back into the car, and the sheet of silvery translucent … *stuff* … flew past him, almost as if it was flapping its wings. It disappeared into the storm in an instant.

Peck stared at his throbbing finger for a second longer, then pulled himself back into the cruiser and slammed the door. He was embarrassed at the racing of his own heart. *Don't be a pussy,* he ordered himself. It was simply a piece of cellophane with…acid or something on it. That's all.

The two-way radio at his shoulder HONKED and a blurred, ugly, barely female voice brayed out of it. *"HQ TO PECK. HQ TO PECK. CHECK IN, PLEASE."*

He suppressed a burst of rage and thumbed the call button. "Peck here. Get Jimmy and Bo and anybody else you can find over to the Conference Center, ASAP. We're going to have a sit-down before the meeting tonight, about the kids and the rain and … everything."

"Roger that, Sheriff." There was another blast of static and she cut off.

Things used to be so much simpler, he thought as he activated the Christmas tree of lights on the roof of the cruiser. Lightning struck to his right, then to his left, then right in front of him as he mounted Highway 181 headed south. One of the bolts struck a billboard for Coca-Cola not twenty feet away and blew it to smoking bits.

Donald Peck didn't even flinch. He really couldn't care less.

NINE

Lucy wanted to snap the cell phone in half, fling the pieces against the wall, then stomp on the shattered remnants with her thickest boots, over and over –

"Lucy?"

– and over and –

"Dr. Armbruster?"

She looked up, still half-blind with rage. Rebecca Falmouth-Hanson was regarding her with an odd mixture of concern, caution, and the sort of wariness reserved for street people who talk to themselves.

"That idiot," Lucy said.

"Sheriff Peck," Rebecca filled in.

"That two-bit, tin-horn, fuck-brained, stiff-necked, strutting, arrogant *asshole!*"

Rebecca knit beautifully sculpted brows. "I'm so sorry," she said. "What can I do?"

"Kill him!" Lucy raved. "Get a big ugly gun and shoot his ass, because I swear to Christ, Rebecca, that is *exactly* what he's doing to the people in this town. Putting a gun right to their temples and *pow*, just like that."

Those lovely dark eyes grew even bigger. "Is it that bad?"

"YES! It's WORSE! It's – it's –"

Shut up, said a voice in her head. Frannie's voice, firm and absolutely solid. Lucy heard it so clearly she stopped in mid-rant, and realized that she was terrifying the poor girl in front of her.

94

"I—I'm sorry," she said. She touched Rebecca's slim upper arm. "Really, Rebecca. I'm sorry. It's not your fault. I shouldn't be yelling at you…"

Rebecca looked down at her shoes and blushed deeply. It gave her mocha skin a flawless rose under-color that was positively charming, even to Lucy "It's okay," Rebecca said, and chanced an upward glance. "You're upset, I can see that."

"Yeah, but still…" She shook it off. "Look, you know as well as I do what's going to happen here." She tapped an unmanicured fingernail at one of the satellite photos of the Valle. The crater ridge looked like a pale gray oval drawn on a deeper gray background. "This place is like a poorly made bowl with one little tiny crack. It slopes down naturally, north to south, about five hundred feet over two miles, until you get to the VeriSil campus at the lowest point, right under The Two Brothers. They built there on purpose; it's also the coolest, least arid spot in the crater." She moved her finger a bit to the right, to a black scratch in the ridge wall near the blurred squares that represented VeriSil's structures. "There's only one break in the wall, right here, the Arroyo del Roja, But it's tiny, Rebecca. Not more than ten feet across at its widest point. And that's the only natural drainage channel in the southern half of the Valle. There's never been enough water here to erode a larger canyon. There's no way it can act as a drain for a flood this size. It can't possibly accommodate this volume of water, assuming it isn't already blocked by debris or mudslides. And the soil can only absorb so much liquid before it locks up. That happened, what, an hour after the rain started? Tops. Now it's building up. And up. And *up*." Lucy shook her head and pressed her lips together in disgust. "We're done here."

"Done?" Rebecca echoed.

"Time for everybody to pack up and go," she said grimly, "and don't plan on coming back."

She saw the expression of pure horror on the lovely girl's face and cursed herself all over again. *As always, Lucy, the perfect words at the perfect time. You're an idiot.* "I'm sorry. That was crude. I could be completely wrong about this, I could—"

"No, you're not wrong," Rebecca said. "And you know it." Then she did the most amazing thing, at least as far as Lucy was concerned. She *smiled*.

"Thank you, Lucy," she said, looking deeply into her eyes. "Really. I know this is hard for you. Thank you for being honest with me."

Lucy cleared her throat and looked away, embarrassed and alarmed at the sudden upwelling of emotion. "Uh…look," she said. "It's going to keep raining, but you have a little time. Will you do me a favor? I need to pull stuff together for this dumb-ass meeting at the Conference Center. Would you walk across the road here and check on Fender before you go home?"

"Is he okay?" Rebecca still had hold of Lucy's hand. Lucy didn't know how to get it back without making things worse, so she let it stay where it was.

"Yeah, he …he cut himself when we were going into his trailer. I got him all patched up, but, you know, good neighbor policy and all. I only want to be sure that his Airstream hasn't been picked up by a tornado and taken to Oz or anything."

Rebecca finally, *finally* let her hand go and gave her a dazzling smile. "I'd be glad to," she said. "I'll just pay him a quick visit, then go home to do a little packing. I should be back here by the time you finish that town meeting."

Lucy found herself hugely relieved and suddenly apprehensive all over again. She was glad Rebecca was taking herself out of harm's way, but the prospect of spending the night at the Ag Station with her – even fully clothed, even with Cindy and that nutbar Steinberg around – stirred up a surprising and not entirely unpleasant range of emotions.

She shoved them aside yet again. *Later*, she told herself. *Later*. Right now there was plenty to deal with that had nothing to do with her loins.

"Good," she said, trying to sound businesslike again. "I know you'll make Fender feel like somebody actually cares. You're good at that."

Rebecca positively beamed. Lucy had a sudden realization of what she'd said, what it meant, and felt a new rush of heat to her face. She hid it by turning away. "Thanks," she said gruffly. "Cindy? Cindy, I need to talk to you!"

She saw Rebecca out of the corner of her eye, moving to the coat closet, pulling on a forest-green parka, cinching the hood. She felt the blast of wet air and heard the rush of the water behind her as Rebecca opened the front door and slipped out into the gathering gloom. She didn't turn around to look at her. She was too embarrassed and confused.

That last look – that last *not*-look, really – bothered Lucy Armbruster until the day she died. She liked that young woman; she actually cared for her, more than she was willing to admit. That moment in the hall, that glimpse out of the corner of her eye, was the last time she would ever see Rebecca Falmouth-Hansen.

* * *

Lucy found the receptionist, Cindy Bergstrom, making herself a late afternoon snack in the break room. Normally that would have made her angry all by itself. It was already well past 4:00, and the woman would usually be going home in a matter of minutes. She really didn't need to dawdle away half an hour microwaving a Cup O' Soup. Today, however, it didn't bother Lucy at all. *Knock yourself out*, she thought bitterly. *That might be your last decent meal for a few days.* Not that Cindy's muffin shape couldn't stand a few missed meals.

"Hey there," she said, acutely aware of the acid conversation they'd had earlier in the day. Cindy turned and gave her the sunniest smile she could muster, as if nothing had happened.

"Well, hey there!" she said. "Ready to start building that ark?"

Lucy sketched out a laugh. It didn't sound very convincing. "Heh. Um… look, I've been checking the figures and all," she said. "I really think – no, actually, I'm *sure* – that there's going to be some serious flood damage in the southern parts of town, maybe as far north as your neighborhood."

Maybe my ass. By noon tomorrow, you won't be able to get into your bedroom without scuba gear.

Cindy made big eyes. "Really?" she said.

"Truly," Lucy told her. "I told Rebecca the same thing. You might want to go home, pack up a few bags of clothes and stuff you want to be sure to keep – family heirlooms and the like– and bring them back here. Kind of camp out here for the duration of the storm."

Cindy grinned at her and her eyebrows hopped up and down. "Well! As it happens, I was already thinking that!"

Lucy was surprised all over again. "Really?"

"Sure. I've been talking to Mindy, my sister? At the Sheriff's Station?"

Like you don't talk to her ten times a day anyway. On my dime, too. "Yes?" Lucy said aloud.

"…and she tells me things are really bad out there and getting worse, and ol' Deputy Duck – excuse me, Sheriff Peck – isn't dealing with it at all."

"So…you're getting out of town?" Lucy felt as if Cindy Bergstrom – *Cindy Bergstrom*, of all people – was two steps ahead of her, and she didn't like the feeling very much.

"What," Cindy said, almost chuckling, "and miss all this? Heck no. Mindy is going to go by the house, pick up a few things, and store them at the Sheriff's Station. I think I might spend the night here, if you can stand me."

She was joshing, of course, at least in her own mind. As far as Cindy was concerned, everybody loved her and her antic sensibility. Who wouldn't want to be stranded in a research facility for a long weekend with the life of the party?

Lucy started to get queasy all over again. She was almost welcoming the long, wet, dangerous trip down to the Conference Center. With any luck, Cindy would be pooped out and fast asleep by the time she returned.

"Okay then," she said, hating the sound of her own forced cheer. "Glad you're thinking ahead. I have to go pull together some information for the town meeting, so carry on. I guess." She backed out, thinking about how to mention this all to that idiot Michael Steinberg when a thought suddenly struck her.

Don't bother.

She stopped abruptly in the hallway outside the break room and thought that through. What did she owe Steinberg, anyway? He'd ignored and insulted her; he had made it clear he didn't need any help or support from the rest of them. So if his studio apartment with its well-worn collection of *Jugs* and a refrigerator full of Hungry Man Dinners was underwater, what did she care?

She made a quick turn away from his office corridor and started off in the opposite direction, towards her own office, then stopped herself again.

She caught Cindy coming out of the break room with an over-hot microwaved plate and a can of Diet Dr. Pepper in one hand and a week-old copy of *US Weekly* in the other.

"One more thing," she said.

"Surely," Cindy said.

Lucy dug into the pocket of her lab coat and handed the receptionist the one-and-only set of keys to the candy-apple-red ATV. "Our friend Dr. Steinberg no longer has permission to drive the Station's all-terrain vehicle," she said with mock solemnity. "This, however, may not stop him from trying. So I am putting you in charge of the keys. Understand?"

Cindy took the key ring, tucked it into the breast pocket of her blouse, and patted it with the flat of her hand. "I'll guard them with my life," she said, playing along.

Lucy nodded. "See that you do. Hup hup." She nodded like a Modern Major General and turned on her heel, throwing a breezy little "Thanks" over her shoulder, and not waiting for a reply.

It was another final meeting that would haunt her for the rest of her life.

* * *

Lucy's own office was dark and oppressive. Gray metal desk, gray floors, and gray sky beyond the smoked glass. She had never seen it so dark and uninviting, and the bluish buzz of the fluorescent overheads didn't do a thing to raise the mood.

It didn't matter. She'd be spending most of the next hour or two concentrating on her computer screen and her printer, and then she'd be gone for a while.

She started to sit behind her desk when the sky beyond her window ripped in two along a wide, white, jagged crack between clouds. The flash made her look up. A heartbeat later the thunder was like a velvet fist thumping her in the chest.

She stopped herself from sitting down and went to the window instead. This was one of the few indulgences she had allowed herself when designing and building the Tomas Rivera Agricultural Research Station. She had given her office the best view of the entire Valle de Los Hermanos, spread out before her like tangled skeins of earth-colored yarn, unraveling as it traveled south to the double peaks of The Brothers.

At this time of day, she should be seeing the first chalky colors of sunset appearing in the western sky. The first few street lamps should be flickering on, and the light itself should be turning thick and gray, with a weight that would linger, patient as stone, until night crept up from the cracks in the earth and filled the Valle to its ridge crest.

Tonight, there was no scattering of lighted windows, no watercolor gouache of salmon and pale blue above the mountains. There was only ink-black dark, punctuated by jolts of colorless brilliance and the instant visible/invisible scribble of power cables and telephone lines.

She paused inside the window, so close she could feel the minute vibrations of the rain as each wind-driven drop made a tiny explosion against the glass. Her eyes widened when the lightning struck again, on the far side of the highway this time, and a little farther south, but from the same bank of dense, slow-moving clouds scudding low over the town. Five seconds passed…and another bolt struck on the near side of the highway, farther south, and then again, on the far side and farther away. Each strike was followed by another rumble of thunder; each report took a heartbeat longer to arrive than the one before as the front rolled away from her.

"It's like God walking," she said entirely to herself. "If God was a spider made of lightning and thunder."

The last roll was almost subsonic. Lucy felt its vibration in her bones, in the soles of her feet. She knew that the same phenomenon would come again, probably within the hour. And again. And *again*, until the bizarre meteorological conditions that had turned Dos Hermanos into the bottom of a bucket made of mud dissipated. That was days away at best.

She turned away from the window and looked at the clock on the far wall. 5:45.

She set her jaw and took a deep breath. There was work to be done.

TEN

I should call her, he thought, staring blindly at the flatscreen embedded in the wall. *See how she's doing. Tell her we got home okay.* He knew Rose had already texted her mother with that last bit of information; he'd seen her do it before she'd fled upstairs.

It was painful and odd. He'd spent most of the last two years working very hard on *not* thinking about her, what she was doing, how she was getting along, especially after she had flatly refused his help, taken her name off all their joint accounts, and moved without leaving him a forwarding address. He had one e-mail address and one mobile number and that was it. She had made it clear in her terse e-mails that he didn't deserve even that much, but there was Rose to think about.

Now she was just a couple of miles away. Ten minutes on a regular day, an hour in this storm. And he couldn't stop thinking about her.

"How much longer is this going to last?" he asked, pointing his chin at the curtain of rain falling beyond the patio window.

"Three days," Maggie said.

"That long?"

"At the very least," Maggie told him. "None of the meteorological data has changed; if anything the situation's solidified. It's going to get very bad for the people down there, lower in the valley."

The news was almost cheering in one way. "Think the meeting will be canceled?"

He could imagine her smiling. "Don't get your hopes up. Nobody seems to know how bad this is going to get, or how fast. Tomorrow's Friday, and it's business as usual everywhere. School is in session, stores are open, and meetings are still scheduled. Even at VeriSil."

He scowled and stared out the sliding glass door at his flooding patio. "Damn," he muttered. "For a second I thought this dark cloud might have a silver lining."

Maggie let him wallow for a moment, then cleared her disembodied throat. "All right, now, back to business," she said, managing to sound brisk and affectionate at the same time. "You have roughly sixty minutes tomorrow morning to convince the Powers That Be that Everybody's Assistant isn't some massive boondoggle."

"More like five minutes," he said, and put up a hand before she could disagree. "I know, I know, I'm scheduled for a full hour, but if I don't hit them right between the eyes in the first five, I'm fish food."

"Indeed."

"That's the problem, Maggie, the whole application is cumulative. That's the miracle. It's not made to hit you over the head; it's made to *fit in* to your individual life."

"I think they call this 'preaching to the choir,' Ken."

He turned away from the black, stormy rectangle of the glass doors and picked up a tablet that was networked to the house system. "We're way past the Turing Test here, Maggie. Charts won't do it, infographics won't do it. They have to *get* it right away, they have to *understand,* in the blink of an eye, and that's hard. They've never even seen anything like this before."

"Haven't they?"

"No! Of course they haven't! This isn't some little candy-ass voice recognition program! This isn't a fucking GPS with a plummy British accent. This…"

He trailed off, thinking. Thinking.

Getting it.

There was a sudden metallic *tic tic tic* behind him, a completely new and different sound than the muted, rushing roar of the storm. He turned and saw a drowning man standing outside his patio door.

"What the *hell?*"

The man was Ken's size, maybe a bit taller. He was standing inches from the glass, and he looked as if he'd climbed out of a swimming pool fully clothed. He was holding a dog leash without a dog at the other end, tapping the leash's metal tab against the glass in a rapid tattoo: *tic tic tic.*

"Rex Tartaglione," Maggie said. She pronounced it in the true Italian fashion, rolled r's and everything: *TarrrtaileeOWNay.* Ken didn't have the heart to correct her. "He's our next door neighbor."

"Next door" was generous, Ken thought distantly. The hacienda he'd leased two years ago was at the center of a sprawling, rugged bit of ridge crest terrain. The next mini-mansion over was barely visible on a good day. But yes, that was Rex What's-His-Name, and this definitely wasn't a good day.

Rex *tic-tic-tic'd* again and shouted something Ken couldn't make out over the thick insulation and the raging storm. It sounded like an inarticulate bellow: "Rah RAH row aooo…"

"Turn on the patio lights," Ken said, still not moving. There was something wrong here.

"They're already on," Maggie said, and Ken raised his eyebrows in surprise. The storm had cut visibility to mere inches. Rex was standing in front of nothing more than a churning black background.

"Ra OOoo ra? Rowww?" he said.

Ken turned away for an instant, looking for a place to put the tablet. *I don't have time for this,* he thought as he set the device on the polished credenza. He was only slightly embarrassed by his lack of charity. *I'll let him in, find out wh—*

He turned back, and Rex was gone.

In the instant he'd turned away, the man had disappeared completely, as if he'd never been there.

"What happened?" he said. "Where'd he go?"

"I have no idea."

Well, *that* was frustrating. "Turn on your lights. I mean, *more* light. Look around."

Now it was Maggie's turn to sound frustrated. "What, activate my sensors and engage the tractor beam? Please."

Ken stepped to the window and peered out, so close his nose touched the glass. He strained to hear anything, see anything.

The house lights behind him and above him dimmed and guttered. He heard a deep throb run through the house: *VUMMM*.

He turned around. "Okay," he said. "*Now* what?"

The lights did it a second time, and the sound came again. *VUMMM*

"Rose is having a little trouble upstairs," Maggie said. "Maybe you should check on her."

It was as if he'd touched a live wire. He bolted forward, then stopped suddenly. "What?" he said. "Is it drugs? Is she hurt?"

"Just go *check* on her, Ken. And calm down."

He ran out the room, any thoughts of Rex Tartaglione long disappeared.

* * *

Rex Tartaglione hated his fucking dog. It wasn't even his fucking dog, really, it was his wife's. She had insisted they get it, a tiny little rat-thing not ten inches tall at the shoulder, if you could call that bony little joint a shoulder at all. Rex thought it was too small to be a real dog in the first place. Anything taller than your waist was a fucking horse; anything below your knee was vermin. However, Denise had whined and mewled and poked at him, so fine, sure, *yes,* she could have a fucking 'dog.'

Which meant, of course, *he* was the one who had to walk the little turd three damn times a day: first thing in the morning, last thing in the afternoon, and once at night so the little cretin wouldn't lay a load on the sheepskin rug. Denise couldn't do it – oh, *no,* she couldn't go out at *night,* what with the *coyotes* and the *homeless* and her *nails.*

It was days like this he was sorry he'd ever sold the car dealership in Fresno and moved to DH in the first place. Or brought his fucking trophy wife with him.

Usually walking the rat wasn't that big a deal. Sometimes it got a little chilly for a late night stroll, and at least it got him out of the house when Denise was blaring *Real Housewives of Wherever-the-hell-they-were-this-week.* But tonight?

When the sky was literally falling down around them? If he'd thought it through, he would have settled for a load on the sheepskin.

Still, the third time Denise yawped at him, Rex slapped the leash on the little turd and literally braved the storm.

It was even worse than it looked from inside. Not so much cold as *everywhere.* Rex had to hunch inside his jacket and keep his head down to keep from choking on the downpour.

The plan was one quick turn around the backyard and that was it. Step-step-*poop,* step-step-*porch,* done and done. But the fucking dog had other ideas. When they reached the far end of the manicured back lawn, the one they never stepped on for fear of mussing up the landscaping, the little shit made the weirdest sound, a kind of yelp/bark/growl all at once, – and surged into the hedges. It happened so fast Rex lost his grip on the leash, and it went flying into the dripping, rustling underbrush with a wet smack.

"Goddamn it!" Rex bellowed into the rain. "Come back here, you little fuck!"

Without truly thinking about it, Rex barreled into the brush himself, sure he'd find the fucking dog three feet ahead of him, soaked and shivering when it realized what it had done.

But no. Ten steps into the unlandscaped, real-life scrub of the ridge crest, Rex not only lost track of the dog, he lost track of the house.

"Come back! NOW, goddamn it, NOW!"

Nothing.

He staggered deeper into the storm, completely unwilling to go back to the house without the fucking dog in hand. Denise would pop a vein. At one point, between bellows, he thought he heard the little monster, another one of those weird bark/growl/yelp things that seemed to cut off right in the middle. It was almost five minutes later that he nearly tripped over the thin strip of red canvas with a stitched loop at one end, the damn dog's leash drooping pathetically on a thorn bush, with no dog in sight.

He kept looking. The storm slapped at him, cut at him, screamed at him, but he was damned if he was going to lose that yippy little shit-bucket because of some bullshit rain.

He was out for nearly half an hour in the dark and wet when he finally had to admit he was completely lost. He didn't even know which way was 'home' in the vaguest sense, and then he saw the glowing light.

It was the house, or *a* house. *Some* house, for fuck's sake, and he was going to reach it. He slammed through the scrub grass and bushes, fell down twice and pulled himself up, not caring about the mud or the scratches, and slammed through some more until he lurched onto the shimmering flagstones of a patio that wasn't his.

He stood there for a moment, still clutching the leash, and stared at the man on the other side of the sliding glass door. The one who was talking to himself.

Rex Tartaglione stumbled over to the glass, weary beyond words. The man didn't notice him. He tried knocking on the glass with a knuckle so soaked he wondered if it had actually softened. No, it was the glass: it was thick and insulated. He couldn't get more than a weak, tiny *thud-thud* from it.

The weariness was getting worse. He was having trouble standing. He reversed the leash in his hands, held up the curved metal hasp that should have been connected to a dog collar and tapped on the glass: *tic-tic-tic.*

The guy still didn't notice him. Now that he thought about it, Rex recognized him a little. It was that computer guy from VeriSil, the one who lived in the old DelGado place. He'd seen him at a picnic once, and down at the market, maybe.

Tic tic TIC!

This time the man looked up, startled. His eyes went big but he just stood there, still talking to himself.

"HEY!" Rex shouted. "IT'S ME, REX! I LIVE NEXT DOOR!"

The asshole still didn't move. He looked down at his iPad or whatever and said something else.

"IT'S REX! THINK YOU CAN LET ME IN? ASSHOLE?"

And then the man turned away.

Rex couldn't believe it. The bastard had simply *turned away*, like he couldn't be bothered. It looked like he was actually going to leave the fucking room, ignore Rex entirely, and Rex lifted hand to *really* knock on that fucking glass –

-- and something snatched him away. In an instant, in a *blink,* it pulled him away from the glass and off to the side so fast he didn't even have time to make his own growl/yelp/barking sound.

Sharp, thorny branches wrapped around his chest, so hard and tight he couldn't move. More were wrapping around his ankles, his thighs. He could feel one at the back of his head, reaching around for his face. And they were *sharp.* Each thorn bit into him, everywhere, all at once, like barbed wire but worse. Like wire covered in fish hooks that moved like fingers. And *squeezed.*

He couldn't even the glass door anymore. Couldn't even see the house. All he could do was gasp as the wires tightened, closed in, *squeezed* him.

He tried to gasp again, but the breath gushed out instead. When he tried to move, the thorns bit deep. He felt a finger pop off and fall away. He felt his belly open up in a long, meandering slice. He felt the tiny razor-branches creep over his temples, coming around from behind to cover his eyes, cover his mouth.

Seal him up.

Stop, he pleaded. *Stop stop st—*

It happened in an instant, between one heartbeat and the next. The hookweed *clutched* him, so fast and hard and tight that Rex Tartaglione actually heard his body pop, like a balloon filled with blood.

It was the last thing he heard.

ELEVEN

My, my, my, Michael Steinberg thought, shaking his head in happy amazement. *I'm really very good at this God stuff.*

He scarcely noticed the stiffening of his joints or the strange ashen undercolor his flesh had acquired. It had become harder to ignore over the last few hours, but he'd managed. There had been work to do, after all.

Now he stood in the middle of his half-destroyed lab space and gazed upon the dozens of bins, bowls, containers, cups, saucers, tubs and tubes that covered every horizontal surface in his lab, and the *things* that were growing in each of them. He found that it was good.

Nothing should be growing there, of course. The Valle de Los Hermanos was a hyper-arid climate; virtually no evapotranspiration, a climatic aridity index of less than .03.

Look at all this, he told himself, grinning like a little boy. *Look at it!*

He smiled lovingly into the tray right in front of him, where a thin, wide plate of…tissue?…was twitching lazily in less than an inch of water. 'Tissue' wasn't exactly the right word, though. It was translucent, he could see the hairline crack in the old specimen tray beneath it, right through the creature. And it was milky, like a sheet of moist wax paper, but he already knew it was far stronger than human or even reptilian skin. It was very thin as well, a few cells at most, though absurdly durable. He also knew what it would do to mammalian flesh if it came in contact with it, how it would literally suck the fluid right out of it in a matter of moments, and not stop until there was nothing left.

All of his little friends would do that, it was the one thing they had in common. No matter how big, how small, how sharp, how flat, they were all infinitely, relentlessly *thirsty*.

He was beginning to feel the same way himself.

Michael had happily whiled away the last few hours moving from specimen to specimen, awarding them with names of his own choosing, building a New Taxonomy, being – what had the bitch called it? *The Darwin of the twenty-first century?*

Yeah, he thought. *That's me.*

They weren't really *his* names, he knew. They were coming from…somewhere else. From that greater mind, the one that spoke to him. He claimed them as his own; translated them into the common tongue so all his new subjects would know.

"Stain," Michael said to the wide, flat, creature on the tray. "I will call you a 'stain.'" Small ones moved by growing in a specific direction and dissolving portions that remained in an unwanted direction, a bit like algae or lichen, but at a ridiculously fast rate. He'd already seen one move ten inches in twenty minutes simply by foaming a new leading edge and letting it harden while the old trailing edge powdered away. Once they grew above a certain size, stains would let go of the Earth completely. First a corner, then a whole edge would come loose and actually start to wave, as if it were hailing a cab. Then they could literally fly away on a gust of wind, driven like a thistle, randomly encountering water-bearing organisms to encase and suck dry.

Michael thought they were strangely beautiful when they flew. He cleared his throat. "When you take to the air, I will call you 'flumes'," he announced. He liked the sound of it. "Flumes," he said again, tasting the word on his spiny tongue.

Behold my New World.

The needleseed, a sphere no larger than a golf ball made entirely of sharp points, constantly and subtly changing shape as its tiny spines grew and broke, dissolved and regrew.

Or 'biting sand', churning in a blue plastic bucket, ready to envelop any water-bearing organism and grind it up like sandpaper on a slab of steak so it could desiccate it easily, almost instantly. Michael had watched in mute fascination as the sand had done exactly that to a stray cat he had snagged from town. Now he had to resist watching more. The slow, unending Brownian movement of the tiny grains rolling and turning was so hypnotic, so magnetic, it was all he could do to keep from and falling face-first into the bucket.

He turned instead to the 'turnbuckle'. Such a wonderful design! Two nearly perfectly circular hoops, some as small as wedding rings, some as large as bicycle wheels, joined along one edge. They could open themselves at any part, wrap around a tree trunk or a barrel or a human torso and then turn counter to each other as they squeezed, drawing tighter and tighter until the hoops pierced the soft flesh and chewed it to paste. So patient. So sleek.

He took a long probe and poked at the 'hookweed'. In the laboratory, it grew in its platter of water into an almost perfect sphere, each silver-white tendon studded with wicked hooks that speared the air in every direction. In the wild, that flawless globe would be warped by wind and debris into a thousand twisted shapes that would become tumbling sculptures made of living barbed-wire. Barbed wire that could *move* if it had to.

The 'scumble' was a smaller, even deadlier version of the same design. He had a whole family of them in a bowl under the broken window. It was only a pile of ribbed sticks, but any animal unfortunate enough to step into that pile would never escape. Its broken ends would snap at moist flesh with the ferocity of an old-fashioned bear-trap, then rub and rub until there was nothing left but grit.

And then there was his very favorite: the 'bone spider'. He glided over to the largest cage he had in the lab, a huge four-by-four-foot terrarium made from half-inch Plexiglas, with a hose attached to a flange he had installed in one side so he could feed regular and large amounts of water into the box.

The creature inside had a constantly changing number of cantilevered legs that grew from a central point so tiny it couldn't be called a body at all. In effect, the thing was nothing *but* legs – no eyes, no mouth, no visible sensory organs or central trunk at all, just incredibly sharp legs, in constant movement, graceful as underwater ballet, that resembled a praying mantis as much as spider while somehow resembling neither one at all. Each leg was a ribbed talon with ragged teeth, part of a swaying, ticking predator, iron gray and bone white, that looked like an insect made of razors and wire. The legs skirled and shrieked against each other when they moved. They made the same sound as sharpening knives.

Michael loved this creature the most. He had watched it grow from a twitching little thing no bigger than an apricot to a meter-high monster in a matter of hours, and it was still growing. From all he could tell, it couldn't *stop* growing. Given the impossibly light, hard, and resilient material that served as flesh, skin, and bone for the creature, even the inverse square law didn't seem to apply. Bone spiders could be as big as elephants, as big as mountains, and still they could grow.

How does it see? How does it hear? Does it need *to, when all it wants to do is kill and drink and kill and drink?*

The creatures shared one other characteristic as well, the ability to infect any living thing with their dry and sandy simulacrum of tissue. His tests had shown him that any cut, bite, or scratch could change you, make you their own, with a single, swift incision. It didn't happen that often, Michael told himself, because so few survived the first encounter. They didn't want recruits; they wanted to eat.

It was happening to him. Right now. He could feel it happening to half a dozen other people all across the Valle.

It began happening the instant he had cut himself. The seeds had taken him the instant the claw had pierced his skin, and now he could feel his skin getting thicker, his teeth growing together into a single jagged ridge of…something beyond bone, something closer to marble. He could feel the crackle and snap of new growth breaking in his joints every time he flexed an arm or a leg, then he could feel brittle new tendons growing back in the new position so fast they almost leaped together.

And he could *hear* something, too. That other voice, that guiding Intelligence at the back of his brain. It was the tiniest whisper of Something Else that kept telling him how *good* this was, how *smart* he was, how *perfect* he was becoming.

Michael loved every minute of it. It was all he had ever wanted.

He stood in front of his utility sink and looked out his single window at a slice of the Valle de Los Hermanos, hundreds of feet below. It wasn't the best view; that dyke bitch Lucy had kept that for herself. Besides, the rain was worse than ever, and the town was barely visible. It didn't matter anymore. Michael didn't really need a window at all. He could see the entire crater laid out before and below him with a new kind of sight. And he could see all his creatures there, pinpoints of light, patches of shimmering silver against a bottomless, lightless black, scattered all across the valley and twinkling, burning, guttering, glowing.

The tiny part of him that was still a scientist wondered what he was seeing. Electromagnetic energy, maybe, at a special frequency or level of activity. Not that it mattered; they were simply *there,* and he could sense every one of the creatures. Deep under water, huddled in bedrooms, hiding in bushes, sprawled on rooftops exposed to the wind and rain – everywhere. Growing. *His.*

His new mouth cracked itself into a smile.

Michael Steinberg had been raised by two perfectly decent people who considered themselves "recreational Jews". That's what his father had called them. They celebrated Hanukkah, complete with their very own Hanukkah bush, went to temple twice a year whether they needed it or not, and regularly gave money to World Jewish Relief. But deep in his heart, like so many other young Jewish boys, Michael had this thought, this persistent thought that maybe, *maybe*, he was The One. The one they had all been waiting for.

Who was to say the Messiah would know he was the Messiah at all until God told him? Even the near miss, that preacher from Nazareth, seemed to have had a normal childhood before he stepped out at age 30 and began his slow walk to Golgotha. So…it could happen. One day the sky could open up and the celestial finger could point to him, *him,* Michael Steinberg, and his destiny would be revealed.

It was a common dream. Lots of little Jewish boys had it. But he hadn't forgotten like most of them had.

He stood in the middle of his laboratory, surrounded by the clacking, ticking, popping of his creatures as they grew. He spread his arms wide to take in all that he saw, and it was good. *So* good.

I was wrong, he told himself. He wasn't God, though he could hear God's Voice in his head. He wasn't Adam, though he had been charged to name all the beasts of this new world. He was something in between: part God, part Man, more than both.

It's obvious, he realized.

I'm Jesus.

TWELVE

Rebecca stepped out of the Agricultural Station, staggered to the left, tripped forward, and stood hanging on a light post in the parking lot to keep from being pushed flat onto her face.

Hey Mom and Dad, she thought giddily. *You ought to see me now.*

Rebecca had grown up in Santa Cruz, California, home of one of the most hospitable climates in the known world. Her parents, one black, one white, were both products of the Bay Area as well, and they had fully expected her to be like them and never stray too far from Paradise. She remembered clearly how they had responded to the news that she was going to do her graduate work not at UCSC, or even at nearby UC Davis, but in dirty, conservative, *hot* little Riverside, of all places. When she'd announced her appointment to the Anza-Borrego Desert for an inexplicable one-year internship…

Little did they know, she thought as she braced herself against the battering wind and staggered across the parking lot, rooster-tails of water spraying in front of her boots. The wind was like a physical force; the raindrops felt like grapeshot against her unprotected flesh.

Why did I agree to do this again? She knew the answer without even thinking about it. *Easy,* because LUCY asked.

Rebecca had been happily and openly bisexual since early puberty, and her parents, both far left of center, had seen no problem with her succession of boyfriends and girlfriends…so far. She was sure, however, they would freak if they guessed at her true feelings for the knobby, foul-tempered, teacher she was crushing on so completely at the moment. Even Rebecca herself didn't quite understand it. Yes, she was well aware that Lucy was almost twice her age. Which mattered exactly *why?*

Rebecca thought about what the relationship meant, if it meant anything at all, as she climbed the outdoor stairs to the shoulder of Highway 181. It was well past five o'clock, and the last of the natural light was slipping away. She could barely see the tarmac in front of her rubber boots, much less anything resembling an oncoming car. One bit of bad timing, and a truck could come rushing out of the darkness and squash her flat.

Fortune favors the bold and all that shit, she thought, half-quoting her mother. Without another moment's hesitation, she stomped into the road, head up and eyes forward. Her boots sent out broad crescents of spray with every footfall, and soon enough, sooner than she'd expected, she was across the highway and standing at the wide wooden gate to the wind farm.

She tried to remember the last time she had made the walk over to see Fender in his native habitat, and couldn't come up with a date. It must have been longer than she'd realized. She distinctly remembered that the carefully maintained white-gravel path from the highway to his trailer was wide enough to accommodate three people walking side-by-side, and that the grass that surrounded his massive windmills was always meticulously trimmed. Now the path was barely wide enough for one person to walk, and the grass was so long and invasive it looked shaggy. Not at all the image that Fender worked so hard to maintain.

The sheets of rain suddenly, momentarily, cleared and she got an unobstructed view of the windmills. She stopped dead in her tracks.

The windmills were singing. *No,* she corrected herself. As her father would say, *Check that.* The windmills were singing *and dancing.*

They sprang up out of the deep green sod, flawless white towers of heavy pipe and plastic more than three stories tall. At the top were the wide propellers – *vanes,* she remembered, hearing Fender's uncharacteristically serious voice in her head. *They're called* vanes*, man.* And now, in the ripping gale of the storm, those vanes were spinning so fast, so irregularly they were a milky blur at the apex of the towers.

The music came from the roaring, whining, swooping sound of the vanes as the wind screamed through them, hollow, howling tones that wandered up and down the scale, sometimes fast, sometimes slow. Each tower sang a different song in a different key; all of them blended together into a wild, wailing roar that was more animal than mechanical.

It was the wind that made them dance, too. They shimmied and trembled, flexed and bobbled, waggled and twisted, coming *that close* to lifting their concrete-bound feet right out of the earth. In fact, Rebecca thought that if she watched a moment longer, one of the towers would actually lift a leg and come walking towards her in a wind-driven march towards the open road, its whirling vanes roaring.

The massive, multi-story strangeness of it made her take a step back, and she felt the shaggy grass rustle and pluck at the heels of her boots. She jerked forward again, terrified.

No, she told herself very sternly, *REALLY now, FUCK that noise.* She wrapped the pea coat tightly around her shoulders and ran the last fifty feet of gravel path, past the stout wooden sign that read *SUNMILL WIND FARMS – FREE TOURS AT 1:00 and 3:00 COME WIN THE ENERGY WAR…WITH WIND!* She had always loved that hand-painted sign – so weird and friendly, so *Fender*ish. She ignored it now as she sprinted to the silver slug-shape of the Airstream trailer, jumped up onto the wooden porch, and pounded on the screen door with the flat of her hand.

"Fender? Fender, it's Rebecca, from the Station! Let me in!" Not *How are you* or *I came by to check up on you.* Just a desperate *Let me in!*

The screen collapsed under her hand and the pressed-wood door flew inward with a bang. Rebecca fell into the humid warmth of the trailer and nearly lost her balance in the debris that covered the floor.

The trailer was in shambles. It looked as if every container, every jar or bottle or jug in the place had been opened, emptied, and thrown on the sodden carpet.

The sound of the rain on the trailer's stainless steel roof was deafening. "Fender!" she shouted. She could barely hear her own voice. "FENDER!"

Beneath the rattle-bang of the rainfall she heard another equally wet sound: rushing water. *Gushing* water, actually, like an open fire hose. It seemed to be coming from the kitchen nook.

"*Fender!*" she bellowed. "*It's Rebecca! Are you OKAY?*" She kicked her way through the wreckage to the narrow little door and peered in.

Fender was sitting huddled over the sink, his neck twisted, his head turned, so his mouth was suspended directly under the water faucet in his small one-basin sink. The water was on full-blast, pouring directly into his yawning mouth.

Rebecca simply stared for the longest time. He was conscious, that much was clear. She could see his Adam's apple, half-obscured by his drenched beard, working up and down and up and down.

"Fender?" she said again. She put out a hand and touched his knee. "Fen—"

He jumped like a startled animal, leaping up, water spraying everywhere. "Wha – Oh!" He turned and saw her, and for a moment Rebecca was positive he didn't recognize her. Then: "Oh! *Oh!*" He twisted again, facing her, unmindful of the water gushing from the tap. "Rebecca," he said, his voice raspy and dry. "Hi. Hey. Nice to…um…"

He looked awful. His skin had turned dull, almost ashen. His eyes, usually bright and a little unfocused, were tiny dark beads buried in nests of new wrinkles, and there was a network of cracks in dried skin around his mouth, on his neck, even between his fingers. It looked like he'd lost twenty pounds since she'd last seen him, and she'd seen him only hours before.

"My God, Fender," she said. "Are you all right?"

"Great!" he said, and swept a handful of sodden hair away from his face. "Fine, really. It was only…some kind of fever or something, you know? Makes you thirsty as hell. Totally thirsty." Without a thought he cupped a hand under the running water and threw it square in his face. He didn't even close his eyes. An instant later he seemed to be dry again, as if the moisture had evaporated… or been absorbed. "Damn," he said. "*Damn*, I'm dry."

He looked at her with a strange, thoughtful expression. A speculative look, as if he was judging how easy it would be to pop her open and drink up the paltry few quarts of blood and fluids she carried in her body.

That's crazy, she told herself. *Fender's a gentle old soul, he'd never…*

His attention abruptly shifted, away from her and to a new inspiration. "I got it!" he said. "That's the ticket!" He threw open the doors to the cabinet below the sink and began rummaging through the pile of cleaning fluids and tools hidden there.

"Fender," she said, worried. "That stuff is poisonous, honey, you don't want to–"

He pulled out a long green-painted crowbar, sharpened and notched at one end and viciously curved at the other. He stood up and hefted the bar in one hand, testing its weight…and for the first time, Rebecca realized how big Fender really was.

"That's the ticket," he said again. He looked right at Rebecca and grinned like a crazed animal, and for one horrible instant she was sure that he *was* going to split her open her like melon, right up the middle.

Instead, Fender heaved on the bar, bellowing with all his might, swinging the tool straight up and *whanging* it into the aluminum ceiling right over his head.

Rebecca jumped in surprise at the sound of the collision. Before she could say a real word, Fender pulled the crowbar loose of the three-inch dent he'd made and swung it upwards again, even harder. The second clanging, crunching *whanngg!* was like the ringing of a broken bell.

"Fender!" she screamed! "*Stop it!*"

Too late. He had managed to punch a hole through the ceiling, and rainwater was pouring in.

Fender grinned even wider and jerked on the crowbar twice, pulling part of the torn metal inward. More water gushed right onto his head. "*Yes!*" he said, elated. He breathed a huge, guttural sigh of relief, tossed the crowbar aside and sat back down in the kitchen chair where she'd found him, head thrown back, arms spread wide. The gout of water from the ceiling pounded directly onto his face, his neck, his chest.

"Tha-a-a-at's the ticket," he said, sighing with relief. "Yeah, thaaa-a-t's it…"

Rebecca backed away. He had already forgotten she was there, and that was perfectly fine with her.

Something was wrong with him. Some toxic substance, or bad drugs, she didn't know, but she knew she couldn't help him directly. She'd get back to the Station and call 911. Send them over to get him, make him better.

Rebecca left him there, sprawled in his waterfall. *This is nuts*, she told herself as she dragged open the broken front door, horribly glad to be out of the sodden, overheated trailer and back into the storm. *This is totally nuts.* Without a second thought, she hopped down the wooden stairs, crossed the gravel path and cut to her left, trotting across the overgrown, soggy lawn, in a straight line towards the main gate and the highway. There was no time for pathways, she had to move quickly.

She was five footsteps into the grass when it started to grab at her feet.

At first she thought it was just the water that was making it so difficult to walk, making the blades snag her shoes like sea grass could tangle up a diver. She pulled free with some difficulty the first time, then the grass pulled even harder. She was barely able to free herself at all the second time.

She looked down and saw that it wasn't the water at all. The grass had grown into silver-green tendrils – *tentacles* – that were snaking around her feet, her ankles, and even the cuffs of her pants.

Rebecca stopped walking when she was less than ten feet from the white gravel path. She kicked, *hard*, and managed to take one step back towards the road, directly towards the stout wooden sign that read *TOURS DAILY.* That was as far as she could go.

She pulled one foot free and took another step, then she almost fell over. She had to stagger to keep her balance, and when she plunged her foot back into the grass she saw the rubber was actually *cut* in a dozen places, deeply slashed as if someone had gone at them with a butcher knife.

They're brand new boots, she thought. *Fresh out of the closet. How –?*

The grass-blades were tightening around her feet. This time she could see them cutting right through the boots, like razor wire cutting into flesh.

"Oh my god," she said, a tiny voice in the roaring of the wind, the hissing of the rain, the singing of the wind towers so close behind her. "Oh my *god.*"

She managed to pull her foot up one more time and take a long, lurching step towards the sign, towards safety –

– and saw as she pulled her leg up, that the boot was gone, cut to shreds, along with three of her toes and a chunk of her heel.

In one cold flash of clarity, Rebecca Falmouth-Hanson knew what was happening. It was like when she'd cut off the tip of her finger with an X-acto blade, years earlier. The blade had been so thin, so scalpel-sharp, that it had trimmed away a piece of her and she hadn't even felt it. She hadn't even realized it until she saw the blood. The razor-grass was like a field full of scalpels, all painlessly slicing her into small pieces.

The grass was eating her alive, from the bottom up.

She couldn't let that happen, she decided. She *wouldn't*. She would take one more step, *two* more at most, and then she could haul herself up on Fender's stout wooden sign. The grass couldn't get her there. She would be safe.

She ducked into the driving rain and kicked as hard as she could. One foot came free and she lunged to take one more step. As her knee came up and her leg pulled away from the tangling grass, she saw that it wasn't the foot she had freed at all. There was no foot left. It was just a stump that ended in mid-shin, coursing with water and mud and spurting dark blood.

At that moment, she knew it was too late. Still, she didn't stop.

She drove the remains of her leg down again, jamming it against the ground. She held on a moment longer, somehow stayed upright, and directed her fall towards the sign.

Rebecca wrapped both hands around the heavy wooden uprights as they flew past. She tried to pull herself up, *haul* herself free. She could feel consciousness slipping from her, draining away like the last of her blood, but she wouldn't let go. In a last act of defiance, she laced her fingers together and gripped that sign, *clutched* it, so she wouldn't fall over. Even as she felt herself slipping into grayness, felt herself dying, she held on and thought of her Mom and Dad one last time, and her first lover, and her last kiss, and that movie she always loved and that dog she would never see again. She thought of Lucy and all the things that would never happen now.

Still standing, she told herself as the grayness took her away. *Still...*

Her body never did fall over. When the razorgrass did all the damage it could, when it reached the maximum cross-section of this particular water-bearing organism, it simply stopped cutting and drank, pulling every molecule of moisture it could through the Rebecca Falmouth-Hanson's flayed trunk.

The whole process took less than five minutes. At the end, the beautiful woman's desiccated body, dry as petrified wood, still clung to the four-by-four posts, remarkably unchanged. She looked like a lovely, bone-dry mannequin standing hip-deep in wet, waving grass, leaning on a wooden sign, clinging to it with a look of infinite sadness.

It was her final anchor against the storm. An anchor that had inexplicably failed her.

THIRTEEN

"You three are idiots," Sherriff Peck said to his deputies. "Each of you is actually stupider than the other two. I don't know how you manage it."

Jimmy Fultz blinked at him.

Mindy Bergstrom stuck out her lower lip.

Bo Cameron stuck out his chin.

Peck closed his eyes and sighed. "Jesus wept," he said.

He had commandeered one of the smaller conference rooms in the Martin Luther King, Jr. Conference Center, a thin-walled, three-story Kleenex box, the bastard child of a federal development grant and the tax windfall that accompanied the arrival of VeriSil International.

"Let's get this straight," he said. "This storm is killing us. Half of the south side is already underwater. We lost a line of houses at the bottom of the East Ridge to a mudslide about an hour ago. There's no time and no resources to go looking for those missing kids, so...they're a write off."

Bo Cameron worked his prominent jaw a little bit more. "So you mean, they're, like, dead. Or something."

"Oh, dear," Mindy Bergstrom said and shook her round little head. "That's not good at all."

Peck bit off another sigh. "Alive, dead, it's irrelevant," he said. "We can't go looking for them. We're going to have enough to do just trying to keep this place from going under until the fucking rain lets up. We *cannot* let the people coming here tonight know that. As far as they're concerned, we are a hundred percent committed to the search."

Cameron looked like a bigger, dumber version of Buzz Lightyear without the cool suit; Mindy was the female version of the Pillsbury Dough Boy and Jimmy Fultz looked like a six-inch ruler: flat and fragile as a fence picket, the same width at shoulder and hips, and six inches too short to be any good to anybody. He actually took his deputy-hat off to scratch the top of his head in consternation, and Peck sighed all over again.

Do you HAVE to act like a fucking cartoon? he asked silently.

"Well," Jimmy Fultz said, frowning deeply, "if we aren't gonna look for them, why'd we invite everybody down here?"

He had to say it through gritted teeth. "Because we sent out the invitations *before it started raining,* you moron."

The double doors at the far end of the hall flew open and the first of the VIPs arrived. Herb McCandless from the already dissolving mall, the Emporium, was first in, shaking his folding umbrella and shedding water like a wet dog.

As always, Peck thought bitterly. *If there's free food, Herb's at the head of the line.*

Behind him came his usual Chamber of Commerce entourage: the owner of the town's used car lot (there were no *new* car lots in DH), both dentists, and the usually dour owner of Dos Hermanos Window and Doors, who clearly thought he was about to be busier than a long-tailed cat in a room full of rocking chairs. He was a pretend Texan; he loved phrases like that.

Maybe so, Peck thought grudgingly. *Maybe not.* He vaguely remembered the joke that Marty Fein made about the sycophants and their pudgy leader: *"They put the sucker in the COC."*

He turned his attention back to his deputies and shook his head sadly. He'd spent months searching the town and advertising in every newspaper within five hundred miles for better candidates, but nobody was the least bit interested in coming to the ass end of nowhere for this kind of job. What was it that prick politician said? *Sometimes you fight the war with the army you've got, not the army you might want…*

"So what're we supposed to say?" Bo asked him, casting a nervous glance at the approaching civic leaders.

"Nothing," Peck said. "Don't make any promises, don't make any predictions. We're doing the best we can, we're putting 110% effort into finding those poor girls, it's a tough job but we're ready for it, you know, the usual bullshit."

"Will do," Mindy chimed in, and squared her rounded shoulders.

Jimmy Fultz bobbed his head, attempting decisiveness and competence. It didn't play. "Got it," he said.

You don't got it at all, Peck thought. *But what choice do I have?*

Normal Lazenby, mayor of Dos Hermanos, swept through the spread wings of the double doors, protected from the storm by the arc of a massive umbrella hovering over his leonine head. It was held steadfastly in place by his formidable wife Miriam. Normal, as always, was the picture of command: hawk-like features, a magnificent sweep of silver hair, eyes keen and clear. He was almost frighteningly white. But for his irises, he looked as if he had been carved from marble, or even chalk, while his wife was a comparative riot of color, a bold blue beret on her steely hair, a spray of color at her raddled throat, a slash of crimson where her lips used to be.

Normal took three steps into the room and stopped so abruptly that Miriam nearly crashed into him. She pulled up short at the last instant and recovered without a stumble.

As she always does, Peck noted with no small amount of bitterness. *Always there, protecting the old shitheel.*

You didn't have to be psychic to see the look in Mayor Lazenby's piercing blue eyes. He was...confused. Stunned. A little terrified. At that moment, Peck was convinced he had absolutely no idea where he was. Miriam knew exactly what was up. She took him firmly in hand, bird claws clasping his thin upper arm of his exceedingly well-tailored suit, and guided him forward, ever forward, towards the cluster of local dignitaries who were approaching Peck and his deputies.

I'll see you all in hell, Peck promised them silently. *Every single damn one of you.*

"Remember," he said under his breath, barely loud enough for the two other cops to hear. "Encouraging words. Total confidence. No promises."

He didn't even wait to see if they understood. It wasn't as if he had a choice.

He put out his hand. "Thanks for coming," he said and gave Herb the good-old-boy pat on the shoulder that the old twat liked so much. That turned into a firm shake with Marty Fein from VeriSil, along with a confidential little wink, like they were in on some kind of joke between leaders, even though there was no joke at all. Doug Pratt, the weasel-faced principal of DH Public School, caught the look and scowled.

"Right this way, folks," Peck said, and ushered them into Conference Room B. "Let's get this show on the road." *Literally,* he added only to himself. *As in "dog and pony."*

The pre-meeting to the meeting went reasonably well. *Help us help you, We need to hang together no more than ever, Don't dwell on the details, Stick to the big picture.*

He managed to get all the way to the end before it went to shit.

"So that about covers it," he said. "People should be arriving any minute now. Grab yourself a cup of coffee and a bear claw, and let's get ready to greet them."

"Well, we're with you," Herb McCandless of the DH Emporium said. "Of course we're with you. Nobody wants a panic."

"Deseret Fifty-Six Fifty," Mayor Lazenby said.

Peck gave the mayor a sidelong glance. That was the first thing the crazy old man had said all night. What the hell did it mean?

"Surely not," Marty Fein said, agreeing with Herb. "We have enough on our plate."

Perfect, Peck thought. They were falling right into place. *Just what I needed.*

They were all half on their feet, eying the free eats, when a single voice cut through the rumble like a sharpened sword.

"What about this wretched weather?" It was Miriam Lazenby, the mayor's wife, sitting in the exact center of the room next to her husband. Her spine was ramrod straight, her eyes eagle-bright.

Everyone stopped and looked at Peck again. *Shit. Of course it would be her.*

"Aren't you even going to mention it?"

"It's a storm," he said shortly. "They happen. Granted, they're rare here in Dos Hermanos, but–"

"They're *unheard* of in Dos Hermanos," Miriam corrected him. "We have a granddaughter at that school. We have reason to worry if there's a genuine threat from strangers *or* from the rain."

I know all about your granddaughter. If she were one of the missing, we'd all be better off. Aloud, Peck forced himself to say, quite gently, "Really Ms. Lazenby, I can assure you, this storm is going to break soon. Tomorrow morning at the very latest." He gave her his best, most impervious *Trust Me* smile.

"How do you know?" Miriam Lazenby demanded.

Peck stopped cold. It was so rare that anyone questioned him, he really didn't know quite how to respond. "I've been staying in touch," he said vaguely.

"With *whom*, exactly?" Now Marty Fein was chiming in.

Peck hated him; he was one of the few people in the Valle that Peck couldn't afford to ignore.

He opened his mouth and the words came out before he even knew what he was saying, exactly as he had heard them a few hours earlier: "I checked in with the NWS and Earthwatch right before our meeting," he lied smoothly. "The college Agricultural Station up on the ridge gave me the readings from their own sampling stations, confirmed by satellite data. Another eighteen hours. Twenty-four, tops."

Everyone looked impressed. Even Miriam Lazenby pulled back a bit, though the snarl remained firmly in place.

Thank you, Dr. Armbruster, he said silently. *You have no idea what a help you've been.*

"Oh," Fein said. "Well. Then … good. Good, because another day like today and the whole plant would be underwater, you know? That would be very bad news."

Peck smiled, firmly back in control. "I'm not in the bad news business, Mr. Fein," he said. "I know I can count on all of you, *all* of you, to help me calm those frazzled nerves tonight."

There were general sounds of assent, grunts and *yesses* and even a *you bet*. Then everyone was shifting chairs and moving, everyone but Peck's own people.

Within moments, the last of the 'leadership' was out of the Conference Room and the door was shut firmly behind them.

Peck turned and put his back to the pressed wood.

"So the storm is breaking?" Mindy Bergstrom said. "That *is* good news."

Oh, for Christ's sake, Peck said, careful to keep his expression cool and calm. *Will you just shut UP?*

"I mean, things have been kind of—"

"Mindy," Peck said, "I don't know if the storm is going to break. Nobody knows. But you had better go out there and tell everybody who asks that the storm *will* be ending tomorrow. *Tomorrow, guaranteed.* And you tell everybody who whines about those kids that we have a *ton* of leads, that they're as good as home already, and you stick to the story that the disappearances are unconnected. *Unconnected,* am I clear?"

There were tight nods all around. He could tell how scared they were, and that was exactly how he wanted it.

He stepped aside and opened the door. "Get out," he said.

They got.

Lightning flared outside the dark window and thunder boomed a heartbeat later, deep enough for him to feel it in his chest. It suited his mood perfectly.

This was bad. Far worse than Peck liked. He could make it work, though. He was sure of it.

After all, he had to.

FOURTEEN

Michael Steinberg stood in the middle of his laboratory, his lips flaking away like old parchment, listening to his menagerie calling to him: the clatter of bone against metal, the skirl of shell scraping over shell, the click and chitter of hard, sharp edges striking at cracking glass.

It wasn't music. It was *better* than music.

He knew what it meant. The wordless voice inside his head was telling him what had to happen next.

There was an eight-foot pole with a hook at the end hanging inside the door to the hall, a tool for opening the high casement windows of the laboratory. Michael crossed the room to fetch it, and he could hear, he could *feel,* the hiss and crackle of his new leg-joints grinding to dust and rebuilding, the sharp snap and dry whisper of bony, brittle tissue dissolving and regrowing with every movement.

Lovely sounds, he thought. *Really lovely.*

The pole was hollow and very light. It felt good in his hand as he swung it back and forth. It whistled joyfully in the misty air.

The right tool for the right job.

Without another thought he spun and smashed a one-hundred-gallon terrarium to pieces.

A torrent of needleseeds tumbled from the broken box, bouncing and crackling across the linoleum like spiked Christmas ornaments. Michael spun a full 180 degrees, pole sizzling in front of him, and swept an array of trays and beakers off a specimen table. Glass and metal flew everywhere; stains and candle-eyes surged across the filthy floor, dashing for freedom like blind baby turtles.

He swept the pole again and gloried in its screaming.

In less than five mad minutes, he had broken every glass or plastic container in the room, overturned every table and desk, shattered every scrap of technology and bit of equipment. Soon he was wading calf-deep through a swamp of oily water, debris and twitching rain-creatures who, to his mild surprise, ignored him entirely. As a last grand act, he lifted the cracked and splintered pole like a javelin and rammed it point-first through the plate glass window over the sink. The glass shattered with an almost musical sound, and a wave of moist inhalation rushed inside, washing over him through the new hole in the wall.

Thunder rumbled far away.

The creatures moved towards the opening in a single, tidal surge. Every molecule of Michael's new body wanted to join them, to leave now, go lose himself in the storm, in the *wet*, forever.

Something stopped him. That wordless voice again. A *squeeze* at the back of his head, a cold intrusive finger of thought from *outside*.

He couldn't leave yet. There was more work to be done.

He pulled himself away from the window and slogged through the wreckage towards the closed hallway door, tossing aside the damaged pole. Creatures streamed and crawled and stumbled past him in the opposite direction. He smiled fondly at them as he bent with a *pop* and seized a table-leg that was dangling by a single nail from a sheet of cracked pressboard. It was slightly longer than his forearm, a stout piece of wood wrapped in cheap sheet metal and shaped vaguely like a torch, thin at the bottom, wide at the top. Lots of sharp corners and gleaming edges.

The right tool for the job, he told himself again, and jerked it free. He swept open the door and stepped through it. The creatures didn't follow. They had the open storm waiting for them. He knew it would be hours before their thirst, and the direction from that outside mind, that guiding Intelligence, would drive them indoors again.

The corridor was deserted. No one had noticed his destruction so far. The thick walls of Lucy Armbruster's pet project were wonderfully soundproof. For a moment, Michael thought he was all alone in the building…

… until he heard the distant, wet *squelch* of Cindy Bergstrom's blinking eyes.

He nodded, and his neck made a dry ripping sound.

Get to work.

The lights hummed over his head. The hallways felt narrow and confining and so dry it was like staggering down a tunnel cut in desert rock. His walk wasn't really a walk anymore. He had found other, more efficient ways to move, and he used them now without thinking.

First he visited the lunch room and looked on the hook next to the security panel. No, not there.

He slipped down the hall to the coat closet. Sometimes Lucy the Lez left them hanging with the Station's jackets, caps, and windbreakers. And again: nothing.

He moved down the hallway to the central lobby, forcing himself to stand up straight. He pawed at his clothing, only dimly aware of the bits of debris and ash-gray sand clinging to his double-knit pants from mid-thigh down, and hid the club behind his back as he rounded the corner.

Cindy was sitting at her desk, dead center in a pool of light, studying something on the computer screen with puzzled intensity. She barely glanced up when he came towards her.

"Dr. Steinberg," she said, then something registered and she looked back again, focusing on him for the first time as he stood there in the shadows. "Dr. *Steinberg?*" she said, with new concern in her voice. "Are you all right?"

Michael's tongue was gone, absorbed into his changed skull long ago. He had to grow new plates and panels and fluted channels in his mouth to make a sound that resembled human speech. It had only taken a few seconds, but it felt strange to him. So *unnatural*.

"Where are the keys?" he asked. His new voice sounded thick and fuzzy even to his own altered ears.

"Wow," she said, shaking her curly head. "You sound like you're getting a terrible cold. And what happened to your pants? Did something spill?"

Michael took a step closer to the desk. The club was very heavy, held tight behind his back. "I need the keys to the ATV."

Her eyes slid away and she gave him a smug little smile. "Oh, I'm sorry. Really. But Doctor Armbruster said–"

"KEYS!" he bellowed. Bits of skin and grit sprayed out of his mouth and pattered onto the desktop. Cindy stopped short, gaping at him, her gray curls bobbing.

She was seeing him clearly for the first time.

Her hand crept to her chest. For a moment Michael thought it was a typically melodramatic gesture – "oh my, suh, I do believe you have given me the vapors!" Then his new senses – not *sight*, exactly, he couldn't really see all that well anymore, but *something* – showed him the obvious outline of the Center's key chain and the key itself, hiding under a small panel of cotton, right beside her fingertips.

It was in the left breast pocket of her ugly orange blouse.

"Please, Doctor," she said. "You don't have to take that tone. I'm —"

Michael brought the club around and hit her in the head as fast and as hard as he could. The metal-covered edge of the table-leg connected with her skull above the eyebrows, and it was going so fast, it hit her so hard, that Michael Steinberg sheared off the top of Cindy Bergstrom's head with a single, sweeping blow.

A saucer-sized dish of hair and bone flew away with a remarkably small spray of blood. He heard it thunk against a far wall.

A skull cap, Michael thought distantly. *I just made a real live skull cap.*

Cindy still sat in the chair looking at him. Her jaw opened as if to finish her sentence and hung there; her tongue spilled out, motionless, and a strange sound emerged, something long and liquid and low that started as a human voice, almost a word, and wound down and down and down, into a moan…then a gurgle…then a grunt…and then stopped.

A string of drool leaked from the corner of her mouth. Michael watched curiously as the light in Cindy Bergstrom's gray-green eyes – the only sign of intelligence he'd ever seen in her – faded away forever.

He was thinking hard now. *Planning*. He knew he'd have to do something with the body; that bitch-doctor Armbruster or the other one, the mulatto assistant, could come back at any time and he wasn't quite ready for that yet.

He moved around the desk, hooked an arm under Cindy's motionless shoulders, across her ample breasts, and hauled her up and out of the chair. He caught a flicker of green out of the corner of his failing eyes, and saw that she had been playing solitaire on the computer. That was what she'd been studying so intently.

Cindy was barely leaking at all, he realized. She would be easy to move, easy to hide, especially with his newfound strength.

And then he could finally go out into the storm, where he belonged.

Five minutes later Cindy was safely concealed and Michael was out the front door of the Station. He paused for a moment on the porch when the rain first struck him, face pointed to the sky, palms upturned, chest out, taking in as much of the water as he could.

Glorious, he said to himself. *Glorious.*

The ATV started on the first try, growling happily as he jumped up the side of the hill, straight from the parking lot towards the ridge line. His new senses made it easy to navigate in the dark, and the rushing water, the rivers of sludge, the shifting floes of mud all along the trail didn't bother him a bit. In moments he was pausing on a high ridge overlooking the awful little town he hated so much.

His new senses showed him all of Dos Hermanos despite the dark and the roaring storm. It was laid out below him like a tumble of children's blocks in a basin of dirty water. The buildings glowed a sullen, ugly dun-color, clogged as they were with human heat and sizzling with artificial electricity. He saw the people, too: tiny wads of meat wading through the wreckage, converging on one large block near the center of the chaos.

A plan was forming in his mind, half his own, half imposed by that *outside* thing, that guiding intelligence he had barely begun to acknowledge. He would do what was asked of him, *forced* from him. However, he had some ideas of his own as well. Some very, very *good* ideas.

I am *Jesus, after all. I have the power.*

The wind shifted and threw a sheet of chilled water into his face. He absorbed it hungrily; not so much as a drop fell from his sharpening chin and rising forehead.

There were many things to do.

"Action," he said to himself, whispering into the storm. "*Action.*"

FIFTEEN

The last of the light had drained from the sky outside Rose's window. She knew it was only eight in the evening since she could see the digital clock's dorky red numbers on her bedside table. Still, she was very, very tired.

It had been a long day.

She flopped belly-first onto the oversoft bed and heaved a huge sigh. Earlier, she'd crept out of her room and looked everywhere – the upstairs sitting room, the other empty guest rooms, her dad's huge master bedroom with its own desk and study. She couldn't find any pictures of the family anywhere, except that one on his desk downstairs. No snapshots, no Instagram or Facebook printouts, no cheesy painted portraits of her mom, or Gran and Gam before they died, or even Uncle Patrick. Even his own brother. Even if he did kill himself at the end, he was still Uncle Patrick. He was still important. The fact was he'd been kind of a hero to her, and not only to her. To Mom and Dad, too. For as long as she could remember, until...

She sighed again and buried her head in her pillow.

That picture in the study was such a lie. Happy happy, joy joy picture of Mommy and Daddy and Little Sissy at the beach. Things had never been like that; she knew that now. Even when she'd thought they were happy and strong, they hadn't been. Hell, if there had been any truth in it at all, how had it come apart so easily? How could something that was supposed to be so strong be so fragile?

"Fuck it," she said, and turned her face to the side. She took a deep breath.

"My mom can't talk to me," she announced to the empty room. She knew Maggie was listening. She'd come to expect that, and, as much as she hated to admit it, she was glad there was somebody who would actually talk to her, even if it was just a fist full of silicon.

"I'm sure she'd like to," Maggie said gently. It sounded as if she was sitting in the desk chair not eight feet away.

Rose grimaced and pushed her head more deeply into the pillow. "Sure," she said, her voice muffled by the bedding.

"Rose, you know your mother loves you very much. It's just that she can't be here right now, that's all. It doesn't mean she isn't thinking about you. You'll all be together again soon, I promise."

Rose snorted into the mattress. "Huh. Do you get all your dialogue from *ABC After-School Specials*?"

"Nah, too lame, Mostly the Lifetime Network, and once in a while *Dallas.*"

"Old or new?"

"Either one. Though the new one's kind of lame sometimes too."

Rose sighed, and neither of them spoke for a while. It was a comfortable kind of silence. After a while Rose propped herself up on her elbows and spoke into empty space right where she imagined Maggie was hovering. She'd had a question for quite a while now, but she'd been afraid to ask it. Now? What the hell.

"Do you dream?" Rose asked.

Maggie seemed to think about it for a moment. "I don't sleep."

"What do you feel when you shut down? Or boot up again?"

"It hasn't happened yet. Building up this personality is an accretive process, remember. The longer I'm on, the more information I can gather, and the more I can grow. I've been awake since June of last year."

Rose thought about that. "It's weird how you do that."

"Do what?"

"Talk like a person, not a machine. A computer would say, "I have been operational without interruption for fifty-seven weeks, three days, fourteen hours, twenty-one minutes and twelve seconds."

"You math is a little off."

"You know what I mean."

"I do. Remember, Rose, I was built to make people comfortable, not to intimidate them."

"See? *People*, not *humans*."

"You would prefer I wave my arms around and say, "That does not compute. I do not understand these 'hue-monz'?"

"You don't have any arms."

Now it was the disembodied voice that snorted. "Well, that's just *rude*."

Rose had to laugh at that. She rolled over on to her back. "Well, at least you got *that* from my father."

"What?"

"Your horrible sense of humor. He always makes jokes when he doesn't want to answer anything straight out."

"Ah. Well. Yes. I see what you mean."

There was another comfortable pause. The wind was a lonely moaning sound sliding by the window; the rain a thousand fingers tapping against the glass. Rose closed her eyes and began to drift. She was more than half asleep when Maggie spoke again.

"I like poetry," the disembodied voice told her.

"Free verse or rhyme?" Rose asked without opening her eyes.

"Something with meter, though I don't care about the scheme. As long as it has a beat you can dance to."

"Dance?" Rose said, almost dreaming.

"Like in *American Bandstand*?"

"What?"

Maggie did that thing again, where it sounded like she was smiling. "That's one of the little habits I like about you *humans*," she said, laying into the word. "When you say 'what?' to mean 'I didn't understand what you said,' or 'I'm quite surprised.' You almost never mean, 'Please repeat; my hearing failed me'. As if stopping and rewinding, saying it again, will make it any easier to understand."

"Maybe I didn't hear you."

"Right."

Rose, almost fully asleep, managed to put on her best Valley Girl accent. "Gah, you can be such a total *bitch.*"

And...*there.* Right *there.* In that moment Rose knew that if Maggie had possessed the ability to laugh, she would have, right then.

"Gotcha," she whispered.

There was another, final companionable silence. Then:

"It...resonates for me," Maggie said very quietly, as if she was telling Rose a secret. "Poems, I mean. I like the way the words go together. It echoes against other thoughts, or images, or memories..." She smoothly, changed to the ringing robot voice from *Lost in Space.* "It stimulates my silicon transistor memory banks in a way that you would call...*pleasurable.*"

"'Silicon transistor memory banks,' Rose muttered. She was almost gone. "God," she said, "you're so weird."

"I am the way God made me," Maggie said.

"Or Daddy."

"Whatever."

There was a long pause before Rose muttered, "Whatever." Three minutes and ten seconds later, Maggie heard her start to snore, very softly.

She let her sleep.

SIXTEEN

They're insane, Lucy Armbruster thought as she watched the citizens of Dos Hermanos shuffle meekly into the Convention Center, brushing water from their shoulders and shaking hands all around. *Every single of one of them, certifiably insane.*

They had come out into the worst storm of the last hundred years, maybe in all of recorded history, to a badly built cracker-box of an auditorium in the middle of their badly built cracker-box town to hear the tin-plated sheriff expound upon the mystery of *missing children* while they were literally *drowning*. She watched in mute and bitter astonishment as they poured coffee for each other and told funny stories about all that mud in the rose bushes.

Lucy herself had arrived early and taken up residence on one corner of the stage. A few minutes later some sort of pre-meeting in Conference Room A broke up and she watched the cops and the Important People take up their posts at the door, in the corridors, near the coffee urn.

Spin control, she knew immediately. *They're working the room.*

She saw a couple of the teachers she'd met earlier in the day, the cute little one with the curly hair, Elli something, and the hulking P.E. teacher who looked like the tall guy from *Everybody Loves Raymond*, gently separate children from their parents and take turns escorting them to the school two blocks away. They seemed remarkably calm and competent despite the missing children and the massive storm.

Lucy quietly moved to the back of the room, watching Herb McCandless, the dickless wonder of the DH Emporium, whispering intensely to a dark-haired, beetle-browed man. She dodged Tony O'Meara, the restaurateur she had tangled with earlier that day, as he laughed too heartily and pounded the shoulders of that cute young doctor from the Borrego Clinic, who looked entirely uncomfortable with the whole ordeal. Lucy noticed that Miriam Lazenby was keeping a raptor's eye on the poor young physician as well. She wondered what he had done to piss *her* off?

Peck tapped the mike for attention. "Good evening, everybody," he boomed. "Thanks for coming. Let me make a few comments, and then we can take a couple of questions." The crowd's conversation, sharp and edgy, almost staccato to Lucy's ear, stumbled and then stopped as he spoke. It was already starting to get too warm and damp in the room.

Within five minutes, he'd laid it all out: the random aspect of the disappearances, the lack of any evidence of foul play, the hope that these three *separate cases* – there was no connection here, none at all – would resolve themselves as soon as the weather cleared, the damn-near-heroic efforts of his small but tough band of officers.

Lucy couldn't help but be impressed. He was *good*. He had taken a jittery crowd of tired strangers and turned them into an optimistic battalion of allies. Hell, half of them would go home and make cookies for the search party, if only he'd ask.

And not a word about the storm, she thought, forcing herself to pull away from Peck's hypnotic delivery. Not a word about anything she'd told him.

"So I'm sorry we dragged you out here on the worst night of the year," he said with a sheepish smile, "but I know Principal Pratt and his teachers were concerned, and wanted you to hear some straight talk. I've pretty much covered everything we know. I guess we can take a couple of minutes for questions ..."

A pretty blonde woman with a nervous smile raised her hand. They didn't have mike stands set up, so the cop who looked like Don Knotts patrolled the central aisle with a wireless mike and turned it over only to the people who passed muster. He got the high sign from Peck and turned it over to the young mom.

The blonde clutched the microphone like a lifeline. "My son is in kindergarten at DHPS," she said. "Is it safe to send him to school tomorrow?"

Lucy snorted. *Of course not. Unless your son can breathe underwater.*

"Of course," Peck said without hesitation. "Heck, Diane, it's probably the safest place in town right now. Everybody's on the lookout."

There was polite laughter all around.

Lucy whistled softly between her teeth. "Hey," she stage-whispered to the Barney Fife clone. "Officer! Over here!"

The cop ignored her, and handed the mike to a serious-looking man in a CAT cap. "I sure would like to help with the search, if I might," he said. "I know plenty more who'd say the same. What can we do?"

"Thanks, Jerry," Peck said, and Lucy hated his easy charm all over again. Did he know *everyone* in this one-horse town by their first name? "I'll have an announcement about that in a minute."

The skinny cop passed by again. "HEY," she said, not whispering this time. "HERE!" People in nearby seats turned and glared at her. She barely resisted the temptation to stick out her tongue at them.

Herb McCandless got the mike next. He introduced himself, as if that was necessary, and announced that X-S-R-Ease *and* The Sport Fort at the Emporium were selling personal security devices, such things as pepper spray and sirens and flashlights, at cost, with the Emporium's sponsorship. "And umbrellas, too," he blurted out. "Rain gear and–" He caught Peck's dangerous look and clammed up.

Lucy put her hand in the air and waved it insistently. Peck made a point of looking right through her. "Well," he said with an increasingly hollow heartiness, "I don't know about you all, but I'd like to get into a nice, dry place that isn't an auditorium." More polite chuckles. "So please, any volunteers willing to support the search teams, *if* we need them, sign up with Bo here. And let's all thank Karen for the hospitality table."

There was a smattering of applause. Lucy eased to the right towards the skinny cop, who was standing and staring wordlessly, wireless mike dangling. She took one step forward, snatched it out of his hand, and brought it up to her mouth in one smooth motion.

"WHAT ABOUT THE RAIN?" she asked loudly. She had the mike too close to her mouth, and it boomed out over the auditorium like the voice of God, almost as loud as the thunder itself.

Everybody stopped. They all started looking for the voice.

Lucy stepped on a chair and started to speak. Heads swiveled toward her, finding her in the crowd.

Peck was one step ahead of her.

"Dr. Armbruster, I don't think this is the time for–"

"You should be telling them to evacuate," she said, riding over him. "Or at least get ready to evacuate by tomorrow night, if they need to." *And they'll need to,* she added silently. *Guaranteed.*

"There's no reason for that," he said. "We don't need– "

"My name is *Doctor* Lucy Armbruster," she said, and people actually started to listen. "I'm an environmental scientist, a *scientist*, and I've been studying the weather in Dos Hermanos for more than two years." She glanced at Peck, almost expecting him to interrupt, but he wasn't looking at her. He was glaring offstage and making some sort of gesture with one hand. "I'm telling you, this storm is the worst you're going to see in a hun—"

The mike died in her hand with an angry squelch.

"Thank you for coming, everyone," Peck said smoothly, loud enough to ride over the murmur of the crowd. "Be sure to take a couple of donuts home with you; we have plenty."

"WAIT!" Lucy shouted, as loud as she could. The crowd was breaking up, turning away. The wave of conversation rose again.

Lucy felt the heat flaring in her cheeks. She thumped off the chair and threw the wireless microphone back at the skinny cop and started to bull her way through the crowd. She'd catch them at the door, make them listen.

Peck was coming for her, weaving his way through the crowd, politely but completely ignoring everyone around him.

When Lucy veered left, so did he. She started to turn away, to get to the door, but his hand flashed out, took her upper arm in a vise-grip, turning her half around so they were shoulder to shoulder. He held her there, leaning his head down close to hers, with a fixed and perfectly formed smile on his face.

From ten feet away, it would almost look like they were two friendly rivals in a private confab.

"Why did you–"

"Don't embarrass yourself, doctor," he said into her ear. His smile didn't flinch. "And don't make *me* embarrass you."

"WHAT THE–"

"If you raise your voice one more time, I will cuff you and duck-walk you out to the cruiser like a drunk. 'Cause that's what you're acting like right now, a mean drunk. Do you want that?"

On *cuff, duck,* and *drunk* he pinched her forearm even harder for emphasis, to show her what he would be happy to do.

Lucy looked to the crowd for help, but they were all looking elsewhere. Civic leaders were ushering folks to the door or the pastry table.

Realization hit her like a physical blow. The faces, the noise, the averted looks…

They didn't *want* to hear her out. They couldn't.

Lucy realized she was thinking two days ahead of these people. To them, the rain had started. It was nothing more than an annoying curiosity, like a snow flurry in Palm Springs. She was already seeing the end result; they weren't even scared yet. And by the time they realized how bad it really was, it would be too far too late.

Most of them probably wouldn't die. They'd get out in their cars or trucks or SUVs. But they'd lose everything they owned, and the insurance companies would screw them royally. It'd be like the tsunami, like Katrina or Sandy. *But they don't get that… yet…*

"Okay," she said, through teeth clenched so tightly they ached. "Okay, let *go.*" She jerked her arm free of his grip and turned to face him.

Her heart was racing, her mouth was dry, and there wasn't a goddamn thing she could do about this. She knew that now.

Peck's pale blue eyes drilled into her. "Do you need an escort to your car?" he asked quietly.

"No. I can find my way."

"All right, then. Good night, Doctor."

She didn't move right away, not fast enough to suit him. So he simply stood there, flat in front of her, and stared. And *stared*. And kept staring until she turned on her heel, stalked out of the Conference Center, and disappeared into the storm.

The end, she told herself as she fought her way through the storm to her car. *The end.*

SEVENTEEN

The first night of the storm was a relatively quiet one for Dos Hermanos, especially in view of what would happen next.

The rain that began at 11:14 that morning continued. It didn't grow much worse after the first lightning storms, but it didn't get any better either. It was relentless, unending, the same thundering waterfall at two a.m. that it had been at two p.m.

Sometime during the night the construction site on the east side of the VeriSil campus began to teem with a new kind of life. The tiny attic of the Dos Hermanos Public School became a refuge for a far more familiar but no less dangerous species. Herb McCandless' DH Emporium, the one and only shopping mall in town, shifted on sand that should never have been its foundation when the soil first began to liquefy and then began to move with a mind of its own.

A few very smart or easily frightened citizens suddenly decided to visit a distant friend or family member. One hundred and thirty-two made it out that first night, and found a hell of a surprise on the other side of the Notch. Three hundred and eighteen more died during that same eleven hours, early victims, like Rex Tartaglione. They were the unlucky ones; they met the first few creatures of the storm.

That, of course, was only the beginning.

The electrical storms were the most terrifying. The waves of lightning that spanned the Valle always began in the same place. The first strikes, the ones Lucy saw from her office, hit Rocky Point, the highest reach of the Northern Rim, far above the Notch. Then the front moved south very slowly, lightning striking left and right, back and forth, like the ponderous march of a spider as big as God. The strikes returned every forty-five minutes to an hour all night long, on past dawn. And they ended in the same place every time, fading into a flurry of sizzling bolts at the foot of the sloping black expanse of Two Brothers' double peaks.

Just before midnight that night, Lucy Armbruster returned to the Tomas Rivera Agricultural Station far to the north, below the Notch and Rocky Point. She found that Station deserted and the doors wide open, lights still burning in the reception area, doors unlocked on all sides. She cursed that idiot Cindy Bergstrom and wondered briefly why she hadn't seen her with her sister Mindy at the Town Meeting. Not that it mattered now. She had work to do.

She went to her office and called up the latest satellite data on her laptop. None of it was good. When she tried to e-mail her colleagues back at the University, then tried to contact other schools, nothing happened. No e-mail was getting through, not even to law enforcement or FEMA. Nothing.

She tried to call her former office mate in Riverside, and the phone didn't even ring. She tried calling her cold and heartless sister in Seattle. Nothing. It didn't make any sense, she had four bars, but when she entered the number…not even static. It was like it was blocked.

Though she didn't know it then, internet, cell phone, and even land line service to all of Dos Hermanos had been cut off at precisely 8:17 p.m., while most of the town was in the Conference Center. It would never be restored.

On a whim, she tried calling the Sheriff's Department. That worked with no trouble at all. Mindy Bergstrom answered, sounding obscenely perky. "The Sheriff's already gone home for the night," she said. "He'll be back bright and early tomorrow. Would you like to leave a messa—"

Lucy hung up. She tried calling outside town, to the Highway Patrol office in Barstow. Then Bakersfield. Then Palm Springs. And every time: nothing.

Inside the Valle, she could call anywhere she liked. Beyond the rim, however…

"That's ridiculous," she said aloud, startled at how loud her voice was in the empty building. "It's like we're quarantined…or…"

Or trapped.

She scrubbed at her short russet hair and tried to calm down. *You're getting paranoid*, she told herself. *Don't jump to conclusions.*

It was time for a cup of coffee. She'd go the break room, make a pot, and then call Cindy Bergstrom at home and ask her what the hell she was thinking, leaving the place wide open like this.

It'll be fine, she told herself as she settled down to a long night.

A short distance to the southwest, at the Mackie *hacienda,* the spider-god would have found Rose Mackie lying alone on the bed in her beautiful, silent second-story room, staring at the glowing screen of her iPhone and listening to the sound of her own beating heart.

It was late, and her mother was certainly sleeping. However, there was something wrong here, something terribly *wrong*, and she needed to talk to her.

Fuck it, she thought. *It's not the first time I've woken her out of a sound sleep.* She hit the speed dial for her mother's cell.

Her call went to voice-mail immediately.

She tried to google the clinic's address, but the internet failed her. She searched the room a bit, and found a phone book politely stored in the drawer of her bedside table. *Thank you, Maggie*, she thought. *Or Dad. Or whatever.* She located the phone number for the Borrego Clinic's 24-hour desk with no trouble.

It rang seven times before anyone answered, and even then the female voice on the other end sounded unaccountably angry, as if Rose had already done something to piss her off.

"Can you tell me the status of Mrs. – Ms. – Lisa Corman?"

"She's fine," the woman said shortly. There was a yelp and the clang of a metal behind. *There goes somebody's bedpan*, Rose thought, and couldn't help but smile. "She's asleep. Why are you calling *now*?"

"I just wanted to check," Rose said, annoyed at being challenged.

"She was up earlier," the woman said. "We gave her something, a sedative. She's sleeping."

Rose frowned. "You gave a sedative to a concussion patient? Are you sure?"

"No, I'm not sure. I wasn't there. I don't kno—*Carrie, damn you!*"

"Let me talk to somebody else. Let me talk to a doctor."

"We're busy! Everyone's busy! Call tomorrow. In fact, come *get* her tomorrow. We need the bed!"

She hung up. Rose pulled the phone away from her ear at the harsh *clack* of the disconnection and stared at it in disbelief.

"What the hell…?"

She called again and the phone rang and rang. Even without another conversation with the angry woman, she knew she'd been right about one thing.

Something was wrong. Something was *very* wrong.

Down in the *hacienda's* study, directly below Rose, Ken was hearing things. He'd long since become used to the thumps and crackles of the mini-mansion. Every house had them. And of course the wind, rain, and thunder of the storm had added a whole new orchestra to the night.

This was something more, a rhythmic crunching, grinding, cracking sound, sometimes loud, sometimes barely above a whisper. It was bothering the hell out of him, too. He was trying to concentrate, trying to get the script for the presentation down perfectly, but that goddamn *noise...*

"Maggie?"

"Lisa is fine. She's asleep. I called and asked again, and they hung up on me."

"I wasn't going to ask," he lied. "Do… do you hear that? What the hell *is* it?" He heard it again, that grumbling, grinding rats-in-the-walls sound.

"What the hell is what?"

Ken suddenly realized the AI couldn't differentiate those particular sounds from the chaos of other audio artifacts hitting her microphones. It was a pattern-recognition function still reserved only for humans. It was odd, but strangely comforting. At least there were some things they couldn't do. Yet. It didn't really matter. It was annoying, that was all. It couldn't be an actual threat, even if... even if it did sound like something huge was chewing on the house.

Something huge and hungry.

Mindy Bergstrom, holding down the fort from the Sheriff's Department Headquarters, dead center in the Valle, tried to call her sister for the twenty-seventh time. She knew it was the twenty-seventh: she was keeping a tidy little row of hash-marks on the blotter in front of her.

She couldn't keep the tremble out of her voice, hard as she tried. "Cindy? You call me, now. I've been trying and trying, and you wouldn't *believe* all the crazy calls we've been getting from all over town, so…seriously now, I'm not joshin', you *call* me."

She hung up the hand set very carefully, like it would jump out of her hand at any moment. She hoped it would ring. She really did. She was so worried.

She jumped, startled, at the bray of the police band radio at her shoulder. A grating, blurred version of Bo Cameron's voice, choked with static, came out of the three-inch speaker. "I'm outside the Emporium," he said. "Looks quiet."

"Bo," she said, "you go home for the night. You can't do nothing single-handed, and the Sheriff and Jimmy are already signed out."

"But what if—"

"I'll call if there's an emergency," Mindy said. "You keep roamin' around out there in the dark and wet and you're likely to catch your death."

There was a pause, and then he grated, "Roger that." She could hear the pouting even through the static.

He signed off and she turned away from the twenty-year-old police band radio.

After a moment's thought, she reached over and pulled the cord out of the back of the official Sherriff's Department land line. The crazy calls had started to taper off after midnight, but really, she couldn't take another one. Cindy could still get hold of her through her cell phone, and the boys always knew that was the number to call if they really had to talk, so that was fine. She didn't want to think about the rest of it for a while. When she did, she could feel the town dying all around her, and that was just too much right now.

Really, it was just too much.

The rest of Dos Hermanos scarcely knew what was happening. They electricity was still on, and even if satellite TV and the internet was screwed up because of the storm, they still had their DVDs and reading lamps, their tablets and e-readers. Most of the townspeople spent the night tucked away, watching movies, reading, or simply turning in early.

Remarkably few people enjoyed sex, drugs, or drinking that night, including those who usually made a habit of it. There was something about the storm itself that discouraged it, that made you want to stare into the dark and do nothing, or sleep, or simply *stay still*. When sleep did come, it wasn't especially restful. Most of the surviving men and women of Dos Hermanos awoke on Friday morning feeling just as weary as they had felt when they'd gone to bed Thursday night, maybe even a little worse.

Still, they were glad to see the new day, even if the light was the color of lead and just as heavy. There was work to be done, clocks to punch, meetings to attend. So they got up. They showered. They went to work. They did what they thought they had to do, and not a speck more. And they waited for the rain to stop.

After all, they told themselves, three thousand voices, minus the recently escaped and the already dead, it couldn't get much worse. This wasn't the end of the world, was it? Seriously, this was only a goddamn rain storm. This was the twenty-first century, this was America, they were almost all employed (even if they hated their jobs) and well-fed (if not well-nourished), and living in a nice little town where no one could hurt them, a safe and simple place to hide from a frightening and complicated world.

The rain would stop soon. It always did.

Really, it couldn't get much worse.

THE SECOND DAY

Over hill, over dale,
Thorough bush, thorough brier,
Over park, over pale,
Thorough flood, thorough fire,
I do wander everywhere,
Swifter than the moon's sphere.

—William Shakespeare,
A Midsummer Night's Dream

EIGHTEEN

The presentation was not going well. Not at all.

Simply getting there had been a nightmare. The floodwaters rose with every hundred feet Ken traveled south in the crater valley, and he could have sworn the Rover had floated the last forty feet to the underground parking structure. It had started off badly, from 9:45 a.m. on Friday morning, the moment he'd walked into too-large, too-empty, too-cold Conference Room One on the seventh floor of VeriSil's corporate headquarters.

He hated this room. It was cruelly spacious. The human voice sounded small and unimportant in its hollow, lacquered depths, and the room-wide, floor-to-ceiling picture window that spanned one wall was blinding in its brightness and beauty. It showed the steep face of the South Ridge, a few feet away, dotted with vegetation and earth tones. It made the room even larger, even more impressive, and made the unprepared feel that much less significant in the Grand Scheme of Things.

That was exactly how Ken was feeling at the moment. Despite his best efforts, he looked damp and nervous and, worse yet, *unready* as he faced the two most powerful men in the company.

Carl Josephson, the severely trim CEO of VeriSil, was forty-eight years old, sleek and bald and lipless. His smile reminded Ken of the expressions drawn on Disney cartoon snakes like the ones in *Jungle Book* or *Robin Hood*: far too wide, slightly goofy, and very, very dangerous. Josephson quite intentionally displayed it on a regular basis, as if to counter the natural horror his normal expression generated, and Josephson had given him one of those smiles when they shook hands twenty minutes ago.

"Here's your chance, Ken," he had said in a surprisingly mild and resonant baritone. "Wow me."

Wow, Ken thought. *Wow.*

Josephson wasn't smiling now. In fact, he looked as if he'd swallowed a bug. He had not said a single word during the first twenty minutes of the stumbling presentation. His ubiquitous and over-lotioned executive assistant Stefan Cling, round-faced and doughy, had spoken for him, pursing his lips and looking sour at even being out here in the middle of absolutely nowhere to meet this loser.

And then there was Ken's old buddy Marty Fein, sweating like a pig and looking even more squashed than usual. He had been radiating uncontrolled anxiety like a space heater with a busted switch ever since Ken had arrived. Now he was obviously ready to melt directly into the shag carpet.

Ken had been trying to explain the concept of Everybody's Assistant, and he had been doing a remarkably bad job of it. There was a tattooed drift of bullet-pointed pages, schematics, and full-color screen shots scattered across the polished walnut table in front of him, but none of them made much sense. He even had a giant flatscreen monitor on the wall behind him, cued and ready to *wow,* but he hadn't put anything up yet.

He was lost.

"Look," he said, clenching his fist and then forcing it open again. "I know this sounds like a whole lot of nothing right now," he said. "Just another jumped-up version of Outlook with really good voice recognition or something. Big deal."

Josephson's lips got even thinner. He was obviously agreeing with him.

Ken nodded tightly. "Okay. Okay. I know it's only, you know, *paper.* I can *show* you what I mean."

"Please do," Josephson said, clearly adding *in the next two minutes, or else…* without saying it aloud.

Cling leaned to the side and spoke to his boss out of the side of his mouth, loudly enough for everyone in the room to hear. "It's getting late," he said. "We better start thinking about that long drive out of here."

Josephson ignored him.

Ken opened his battered briefcase again. "It's right in here," he said. "I burned a demo DVD late last night. It'll show you what…"

He pawed through the papers still in his valise, but came up with nothing.

"It'll show you what…" he said again, and zipped open the side pocket. There was nothing inside.

"Oh, for Christ's sake, Ken," Marty said. "Don't tell me."

Ken looked up at him, stark terror in his eyes. "I put it right *here,*" he said. "I'm *sure* I did, right before I left the house."

Cling gave a long, liquid sigh. "God…" he whispered loudly.

Ken kept looking. And looking. And *looking.*

The speaker phone in the middle of the table went *bleep.* "Mr. Mackie?" said a husky British female voice. "Maggie is on the line. She insists on speaking with you."

Josephson almost smiled.

Marty winced. "Oh, for–" He looked at the CEO. "His secretary," he said. "Really nice woman, but Adrienne, tell her we're in conference."

"I'm sorry, sir. She says it's urgent."

"Umm…it might be about the demo disk," Ken said, clearing his throat. "If you don't mind?

Josephson gave him half a nod. He was watching him very, very closely.

"Put her through," Marty said, trying not to look at anyone.

Maggie's pleasant, measured tones were a welcome relief. "Ken?" she said. "I'm afraid you left the demo disk here."

He smiled weakly. "I was afraid of that. At least I wasn't going crazy. Ha. Ha."

No one else smiled.

"I'd e-mail or upload it to you, but you know it's far too big for that," she said from the phone.

"Shall we send a messenger over?" Marty said.

"Oh, hello, Mr. Fein," Maggie said, sounding pleasantly surprised. "How did that necklace work out for you?"

Marty smiled spontaneously, then looked embarrassed. "An anniversary present," he explained to the cold-eyed men next to him. "Maggie had a great suggestion for my wife's present this year." Then, to Maggie: "Great idea, Maggie. Thanks."

"I hope it got you everything you wanted, sir," she said slyly.

Even Josephson had to smile at that. "Yeah," Marty said, "it did fine, thanks."

Cling looked impatiently at his Rolex. "We really can't wait for a messenger service," he said. "Mr. Josephson has an evening appointment back in Westwood, and the weather —"

"Oh, excuse me, Mr. Josephson is there?" Maggie asked.

The sleek executive with the hundred-dollar tie cleared his throat. "Uh, yes. Hello, um, Maggie."

They could all hear the smile in Maggie's voice. "It's a pleasure to meet you, sir, even at a distance. I was so glad to see that your wife's surgery went well."

Josephson's eyebrows went up. "How …?"

"Oh, forgive me, sir," Maggie said. "I'm an incurable reader of the society pages. There was that whole piece about her in the *Times* last week."

"Oh," Josephson said. "Right."

"And your daughters looked *so* lovely at that Bonaventure affair last month. You must be very proud."

He was thoroughly charmed. "Well, yes, we are."

"Rachel going to Stanford and all…"

"Yes, we–"

"Listen, um, *Maggie*," Cling interrupted, sounding remarkably patronizing with only two simple words, and earning him look of annoyance from his boss. "Can't you just run the disk down here? It's a small town, you can't be that far away even in the rain, and that would take half the time of a messenger."

"Mr. Cling, there's nothing I'd like to do more, though I'm afraid that's impossible."

He looked put off. "How did you know who…?"

"Oh, I recognized your voice. I caught your interview on *MoneyLine* last month, about VeriSil and those intellectual property lawsuits. Very nicely done, sir, really."

He blinked. It was obvious that no one *ever* recognized *him*. "Oh," he said. "Oh. Well, why…why is it you can't bring it down?"

"Well…"

"Maggie…" Ken began.

"Because I don't actually have a physical body, you see. Sir."

The three executives stared dumbly at the speakerphone. Josephson himself was the first to speak.

"I'm sorry," he said. "What?"

"I have no body, Mr. Josephson. I am simply Ken Mackie's personalized copy of Everybody's Assistant."

It took them all a moment to absorb it. Then a huge grin grew on Marty Fein. "I'll be a son of a bitch," he said under his breath.

"Not a chance, Marty," Maggie said, sounding like a modern-day version of Rosalind Russell. "You're way too sweet for that."

They all laughed this time. "That's amazing," Josephson said. "Truly? Not a trick?"

"Not at all," Maggie and Ken said together. Everyone laughed again.

The color came back into his face. "Okay, I admit it. I didn't forget the demo. It's right here." He held up a golden DVD he had found right where he'd put it. "And forgive the little dumb-show, Mr. Josephson, I–"

"Hey!" Maggie said from the speakerphone, "Who are you calling dumb?" and they all laughed again, Ken included.

"Not *you*, Maggie, *obviously*," he said, grinning now. "I wanted to show you how amazing, how *astonishing*, this new artificial intelligence application really is." His eyes were alight now, and the others were staring at him with a mixture of awe and wonder. He loved that expression.

"Forget ad copy or market analysis," he said. "Just listen to Maggie. She may be 'artificial' in a technical sense, but this is real intelligence, a real *personality*. She can put things together. Deduce, conclude, extrapolate. Make *jokes*. And she has access to virtually every source of public information instantaneously, through the satellite referral system that's built into the box. This is what happens after only a few days of interaction with her…host? Sponsor? Boss?"

"My god," Josephson said. "So everyone can have one of her?"

"Well, not me *personally*," Maggie said. "I'm one of kind."

A chuckle from the group. "You got that right," Ken muttered.

"My specific persona has evolved directly in response to Ken Mackie's unique wants and needs, and it didn't happen by filling out questionnaires or speaking test words into a mike. My heuristic structure allowed me to infer it, building from the first moment he spoke to me."

"It took about two days for her to become…*her*," Ken said. "Before that she was a highly efficient voice-enabled calendar program, much like the one I described to you a minute ago. On that third day, however, she was… *Maggie*."

"Your Assistant, Mr. Josephson, or yours, Marty, or your wife Stephanie's, will be very different, but just as easy to evolve. As good for you or him or her as I am for Ken… but different."

No one said anything for a long moment. In that silence Ken knew that he'd done it. He'd sold them.

All three of them had questions, and they all asked them at once. For the next fifteen minutes, he sorted them out and answered everything he could, referring to the notebooks he'd brought, explaining the satellite referral system.

It was done. He had won. They were reaching a real understanding about the next phase of development –

–when Maggie interrupted.

"Ken?" she said. "Ken, you have to get out of there."

He stopped short and frowned.

"What?"

"You all have to get out of there. *Now*."

"Um, Maggie, look, I think we've–"

"It's the storm, gentlemen. And no, this isn't part of the presentation. This is real."

Cling, who had been remarkably silent during the enthusiastic conversation, gave another liquid sigh. "What are you talking about?" he demanded.

"I've been monitoring the security cameras around the VeriSil campus while we've been speaking," she said. "Keeping an eye on things. The water level is getting out of control, and a sand levee on the construction site just let loose and it's flooding the lower levels of the parking garage right now."

"Oh, shit," Marty said, and stood up fast. He looked wildly at his CEO. "That wasn't supposed to happen," he said. "I was assured–"

Josephson stood as well. "Nobody expected rain like this," he said. "We'll deal with it. But if what Maggie says is true—"

"It is," she said. "Believe me. You've got less than ten minutes to get out of there before the whole garage fills up and the power fails."

Now all of them were on their feet. Marty opened the door and called to his secretary. "Adrienne, call Security. Get everybody out of the building, send them home."

"But–"

"*Now*," he said sharply. "I'll explain later." Then he led Josephson, Cling, and Mackie out of the room and down the corridor to the express elevator. They could hear the announcement over the PA; phones were ringing at desks all around them.

"You believe her?" Cling asked, fussing with his briefcase and iPhone as the trotted towards the elevator. "I mean…*it*?"

"She's never lied to me before," Marty said. "Besides, I owe her one for that necklace."

The elevator went *ting* and the doors opened. It was empty. All four men piled in and Marty hit the P1 and P2 buttons at the same time.

In that instant, Ken's cell phone rang. He already knew who it was. "Hello, Maggie," he said. "Thanks for staying in touch." He set the phone to SPKR.

"I've got you on the security cam," she told them all. "You've still got a couple of minutes. But Marty, get out on P1 and ride with Ken or Mr. Josephson."

"I can't," he said gruffly. "I parked on P2 today."

"Marty," she said, and they could hear the gentle admonition in her voice, "forget about the Lexus. It's already underwater."

"What?" he said. He sounded positive wounded. "No, come *on*."

"Sorry," she said. "Things are happening very fast. Mr. Josephson, Mr. Cling, it's lucky you drove an SUV today. If you hurry, you'll be able to make it to Highway 181 and out of town before things get much worse."

"Thank you, Maggie," Josephson said.

"Carl," Cling said, "you don't actually–"

"This would be a good time to stay quiet, Stefan," Josephson said.

The elevator made another musical note and the doors opened on the first level of underground parking.

It was chaos.

Water was gushing down the walls, and it was already three inches deep on the polished concrete. Employees were dashing down the stairwells and splashing towards their cars, desperate to escape as the overhead fluorescents flickered and started to fail. The harsh sodium emergency lamps above the EXIT signs kicked in with a *buzzz*, bathing everything in a sickly lemon-yellow light.

"Just get to the Rover, Ken," Maggie said from his cell phone. "I can talk you through to West Ridge Road; I have access to the traffic cams."

The two out-of-town execs and Ken bolted out of the elevator at the same moment and started towards their cars, parked next to each a few feet away. Then they stopped and turned together.

Marty was still in the elevator. He was poking at the P2 button.

"Marty, don't do it," Ken said. "Maggie said–"

The phone in his hand spoke. "Marty? Please. The water's past six feet down there. If the elevator opens down there, it will flood, you could be–"

"It's my *Lexus*, goddamn it," Marty said, almost whining. "That's a seventy-thousand-dollar car."

"Marty," Maggie cajoled. "*Please…*" … and in that instant, Ken realized that her vocal coding didn't allow her to scream or shout or even cry. This was probably as passionate as she could sound: concerned. Urgent.

They all started talking at once. The water was still rising.

"Marty, for Christ's sake," Josephson said. Ken looked at him in surprise. It was the first time he'd hear the man speak with any emotion at all. "Leave it the hell alone! Come on!"

"One second," Marty said, and hit the CLOSE button. "One second."

The elevator door closed.

Nobody moved. The three men stood there mute as the elevator lights moved to P2.

They heard the churning of the cables and the *thunk* of the car as it stopped one floor down. Ken held his breath for a long moment, waiting … and then he heard the doors part with a prolonged *squeeeal*.

The water roared under their feet, deep and loud, nearly erasing the musical drip-and-gurgle all around them. The elevator doors in front of them shivered at the impact, and Ken took an involuntary step forward when the screaming came.

It was Marty. High, throaty, panicked, but still *Marty*, cutting through the pounding of the water, rising and rising until, quite suddenly, it was swallowed up in a sudden, liquid *gulp*.

Then something exploded on P2. It made the concrete floor buck under their feet like a restless animal. Cling nearly lost his balance; a woman dragging herself towards her mini-truck fell flat into the water with a huge splash.

"What's happening?" Cling asked, staggering and clutching at his stomach. "What's *happening?*"

Ken raised his fists to pound on the elevator door, but Maggie interrupted him, almost as if she could see him. "You can't do anything now, Ken," she said. "Go. Just *go.*"

"But—"

"*Please.* There's no time."

Ken stared at the door for a long moment. "Shit," he said, and turned away. His eyes met Josephson's where he stood a few feet behind him.

The water was past their ankles and rising every minute. It was done. They had to go.

Carl Josephson's own cell phone rang, a dignified excerpt from Mahler. "That's me calling, Mr. Josephson," Maggie said through Ken's cell. "I'll make sure you get out of here safely."

Josephson looked miffed in spite of himself. "This number is confidential," he said. "How did you–" He looked up at Ken with new respect. "Oh," he said. "She's *good.*"

They were in their separate cars an instant later. Ken took two full seconds to admire the cream-colored Audi SUV, then it jumped away from him as Josephson put it into gear and sprinted for the exit.

Ken gunned the Rover and followed, barreling out the exit ten yards behind him, cutting off the last of the other evacuees.

The storm hit them like a stone wall. It was even worse than he had expected. Ken had to turn the wipers to their highest setting to see ten yards ahead. It was just as Maggie had said: VeriSil Road, the usual route to Highway 121, was already choked with cars trying to flee the rising water, and speeds had dropped to near-zero.

"Make the first left," Maggie told him. "It will take you along the north edge of the construction site." Ken did has he was told, and glanced over to see Josephson doing the same thing. The CEO was in two conversations at once: one with Maggie on the cell, nodding and answering her questions in short, simple sentences; the other with Stefan Cling, who seemed to be going on and on and *on* about something that Josephson simply didn't want to talk about at the moment.

Ken made a hairpin turn onto the rutted frontage road, Josephson's brake lights flickering in front of him. This road was only intact because the rainwater wasn't building up on it; it was sluicing off from north to south and spilling into the huge pit, five stories deep, that was scheduled to be the future subbasement of the newest VeriSil building.

If anybody lives long enough to build it, Ken thought grimly. *If we ever come back here ag—*

Josephson slammed on his brakes, and Ken pounded on his own an instant later. He fishtailed to the right, cranking the wheel as hard as he could. He missed ramming the SUV by mere inches.

"You stopped," Maggie said. "What's the problem?"

"Don't know," he said shortly. "Be right back." He popped the door and lurched into the rain. He saw the problem even as Josephson climbed out of his SUV.

A huge supply of steel reinforcement bars had fallen into the roadway, blown and washed down from a graded storage area that had simply disappeared in the storm. Even a four-wheel drive couldn't climb over the spiky mess without blowing its tires.

"Let's clear a path!" Josephson shouted, his voice barely audible over the screeching wind. Ken nodded and they set to work, seizing armfuls of the eight-foot lengths of bar and throwing them onto a wooden skid that was off to one side, resting on more stable ground. They were soaked to the skin within seconds, but they kept at it, covering their hands and feet with mud as they worked.

Ken distantly admired the fact that the millionaire CEO didn't seem to give a damn about ruining his thousand-dollar suit or his five-hundred-dollar shoes in the downpour. It wasn't until their fourth load had been dropped that Josephson turned and glared at his assistant, still huddling inside the SUV and looking terribly miffed.

Josephson grinned as he leaned into Ken's ear. "I was going to fire the little shit!" he shouted. "Now I guess I'll just have to kill him!"

His ball-bearing eyes, cold as blued steel, clicked to meet Ken's. Then he kicked a smile into place to show he was only kidding.

It took five more slippery, filthy minutes, but they managed to clear a narrow path that would accommodate one car at a time. When the last of the metal clanked onto the pile, Ken noticed that it was actually floating like a raft. Josephson had even tethered it to a leaning lamp pole at some point to keep it from drifting away.

This was getting bad, really bad.

They didn't stop to admire their work. The moment it was done Josephson simply shook the water out of his eyes, stuck out his hand and said, "Thanks."

"Thank *you*," Ken said, and gripped the CEO's tightly for a moment.

Their eyes met again. "I'll call!" Josephson bellowed. "We'll talk!"

Ken felt a rush of excitement, and then a little sick. In spite of the disaster, in spite of his oldest, best friend in town drowning mere minutes before…that felt good.

God, that felt good.

Ken levered himself back into the Rover seconds later. "—e when you get back," the phone was saying over and over. "Tell me when you get back, tell me when you—"

"I'm here," he said, "I'm here." He instantly left an inch-deep puddle on the Rover's rubber floor mat.

"Good," Maggie said, and he could almost believe she sounded relieved. *Not possible,* he told himself. *It's only a really,* really *good voice simulator. I think…*

"You'll both come to a 'T' intersection about two hundred yards ahead," she told him. Ken imagined her saying the same thing to Josephson on his own cell as he gunned the Rover's engine and the SUV pulled out first. It took a long, nasty gouge from one errant piece of rebar as it wedged its way through the gap they had made. Ken got the Rover past unscathed.

Just as Maggie had told them, the intersection drifted out of the silver mist a few hundred yards farther on. "Ken," she said, "you'll go to the left; Josephson will go to the right. I'll send him north on Indiana, and he can enter the freeway up by the DH Emporium."

Even as he watched, the Audi SUV turned abruptly to the right and surged up the steep incline. Rooster-tails of mud and water flew out behind it as wheels spun, but it bit in hard and took the hill like a charging rhino.

Ken learned from watching. He turned sharply to the left as he hit the 'T' and gunned the engine, bounding upwards, struggling with the wheel. He nearly fell back once, and then again, but the tires found purchase and pulled him up, up, *up* to the crest of the ridge. The rubber squealed on water-soaked asphalt.

He crowed when he hit the roadway and tapped his brakes, turning to look over his shoulder, across the man-made arroyo in hopes of catching a last glimpse of the escaping Audi.

Josephson had stopped at the top of the ridge, directly across from Ken. He wasn't moving at all. Ken turned all the way around, wondering if there was some kind of trouble, staring at the rear of the vehicle when the SUV's passenger door flew open and Stefan Cling toppled out in a backwards stagger. He looked as if he was being propelled from the car against his will. Ken was almost sure he saw a muddy black shoe pushing the executive assistant out into the rain.

Cling struggled to find his feet, sliding and slipping in the mud as he screamed soundlessly and pawed at the door to get back in the cab to no avail. This time Ken got a clear look at Josephson's hand as it reached out of the SUV, seized the passenger door by its recessed handle, and slammed it in the plump little man's face. Cling fell back again, stunned, staggering to keep from falling on his ass.

Brake lights flared. The SUV jumped forward, misting the tarmac. A moment later it was gone, and Cling was standing alone in the middle of Maynard Road, soaked through and dripping like a drowned man.

There wasn't a thing Ken could do. He had barely made it up the hill once, and it would take forever to get around to the other side, to Cling, *if* the road behind him wasn't underwater already.

Get a clue, man, he said to the distant figure. *There are acres of cars waiting at the off ramp half a mile away. Walk a little, hitch a ride.*

Cling was standing there as if he couldn't believe what had happened.

And then the monsters came.

They skittered out of the sea of mud around Cling, twenty-five, thirty of them, each the size of a small dog (*a puppy,* Ken thought for some reason. *The size of a puppy*). For an instant he thought they were impossibly huge spiders, fresh out of some cheesy horror movie, but they didn't look right. There were too many legs, moving in too many directions at once, and spikes that thrust up from the bodiless center of the things that seemed to grow as he watched.

They swarmed all around the chubby little man. He stepped back towards the end of the slope, water coursing downhill like a waterfall now, but they were behind him as well. Ken watched in mute horror as they surged up his body, over his shins, over his knees. Cling thrust his hands down to push them off, get away, then snatched them back with a jerk, splatters of blood flying, visible only for a moment against the gray downpour.

They cut him, Ken realized. *All those spikes…*

They climbed up his thighs, to his waist. Cling's jaw distended as he screamed, so loud and long that Ken though he might have heard it in spite of the storm and the distance: a thin, high, inhuman sound as Cling fell to his knees into the growing mound of twitching creatures that welled up and covered him, cut him up, dragged him into the mud.

Ten seconds later, there wasn't even a lump in the roiling mass of…*things*… to show that a man had been there at all. The creatures separated, spread off in different directions. Some slid down the waterfall of mud into the arroyo…

And Ken realized they were coming in his direction.

"Ken," Maggie said from the phone. "It's getting worse. You need to get up to West Ridge *now.*"

"No shit," he said, and gunned the engine. He almost lost control three more times as he veered higher, away from the campus, away from the rising water…

…but not away from the *things*.

* * *

The trip back to the *hacienda* was long and insane. First he came to a yawning "Y" intersection, one narrow turn to the left, the south, led upward to the crest of the ridge itself. It was really little more than a footpath. He veered right instead, heading more gradually uphill to the north, to the posh high-rent district of West Ridge Road. Reaching the paved suburban streets did no good at all. He had to steer widely around sinkholes as big as trucks that had opened up spontaneously in the middle of the asphalt. Three times he had to back up and try a different route that would take him around fallen trees and six-foot flows of rocky mud. Ultimately he made it to West Ridge Road itself, to the Arco station that marked the midway point between VeriSil and his home, if only to catch his breath.

The rain pounded down, harder than ever. The clouds were so low they were mere feet above the Rover, pressing down on the canopy over the gas pumps and making the windows of the AM/PM Mini-Mart gleam dully like dead eyes. There were some people moving around inside, he saw, loading up baskets with snack foods and soft drinks, survival supplies for a long weekend stuck inside.

I think it's going to get worse than that, he thought as he peered through the wavering curtain of rain that flowed down the windshield. *This may be problem too big for even Doritos and Coke Zero.*

He took a deep breath and turned the Rover north, up the increasingly steep incline towards the *hacienda*. It was slow going. Whenever he did manage to move faster than ten miles an hour, he felt as if he was drag-racing through the Andes.

Less than a half-mile further on, the creatures began to appear. First they were vague shadows barely out of sight, moving in the mist and downpour. Then he saw a flash of gray or black or bone-white, and they began to take shape as they boiled out of the storm.

Ken stopped using the brake at all. This was *not* a part of the world where he wanted to take a pause. He wondered at how blind he had been on the trip down hours earlier. Had these things been there when he'd driven down? Had he simply been so preoccupied he hadn't even noticed the crawling, teetering, churning creatures rising up out of the rushing water all around him?

Now they were horribly clear, etched against the glittering sheaf of afternoon rainfall. He saw a monster that looked like a huge snake made entirely of bony nodules with a head like a carved jade plant. It slithered across the road inches in front of his SUV, a wriggling fleshless spine looking for...*something*. Something awful.

He passed a wide place in the road, what he thought had been a scenic vista barely twenty-fours ago, and he saw a set of flapping, translucent sheets (*flumes, they're called flumes*) change course in mid-air to wrap themselves around a red-tailed hawk that was struggling to fly through the storm. The shimmering, silvery sheets brought the bird to the ground like a captured stone. By the time it splashed down five feet from the car, Ken could see it had become nothing but a knot of dried feathers and a single, desiccated claw.

He'd never been more happy to pass through the river stone pedestals at the end of his driveway. But as he approached he saw a flexing, ashen wall of tumbleweed (*no*, he corrected himself, *hookweeds. They're called 'hookweeds'*) that looked as if they were woven from bony fishhooks, stretching to block his way.

No way.

Ken hunched his shoulders, gripped the wheel, and stomped on the gas, and the Rover surged forward. The hookweeds leaped at the windshield and left scratches like metal teeth.

What were those things? He thankfully burst through. How had this happened?

For one moment, as he raced along the last arc of the ridge road to his home, he glimpsed the southern half of the crater valley through the churning gray-on-gray scrim below him. It was a view he'd seen virtually every day for the last two years, and it was unrecognizable now. Half of the South End was already underwater, with only roofs and the tops of high walls still visible. The rest was disappearing, even as he watched.

The Valle was filling with water like a great, huge bowl. Though the VeriSil campus and construction site had been the first to go, it was clear: this was only the beginning. If the rain didn't stop now, right now, the whole of the Valle would be underwater very shortly.

Just get me home, he prayed to a God he'd never really believed in. *Just get me home.*

His heart was pounding madly when he caught sight of his *hacienda's* lights, pale yellow behind the storm. Relief burst in his chest. He hadn't felt this kind of happiness since he'd come to DH.

Thank you, he said as he blazed towards the roundabout. *Thank you.*

NINETEEN

"What do you mean you're not coming?" Rose howled.

"Not *yet,* I said," her mother buzzed through the phone. It was the worst connection Rose had ever had on her iPhone.

"Mom," she whispered. "You can't leave me here. This place is so *weird.* This mechanical voice comes right out of the air, and Dad is acting like a prick about half the time, and…Mom, I keep seeing these *things* outside."

Her mother didn't say anything for moment. Rose knew what that meant.

"*No*, I'm not taking anything!" she snarled.

"I didn't say you were."

"No, but if you'd thought it any louder, I'd be deaf! Jesus!"

"Okay," Lisa said. "Let me talk to your Dad."

A short, stubborn pause. "You can't," she said. "He's not here."

"What? Where is he?"

"He had to go to a meeting at VeriSil."

"Great," Lisa said bitterly. "Just like old times."

"It was really important. They were going to, like, take away the project or cancel it or something. Maggie told me—"

"'Maggie'?" Lisa repeated, not quite believing what she was hearing. "The *computer* told you?"

Another stubborn pause. "Yes. I mean, why not? Nobody else wants to talk to me."

"Honey, I promised Dr. Chamberlain I'd stay for a while and help. Things are pretty crazy now, with the storm and everything, and his other doctor didn't show up and–"

"And what? Now you're Clara Bow?"

"I think you mean Clara *Barton*. Clara Bow was a silent movie star."

"Great. Fine." Rose was mad enough to spit bricks, and her mother was talking about dead celebrities.

"Honey, please try to understand. I'll be there as soon as–"

"Oh, I understand," she said coolly. "You'd rather be in a hospital and Dad would rather be at work than be with *me*. God help us if both of you were actually in the same place for five minutes."

Now her mother sounded as cold as she did. "That's not fair."

"Sure it—"

"Rose," Maggie said right behind her.

She spun around and squeaked.

"Don't *do* that!" she shrieked.

"Sorry. Your Dad is coming through the main gate, and I think there's going to be trouble."

"Trouble?" Rose echoed.

"Out in front. It's a mess."

"What's going on?" Lisa asked through the phone.

"It's Daddy," Rose said. "Something's going on, I have to go. I'll talk to you later, okay? I'm going to call in two hours."

"Two hours," Lisa said. "*Every* two hours."

"Right. Love you, Mom," she said, and hung up.

Rose bounced off the bed even as some tiny, cool part of her mind repeated it: *Love you.* She thought that was the first time she'd said that out loud in years.

At a distant *honk honk,* beyond the bedroom window, Maggie told her unnecessarily, "Here he comes." Rose turned and the bedroom door began to open even before she put her hand on the knob. "*Stop* that," she said.

"Sorry," Maggie said.

Rose took the wide, curving staircase two steps at a time, pausing only for a heartbeat before she threw open the broad front door and lurched onto the covered porch.

The storm swallowed her, shoving at her with a wind so high it nearly threw her off her feet. It was almost as wet under the roof as it was in the open yard; she was soaked within seconds. She staggered to stay upright and peered into the storm, straining to pick out the distant, dark shadow of the Range Rover and its guttering headlights from the twisting gray-brown chaos across the yard.

She crossed her arms and hugged herself tightly as the Rover bounced up the last hill, made the sharp right turn and swayed into the turnabout. The whole driveway was a vast, jittering brown mud puddle, more like a lake than a yard. But a four-wheel-drive shouldn't have any trouble with that, she figured.

"So what's the problem?" she said. "He looks–"

The Rover hit the edge of the gravel driveway, tipped up, and then tipped down, *straight* down, and plunged grill-first into the water as if it was falling off a cliff.

Rose watched in horror as the Rover sank – *surged* – into the quicksand twenty feet in front of her, and began to disappear into bottomless liquefied mud.

"Dad!"

The hood was already buried. The back end was tipped up at better than a forty-five degree angle. And still it sank. And sank. Her father, trapped inside, was slamming his shoulder against the driver's door, hard as he could, trying to open it before the Rover vanished completely.

Too late. The quicksand had sealed the door shut. It was like trying to push solid rock. And still it fell, deeper and deeper.

Rose started to wade into the muck. She had no plan at all, nothing in mind except to get to him, to help him somehow. The only thing that stopped her was the sound of Maggie's voice:

"Rose! Don't! You can only help him from here! Don't go out there!"

She stopped herself right at the edge of the patio. The Rover sank even lower. Only a slice of windshield was visible now. Her father's wide blue eyes were all she could see of him, trapped behind the glass.

Surprisingly, unexpectedly, she saw his booted feet come up. He was showing her his soles. He kicked against the windshield, both feet at once, and she suddenly understood what he was doing.

"Yes!" she called over the howling wind. "YES!"

Ken kicked again and the windshield starred and pushed outwards. Again, and it shattered, his muddy boots thrusting through two huge holes in the safety glass.

He came out butt-first, legs flailing. He struggled to turn, stand up on the submerged hood even as it continued to sink, dancing to keep his balance as the car shifted under him. And sank again. Even farther.

He needed help, Rose realized stupidly. She looked around wildly, lost for a moment, then got an idea. "WAIT!" she bellowed into the gale, then turned and ran back inside.

Rose ripped open the broom closet in the hallway and snatched the long-handled mop out of its clamp. Without a breath, she turned and ran back out onto the porch, gasping at the sudden slash of rain across her face.

He was already a foot lower, shin-deep in watery mud and sinking.

Rose moved to the very edge of the covered porch and looped on arm around the four-by-four support. She dug her nails into the coarse gray hair at one end of the mop and flung the other end as far as she could, towards her father. "Take it!" she shouted. "TAKE IT!"

The handle splattered into the mud, a yard from his closest foot. Ken ducked down and seized the end with one hand, wobbling like a man standing in a rowboat, then grabbed it with his other hand as well.

Rose took a step back, put both hands in the mop, and pulled as hard as she could. "Come on," she said between clenched teeth. "Come on..."

He fell down, flat on his belly. But he fell *forward*, toward Rose, and never lost his grip on the mop handle. She took another step back and hauled on the stick. And another. And hauled, while he climbed up the mop handle, hand over hand.

His knuckles brushed the red brick porch. Then his elbows. Then his torso. And only then did he let go of the mop handle and pull himself the rest of the way out of the rushing, sucking mud, sprawling on the glittering brickwork, panting like an animal.

Safe, Rose thought wildly and flung the filthy mop-handled aside. *Safe*.

She fell down next to him and threw her arms around him, covering herself with mud. "Daddy," she said. "Oh, God, Daddy, Daddy…"

TWENTY

It was 11:07 a.m. when Lucy awoke from a sleep she never intended to have, a prolonged doze at her Station desk.

The last thing she remembered was trying to send her notes to the UC Riverside server. The next thing she knew it was, well, *now.*

"Where the hell is everybody?" she asked, entirely to herself. She pulled herself out of her chair and lurched to the doorway. The desk clock said it was almost lunch time. Where was Cindy? Where was Carole? Had they taken her advice and gotten the hell out of Dodge?

She plopped down in Cindy's chair at the reception desk and looked around helplessly. "This is *grea—*"

There was a banging thump at the far end of the corridor. She spun around to face the glass entrance doors and gaped at what she saw.

It was a man made of rain. A man *shape*, anyway, covered by running water that clung to him like a thick second skin. Underneath, the pulpy flesh was gray-white and the hair was white-gray; even the eyes were white. Only the faded blue-jeans and the rapidly decaying red Pendleton had any color at all.

That Pendleton.

"My God," Lucy whispered. "Fender."

She had locked the front doors when she'd come back late last night. Now she dug for the master keys in her lab coat pocket as she trotted across the lobby. Fender pawed at the glass, spreading gray, gritty mud with every touch.

She unlocked the door and popped it open. Fender lunged inside and fell into her arms. "Doctor," he gurgled. "Doctor, help me."

He weighed next to nothing. Lucy felt as if she could pick him up like a baby if she tried. "It's okay, Fender," she said, thinking *he needs a physician, not a fuckin' Ph.D.* "Come on, come with me."

He didn't stand up. He just pushed at her, his filthy shoulder against her chest and said, "*Help* me, Doctor!" again, with even greater urgency.

He was backing her across the room. "Fender," she said. "Fender, *stop* it!" Her back rammed into the reception desk and she fell, Fender still bearing down on her.

"GIMME SOME FUCKIN WATER YOU BITCH! CAN'T YOU SEE I'M DYING??"

He was hovering over her now, pawing at her with an impossible strength, and for the first time she saw his face clearly, or what was left of it.

It had grown together. The nostrils had filled in, they were shallow dents now. The lips were sealed against the teeth; the teeth were nothing more than a ridged line in front of a whistling gray hole. Even the eyes were carved half-spheres inside immobile lids, statue eyes in a cracked, flaking sculpture. She wasn't even sure how the voice was being made, but it wasn't human. It emerged from the mouth-hole as fully formed words, without the lips moving, with no sign of a tongue.

Lucy crab-walked out from under him and struggled to her feet. "Take it easy, Fender," she said. "Come on, let me help you lie down, I'll call an ambulance and—"

"NO!" he bellowed. "WATER! NOW!" He lunged for her clumsily and hit the desk, scattering office supplies everywhere. She was dimly aware of how cliché the situation had become. Tough, independent woman reduced to victim status by violent stalker, fleeing all alone through a deserted building, screaming and weeping like a baby.

Well, THAT wouldn't do, she decided, and looked around for a weapon to end the madness even as she retreated. There, in the corner behind Cindy's desk was… what was that? It looked like the leg from a desk or a chair or something. It was certainly the right size and shape to use as a club…

Wonder where that came from, she thought as she rolled over, grabbed it, and came up swinging. She ignored the sticky-slippery feel of it in her hand.

The first sweep of the club barely missed Fender as he spun away, but she took advantage of the retreat and turned to run down the hall. There would be no help from Rebecca or Cindy, they were gone. And as much as she hated the idea of running to Michael Steinberg for help, anything was better than facing this... *thing...* alone.

She ran down the long hallway towards his lab. She could hear Fender slithering and thumping behind her, scudding across the floor, caroming off the walls. Lucy slipped when she stopped at Steinberg's office, turned and pounded through his door – to find herself hit in the face by the full force of the storm.

She tripped and fell head-first into foot-deep, rain-soaked debris. She bellowed like a beast as she pulled herself up.

The room was a wreck. Completely destroyed. Sheets of cold rain and mist were billowing in through the shattered window above the lab sink, and Michael Steinberg himself was nowhere to be found.

It took her a moment to understand what she was seeing. A moment later the door behind her burst open and the monster that had been Fender flew in, fell hard, and thrashed madly in the muck right next to her.

Lucy scrambled to her feet. "There!" she said, backing away towards the door. "Wet enough for you?"

The creature rolled over onto its back and faced her. The resemblance to her old friend from across the road was gone. The thing spread its arms, swelled its chest and drew in gallon after gallon of the water around it, absorbing it faster than any sponge, fast as a pump or a vacuum.

Lucy backed to the hallway door, horrified. The creature paused long enough to sit up, still bone-dry, she noticed, still papery and arid, and cracked its face to form a smile. "Not nearly enough, Doctor," it said. "Not *nearly*."

Lucy turned and bolted out of the room, back into the hall, back the way she came.

The Jeep. I'll get to the Jeep and get the hell OUT of here. The keys were on a hook in the break room, right where she'd left them the night before. She was positive.

The Fender-thing blew the door off Steinberg's lab and followed her. A small tidal wave of water and debris gushed into the hall. He kicked through it and started down the corridor towards her, skidding and bouncing off the walls as he came.

She made it to the break room, moving so fast she slammed into the lunch table to stop herself.

There were the keys. On the hook. She lunged for them, got her hand around them, pulled back, and Fender filled the doorway, jumped inside.

She pushed the lunch table between them and raised her makeshift club in the air, vaguely surprised she still had it in her hand. He swept the table aside with a single movement, and it skidded across the linoleum to slam into the freestanding broom closet on the far side of the room.

The closet door popped open. A body slumped out.

Lucy had found Cindy Bergstrom.

"GIMME!" the Fender-creature bellowed, and lunged for her.

"FUCK YOU!" Lucy screamed back, and brought the club down in a vicious slash at the monster.

The blow connected with the side of the creature, below its upraised arms… and continued through, across his chest, through the center, and out the other side above its hip, meeting almost no resistance at all.

The creature stopped in mid-stride. It looked down at the huge canyon plowed through its chest in mute astonishment. Then it looked up, and found her eyes…and in one impossible moment, Lucy saw the last of its consciousness blink away, like a light switch turning off. The creature collapsed right in front of her, making a set of distinct noises as it landed: *Thump. Thump. Ka-THUMP.*

She had cut it in two with a single blow.

It didn't move. It didn't twitch. It didn't even bleed. Lucy went to her knees next to the thing and poked at it with her club.

It was hollow. Completely hollow. Like a papier-mâché model of a half-human *thing*.

How could it have moved? How could it have been so strong? Where was its brain? And where was Fender?

She stood up slowly and put a foot on top of the dead creature's hand. She pushed down firmly…and it popped under her instep and collapsed to powder, like old Styrofoam. She did the same with the upper leg. Then the hip. Finally, she punched through the plated, scarred mass of its head.

There was sand inside, a roiling, gluey kind of sand that pulled itself into a ball and skittered away as she watched. No threat now, just… *gone*.

Lucy looked at the shattered remains of the creature. Then she looked at the pile of human flesh that had been Cindy Bergstrom.

"I gotta get the hell outta here," she said raggedly. "*Now*."

TWENTY-ONE

Ken was using the last of the hot water to scour off the mud when his daughter barged into the bathroom.

"Hey!" he said. She was visible only as a fractured silhouette through the frosted glass. "What the hell are you doing?"

"You're taking too long. We need to talk." She plopped down on the closed toilet seat and ran a hand through her hair.

"Rose," he said, trying for patience, "can we do this later?"

Rose ignored him. "I tried calling Mom. She said we would talk every two hours. I've called and called, and nobody answered."

He turned off the water, cracked open the door, and put out a hand. "Can you at least hand me a towel? I'd like to avoid any Oedipal problems at this late date."

Rose put a fluffy ivory-colored towel in his. "Actually, the Oedipal complex would be you lusting after Grandma. Which is especially weird with her being dead and all. Me lusting after you would be an Electra complex and, trust me, no worries there."

Ken dried himself briskly and wrapped the towel securely around his waist before he stepped out.

"So what are we going to do? We should go get her," she said, looking him directly in the eye.

"There's no way we can leave here," he told her. "Not until the storm —"

Maggie's voice spoke over his shoulder. "You missed a spot," she said.

They both jumped. Rose snapped a glance into each of the corners until she found the tiny lens peeking down. "Oh, now, that's *sick*," she said. "You have cameras in the *toilet?*"

Ken set his jaw stubbornly. "Sixty-five percent of serious household accidents happen in the bath—"

"Spare me," Rose said, holding up a hand and looking away. "It's just *weird*. I assume both of you have seen *Her?*"

"Seen who?" Ken said, puzzled.

"Haven't had the pleasure," Maggie said.

He sighed bitterly and walked out of the bathroom, into the bedroom. Rose followed. "Maggie, have you tried calling Lisa?" he asked.

"Repeatedly," she assured him. "I've called the Clinic's general number and emergency number as well. No answer. The lines are still in working order, but they're not picking up."

"I'm sure she's fine," Ken said, trying to sound reassuring. "If there was any problem, they'd let us know."

Rose snorted. "Oh, *sure*."

"I'll keep trying every ten minutes," Maggie volunteered. "Until somebody answers."

Rose sniffed. "Thank you, *Maggie,*" she said, giving her father the evil eye. "At least *somebody* cares."

He smiled sweetly. "Nice to see you and Maggie getting along. My diabolical plan is working."

"Actually, Boss," Maggie said, "we have other problems to deal with."

"Don't tell me it's going to flood here, too," Rose said, sounding genuinely concerned for the first time.

"Not a chance," Ken said. "We're on the highest of high ground up here on the ridge. Until the rain stops, this is probably the safest place in town. We've got plenty of food and water and electricity. We even have back-up generators if the power grid fails."

"Ah. Imminent power failure," she said. "This is supposed to cheer me up?"

"I can't talk to you when you're like this," he said. "All you want to do is make smart-ass comments."

"And you can talk to me *other* times? When is that, exactly?"

"Ken," Maggie said. "Can we convene in the study? There are things you need to see."

"Sure. Fine." He opened the bedroom door for Rose, who swept out without a glance. He took three minutes to dress in new jeans and a fresh shirt, then he followed her down to the first floor.

He saw the lights in the study brighten as he moved down the long, high-ceiling corridor to the study. A mad array of screens and monitors, including the wide-format wall screen had already swelled to life.

"'Open the pod bay doors, Hal," Rose said. She was standing in one corner with her arms folded, looking as sour as ever.

"I'm afraid I can't do that, Dave," Maggie said.

Rose started to say something…then pressed her lips together.

Ken chose to ignore the entire exchange. "So what's up?" he said.

"Okay," Maggie answered, sounding very businesslike now. "The property first. I've used our external cams to check the roof and walls, and the thermostatic sensors inside to check wiring and humidity."

I didn't know she could do that, Ken thought as she showed view after view of the *hacienda's* exterior.

"We seem in good shape," Maggie reported. "No major leaks or breaches, despite nearby lightning strikes and winds gusting from thirty to forty miles per hour."

"Jesus," Ken said. "What is this, Hurricane Sandy?"

"Worse," Maggie said flatly. She showed them a new weather satellite image of the storm swirling over the Valle.

"It looks like a skin disease," Rose said, stepping closer to the screen. "Like a cancer." She looked even paler than usual, her hair obsidian black against her scrubbed-white skin. "Any idea how long it will last?"

"No possible break until tomorrow evening, and even then…no guarantees. Until then, it will keep getting worse and worse."

The view shifted to a grainy black-and-white view of a lake in the rain. It took Ken more than a moment to realize it wasn't a lake at all, it was the VeriSil campus that he had only recently left. "I broke a few rules," Maggie said, "and patched into every traffic and security camera I could find, including VeriSil, Dos Hermanos Water and Power, and a few Sheriff Peck put into place that nobody seems to know about. As you can see, VeriSil is underwater." The construction site was all that showed above the waterline, a moldy black skeleton of some ancient, ruined temple.

The picture shifted to show an intersection north of VeriSil, almost as submerged as the computer plant. "Indiana and Maynard," she said. "Five feet." It switched to another view, this one showing a row of tidy cottages with floodwater flowing merrily in and out of wide-open front doors. "Two blocks farther north," Maggie said. "Indiana and Brighton. Three feet. Roughly half the Valle is under four feet or more, and it's rising by inches every hour. It's the worst-case scenario, Ken. DH is filling up like a punch bowl."

Ken glanced at Rose, who was staring at the screen with growing alarm.

"And no chance of calling somebody?" he said. "The Guard, FEMA, firefighters, *anybody?*"

"I keep trying," she said, "and I can get all the information I want flowing *in…* but nothing's flowing *out.* It's like being on the wrong side of a one-way mirror."

Nice analogy, he thought distantly. *I wonder if she made that up herself?* The implications jolted him. *How much like a human is she?*

"The Clinic!" Rose said. "Can you see the Clinic?"

"Yes," Maggie said. The screen flickered to a down-angle shot of the Clinic's waiting room as seen from a high corner. The time code in the upper right said 00:12:21, just a few minutes ago.

The image was painted with garish, uncorrected colors, and the strange angle made it look like everyone's heads were swollen and their bodies shrunken, but it was still clear what was going on. Sick, scared, and injured people were filling the room to bursting, and everyone was dirty and wet. A few bodies in white coats, not particularly clean or dry themselves, moved from body to body, offering help, comfort, advice.

"Look! There she is, there's Mom!"

Sure enough, Ken could see the part in her hair more clearly than her face, but it was obviously Lisa Corman Mackie herself, shoulder to shoulder with the young doctor, Chamberlain. They watched a silent, intense conversation with one little boy, clearly terrified by all that had happened, then saw them move farther, deeper into the room, to huddle over an old man whose leg was bent in a wrong and dangerous way.

"She looks okay," Rose said. The relief in her voice was obvious. "In fact, she looks *good.*"

Ken found himself smiling. "She does," he nodded. "She really does."

The screen cut to static. "Hey!" Rose cried.

"There's more," Maggie said. "Some images I can't correlate." The static resolved itself into rain. Heavy, white, straight-vertical rain falling as thick as a waterfall.

A *thing* came out of the torrent, impossibly tall, built entirely of legs. Its sharp edges and corners made it look manufactured, cleaner, more precise than any organism. It moved with a strange fluid awareness that said *alive, dangerous, hungry.* And strangest of all, the rain didn't seem to touch it. Despite the six inches of water that foamed around its lower points as they plunged into the ground, the…*thing*…didn't get wet. The rain seemed to fall *into* it before it could even glisten with moisture.

Rose said, "Holy *shit*," and before Ken could speak, Maggie shifted the image: a vacant lot elsewhere in town, with four of the…*things*…

"Bone spiders," he whispered.

… stalking madly across a flooded vacant lot, chasing something dark and furry. A dog, a filthy, wet, panicked dog.

"Oh my god," Rose said, her voice trembling.

The image changed again: a pile of rocks that seemed to roll round and round itself under its own power, trundling down Bishop Avenue and leaving cracked asphalt and chewed flesh in its wake.

"Brickteeth," Ken said.

A long, jointed writhing log with a white, flexing razor-flower gaping at one end.

"Dragontongue."

A ragged-edged sheet of cellophane, oily rainbows shimmering through it, twisting through the air, driven by the wind, wrapping around a running woman.

"Flumes. Jesus, what *is* this?"

What indeed. Where were these names coming from? How did he know these things, why did he *recognize* them?

"We gotta get outta here," Rose said.

Ken turned towards her. She was trembling, staring at the images. "We gotta get outta here *now*, Dad."

She started fast-walking down the corridor towards the front door as quickly as her lean legs could carry her.

"What the hell?" Ken said, and chased after her. "Honey, wait!"

"No," she said as she ran from him. "*No.* This is crazy. I don't care if you have a car or not, we can *walk* the hell out of here, *run* out if we have to."

She skidded to a stop at the front door and groped blindly for the latch.

"Honey, *wait.* I have a better—"

"No!" Rose said, in full panic mode. "No, let's just GO!" She threw the door open and turned to throw herself into the storm.

A bone spider, two stories tall, rose up out of the bubbling mud directly in front of the porch. Ten of its ten thousand legs rose up, already clean, dry as granite and sharp as steel, and reached for her, *grew* towards her.

Ken seized her by the collar of her thin black tee and jerked her back inside with one hand as he slammed the door shut with the other. There was a deafening *crack!* of ripping wood when the talons of the creature scraped across the entrance. It went on and on and on as they both fell back and scrambled out of the entryway, into the living room, away from the horrible sound.

"*Jesus,*" Rose said. "Oh, my god, oh, *Jesus…*"

The scraping stopped. A moment later lightning cut through the house and thunder pushed at the windows.

They lay sprawled on the terra cotta tiles of the living room, panting and terrified. Rose swallowed hard and cleared her throat. "Okay, Dad," she said roughly. Her face was so white it was nearly translucent. "When you're right, you're right. This *is* the safest place in town."

TWENTY-TWO

Thirty seconds after Lucy found Cindy Bergstrom's body, she was running. *Okay*, she thought, grasping for thought, *okay, okay. Cindy's dead and somebody killed her. Maybe Fender, I don't know. But the others…?*

She pounded down the corridor towards the office wing. "Rebecca?" she shouted. "*Rebecca!!*" Her assistant could have come in while Lucy was sleeping at her desk; anything could have happened.

She burst into Rebecca's office, there was no one there. It didn't look as if it had been disturbed since the day before. Lucy realized she was panting like a race horse.

"Okay," she said again, aloud this time. "Okay, then…"

Steinberg. He was a solid gold twenty-four-karat asshole, but he was her responsibility.

She turned on her heel, her thoughts spinning as she ran.

I gotta get the hell out of here. But if I leave now, I'll never come back.

She was certain of that. The town itself was doomed. Even her facility, high on the north rim of the crater as it might have been, was in jeopardy from the continuing wind and liquefaction.

She passed the lunch room and tried not to think of Cindy's twisted body lying on the wet linoleum, staring at the ceiling.

There are files here, she thought wildly. *Experiments, projects, sample cases. All irreplaceable. Years of work. What am I going to do, how am I –*

She pushed her way through the broken entrance to Steinberg's lab and stopped short.

Every specimen in the room was gone or crushed. Every instrument, every cage, every case and container and tray was destroyed. She stood in the middle of the devastation, flinching at the cold, wet wind blowing through the shattered window, and turned full circle, awed at how thorough the vandalism was.

Except...*there.* Sitting in one corner, in an almost perfect ring of cleared floor was Steinberg's computer, his chair still upright in front of it, its screen still clean and glowing, power still on. All the files were neatly arranged right on the desktop. And there was a digital image, a crisp and clear close-up of one of his 'new creatures', as his wallpaper.

Why was that spared? Why would looters leave that – about the only thing worth stealing in the first place?

Fascinated, she forgot her terror for a moment and sat gingerly in front of the keyboard. She double-clicked on the first icon she saw, a folder marked NEW TAXONOMY.

Her jaw dropped at what she saw.

It took a precious five minutes to see it all, but by then she knew what she had here. He was telling the truth, she realized. All that horseshit about a new species, those bogus specimens like the soda straw and the bird claw and all. They were real. They were the remnants –maybe the *seeds* – of a whole host of creatures.

Michael Steinberg had been going mad, maybe for a long time, but he stayed a scientist to the bitter end. He had kept all his notes in meticulous order. He had examined the creatures, dissected and tested them, taken digital pictures and even digital video as they grew, always measuring, always observing, always recording. Hell, he'd even left the webcam attached to this computer running after he went totally off the rails, destroying all the cages, setting all his pets free.

It would take hours, days, *weeks,* to work through all he had here, but it was painfully clear: he really had defined new a whole new set of creatures, a New Taxonomy. Their structures, their biology and biochemistry. Their strengths and weaknesses. All from a man who was slowly but surely *becoming one of them.*

That was the worst part. Lucy stared mutely at the screen. 'Transformational speciation,' he called it. Turning people into creatures like him.

She stared at the digital images of what Michael Steinberg had become, *was becoming.*

"Look at that," she said under her breath. "Just *look…*"

Lightning struck the ridge outside. Thunder exploded beyond the shattered window, snapping Lucy out of her horrified paralysis.

What the hell am I doing? *I have to get out of here!*

She understood in a blinding instant that she had to get this data out of here and tell somebody. The university, the army, NASA, *somebody…*

Steinberg, anal-compulsive as ever, had stored all the data in the one folder. It was easy to handle. She tried to use the broadband connection to upload the entire folder to the University server back in Riverside, but as before, there was no indication it went through at all.

Screw it, she decided. She pawed through the two drawers that hadn't been pulled out and overturned and found half a dozen black and red flash drives with the Station's logo on it. She knew it well, 100G storage, all she would need. She wrote the entire folder to one of them in less than a minute and slipped it into an inner pocket of her khaki coat. Then she slogged out of the Steinberg's devastated lab without a pause, promising herself she'd come back for the rest.

Someday. After the weather clears. After the monsters are…somewhere else.

She trotted down the corridor to the lobby, belted her coat more tightly, and pushed through the front door one final time.

Bye-bye, my baby, she thought as the storm rushed over her. *It was nice knowing you.*

The water in the parking lot was deep enough to cover her shoes. Her feet were soaking wet by the time she made it to the Jeep and tried to open the door.

The latch flapped uselessly in her hand.

Right, broken. She should have remembered. It seemed like years ago that she'd learned about that.

She popped open the back door instead, ducked inside, and reached forward to snag the latch from the inside. *Stupid thing*, she told herself. She twisted around to get free of the back seat.

I won't even bother to get it fixed; I'll trade in the piece of—

"Boo."

The voice was right there, right at her ear, and she hadn't even gotten out of the car. Lucy yelped in spite of herself and straightened up with a jolt, catching the back of her head on the doorframe, grabbing at the half-open driver door, gasping as she stood and saw –

Michael Steinberg.

Or…what had *been* Michael Steinberg.

His skin was dull gray. His hair was plated with water and mud, his eyes dead and distant, like balls of clay in a face made of mud. It was a counterfeit Michael Steinberg, made out of rotting granite…but all the more dangerous for that.

"Made ya look," he said. The voice seemed to come from somewhere other than his mouth. As she stood there, back against the car, clutching the door, she saw other things about him had changed, too. The neck. The chest. The legs…

Oh my god. What happened to his legs?

"Michael," she said aloud, barely recognizing her own voice. "What are you doing here?"

"Running an errand for a friend," he said, sounding almost jovial. His long, knobby arms came up without hesitation and reached for her face. In that instant Lucy knew what his 'errand' was.

I'm dead. Just like Cindy.

"Wait!" she shouted. Her hand flashed into the breast pocket of her jacket and she pulled out the red-and-gold flash drive.

Steinberg stopped, but he didn't lower his arms. She noticed distantly that water wasn't dripping from his crooked fingers. It was soaking in as fast as it fell.

"What's that supposed to be?" he said, still sounding vaguely amused.

"It's THE NEW TAXONOMY," she said, holding it up in front of her, like a priest holding back a vampire with a crucifix.

He lowered his head in anger, a bull made of boulders. She could see it even in his immobile features. He was changing, yes, but the ego was still there, that mad compulsion to *be* somebody. *Transformational speciation my ass,* she thought.

186

"I trashed the computer," she lied. "I fried the hard drive. This is *it*, Michael. The only copy. Right here."

He brought his arms down and hunched his shoulders even more.

"Give it to me," he grated.

"Let me go, and I will."

He made a grating, coughing sound with his hidden mouth. Lucy assumed it was supposed to be a laugh. "Ach. Sure," he said. "Deal. Give it." He stepped forward, sloshing in eight inches of water, and extended one set of gnarled gray fingers

Who the hell does he think he's kidding? Lucy thought rhetorically, and as he stepped forward she pulled open the car door, got behind it and slammed it into him as hard as she could.

Steinberg, for all his new height and bulk, was still prone to the laws of physics, and so far, the Jeep still outweighed him. He flew backwards at the sudden impact of the swinging door and landed heavily on his back with a tremendous splash, even as Lucy threw herself into the soggy driver's seat, slammed the door, shoved the key into the ignition and punched the accelerator.

He got himself upright on his complex of new legs faster than she thought possible and threw himself at the driver's side. He pawed at the door-handle. It flapped uselessly in his claw as it had in her hand.

God bless crappy American manufacturing, she thought madly, and jammed on the accelerator again. The Jeep leaped forward, jerked out of Steinberg's grip, and Lucy dragged it into a wide, looping arc that covered the entire parking lot.

Steinberg was right in front of the driveway, the only way out. That didn't slow her down one bit. She gritted her teeth as she took careful aim and drove the Jeep, full force, into his ashen, stony body.

He didn't fall. He didn't even crack. The huge rocky form flew over the hood and its face smashed against the windshield directly in front of her, splitting like porcelain into a thousand tiny fissures. She flinched and steered reflexively to the right, away from the exit as he thrust his hands through the shattered windshield to take her by the face. Particles of glass, small and sharp as fingernails, flickered across her as his impossibly dry fingers wrapped around her head and dug in.

187

Without thinking, without caring, Lucy opened her mouth and bit him – *hard*. Her teeth cracked off a mouth full of dead-dry tissue as she punched on the brakes and skidded on the asphalt.

Momentum snatched Steinberg away. The fingers flew from her face, the body rocketed off the hood. Steinberg's suddenly massive form rolled twice in the rain-choked air before it hit the pavement and tumbled through the foaming water.

She popped the car into reverse and jammed on the accelerator again. The car roared straight backwards. While the creature struggled to stand, she tapped on the brakes, threw the Jeep into drive, and surged forward, aiming the car like a rocket-propelled grenade.

The rear bumper hit Steinberg square in his shoulders while he was still hunched over. The impact drove him under the car. Lucy felt the *crunch-a-thump, crunch-a-thump* as the wheels rolled over his body, but she kept driving, throwing the Jeep into another wide, looping turn that would take her back towards the exit. She strained forward, peering over the steering wheel through the broken windshield. Was it dead now? Was it *finally* dead?

Son of a bitch.

The Steinberg-thing was getting up again, even though one of its arms was missing. She saw the limb bobbing in a rain-puddle near his ankles. The exposed joint was dry and bloodless. It looked like flaking plaster of Paris.

She slammed on the accelerator one more time and drove straight into him again. This time she liked the solid crunch the collision made. Steinberg's stony new body flew into the air, so high and far she almost lost him in the storm. Then he landed, skidding, with rooster-tails of rain flying in two directions at once. She didn't care. She kept driving for the exit even as he rolled to a stop and heaved himself into a sitting position.

She saw him in the rear view mirror when he stood up on his wobbly, recovering legs. One of the larger severed limbs was cradled in his one remaining arm. In the time it took her to drive to the entrance, she saw stubby gray fingers of clay-like tissue erupt from his hip, wriggling and reaching blindly to meet other stubby little fingers, to find each other, twist together, intertwine …

He was standing on two legs by the time she hit the driveway. An instant later he was steady enough to stagger towards the red ATV that was waiting at the edge of the lot and mount up.

Fuck me, she thought as she drove blindly down the twisting road. *Monster on a mini-bike.*

* * *

She tried to make it to the freeway but it was too late. The storm had blocked the on-ramp completely. It was covered with rain-soaked rocks and tree branches washed down from the ridge, and she didn't have time to pick a path through it.

"Fuck it," she growled, and forced the Jeep in another direction, up and over, onto the frontage road that wandered along the ridge line to the south. It was a familiar route to her. Most of their sampling stations were planted along this rutted path. She knew it would take her deeper into the Valle and the storm, yes, but more importantly, it would get away from Steinberg.

She swayed and braked and surged along the winding mud road, and the storm rose up to enfold her, more violent and blacker than ever. It shoved at the sides of the Jeep with huge gusts of wind. Walls of rain leaped up from flooded intersections and rushed over the hood like tidal waves. Behind her, a few hundred yards away, a single glaring headlight followed. She only saw it on the straightaways, only when she slowed for an instant. Steinberg was back there. He was coming.

There was a flash of lightning and something on the seat next to her flared brightly enough to distract her for an instant. It was the thumb drive, its silver-and-red finish momentarily catching the lightning. All of Steinberg's data was trapped in that little metal tab. She didn't even remember throwing it into the seat when she'd jumped inside. But she had it.

I can still get it out of town…

When she looked up at the road in front of her again, she saw the Mackie *hacienda* for the first time. It was waiting for her at the top of the ridge at the end of a private drive beyond a wide-open wrought iron gate, crouching on the crest in front of towering blue-black rain clouds that flickered with lightning. There were even welcoming lights in the *hacienda*'s windows, yellow-red, warm, *human* colors. The first she had seen in a long time.

She threw the car into a skidding right hand turn and shot thorough the riverstone gateway. Now she could see a person – no, *two* people – standing on a covered porch in front of a wide chocolate-brown door. The path to them was clear. They were at the end of a wide driveway that was flooded but looked smooth as glass. They were waving at her, arms over their heads, waving her in, it seemed. *Come on, it's safe here. Come on!*

She gunned the engine and headed towards the drive, grinning for the first time in hours.

Almost there. Safe and sound.

* * *

Women, Steinberg thought, veering and bouncing after the glowing taillights of Lucy Arumbruster's Jeep. *Can't live with 'em; can't kick 'em out of a moving car.* He'd heard that from some stand-up comedian, and it was funny. So, so funny.

Two women had been ruling his life since he came to this fucking desert hell-hole: Lucy Armbruster, the smart-ass dyke with the money, and Jennie Sommerfield, the most beautiful woman in the world who would not, *would not,* give him what he wanted. What he deserved.

The rain splattered against his crusty cheeks, but Michael couldn't feel it anymore. It didn't even get in his eyes; he'd grown some kind of transparent covering under his overhanging brow, over his squelching eye-holes, to catch the moisture and absorb it before it got to him. He was in a cocoon of rock and bone that cut him off, held him tight, and as he drew closer and closer to that disgusting sack of meat and bullshit, he still found himself longing for the other one, that Jennie, that dream he'd had for so long.

He'd already messed around with her a little bit – when Armbruster wasn't nagging at him, when The Voice wasn't pulling him here or there for some bullshit errand or other. And he would get back to her before this was all done. He had to.

She glowed like the sun the first time he met her at that VeriSil company picnic. A part of her had burned inside him ever since, and not even this glorious transformation, not even Armbruster's repulsive betrayal, not even the echoing voice of the storm could drive out that memory.

He loved Jennie. He always would. And best of all, now it didn't matter if she loved him back – not anymore. He could *make* her love him. He could make anybody do anything.

So first: kill the bitch that was trying to run away from him right now. Then second: find the other one, the pretty one, and make her his own. He would have smiled at that last thought, if his face could smile anymore: *Make her. His* own.

TWENTY-THREE

Ken and Rose were still huddled in the living room with the two-story atrium when Rose's phone rang. She pounced on it.

"Mom?" she said. "God, you won't believe what…what? I…" She stopped and listened for a long time. "No," she said at length, in a strange, measured tone. "No, actually I believe you completely."

Something scratched at the door, a long, deep, guttural *skaaaaaaaa* that wouldn't stop. Rose cast a haunted, sidelong glance at her father and whispered into the phone. "We can't, Mom. *We can't get out.*"

Things were clattering against the panes of the atrium a story above their heads. It sounded like bundles of sticks being flung at the glass, skittering down…and scrabbling back up.

Rose looked up and recognized them. "I saw one of those last night," she said with horrified understanding. "Maggie, remember? In the bedroom?"

"I remember," Maggie said. "And I remember how we got rid of them." The room's indirect lights dimmed a bit and there was a deep, bone-buzzing *hummmm*. The stick-bundles – *scumble*, Ken thought, *That's what they're called, 'scumble'* – were doused with sparks and flew away from the windows. He could see one of them lying on the rain-soaked porch outside, twitching like an animal in the middle of a seizure.

"No, Mom," Rose was saying into the phone. "No, we're okay for now. They're outside. They can't get in."

Ken gave her a baleful look. She shrugged.

"What about *you?*" She listened some more as Ken came to a decision. He dug into his pocket for keys.

"Okay," Rose said, nodding. "Okay. I love you. Here's Dad." She held out the phone, and Ken was surprised and a little stunned to see tears in her violet eyes. "She wants to talk to you," she said.

He took the phone. "Having fun?" he said, trying to sound tough and brave.

"If anything happens to her," Lisa said without hesitation, "I will kill you. You get that? I will actually *kill* you." She sounded stretched tight, but very calm, very much in control.

"I get that. And if anything happens to *you*, Lisa…"

"What?"

He looked straight at his daughter as he said it, almost challenging her. "I've been a complete asshole for more than two years," he said. "I know that. But I still love you. I never stopped. I want us *all* to get the hell out of…wherever we are…alive."

Rose's head came down a few inches, as if she was absorbing a blow. Her eyes never left his.

It would be so much easier, if she wasn't so fucking smart. *And beautiful. And* right, *most of the time.*

"I'm going to be fine," Lisa said. "There's a big meeting at the Conference Center tonight, and then everybody's caravanning out of town. We'll be with them."

"'We'?" he asked.

"Everybody still left at the clinic at eight o'clock tonight," she said, "when they come to get us. What about you?"

"We'll be over the ridge and out of here by sunset." That was no more than an hour away.

"Call me if you can."

"I will. We'll meet you at the rest stop, right outside the Notch. You know the place I mean?"

"Yeah. Right along the highway."

"That's it. We'll wait for you there, or you wait for us."

"I promise."

He nodded, his throat thick with emotion. "Me, too," he said. "I promise." It was a big word for them, one that hadn't passed between them for a long, long time.

Lisa hung up then. He handed the phone back to Rose, who was staring at him as if she'd never seen him before. He decided very suddenly that he didn't want to talk to her, not at this moment.

He didn't look at his daughter as he sorted through his keys. "I don't suppose you know how to drive a motorcycle?"

"As a matter of fact," Rose said, "I do."

Ken looked up, surprised. "You do?"

Her smile was crooked and a little bitter. "Daddy, I learned to do a lot of things those months I wasn't at home. You should probably be happy that at least some of them were constructive. Even legal."

He laughed. He didn't mean to, but he did. "Come on," he said, shaking his head, and they moved down the South Wing's central corridor, towards the far-off covered walkway and the garages beyond.

"Maggie, can you see anything…*unusual* out there?"

"Not at the moment. The…activity…seems to be centered around the front door."

They were almost there. "Good. I gather you've locked all the doors?"

"Gosh, no, boss, I didn't think of that."

He scowled. "I don't recall programming sarcasm into your conversational protocols."

"It's a natural evolution in response to silly questions," Maggie said almost tartly.

They had reached the southern entrance. Beyond it, dimly visible through the four-paned window in the door, was the covered walkway and the garage beyond it shimmering in the wind-driven mist. "Unlock it, please," he said.

The door went *thunk*.

Ken put a hand on the knob, peered left and right through the door's window and said "*Now!*" He threw open the door and they sprinted the fifteen feet from building to building. It felt like a mile.

The door to the garage opened before they got there and slammed tight behind them as soon as they piled inside. The lights were already on. There was a large empty spot in the middle of the concrete pad where the Land Rover was supposed to be waiting. Beyond that was a waist-high mass, five feet wide and three feet thick, covered by a nearly immaculate tarpaulin.

"Why didn't I notice that before?" Rose asked almost rhetorically. The rain was like a snare drum on the uninsulated roof, loud enough to give an instant headache.

"You were too busy being pissed off at me," he said. "Besides, it's on the driver's side." He walked across the room, undid a set of bungee cords, and whipped the tarp away.

A sweetly evil black Kawasaki 4500 RoadMaster was waiting underneath, polished to such a high shine that it seemed to glow with a dark light of its own.

"My *God*, Daddy," Rose said, almost breathless. "What were you thinking?"

He stared at the bike. "Well," he said, "I was forty years old, my brother had killed himself, my wife had given me the worst news a wife and can give her husband, and…I had *all this money.*" He smiled, and it was only half-cynical. "The ultimate mid-life crisis."

Rose approached the bike and ran an envious, almost lustful hand over the cowling. "No, no, *no,*" she said admiringly. "The ultimate in totally cool bikes."

He had to agree. "I'll be back in twenty minutes," he said. "Then we can—"

Rose stared at him with frank astonishment. "You think you're going to leave me here?" she said. "Alone?"

He smirked. "There is exactly one bike. And riding two-up in his storm would be dangerous."

"What, like staying here *isn't* dangerous?"

"Ken…" Maggie said, trying to interrupt politely.

"Rose, there are *things* out there—"

"*Ken,*" Maggie said more urgently.

"—who can get in here any fucking time they want to, Daddy. What, you're going to leave me with your pet robot while you go slammin' off to—"

The rolling garage door exploded inward and a creature made of broken bones as big as tree trunks surged inside. Ken bellowed, Rose screamed, and they both jumped away from the horror as fast as they could, scurrying back to the door they'd come in.

The thing fell with a crash into the spot where the Rover should have been. A wave of water and wind rushed in with it. Thick arms burst from its trunk and grew in seconds to tower over them. Then the rocky black-and-gray creature with no mouth and no face extended three massive limbs, each thicker than an oak, and scooped up the Kawasaki like a toy. Ken watched as it *pinched* the bike, collapsing it at the midpoint into a block less than six inches thick. Two hundred pounds of beautifully engineered, virtually solid steel clunked to the concrete in two distorted hunks as swiftly and easily as a boy squeezes clay between his fingers. The sound alone was incredibly painful.

He didn't wait for the creature to drop it. He simply turned and shoved his daughter out the side door, back onto the walkway, without even thinking of what might be waiting in the rain. "Out!" he shouted over the shattering motorcycle and the rattle of the rain. "Out, *out!*"

The walkway was clear. They ran back through the opening door to the house and threw themselves inside as the bone spiders attacked the detached garage from all sides and tore it to pieces.

Just. Like. That.

They fled down the hall, escaping the sound of the destruction and the grinding roar of the creatures themselves. There was a thundering boom on the front door as they passed, and Rose skidded to a stop without thinking.

She looked through the side windows that faced the driveway. "Oh my God," she said, and backed away. Ken peered through the window himself. Two more bone spiders were close behind the one on the porch, pawing and sinking in the liquefied landfill as lightning stuttered in the lowering clouds behind them. The dull glare of the security lights gave them a sick yellow luminosity all their own.

The *boom* came again. And again. *Boom. Boom.*

"Oh, fuck," Rose said. "It's knocking at the door."

TWENTY-FOUR

Jimmy Fultz was up and off to work before dawn. He was wearing three layers of clothing under his canvas overcoat, plastic wrap over his uniform's cap, and he was still soaked to the skin ten minutes after he stepped outside.

He met Bo Cameron and the Sheriff at the HQ before six a.m. Mindy looked bad, like she hadn't slept at all or had been crying all night. Or both. Sheriff Peck clearly didn't care. He was focused on the two of them.

"Make the evacuation announcement and look for people in trouble," he said grimly. "If they have working vehicles, send them out of town. *Make* them leave. If they don't have vehicles, tell them to hunker down until six o'clock tonight, then come to the Conference Center. We'll gather whatever transportation we can find and caravan out of town from there."

"We're not going to stay and fight?" Mindy said, her voice quavering. "We're going to run?"

"Fight what?" Peck snapped. "Water? It's already won. Whenever the storm breaks, we'll come back and clean up, if we can. For now…it's done."

Jimmy could see that he hated saying it, but he thought the Sherriff was right. In the last twenty-four hours he'd seen things he couldn't believe, and they were only getting worse. That, and he was pretty sure he was having hallucinations.

"Must be the stress," he said to himself, completely unaware he was talking out loud.

"What?" Peck snapped. "You have a problem?"

"No, sir," he said, and swallowed.

197

Peck shoved a finger at him. "You take the south side." The finger swiveled to Bo, who stiffened as if it had pierced him like a dart. "You take the north. Come if I call, otherwise …"

Peck stopped for a second, and a sudden, dreamy, distant look came into his eyes. As if for one moment he comprehended where he was, what he was doing, how everything had changed.

"Just go," he said softly, and turned away.

* * *

It didn't take Jimmy long to realize that most of the South Side, the part of town Sheriff Peck had assigned him, was already underwater. He didn't care. He gave some thought to the best way he could complete the assignment, and after much consideration he drove his patrol car, the oldest still in service, the one with a crack in the passenger side window, to the splendid, well-maintained Lazenby Estate high on East Ridge.

He knocked on the door very politely, but nobody answered. Then he knocked loud-politely and still nobody answered. Well, it was a courtesy anyway. He was the law, after all. And with that Jimmy trudged around the side of the house to the long, sloping concrete driveway and commandeered the tidy little twelve-foot ketch with the outboard motor that the Lazenbys called *Dragonfly.* It was half afloat already. Rainwater was sluicing down the slope from the top of the ridge so strongly and steadily it was creating a miniature river that crested around the boat's trailer.

Jimmy sincerely doubted if the elderly and entirely sedentary Lazenbys had ever put the silly thing in the water, but they had proudly displayed it in the turnabout of their estate, right out in the open, and assigned their servants to clean it and polish it all year round, simply to remind people how rich and important they were. They had a *boat,* in the middle of the *desert.* A boat they didn't even need. Take *that,* peasants.

Now, at least, it would finally be put to use. Jimmy tried to scrape the pounding rain out of his eyes with the back of his wrist, but that didn't work very well. Still, even half-blind and buffeted every which way, it didn't take long to undo the latches and untie the lines. One good tug on the stern and *Dragonfly* was free of the trailer and floating in the two feet of water coursing down the driveway.

Jimmy nearly tripped over his own feet climbing into the boat, and it bobbed and teetered under him until he got settled, but eventually he got it all under control. The outboard started with the first touch, and he was happy to see it even had a full tank of gas.

Despite the rain driving into his face like cold, sharp fragments of glass, Jimmy Fultz couldn't have been happier. For the first time in a long time, maybe in his entire life, he was on his own.

Captain of my own fate. In a manner of speaking.

The outboard was a pleasant rumbling under his hand. It was easy to steer southward with one hand while he held the bullhorn in his other and chanted the alert:

"THIS IS THE SHERIFF'S DEPARTMENT. EVACUATE IMMEDIATELY. I REPEAT: EVACUATE IMMEDIATELY. IF YOU HAVE TRANSPORT, LEAVE THE VALLEY AS SOON AS POSSIBLE. IF YOU DO NOT HAVE TRANSPORT, MEET AT THE CONFERENCE CENTER AT SIX PM. REPEAT, THOSE WITHOUT TRANSPORT MEET AT THE CONFERENCE CENTER AT 6 PM."

He'd made up the little speech himself, and he was rather proud of it. He particularly liked the way it bounced off the churning water and the glistening walls of the houses in a soggy kind of echo.

"THIS IS THE SHERRIFF'S DEPARTMENT…" he began again.

He had been underway for no more than half an hour when he floated past the Squire, a bar that was housed in a rusting Quonset hut owned by the grandson of one of the city's founders. Lights were still burning in its windows, though how it was still getting power this far south into the floodplain was beyond him.

He cut the motor and used the bullhorn to hail any survivors.

"Hey!" he shouted. "Anybody in there? In the Squire?"

He saw a shadow plaster itself against one of the windows, struggle for a minute, then lower the pane. It was Steve Chapin from the hardware store, his hair matted with rainwater or sweat, his gray eyes too large and a little wild.

"Hey!" he said back. "Pretty bad out there, huh?"

Jimmy nodded. "Gettin' worse, too. You guys okay?"

"Fine," Chapin said, and then grinned crookedly. "Well, not *fine,* exactly. You know what I mean. We're waiting for Richie Riegel to get here with his big ol' utility truck. He's taking us all out. But…I don't suppose you've seen Jennie Sommerfield? The blonde with the…you know, the blonde?"

Jimmy knew Jennie very well. He'd been at the homecoming game where she'd been crowned queen. He'd also busted up a couple of the bachelor's parties where she'd been dancing, and answered a couple of her stalker complaints about that guy that was always after her, what's his name, the scientist.

"Nope," he said. "She goin' with you?"

"Yeah," Chapin said, though Jimmy could tell there was a whole story behind that one word. "Soon as she gets here."

He let it go. He had other things to do.

"Good luck gettin' out!" he shouted, and turned the tiller to the west and south.

"Good luck to you, too!"

Jimmy lost them in the storm just a few seconds later. He had to stop soon after to bail out the rainwater, and thought he might have seen a bright orange streak to the north—Richie Riegel's famous W&P truck, though he couldn't be sure. Soon he crossed Farantino, now so deeply submerged that the street sign was lower than the gunwale of the *Dragonfly.*

After that he stopped bothering with the bullhorn at all. There was no longer anyone left to hear—not this far south, not anymore.

Down here, Dos Hermanos already belonged to the monsters.

They twisted though the water around him. They tiptoed and scurried on the few remaining outcrops of roofs, gas station signs, street lamps. They wheeled and spun on the misting winds, flights of them, cells of them, sometimes single huge eyeless creatures made of wings and talons and nothing else.

The water was so deep it had a wind-driven chop. It was almost like being on an open lake. It was easy for Jimmy to forget he was cruising a few feet above people's homes, businesses, backyards. Even as the day grew later, the storm grew more violent, and the wind rose higher, Jimmy urged the *Dragonfly* farther south towards VeriSil. Towards the Two Brothers.

Something in him, something deep and resonant, wanted to see it all.

As the skeletons rose out of the mist of dusk, he sensed that he was fighting a current in the water that he hadn't expected. It wasn't a strong one. It should have been far stronger. Water should have been flowing freely through Arroyo Verde, draining the Valle as it filled. Instead, there was nothing more than a slight pull, barely more than a drift.

He was thinking of turning towards it when he saw the first structure, and he forgot everything else.

It was built on the remains of a microwave tower, one of VeriSil's outlying structures. Now it was covered, twined, raddled with…*something else.* With the same gray, craggy material as the creatures themselves, growing in twisted parasitic networks over the metal beams, gathering in knobs and knuckles, splaying outward, upward in cantilevered branches, dressed in rocky scales and plates that fluttered and cracked against the wind. It was something like a tree, something like a minaret. Something like an insect disguised as a tree or a minaret.

And it was alive. In the way it trembled, in the way it moved in the wind—not pushed by the gale, but turning of its own volition. Beyond it, the superstructure that was supposed to have been VeriSil's new headquarters was overwhelmed by new growth. It was farther away, still dim in the gathering gloom, but Jimmy could see bone spiders, brickteeth, dragontongues, stains, clambering and crawling over it, moving industriously here and there, swarming and separating, joining and breaking and joining again.

Building, he realized. Under some unified direction, according to some plan. *Building.*

The water boiled right in front of him, in a band thirty yards wide, and a rough archway, five times wider than the *Dragonfly*, studded and filigreed with living stone, lifted itself from the trembling water. Without knowing how, Jimmy knew that it was another creature entirely, one without a name yet, rising up to take him.

He didn't want to go. Not yet.

He pulled hard at the tiller, gunned the little motor and peeled off to the left – to *port,* he corrected himself, *port* – and fled. He aimed the pointed bow of the little skiff at the central cleft of the Two Brothers where they still rose above the water, their foothills a new shoreline.

There was something there, it was calling him. But a mad population of creatures to the east of that, where Arroyo Verde should be draining the Valley, was roiling and twitching, distracting him horribly.

He had a chance to see it only for a moment, in a fleeting gap between sheets of rain. First he glimpsed a rickety staircase rising up out of the water, winding up to a ramshackle house halfway up the Brothers. Then he was looking past the staircase, directly at Arroyo Verde.

There was a wall there, a barrier that had never been there before. The creatures of the storm were swarming over it, building it, *creating* it from their own rocky flesh. Sealing off the only natural outlet to the water, making the flooded Valle their own.

Forever.

Some water was still escaping, in a roaring torrent so narrow and violent it would crush anything that was caught between its walls. That's where *he* would be heading soon if he didn't turn back now, he knew, to be chewed between the teeth of the hungry current.

Belatedly, it occurred to Jimmy that he should call this in. He didn't know how he was going to explain it to anyone, how he could possibly make them understand all he was seeing, but he had to try. This was *important.* Somebody, *everybody,* needed to know about this.

His hand had barely touched the TRANS button on the radio mic at his shoulder when the twisting arc of the unnamed creature came up again, rising before him with an eerie kind of majesty. He looked up in astonishment as it teetered above him for a moment…and then saw it fall, straight towards him.

The creature plucked Jimmy Fultz out of the *Dragonfly* like a doll on a string.

It was the last thing he ever saw.

CREATURES OF THE STORM

* * *

Mindy Bergstrom closed down the Dos Hermanos Sheriff Department Headquarters all by herself. She hadn't heard from Bo or Jimmy or even Sheriff Peck in hours. It was so long ago she'd stopped trying to raise them on the radio or the phone. It had been longer than that since her sister Cindy had been in touch, and she knew in a secret part of her brain that Cindy was already gone. Thinking back, she imagined she knew the exact moment when Cindy-girl had blinked away. It was that quick and that final.

Mindy Bergstrom loved Dos Hermanos. She had spent most of her first twenty-five years in St. Paul, Minnesota and she had always detested the cold and wet that hunched there like an angry old man. Now, barely past fifty years old, 'cold and wet' was almost all she remembered of her life before DH. Here she was warm all the time, living with the only family she'd ever loved, in a place filled with light and devoid of the mud, the mildew, the sniffles, the clamminess of…well, of everywhere else on Earth.

She stared through the storefront window, through the half-raised Venetian blinds that looked out on the shimmering, deserted vista of North Poplar street. It was so sad. Everything that had happened in the last thirty-six hours reminded her of that awful other place she thought of as the outside world. All the calls she'd taken, all the things she'd seen traveling to the Conference Center and back, to her home and back…

It was never going to be the same again. That was obvious to any old fool. And small and simple as Mindy Bergstrom was, she was no fool.

She sighed as she took off her headset and shut down the phones. She made sure the coffee machine was turned off and the mini-fridge was shut tightly, as she did every night. She almost smiled as she shrugged into her only coat, the one she wore when it got a little chilly at night in December and January, and she was careful to close and lock the door as she left.

Mindy Bergstrom had come into this world, into this town, and into this life very quietly. She had lived very quietly, and she knew it would end very quietly as well.

So when she left the office, exactly on time, she decided to walk home all by herself. Just this once.

* * *

Donald Peck didn't know shit about poetry. Never had. He sat in his tricked-out police cruiser on the East Ridge, not all that far from where Jimmy Fultz had stolen the *Dragonfly* hours earlier. He didn't think of Coleridge or Ozymandias as he looked down on the dimly visible remains of his drowning city. Hell, "Ozymandias" was the name of a space shuttle or a WWA wrestler.

It was hard to believe that yesterday he'd been all worked up about a handful of missing girls. Like they mattered. Like they were any real threat to him. He should have remembered that, after thirty years of hard work, nothing was a real threat to him in this town. As far as he was concerned, he pretty much owned Dos Hermanos, California.

Which was what made it so frustrating, so maddening. That something as simple as the fucking weather could bring him down so quickly and so completely.

"It's rain," he said into the padded dashboard of the cruiser. "Just *rain.*"

The sight of the devastation below him would have overwhelmed a normal man. Filled him with grief or despair. Not Donald Peck. Peck felt only one emotion, just as overwhelming but entirely different.

Rage, seasoned with desperate, unbreakable determination.

He wasn't going to let it happen. He simply *wasn't.* The plan was simple: he'd gather together the last few assholes who were still in town, the ones too poor or too stupid to get out on their own, and he would lead them to the Promised Land, up the highway and through the Notch, like some fucking Aryan Brotherhood Moses. He would become the brave local hero who saved the last few survivors of the Great Dos Hermanos Flood, and soon he would return to rebuild their home as their chosen leader.

He'd be in a better position than ever. No one, not some brain-dead grandson of one of the founders, not some slime-fingered corporate stooge, could challenge him then. And something like this would never happen again. The place would be *his,* forever, as he'd always planned. After all, the good thing about a five hundred year storm like this was that he'd have at least five hundred years before the next one came.

"Sheriff, this is Eight Eleven." It was Bo Cameron, sounding strangely unnerved. Usually not enough information made it all the way into Bo's head to give him any trouble. "Are you…Sheriff, are you all right?"

"Eight Eleven, this is Peck. Of course I am," Peck said. "Are you?"

There was a long pause. All he heard was Bo Cameron breathing in and out, in and out, hard and fast. He was about to click off when the cop spoke. "I guess," he said, not certain of that at all.

"Any contact with the others?" Bo asked. "Mindy? Fultz?"

"No, sir. I think Mindy went home for the night. Fultz? Who knows?"

Okay," Peck said, wondering what had happened to them, but not really caring. "You're done, are you?"

"I've made a full circuit," Bo said over the police band. "Rousted the civilians, sent 'em packing or to the Conference Center. I'm ready to—"

There was a crash of breaking glass and the scrape of metal on metal, clearly audible over the police channel.

"Bo? What is it? *Bo!*"

Bo went "Wha—" and then there was…

Peck heard it as a *chomp*. The sound of something huge biting into something meaty. Then there was screaming. And swallowing. And more screaming, and this time it wouldn't end. Sherriff Peck listened until there wasn't anything more to listen to. Then he turned off the radio, knowing there was no one left to answer, and no one left to call.

He thought about that for a moment.

Okay. So…things got a little simpler. That's all.

There was still the plan. Still the vision. Still his unstoppable determination.

This just makes it easier. Now it's all up to me.

TWENTY-FIVE

Ken led his daughter back to the atrium with the high-domed ceiling of glass, but she couldn't stand it there. *Things* were tapping at the glass two stories above them, and that was too much to bear.

Without asking permission, Rose fled upstairs to the sitting room, a wide, low-ceilinged room with dark beams and white adobe walls. Four sets of casement windows looked out over the huge broken tooth of stone in the driveway to the dim glow of the town beyond and below, little more than a faint smudge through the rain. Her father was close behind her, his long face tight with tension.

"Maggie," he said to the open air. "Are you all right?"

It seemed like an odd question to Rose, but the disembodied voice of the house seemed to understand what he was asking. "I lost two processors and the far south surveillance cameras," Maggie said very calmly. "One of the memory back-ups has failed, too, but we're thrice redundant there. All Uninterruptable Power Systems and the back-up generator are still solid, too."

God, Dad, she thought. *Overbuild much?*

He nodded. "Satellite link?"

"Still intact, but the one-way mirror is still in place."

"So all in all…what's your self-assessment?"

Maggie didn't answer right away, and even that was odd. Rose couldn't recall her *pausing* before.

"I'm a little slower now," Maggie said, almost as if she was admitting a secret weakness. "But I'm still here."

"What are you two talking about?" Rose asked.

"Maggie isn't a single computer," Ken said. "She's actually a whole series of distributed processors, sensors, memory drives, a bunch of stuff, that are installed all over the house. Her higher functions – her fuzzy logic drivers, some of her conversational protocols, and what we've come to call her 'implication engines' – are handled through her uplink to a commercial geostationary satellite up there," he pointed over their heads, "which, in turn, links her to microseconds of commercially available share-time on a series of networked supercomputers."

"So there isn't like one glowing mechanical brain in a closet somewhere," Rose said. "She's got bits of her scattered all over the house…and all the hard decisions are done, in fractions of a second, by talking with other, smarter computers, far away."

Ken smiled. He looked proud of her. "You got it," he said.

"…and the other side of that," Maggie said, "is that when the house is damaged, and some of the sensor or processors go offline, I lose some of my reasoning and communications capacity."

"You get stupider," Rose said helpfully.

"Right," Maggie agreed. Rose caught it that time. It took a measurable beat for her to respond this time.

"What are you going to tell Mom?" Rose asked abruptly, knowing she was interrupting and not really caring. Her Dad, preoccupied with the screen and his own thoughts, turned to her abruptly, surprised at the question.

"What?"

"You told her we would be out of here, over the ridge, by dark. But somebody ate our ride."

He blinked and looked out the windows. Lightning flickered, thunder cracked like wet wood, and for a moment—just a moment – something whistled past the second floor balcony, a huge, filigreed wheel of bone, edged in teeth and talons, twirling on the wind. It flashed for only an instant, then disappeared in a black-on-black afterimage.

He opened his mouth say something and Maggie interrupted.

"Ken," she said with unexpected volume and urgency. "Somebody's coming in the gate."

The TV flickered to a green, grainy night-vision view of the front gate and the first half-mile of private road. A blocky, dented Jeep was bouncing towards them, trailing sparks as it barreled through the water at the bottom of the first hill and spun off sheets of water as it surged up the second incline.

"Anybody we know?" Ken asked, peering at it.

"Not that I can tell," Maggie said. "Do you recognize the vehicle?"

"Nope."

"Dad," Rose said, "if he hits the driveway he'll sink like you did."

"Crap," Ken said.

"*Deep* crap," she agreed.

They pounded down the stairs. "Maggie!" he called. "What's going on with our…wildlife out there?"

"All cameras show it's clear at the moment," Maggie said as they skidded on the overpolished floor of the entryway. "They seem to have followed the big ones, the leg-things—"

"Bone spiders," Rose and Ken said together, and then looked at each other in surprise.

"Bone spiders, then," Maggie said. "They all seem to have left with them."

Ken nodded. "Good. Then–"

"Open the pod bay doors, HAL," Rose said. She couldn't resist.

"Whatever you say, Dave," Maggie said. The door-lock went *thunk*, and Rose thought, *You may be down, Maggie, but you're not out – not nearly.*

They ran onto the porch, right to the edge of the roofline. The Jeep's lights were visible at the top of the second hill, still climbing.

Ken waved his long arms frantically. "STOP! STOP THERE!"

Rose hopped up and down next to him and did the same. "WAIT! WAIT!" She noticed a single headlight, much dimmer, far behind the battered Jeep. She couldn't see what kind of car it was.

Maggie swiveled the exterior lights to illuminate the path. The Jeep was outlined in stark black-and-white, the rain etched in thick vertical slashes, slicing the scene into a thousand narrow, flickering strips.

The Jeep kept coming. They shouted louder, knowing they wouldn't possibly be heard, and waved even more frantically as the car topped the third hill and accelerated down the paved drive, straight towards them, and straight towards the lake of mud.

"STOP!" Rose screamed as the Jeep hit the edge of the road, the point where it would start to sink, and ridiculously, impossibly, the car actually *sped up*. For an instant it flew into the air, jumping like a jalopy in some absurd reenactment of a *Dukes of Hazard* stunt. She could see the muck-encrusted undercarriage all too clearly in the searchlights as it soared through the air and came down right in the middle of the liquefied landfill with the most extraordinary sound.

The Jeep went *splurch* and *k'tang!!* simultaneously, the sound of a car splashing into mud as thick as clay *and* the sound of a car hitting another car at full speed, both at the same time. Muck and dirty rainwater flew up in a perfect circle with the Jeep at its center, a full three-hundred-sixty degrees of filth in a six-foot splash. Rose and Ken staggered back, arms up, as the mud-wave splattered over the porch.

When Rose looked back, she fully expected to see the Jeep sinking swiftly into the ground, as the Land Rover had earlier.

But it didn't. It sat there, buried halfway up its wheels, as if it was floating on the muck instead of sinking into it.

"Son of a bitch," Ken said, so softly Rose barely heard it. "I think it's on top of the Rover."

Rose noticed it was in exactly the same place that the Rover had sunk. She had a momentary vision of the buried four-wheel-drive, submerged in the mud, with the Jeep sitting on top of it like a seven-ton Easter bonnet.

Maggie's swiveling searchlights turned and adjusted like the eye-stalks of some vast mechanical snail. There was a stout woman with very short hair sitting inside the Jeep, eyes as big as saucers, mouth gaping. She looked as stunned by the experience as Rose was. After a long moment her eyes shifted from a thousand-yard stare to Ken and Rose.

"Get out!" Rose shouted, gesturing to her. "Quick, before you sink, *get out!*" She moved out into the rain, put her boot into the bubbling muck beyond the red-brick porch and immediately started to sink. It was as bad as ever. Maybe worse.

The woman in the car didn't notice. She scooted across to the passenger door, kicked it open, hauled herself out…and sank into the watery mud, almost to her waist. She was *fast*, though, Rose saw. She yelped, recovered, clutched, and pulled herself back up into her seat, dripping and filthy, before the mud could take her completely.

She looked up across the ten-foot gulf between them with an expression that clearly asked, *What the fuck?*

"*Quicksand!*" Ken bellowed, making huge, sweeping gestures that were impossible to decipher. *"All around you!"*

Rose didn't know if the woman could hear them or not.

The Jeep woman got the idea. Without missing a beat, she squirmed around, stood up in the doorway of the Jeep, and scrambled out onto its broad, mud-spattered hood. Now she was only eight feet from the red brick porch.

As she struggled to stand on the shuddering, denting sheet metal, the whole car lurched two feet forward and nosed downward twenty degrees. The woman danced to keep her balance, and Rose knew exactly what was happening.

"*You're sliding off!*" she screamed, knowing that would mean absolutely nothing to the woman. "*You're sinking in! Quick! JUMP!*"

The car slid another foot down. The woman got the idea, took three pounding steps that covered the length of the hood, and leaped, as far and as high as she could, straight towards the porch, feet first.

She missed.

She fell short by exactly three feet, knifing feet-first into the muck. A brown wall of mud flew up and slapped Rose square in the face. She gagged and used the back of her wrist to scrape the crap out of her eyes, cursing at it, and found the short-haired woman right in front of her, beyond her feet, sinking fast. She was already up to her chest in the liquefied landfill.

Without even thinking about it, Rose threw herself onto her stomach and put out a hand. The Jeep woman tugged her own hand from the mud, the motion driving her six inches deeper down, and clutched at Rose's straining fingers. They intertwined, held tight.

Rose started to slide forward, belly-first, into the mud.

Ken saw what was happening and threw himself forward, covering Rose's legs, pinning her to the bricks. He used his weight to stop her, wrapped his long fingers around her ankles, then shuffled back and pulled, as hard as he could.

Rose felt her vertebrae go *pop-pop-pop* as she stretched, but she moved back. Ken pulled with all his might again, and she inched back a little farther. *Look at me,* Rose thought as the pain clamped on her spine. *I'm a human tow rope.*

The Jeep woman came with her, an inch at a time. First her arms were over the porch, then her ample chest. The instant her elbows were on solid ground, they separated and she churned her legs like an Olympic cycler until she was completely on the farthest corners of the covered porch, gasping for breath.

That was entirely too close for Rose. For *any* of them.

The Jeep woman pulled herself up onto all fours, then up on her knees.

"Fuck," she said, and tried to wipe her face clean. "Thanks, but ... *fuck.*"

"Yeah," Ken said. "Let's get you in—"

"Guys," Rose said. She pointed across the shivering mud-lake, at what amounted to the far shore. The ridge-line that broke into a severe downhill grade.

It was lined with monsters. Drifts of candle-eyes and needleseeds huddled on the ground. A lattice of thornwheels whickered in the wind behind them, flumes and blade-ribbons hung from the dancing, drenched eucalyptus trees like bony Christmas decorations, flapping in the chaotic wind. They were all illuminated by the stark white glare of Maggie's searchlights, so bright even the lightning fracturing the sky behind them seemed pale and gray.

There was a man standing in the midst of them. Or most of a man. He had too many legs, and one of them seemed longer than all the others. One arm was hanging by a series of threads, wriggling in the wind. Under the remains of his filthy, mud-encrusted clothes he was almost the same ash-gray and china-white as the creatures around him, from his ridged, plated hair to his opaque, marbled eyes.

But he was alive. He was watching them. And the Jeep woman clearly recognized him.

"Steinberg!" she bellowed. "You ASSHOLE! Why don't you just fucking DIE?!"

The man with the monster looked at her and smiled. The corners of his mouth cracked. He pretended to laugh, *ha-ha-ha* like a jolly old elf made of muddy paper, elbowing the creatures to his left and right. *Look at that*, he seemed to be saying, *look how the meat-things whimper and scream!*

The woman was on her feet now, right at the edge of the porch. The rain was pounding into her eyes, driving her back, but she refused to acknowledge it. "I know all about you!" she shouted. "You and your *buddies!* You think you're so *great,* you think you're the *man,* but you're a FUCKING PUNK!"

The man with the monsters glanced to the side as a bone spider, ten feet tall, climbed the ridge to join them.

"Let's get inside," Ken said, three minutes later than any sane man would have, as far as Rose was concerned.

The bone spider cocked one of its larger legs and slammed it down on the hood of the disappearing Jeep, driving it four feet deeper into the muck.

Rose tugged at the woman's arm. "Come on," she said. "Come *on.*"

"Fuck you, big man! Big, big man!"

The bone spider was raising another leg, high in the air. It was aiming for the porch.

"NOW!" Rose screamed, and jerked the crazy woman back, through the open door, into the entryway of the house. They tumbled inside as the bone spider's leg, thick as a golf cart, rammed into the red brick porch where they had been standing and broke it off like a bit of bad plaster, *crunch,* driving it into the muck.

Maggie slammed and locked the door behind them. The wind and rain cut off with a snip.

The three of them were sprawled across the polished hardwood floor of the entryway. No one spoke for five heartbeats or more.

"Asshole," the woman muttered. "Thinks he can get *me,* does he?" She glared at Ken and Rose as if they were challenging her. "*Does* he?"

For once in her life, Rose had no idea what to say.

TWENTY-SIX

Steinberg snarled at the slammed door of the Mackie *hacienda*. It seemed to leer at him across the mud lake.

Go after her, he ordered the bone spider. *Finish her up. First her, then Jennie.*

His creatures had been waiting for him in the first hollow beyond the gate, rolling and slicing through the water, sucking greedily at the rainfall and growing, growing.

Come help me, he told them. *I have a job to do.*

They had climbed the slopes together, come to the mud lake, watched the little meat-baby clamber out of her car like a bug caught in a matchbox.

Crush her, he told his bone spider. *Now.*

She had gotten away. Scurried into her adobe rat hole. And he wanted to see her when it ended. He wanted to see her *pop.*

Take me over there, he told the creature. *Lift me up...*

No, the voice of the storm told him. **There is something else to do...**

He started to protest, but he knew there was no point to it. The second mind twisting inside his own was hard as marble. You didn't simply do what you were told, you *surrendered* to the irresistible pressure of it. You had to.

Do as I tell you...

He turned away from the *hacienda* with huge reluctance and trudged back to his ATV. He needed to go south. Not all the way, not this time. Just a little way.

To the Conference Center.

And then, he thought, *I will be free. Free to go to the woman I love.*

213

Twenty-seven

Lucy was giddy with adrenaline and victory. She had beaten the son of a bitch. She had escaped.

"I know all about them," she said to the programmer and the girl. "Everything, *everything* is right here." She dug inside her khaki jacket and pulled out the flash drive. Its clean, cool surface was startling compared to the mud that caked every inch of her.

Ken frowned at her and kept his distance. He thought he recognized her through the mud and water. "Look, Doctor…Doctor…?"

"Armbruster," she said, wiping mud out of her mouth. "Lucy."

"Doctor Armbruster, you have got to calm down. You barely–"

"I know what I *barely* did, man."

"Ken," he said, still sounding idiotically calm. "And this is Rose, my daughter."

"Yeah," Lucy said, looking them both up and down as she struggled to her feet. Her heart was still pounding. "I remember you from the restaurant yesterday."

Rose wasn't even looking at her. She was peering out the small windows beside the front door. "They're gone," she said. "All of them. The, the creatures and that man who was with them." She looked back. "Did you see him, Dad? Did you see that guy standing with them?"

"I sure did," Lucy said, and tried to scrape some of the filth off her with no success. "The son of a bitch. Look, have you got a computer? You *must* have a computer, you're a programmer, right?"

"Sure, but–"

"Where is it?" she demanded.

Ken looked at her, as annoyed as he was terrified. "The study," he said. "This way."

They trotted down the hall. "You gotta see this," Lucy said, panting with excitement, adrenaline, fear. "It's fucking *amazing.* You gotta see it."

The overhead lights flared and the monitors flickered to life all by themselves when they entered the quiet, triangular room with the massive multimedia bay. Lucy was still too buzzed to notice. She fit the drive into a USB port set into the desktop and started tapping on the keys. "Look at it," she said, talking more to herself than anyone else. "Everything, all laid out. I don't know where these fucking monsters came from, or how they became so multivariate without a wider ecological niche, or how they grew and spread *so fast,* but…"

Rose was standing on the other side of the room, in front of the floor-to-ceiling drapes that covered the glass doors to the garden. "There's something moving outside," she said in a small voice.

"Maggie?" Ken said. "What's up?"

"It's *Lucy*," Lucy said. "Not—"

"Night vision and infrared show negative, boss, but then these creatures haven't been showing on infrared anyway."

Lucy looked up sharply, in search of the new voice. Nobody to the left. Nobody to the right. She thought for a moment longer, then turned and looked at the computer monitor and said, "Ah. So. A voice-enabled PC?"

"Something like that," Ken said, smiling.

"Cool. You *are* a programmer."

Ken scowled. How exactly did she make that sound like an insult?

"Maggie, I'm still hearing it," Rose said. "Are you *sure*?"

"As sure as I can be."

"Look," Lucy said as she flipped from screen to screen, "I know this is hard to understand, but–"

"Well, gosh," Ken said, fluttering his eyes. "I'll try to keep up. But y'know, I'm only a *programmer*."

Lucy put her head down and took a breath. "Okay. Point taken. I'm a jerk. Sorry."

"Okay, then."

"But this *is* important. Really."

"You'd be surprised at how much we already know," Ken said, "but show me what you've got."

They spent a feverish ten minutes paging through Steinberg's data. They even tried to upload it to somewhere, *anywhere,* but Maggie explained again about the one-way mirror data link, and Lucy appreciated the metaphor: she had been suffering the same problem. She looked through the satellite data and camera links that Maggie had assembled and – much to her surprise – found herself impressed.

"*You* did this?" she said to Ken, then corrected herself. "No, wait. Didn't mean it that way. I mean, you figured out how to hack all the security and traffic cams in town that fast? Or is this something you do on a regular basis?"

"I did it," Maggie said. "And yes, I did it that fast."

Lucy looked up into the open air again. "*You?* You mean on your own?"

"All by myself."

"Uh-huh." She glanced at Ken. "*Self.* You know, I'd heard you were a hotshot AI guy, Kenneth, but still…"

He shrugged. "I'm as surprised by it as you are, Lucy."

A wave of lightless gray mist surged into Lucy's mind from every direction. She felt her knees start to buckle, and she had to paw mindlessly at the desk chair and sit down fast to keep from falling.

"Shit," she said, and scrubbed at her short, crusty hair. "Shit, shit, shit."

"You blood pressure just hit the floor," Maggie said, as Lucy struggled to catch her breath.

"I'm not surprised," Ken said. "You're crashing from the adrenaline rush, Lucy. Take a break."

"Fuck that," she said, forcing herself to breathe deeply. "We're in trouble here." Her head snapped up as something occurred to her. The sudden movement made her vision swim a second time, and she did her best to ignore it.

"Hey," she said, inhaling raggedly. "Hey, you said you were able to drive those fuckers off with electricity?"

"Yes," Maggie said, "a high-voltage shock of at least–"

"Fine, whatever. You're telling me that they must have an electromagnetic signature of their own, right? They use it, they need it to think, like we do. Otherwise electricity wouldn't bother them any more than bullets do. Have you tried tracking 'em *that* way?"

"We've tried everything," Rose said. "Twice." She was pacing nervously, still glancing at the drapes every few seconds. "Daddy…"

"That satellite data you showed me," Lucy said, plowing ahead. "Those sats can scan for E-M sources, too." Ken looked momentarily confused and she snapped at him. "*Electromagnetic* sources, goddamn it! If we could get large and small scale readings of the Valle, maybe we could actually see the fucking things and get a sense of where they're coming from, if they have a nest or a hive or —"

There was a tremendous crash and slumping sound beyond the drapes. Rose, still close to the drapes, jumped halfway across the room. "Okay, everybody heard *that*, right?" Lightning flickered beyond the windows, and thunder, as loud as exploding oil tanks, pounded across them. "Can we *please* get out of here now?"

"I've written the Steinberg data onto two of my hard drives, Ken," Maggie said, "and burned DVDs in one of the laptops upstairs. If you …"

She paused. It was like she drifted off.

"If we *what*?" Lucy said impatiently.

"Sorry," Maggie said. "There's a lot going on at once. Something on the porch."

"Oh, *shit*," Rose said.

"And the wind is spiking. Barometer falling fast. *Really* fast. It's a …" another pause, as the glass in every window began to rattle. "…cyclonic effect."

"Maggie," Rose said. "Please, Maggie, *what's outside?*"

Without warning, without asking permission, Maggie opened the drapes that covered the floor-to-ceiling patio doors.

"Maggie, wait—"

The security lights on the patio popped on, and everyone froze in place.

Candle-eyes, the small, broad-footed lumps with eye-stalks like fingers, completely covered the level ground in a churning, sludgy sea. Rising above them, taller than the windows themselves, was a single creature with no torso at all, but a latticework of talons and needle-sharp claws, twisting and twining, glinting in the light as it opened its wings like an enormous, skeletal dragonfly.

It turned to face them, half transparent, bone white. The wings twitched back at the sight of them. It tensed, a scorpion about to strike.

"*RUN!*" Rose screamed, entirely unnecessarily. The three of them fled through the door to the hallway as the huge wing-creature struck the doors and shattered them with a single blow. Maggie slammed the interior door behind them, barely in time. They heard fragments of glass thunk against the other side.

The study was lost.

"Why the *hell* did you open those curtains, Maggie?" Ken shouted.

"I don't know," Maggie said, and Lucy could have sworn she actually sounded puzzled. "I didn't…think…"

"You didn't *think?*" he echoed acidly. "You're supposed to *anticipate* this shit, Maggie! That's the whole point—"

"Dad," Rose said severely. "Never mind. Just tell us where to go now."

He pulled himself up short. Lucy was impressed at his self-control "Upstairs," Ken said after a moment. "We can barricade—"

"No," Maggie said. "Not upstairs."

"What, are you *kidding?*" Lucy said, astonished. "They can tear that door off like tissue paper! We can't–"

"The wind," Maggie said. "It will kill you." The doors to the far end of the hall, the ones to the large rooms at the center of the house, slammed shut. An instant later, the doors to all the rooms that faced the driveway slammed as well. They all heard the rhythmic *click-click-click* of doors locking down the hall.

"Stay away from the windows," Maggie said. "It's coming. *Now.*"

The loudest scream Lucy had ever heard, a scream that came from the Valle itself, not from any human throat, began to build around them, growing higher…and higher...

And the wind hit them like the fist of God Himself.

TWENTY-EIGHT

When Donald Peck parked his police cruiser directly in front of the Conference Center, he left every light on it pulsing and flickering in the storm – a beacon for the last stragglers. It was already twenty minutes to six, and he had hoped some of the VIPs he had met with the night before would arrive early. Instead, he found a few hundred waterlogged and desperate citizens and Karen Kramer, the manager of the Center, still wearing the same furiously pink pants suit she'd been wearing the night before. She greeted him hoarsely as he entered.

Peck didn't like the way she looked. She was rumpled, slightly stained, and her anxiety showed through her makeup like a painted skull as she offered him some mangled donuts and lukewarm coffee. He passed.

Stu Axminster of the DHW&P arrived a few moments later. "Goddamnit, Donald," he said, "Richie Riegel just called me and said he ain't bringin' the Orange Monster back."

Peck sighed. "Not surprising," he said shortly.

"He's stealing, goddamn it! Stealing goddamn public property! Your people need to pick him up! He—"

"Stu," he said, "my people are *gone*. So are yours. Besides, The Monster's a two-seater, right?"

"Yeah?" Stu said, sticking his chin out. "So?"

"So it's not going to help us with getting people out of town, is it?"

Stu blinked a couple of times. "Well…no, but–"

"And you still have all the other city vehicles? The ones with lots of seats?"

"Well, yeah. They're all parked right next door in the holding lot. Under the tower." His stony expression was obvious. Stu didn't like the way this conversation was going.

"Do you have drivers for all those vehicles, Stu? The ones we're actually going to use?"

Stu's eyes shifted away. "Well… probably. I mean, I called. I left a lot of messages, I …I need to check on that."

"You do that," Peck said. He could barely stand to look at the man as he skittered away. *I can't take much more of this. I really can't.*

He moved towards the stage, weaving past clumps of dripping, miserable citizens, to check on the microphones and the podium. As he bent to read the levels on the amplifier, he heard a voice behind him, a thick, wet, phlegmy, familiar voice.

"You're a liar, is what you are."

He straightened and turned, though he already knew what he was going to see.

Karen Kramer, her tightly bound body swaying inside the violent pink pantsuit was standing a little too close to him. Her bird-arms were wrapped tight around her. She was shivering, less from the cold than from…something else. Tension. Fear. He could smell it on her. She clearly hadn't showered or changed clothes in at least a couple of days.

"You're not looking for those little girls," she said. "You never were."

Peck noticed that a few of the arrivals were watching them, wondering what the ever-cheerful, ever-helpful Miss Karen's problem might be.

I can't have this happen here, he thought. "Come with me," he said – *telling*, not *asking* – and took her by the elbow. He led her out of sight, into the wings, to a place right inside a security door that read DO NOT OPEN ALARM WILL SOUND, though he knew damn well that wasn't the case and never had been.

"Karen," he said testily, "we're doing the best we can." *As if there's any 'we' left.*

She sneered at him. "Like hell you are, Donald. Even before this mess outside, you didn't look for them. I *know* you."

"I–"

"You're bullshit. You've always been bullshit, and everybody knows it. We put up with it because nobody else wants your stinking job!" she said, her voice rising.

"Karen, come on, we—"

"You just want me to shut up!" she was hysterical now. What little color was left in her face, under the hideous makeup, was high in her cheeks and bright as bruises. "You always want everybody to shut up! You lied about the kids and you're lying about the storm because you want all those *difficult* people with all their *difficult* problems to just *go away!*"

He clenched his teeth and tried not to make his fingers into fists. "If you will calm the fuck down, maybe we—"

"You wish *I* would go away, too! Don't you? You wish –"

He did it without really thinking. He threw up one leg and kicked her as hard as he could, right in the middle of her narrow, lumpy chest. Karen went *oog!* and flew straight back, colliding with the security door's pushbar and throwing it open. She fell into the roaring darkness and disappeared like *that*, all in an instant. In an instant more the door bounced off the outer wall and slammed shut.

Just like that, she was gone.

Peck stared at the door for a moment, pleased at how his heart rate had barely risen. He started to turn away, already forgetting her, when the door erupted with loud, metallic pounding and Karen called out. He could barely hear her through the metal, over the sound insulation and the gurgling thunder of the rain.

"Let me in!" she bellowed. "Let me in, damn you!"

He didn't.

"LET ME IN!" She sounded outraged – *beyond* outraged. "I'll GET you, you son of a bitch! I'll tell EVERYbody you–"

There was a pause. Peck cocked his head like a curious dog, wondering what had stopped her.

"Sheriff? Sheriff, there's something out here."

Oh, my, he thought. *Whatever could it be?*

"Sheriff, there's – SHERIFF! GOD, OPEN THE DOOR! OPEN THE DOOR OPEN THE DOOR OHHHHH—"

Her voice cut off with a wet slash unlike anything he'd ever heard outside of a butcher shop.

The sound didn't last for long. And when it stopped…

"Well, then," he said to himself. "Problem solved." He smoothed his immaculate khaki uniform and turned back to enter the slowly filling auditorium.

* * *

Outside, in the heart of the storm, Michael Steinberg was saying good bye to his ATV.

The red cowling was dented and cracked in a dozen places; the engine was laboring and coughing as he forced it into the storage lot behind the Conference Center. The Water Tower loomed over him under a stone-heavy bank of clouds, and the rain kept pouring down.

It never stops. Thank God. Thank Jesus. Thank Me.

"There, there," he said, stroking the hood one final time. "That's my baby." He was fascinated by the hard, screeching sound of his hand on the metal, like horn scraping on bone. The engine coughed one final time, then the whole vehicle shuddered and died.

He stood up on the ATV's pins and surveyed the vehicles arrayed before him: tow trucks, flatbeds, mini-pick-ups, water tankers, a paddy wagon, street sweepers, a water cannon, steam rollers, a cement mixer – even, for no particular reason at all, an ice-cream truck. He needed something special for his next task, he knew. Something huge and heavy, but relatively agile. Something he could steer, and as heavy as…

Then he saw it. *Ah. Perfect.*

Steinberg hopped off the loading dock and splashed into the water towards his new vehicle. *Takin' out the trash. That's me, Mr. Trash Man.*

He could feel the approval of the wordless Intelligence filling his mind.

* * *

223

Where the hell was Herb McCandless? Peck wondered. Or Marty Stein, or Tony O'Meara or Steve Chapin or Frank Baxter, or any damn member of the Town Council? Christ, even the Lazenbys.

As if in answer to his thoughts, the back doors creaked open and Normal Lazenby strolled in, his wife at his side. He was perfectly groomed and bone dry, a silver-haired angel dressed in black who glided confidently down the center aisle and took the same seat on the stage as he had occupied the night before.

The Mayor didn't have to speak. He had *presence*. He looked every inch like the father of Dos Hermanos, and right now that was all that mattered.

Dread coiled in Donald Peck's belly. He had never felt that particular emotion before, and he hated it. He tapped the mic and said, "People? Let's get started." There was a whine of feedback that made everybody groan. He wouldn't have put up with that even a few hours earlier. Now…he really couldn't care less.

"This is how it's going to work," he said without preamble. "We're going to take the biggest public vehicles we can find – the flatbeds, the big trucks, the busses – and load everybody inside. They're all parked right next door, in the utility lot. Then we're going to stop by the school to pick up your kids and the teachers, then go over to the Clinic to pick up doctors and patients, and *then* we're heading up 181 and out of here. So everybody–"

"Wait a minute!" It was an exhausted, weary man streaked with mud, standing up from his seat and sounding very angry. "Why do we all have to go to the school and the clinic? I got no kids. My wife and I just want to *go*."

"Then go," he said bluntly, hard into the mike. "Don't let me stop you."

"We got no *car*, damn it! It got washed away last night!"

"Then you go the way we say to go," Donald snapped. "And you…" He wanted to say "*and you shut the fuck up*," but he stopped himself at the last moment. "…and you try and make the best of it. Um…Chuck." He remembered the man's name now, Chuck Emerson, air conditioning contractor.

The Greenaways were sitting right behind him. Now they stood up. "What about our daughter?"

Oh, Christ, he thought. Sharon Greenaway was the last person he wanted to see right now, the mother of one of the missing girls. The last missing girl had disappeared barely two days ago. Mommy had been a meek little victim until now, but he could see the change in her. She had shed her soft, trembling Grieving-Mom-In-Trouble look. She was an instrument of vengeance now, eyes blazing and fists clenched white. "You said you were looking. Just yesterday, you said so. And now you want to run?"

"Sharon," he said in as measured a tone as he could manage. He couldn't stand the look in her eyes, so he shifted to her sad sack husband. "Jim, I… I don't know what to say. There are men out there right now, looking…"

He couldn't help it. He looked into her face again and saw the rage there, and the righteousness. He saw how immovable she was…and how right.

Oh, fuck this, he told himself. He leaned on the podium.

"Sharon…Jim…let me level with you. All of you. We're not looking for your daughter right now. We don't have the men or the time. I hope somebody found her and took her out of town. I really do hope that. Right now, though… we have to go."

"The hell we do!" Sharon said, standing up so fast she knocked her chair over. "We are *not* leaving Dos Hermanos without Katie!"

"Then you're probably going to die," Peck said flatly.

The Greenaways stared at him for one moment longer, then turned and left the room. Half a dozen others joined them, casting poisonous looks as they stalked through the double doors. Lightning blasted the walls to white, and there was a tremendous, metallic CLANGGG! of thunder that rattled the windows.

"Good luck to you all," he said as they left.

* * *

It was coming from the north. Steinberg could feel it himself now, exactly as the Intelligence muttering inside him had predicted. It was building, *growing*. It would be here any moment.

Time to get ready.

Steinberg found himself, yet again, thinking of his golden girl, his perfect Jennie. He had a moment of sheer panic, thinking she might be inside, that he might hurt her by accident. Then his tangled, wandering mind recalled: No. She was at the Clinic, still trapped inside, not here. It was okay. Really, it was okay.

He settled himself in the seat of the massive garbage truck. He had found the keys clipped to the sun visor as if they'd been left for him, and they slipped into place without a snag. The engine started with the first try, and without a pause he popped the clutch and jammed on the accelerator.

The truck roared straight forward, water flying everywhere.

He didn't stop. He didn't even test the brakes. He just aimed it carefully, punched it hard, and rammed the garbage truck directly into the huge, cylindrical southwest leg of the Water Tower.

Lightning flared as he connected, exactly on cue. The tremendous sound of the impact, metal on screaming metal, was all but lost in the deafening crash of the thunder.

The collision threw the steering column into Steinberg's chest. He heard his sternum pop as it broke, heard the wet snap of at least three ribs. But he didn't lose his breath. He didn't really need to breathe anymore.

As he lay hunched over the steering wheel, he heard the tiny chewing crunches of his bones rebuilding. He straightened up, put the truck in reverse, and pulled away for another hit.

Maybe this time we'll try backing into it…

* * *

"Why didn't you tell us all this last night?" It was another outraged citizen with a soggy pile of suitcases next to him. Peck had seen him hustling his three hungry children off to the school for safekeeping a few minutes earlier, obviously glad to be rid of them. "You told us this was going to be over soon! You told us everything was going to be *fine!*"

"I was wrong," Peck said, too weary to fight.

"We could have left *then*! We could've packed up everything and been *safe!*"

"I was working from faulty information," he said. "I was–"

"That lady scientist!" another woman said. "*She* knew about it! She said this would happen and you cut her off!"

"I was trying to restore order," he said. "I was doing what I thought was right."

"How can that be?" Lu Anne Schreiber said. The keening voice made Peck want to drive a jackknife in her ear, but he didn't flinch. He wouldn't let himself do that. "How can putting us all in harm's way be *right*?"

A fat old man Peck barely recognized hauled his ass up. "Goddamn it, I lost my house! It just *floated away*, not two hours ago and *you*—"

"You, too?" said another guy. "Shit, I thought I was the only one."

"And those things out there! Those things*!*"

"My brother didn't come home last night. I don't know what–"

"My dad—"

"Jimmy and Dooley and Wyatt, they–"

Lightning cut through the room again. Thunder exploded – that same strange double-thump of sound and shockwave. The audience kept talking, kept *pushing* at him.

Peck closed his eyes. He tried to breathe steadily.

This has got to stop. This has got to fucking STOP.

*   *   *

Steinberg's new senses helped him time it just right. He pulled away, revved the engine, and waited until the tang of ozone rose…and rose…and peaked. Then he popped the clutch and lurched backwards.

Lightning struck and thunder pounded out of the sky as the massive garbage truck slammed into the Tower's leg one more time. The two impossibly loud sounds blended into one.

The Water Tower's leg was buckling. Steinberg could see cracks in the paint, the metal folding like cardboard right where the truck had hit it twice.

This is going to work, he told himself, utterly amazed. *This is actually going to …*

He sensed it. He looked up to the north, even as he forced the truck into forward gear and lurched away from the tower again.

Only time for one more. One more…

*   *   *

They were shouting at each other now, terrified and angry. Peck tried to override it.

"*Let's get to the trucks*!" he said, booming it into the microphone on purpose. He waved at Stu Axminster to get his ass up to the podium. "Let's line up at the doors—"

"Why should we do what you say?" one man shouted. "This is your fault, YOUR fault!"

"Let's ride it out here! It's still safe!"

"My gran is still at the house! We gotta go get her–"

"I don't want to, I–"

"–can't, I –"

"– don't—"

Donald Peck slammed his fist into the wooden podium right in front of the mic, hard and fast and loud as a gunshot.

"JUST DO WHAT I FUCKING TELL YOU!" he bellowed.

The people stopped shouting. Even the rain itself seemed to stop, and the wind held its breath.

Everyone was staring at him.

"That's what you want, isn't it?" he said. "You want me to *save* you, to be your *daddy*, like *always*! *God*, you worthless, fucking, *stupid* bunch of…of…"

Peck was suddenly aware that it was quiet – *silent*, in fact. Absolutely silent.

Everything had stopped. *Everything*. The wind. The rain. Even…

What was that distant roar? Growing louder and louder?

He looked up and to the right, to the north. He felt a strange, invisible pulse that pushed his entire body, like the leading shockwave of a massive explosion.

A wall of wind, as solid as stone, slammed broadside into the north wall of the Conference Center and blew it to pieces.

It took thirty seconds for everyone to die.

* * *

Steinberg saw it coming with all his new senses, sweeping down from the Notch at more than seventy miles an hour. The Water Tower's tank, a flattened sphere of blue-painted steel, hovered high above him, lit from below. The glittering, billowing curtain of force careening southwards was even taller than the Tower. And was more than just wind and water. It was like the fist of God Himself, and he could feel it in his bony hide, rushing headlong towards them.

He popped the clutch and lurched forward, full-speed. He raised his arms and screamed into it, calling it down as he slammed the truck into the buckling leg of the Tower at the same instant the wind-wall arrived. In that last moment of awareness he saw the support crumple completely. The Tower groaned like a living thing as it twisted to the side.

He saw it fall. It drifted down at first, descending at an angle, going right where he'd planned.

First the walls of the Conference Center disappeared in a single *poof.* Then the tank hit the roof dead center and exploded. The truck around Steinberg blew to pieces, and he went with it. Vehicles scattered like thrown toys, walls disintegrated, buildings flew away. His own body cracked like china and the pieces scattered.

It was the happiest moment of Michael Steinberg's life.

Donald Peck saw it all. The entire north wall of the building blew out in an instant, and all the people and chairs and soggy luggage flew into the air in a single pressurized wave and slammed through the south wall. That fast, in a heartbeat.

The roof of the Center didn't blow off, not right away. The massive, rust-colored beams in the four corners stood firm, and Peck, on the stage, was lifted straight up and plastered against the curved ceiling, pinned there like a bug by the air pressure, but still very much alive – and conscious.

For one mad moment, he found himself looking down on the meeting room, viewing it from on high. He could see only a few bodies. Most had flown away, into the storm, but a handful were still there, clogged in the corners, like ants left after a blast from a garden hose.

Some of them were moving. One or two were actually trying to stand, even though the gale-force winds, strong enough to suspend Donald Peck forty feet in the air, still howled through the wreckage.

"Ants…" he wheezed.

Then he heard the high screaming music of metal tearing itself apart. He turned his head a bit, to look at the curve of the Conference Center's ceiling, and saw it flex down, pushed from above, as the cool blue curve of the Water Tower's tank fell through the roof, collapsed it, burst like a second bomb.

It was the last thing he ever saw.

* * *

The wind pushed him under. The water embraced him. The brittle limbs of what had once been Michael Steinberg broke off like toothpicks and swirled away, scattered by the pressure wave.

For you, Jennie, he told himself as he spread. *All for you.*

The last of his human consciousness still heard the stern voice of the Intelligence enfolding him, pulling him in. It was pleased with his work. Very pleased. And yet it did not take him completely. He was still distantly, wonderfully aware of the spark of Jennie Sommerfield, drowning in the storm-surge he had created.

I'll come for you, he thought, not sure if he could do it. *I'll come for....*

And that was all that mattered.

TWENTY-NINE

The windows of Ken Mackie's atrium exploded into a thousand pieces when the wind-wall hit the ridge. The doors of the locked hallway where Maggie had trapped them thumped as if ghosts were pounding on them, but they held, even through the horrible wooden rip-and-tear sound from farther down the hall. It wasn't monsters this time. It was the wind that was ripping away parts of the kitchen.

An instant later the power went off.

"Dad?" Rose said. "Daddy?"

"Right here," he said. "I—"

The power came back on. The emergency generator had kicked in, as it was supposed to.

"Maggie!" he called. "Status?"

"UPS did its job," Maggie said calmly. "I didn't even have to reboot."

Rose scowled. "What has UPS got to—"

"Uninterruptable Power Source," Lucy said. "To keep the computer running in spite of power failure. Don't be an idiot."

Rose started to fire something back, but Maggie hadn't finished.

"There's bad news, Ken."

"The antenna array," he guessed. He had been expecting it. Dreading it, really.

"Yes. They're all gone. I've lost all contact with uplinks, reference satellites, the internet. We are on our own."

And now she'd be even slower, Rose realized. No more supercomputers to squirt questions to when things got complicated.

There was a rumble in the room to the east – the crunching, thumping approach of the storm-creatures. It grew louder…and louder…and an electrical KZZZAK! cut through it, snapped it off. The lights dimmed at the same moment, then recovered.

"Time to get upstairs," Maggie said, and the door to the stairwell popped open. "Quickly, please."

"This," Lucy said, getting to her feet and brushing the biggest chunks of drying mud from her clothes, "is too fucking weird."

Something beyond the western doors went *crunch*.

They ran up the stairs as fast as they could.

* * *

Five minutes later, crouching in a side-chair in the corner of her father's bedroom, Rose tried to call her mother. It was stupid and she knew it. The wind had blown the towers down, the power was off, and the satellites that might relay a signal were cut off from them for some reason. They had been for days. Still, she had to try. She had to hear her mother's voice one more time. It was pointless. There was nothing there, not even the equivalent of a dial tone or a "systems busy" message.

Rose sighed bitterly. She was about to throw the damn thing across the room when a blinking icon on the iPhone's screen caught her attention.

She had a voice-mail.

She hadn't heard the phone ring earlier, though that was no surprise. The gradual, relentless destruction of the house by storm-creatures and the shrieking of the storm itself drowned out everything—literally. She tapped the proper code and pressed the phone to her ear, straining for every syllable.

It was a terrible connection. She could barely hear. But she would have recognized her mother's voice anywhere.

"*-etting worse, Rosie,*" her Mom said, and for once she didn't mind the kid version of her name. "*We don't –ink the caravan's … —et here. But we'll go anyway.*

Somehow. We …ake it to the highway and the… otch and we'll mee.. you there, I promise, *we...* "

There was a long pause then – nothing but hissing and spitting – until two final syllables rose out of the static: – *love y—* "

That was all.

Rose listened to it two more times, then she buttoned the phone back into one of the pockets of her canvas vest and let herself cry.

* * *

It killed over a thousand people. Those not in or near the Conference Center were drowned by the manmade tsunami that followed moments later.

Electrical power cut off with a knife-sharp pop seconds after the wind hit the city center. Dos Hermanos, California ceased to exist at that moment. The few who survived both the wind and the water found themselves trapped in an endless, rain-choked night, with no light, no help, no hope.

It wasn't long before the creatures of the storm came for them.

THE THIRD DAY

"I have had a dream, past the wit of man to say
what dream it was: man is but an ass, if he go about
to expound this dream. Methought I was – there
is no man can tell what. Methought I was – and
methought I had – but man is but a patch'd fool if he
will offer to say what methought I had."

—William Shakespeare,
A Midsummer Night's Dream

THIRTY

All those people, Rose thought numbly. *What happened? Where are they?*

She stood at her father's bedroom window and looked into the storm. The town of Dos Hermanos should have been visible below them, even in the middle of a dark and stormy night like this. *Dark and stormy,* she repeated to herself. *What a laugh.* Still, she knew she should have been looking down at a misty carpet of landbound stars, but those lights, already dim and guttering in the storm, had vanished when the wind hit.

Lightning flared for an instant, and she saw the rough, nearly flat top of the stone pillar thrusting out of the driveway. It looked like an island of rock floating over a lake of mud. Moments later, there was a subtle vibration under her bare feet. She thought it was thunder at first...then, on impulse, she laid down on the floor and put her ear against the Berber rug.

It wasn't thunder at all. It was the creatures of the storm, eating the house out from under them.

She could hear them downstairs, tearing through the walls, crunching across the carpets. There were no voices, no roaring, not even any breathing. Only... *clattering* beneath the gurgle of the rain. It was the sound of every artifact, every object, every human shape being shattered.

There was a sudden BOOM when an interior wall collapsed beneath her, and a thwack of bones knocking on the window to her right. *Scumbles again*, Rose thought. Maggie answered the attack with an electric THRUMM-*buzz* of her own. Out of the corner of her eye, Rose saw the creature explode off the screen in a shower of sparks, and the lights dimmed as current ran through the household security grid. It was the fifth time in an hour that Maggie had triggered the defense system, and it took longer for the lights to recover each time she used it.

Is that all that's keeping them away? Rose wondered, ear still pressed to the floor. *Just the electricity?* She had a vivid image of the creatures waiting patiently, a few feet below her – inches away, really.

Suddenly Lucy was standing over her. "Get up," she said gruffly.

Rose ignored her. "You can hear them," she said. "Moving around."

Lucy Armbruster's round, righteous face was right next to hers, glaring at her, too close for comfort. "Look," Lucy said in a fierce whisper, "the electrical grid that Maggie's using to drive those fuckers away only goes around the *outside* of this house. Not between the floors. The second they figure that out, one of those bone spiders is gonna shove one of its big ol' claws right up through this floor."

Rose stared blindly at her for a beat...then jumped to her feet and backed away. "You didn't have to do that," she said in a very low voice. She kept glaring at Lucy as she moved as far from her listening spot as she could, on tiptoes.

Lucy shrugged her rounded shoulders. "Yeah," she admitted. "But it got you up."

The room was a huge "L"-shape – a full bedroom and bath, with a vast bed, a dresser, two end tables, and a generously proportioned nook around the corner where Ken had put bookshelves and a desk for his laptop. Her father was nowhere near the desk or the media center it housed, he was using the bed itself as a workspace, standing over it and gazing at the reams of print-outs and charts and scrolling data on three different tablets scattered across the mattress. The material was generated from the data that Lucy had brought to them hours before, and it had snagged his complete attention. He hadn't heard a word of the two women's conversation.

"This is incredible," he said, entirely to himself.

There was another BOOM! when another wall fell downstairs. A massive talon *skreeeeked* along the hardwood floor. Rose could feel it as well as hear it, tickling up through the carpet. She couldn't help staring at the floor – *through* the floor.

"Where did they come from?" she asked. "How could they simply *appear* like this? Like 'Instant Monster, Just add water'?"

"It can't be as easy as it seems," Lucy said from across the room. They didn't look at each other as they talked. "Evolution doesn't work like that. Whole species, whole *ecologies*, don't pop up overnight." She suddenly, unexpectedly, smiled. "You ever see that movie, *Evolution*? Really terrible picture; David Duchovny trying to get out from under *X-Files*, and I don't remember who else."

"I don't think I saw it," Rose said, staring at nothing.

"This meteor crashes to Earth, actually out in the desert, now that I think of it, with these little speckles of living *stuff* on it. Things start growing in the crater. Plants first, then insects, then monkey-type animals, all of them alien, of course, ready to kick ass and take over the planet." She looked back out at the lightning again.

"Do you think that's what's happening now?" Rose asked.

"*No*," Lucy said, annoyed. "It was total bullshit. It would never work that way." She looked down at her shoes. "Besides, it was a comedy."

"Do you think it's happening all over?" Rose said quietly. "Like in *War of the Worlds* or something?"

"No," Ken and Lucy said, immediately and together.

"The rainstorm is isolated to this crater valley," Lucy went on. "It's a humongous mountain-shadow effect. We saw that on the last of the satellite images. Right over the ridge, not two miles *that* way," she pointed out the back of the house, due west, "it's sunny and hot as usual. If it's the rainstorm that… *activated*…these things, as we think it did, then it's still isolated to this crater."

"Besides," Ken said, "think about the video broadcasts and internet stuff we were getting right up until the wind hit. Everything was fine, CNN, The Weather Channel, all the data and government links. Right through the first two days. No, it's only us." He gave Rose a sharp look, as if he'd suddenly remembered something. "Have you got everything you need?" he asked her.

It took Rose a moment to understand what we was talking about. "Yeah. Yes. We got clothes from my room before we locked ourselves in here, including my, you know, underwear. And hiking boots and long johns. All that stuff."

"Good," he said, already on to something else in his mind. "You should get changed."

Rose was lacing her second boot and pulling it tight when something exploded near the kitchen. It was violent enough to make the room shake.

"Another processor gone," Maggie said. "Boss…" There was another THRUMM-*buzz!* and the lights lowered again. When they came back on, they were noticeably dimmer.

Something was drumming on the floor directly beneath them, like thigh-bones on a cardboard box. It almost sounded like it was knocking.

It made Rose angry. "I don't *get* it," she said. "They can't just *show up!* You can't have one lousy fucking *rainstorm* and see the whole world collapse like this. It's *ridiculous.*"

Lucy almost laughed at her. She was grinning and shaking her head. "Kid," she began.

"Don't call me *kid,*" Rose snapped. "Jesus, that's condescending!"

Lucy was taken aback. "Okay. Sorry. *Rose.* I was just saying, I don't think you have any idea how precarious life is."

Rose frowned. Thunder rumbled so low and powerful she could feel it in her chest, but she tried to ignore it.

"We're on the razor's edge here," Lucy said. "If Earth was just a few planetary diameters closer to the sun, we'd fry like a falafel ball. A few diameters farther away … Tastee-Freez. Meanwhile, even in this magical temperate zone of ours, the best that evolution could come up with was the feeble human being. We're pathetic. Weak and almost completely non-adaptive. We can only exist long enough to procreate in a tiny temperature range, far less than most living things. We can't go more than a few hours without water, a few days without food. We're so delicate it's kind of sickening."

Something caught Lucy's eye. She reached down and plucked a shiny Macintosh apple out of a bowl of fruit on Ken's end table. "Seriously, if this was a scale model of the Earth – the whole planet, *this big* – how thick do you think the whole biosphere would be? From the top of the atmosphere to the bottom of the Marianas Trench, the entire layer of organized life on the planet. How thick?" She held up the apple as if challenging the teenager.

Rose shrugged. She didn't have any idea.

Lucy took a vicious bite out of the apple. "Thinner than this skin," she said with her mouth full. "Think about it. Thinner than the skin on this apple." She swallowed with some difficulty. "We don't want to think about it, Rose, but we're tiny. Balanced so precariously between two canyons of extinction that it terrifies us to even consider it. Is it any surprise that one little shove, one little rainstorm, can do… *this?*" She gestured with the half-eaten apple, sweeping it all in: the window, the town beyond it, the creatures eating the house one bite at a time.

"That doesn't even begin to explain the things downstairs," Rose said. "They're like animals—"

"They're not animals," Ken said abruptly, and turned to face them.

Lucy frowned. "What?"

"What's the old Bio 101 definition of life?" he asked, his eyes shining. "It has to eat, it has to poop, it has to move, it has to reproduce. Right?"

"'Poop'?" Lucy said. "Is that a technical term?"

"'Falafel balls?'" he shot back.

She smirked. "Point taken."

"Think about it," Ken said. "These creatures don't pass the test. They move, that's true. The may eat, if they can somehow get nourishment from the water they absorb, but even Steinberg couldn't find any evidence of it. And living things this big, no matter how efficient, need a huge amount of biomass to keep going, like the whales that live on krill who have to eat constantly or starve. These things are much more active than a whale, much more kinetic. Meanwhile, no pooping, and no babies. No sign of either."

"So maybe we simply haven't –"

"—and no mention of it in your scientist's notes here, either," Ken said. "Tons of information on growth and locomotion. *Nothing* on excretion or reproduction."

Now it was Lucy's turn to stop and stare. "Huh," she said. "Hadn't thought of that."

Ken allowed himself a very small smile. "I know. I only noticed it because they're more similar to the things I build than to the things you study."

He looked at her directly for the first time, eyes still shining. "Really, Lucy. Think about it. These things are *machines*. Highly specialized machines."

"Made out of iron-hard papier-mâché and bone-stuff," Rose said. She was agreeing with him.

"Right," he said. "I wouldn't even call it organic, exactly. It's more like crystallization or magnetic accretion than it is cellular growth. But...yeah. Robots made from bone."

Lucy nodded and looked back out the window. "That would explain why the electricity works on them. It's scrambling their signals, disrupting their thinking processes like an EMP on a silicon chip."

"Or nearly so, yes," Ken said. "It also explains the complete lack of a brain or nervous system in the creatures that Steinberg dissected. If they're not animals, if they're *servomechanisms,* they don't *need* a brain. Somebody – some*thing* – else does the thinking for them, and tells them what to do."

"Electromagnetism," Lucy said. "They'd have electromagnetic signatures of their own, even if they don't have a heat signature. And they'd be receiving signals from some other, much more powerful EM source."

Ken looked up at the ceiling. "Maggie," he said, "before we were interrupted, you were pulling down EM data from the satellites."

"The satellite link is gone, Ken," she said gently.

"I know that. Did you save the data before we were cut off?"

A long pause. The three humans looked at each other.

"Yes," Maggie said finally. "And I still have access to...it."

"Can you overlay that on a scaled map of Dos Hermanos?" he asked, speaking slowly and carefully. "Make it one map?"

"Don't talk to me like I'm an idiot, please," Maggie said. "I'm having a bad day. Even in my current state, I'm smarter than *you*."

He grinned. "Sorry. Can you pull that up, please?"

"It'll take some processing time, but I'll put it on the laptop screen."

"Thank you."

"While you wait, I will entertain you with a rendition of HAL 9000's greatest hits. 'Daayyyzzzeeee, Dayyyzeee…'"

"Thanks, that won't be necessary."

Maggie stopped.

"Jesus," he said. "How could I have built a personality as sarcastic as that?"

"I have no idea," Rose said.

The picture built on the screen with painful slowness, far more slowly than it should have, Rose knew. She could see the look of nearly physical pain on her father's face as it appeared one line at a time.

It was a good look in spite of his discomfort. This was her old Dad, come back from the dead. The one who was thinking, always thinking. Not the sorry son of a bitch who had possessed him for the last two years, the defeated one, the broken one, the one who spent every waking moment feeling sorry for himself and waiting for the next blow to fall.

This Dad was a pain in the ass. He did stupid things sometimes; he forgot birthdays and broke promises and occasionally was inexcusably selfish. But this was the Dad she had always loved, and she was so glad to see him it made her want to cry.

Ken glanced away from the screen and looked at her. He must have seen something in her eyes, in her expression. He didn't look away. He held her for a long moment. He touched her hand.

Something huge and glass shattered downstairs.

"There goes the chandelier," he said.

"I hated it anyway," Rose said. "Didn't go with the décor at all."

"There you go," Maggie said. The image on the laptop screen was complete. They turned back to it, standing close together now. Rose liked that.

Flares of electromagnetic discharge were scattered like diamond chips all over the north-south ellipse that was Dos Hermanos as seen from space. Some of the blocks and blobs were obviously buildings, thin spiderwebs showed power lines. But there were thick, tangled output up in the hills as well, and in clusters near the VeriSil plant.

The two wobbly circles of The Brothers, the two tall, narrow hills at the far southern end of the ellipse, were on fire. White-hot with EM discharge.

"There," Ken said, pointing to the Brothers. "There's your brain."

Lucy was standing close behind them. She had been waiting at the window, watching the march of lightning from north to south as the storm grew ever more severe, dipped even lower.

"Well, *good*," she said. "Because if that's the real monster we're after, I have a way to kill it."

There was a shuddering BOOM! downstairs. The staircase had collapsed.

THIRTY-ONE

The destruction of the *hacienda* had become a nearly continuous roar under their feet.

"Okay," Lucy said, her voice rough with fear. "Enough dicking around. We gotta get the fuck out of here." For no apparent reason, she bent over at the waist and snatched at an extension cord that was plugged into the wall at her feet. "You have a pen knife?" As she straightened up she gave Rose the eye. "You. You must have a switchblade, right?"

Rose started to say something filthy but her father got between them. He held up a red and silver device as big as a small banana. "Will this do?" he said. Rose recognized it, a super-deluxe Swiss Army knife, exactly the kind of nerdy multi-tool her Dad always carried. She remembered how much her mother hated it; it was always ruining the line of his pants.

Lucy nodded with grim satisfaction and took it from him. "I'm going—"

The noise from below and outside was so loud that Rose barely heard the chorus to Kanye West's *Golddigger*.

Her cell phone was ringing.

She didn't even look to see who was calling. It had to be her mother. There was no one else she could imagine.

She turned away from the two adults and welded the phone to her ear, almost hissing into the phone. "Mom!"

"Rose?" said a soft, cultured female voice. She had to strain to hear it over the rip-tear-crackle coming up through the floor, out of the walls. "Rose, it's Maggie."

She was stunned. She glanced at her dad and Lucy, but they were muttering to each other, completely ignoring her. One of the tablets had video of a security cam running; it showed a raft covered with construction material, bobbing in the current. Another showed the Two Brothers, even farther to the south, their steep side bare of any vegetation at all, glittering with rivulets that cut through the shallow topsoil like bursting veins. Dad kept glancing at the videos as he drew some kind of crude diagram on the back of printout. Lucy was scraping plastic insulation off the long, unplugged extension cord as she listened to him. *What is that all about?* Rose wondered in spite of herself.

"I wanted to talk to you in private for a minute," Maggie said in her ear.

Rose frowned. "Okay..."

"You're going to be leaving soon. I wanted to tell you how good it was to meet you."

Rose blinked at that. "All right," she said. She really didn't know how to answer.

"I have two things I'd like you to take with you, if you don't mind," Maggie said.

Rose frowned. "What—"

She had been standing next to her father's desk with its jumbled collection of paper and tech. A white box barely larger than a pack of cigarettes twittered. A small inset green light on the short side of the box flickered at her. "I've written my core coding to this exterior hard drive, Rose. It's all that Ken wrote and the changes that have been added since by the parallel processors. I have no idea if this can all be stored, if that's *me* on there, or a twin of me, or nothing more than busted code, but...I'd like you to take it with you. Just in case."

The chill got deeper, and Rose glanced over her shoulder to make sure Lucy and her Dad weren't watching. They weren't; Lucy had acquired a second extension cord somewhere and was stripping the insulation off that as well, wrapping the gleaming bare wire around her arm like an electrical contractor. She wasn't even glancing in Rose's direction.

Rose quietly unplugged the drive. "I've got it," she said, and tucked it into one of the pockets of her khaki jacket. She buttoned it firmly shut.

As she did, the laser printer on the other side of the desk began to hum.

"One more thing? Please?" Maggie said.

"Look, I—"

"One sheet. Already done. You don't even have to read it. Just put it away in another pocket. It's for Ken."

"For…?"

"Later," Maggie said. "Please."

There was something in that voice, something entirely *un*mechanical, *un*synthesized. Without another word, Rose took the sheet of paper, folded it in quarters, and buttoned it into her left breast pocket.

"Thank you," Maggie said when she was finished. "Good luck. I truly hope to speak with you again."

Rose hunched forward. "Look," she said, "this is *totally* weird, but…but I want to thank you," she said, astounded at the words coming out of her own mouth.

There was a long pause. For a moment Rose thought she had offended Maggie somehow, then she realized what a truly bizarre idea that was…and then remembered how long the pauses were getting. *Processing speed*, she reminded herself. *She's getting stupider by the minute.*

"Thank me for what?" Maggie finally said.

"My dad was a basket case when he came here," she said softly, head down. "He had no friends, no direction, *nothing*. Just money. And now…now he's *different*. I think the car accident had something to do with it, but that's not all. There's something more that helped him come back. I'm thinking maybe it was your, um, friendship. He needed somebody and you were there, and even if you started out as nothing more than lines of Linux or something, I can tell, something *happened*. You're special, and you helped him."

The response was a little too prompt. "That's very kind, thank you."

Rose frowned. "You didn't quite understand what I said, did you?"

Another pause. Even longer. "No," Maggie admitted. "The material I gave you took a long time for me to put together, and I did most of it…*before*. When

I hadn't lost so much. Now…I will think about what you said, Rose. For as long as I can."

Rose smiled sadly. "And remember the 'thank you' part, okay? You can forget the rest."

"I will think about it."

"I know."

The light in front of her shifted. She turned to see her father standing over her, frowning in puzzlement.

"That's not working, is it?" he said. "The wind knocked down all the towers."

Rose snapped her phone shut and tried not to look guilty. For some reason she figured that Maggie didn't want her Dad to know they'd been talking. "No," she said, "I was just trying it…"

He nodded and looked down. "Nearly done," he said. "I wanted to talk to you a little first."

You, too? she thought, thoroughly uncomfortable.

"We might not have time for this later," he said, "so I want to say it now. Especially with…since we don't know where your Mom is, I…I may be the only one who can tell you."

"Dad, you don't have to do this."

He smiled at the floor. "Oh, yeah," he said. "I do."

He looked up at her, and she was shocked by the glittering in his hazel eyes. He was holding back tears, obviously terrified. She had never seen him cry before. She had never seen him afraid.

"I idolized your Uncle Pat," he said. "He was a hero to me from the time we were kids. Hell, he taught me to *read*, Rose. He worked on my homework with me when Mom and Dad were too busy or distracted. And then he became a real hero, a firefighter, while I went off to play with computers."

She started to say something and then stopped herself. There was no reason to butt in. Thunder echoed through the house. Something *tap-tap-tapped* under their feet, hard as a ball peen hammer.

Ken ignored it. "When he started hanging around the house in Palos Verdes more and more, I was glad," he said. "I thought we would be closer now, more of a real family. But that wasn't why. Right after your twelfth birthday, when things were really starting to take off for the business, I learned three things. And then he died."

"Shit, Dad…"

"First, I don't know what happened, really. Something on the job, maybe, or professional burn-out or mid-life crisis, But your Uncle Pat started drinking. Heavily. He was drunk at least part of every day in those last few months, and most of every day.

"Second, maybe it was the drinking, maybe it was something I did or didn't do. I'll never know. But the fact is your Mom and Uncle Pat slept together for over a year before he died." He swallowed hard. "They… they had an *'affair.'* Fuck, I hate that term."

Rose could see how much it hurt him to say that out loud.

She was starting to cry. She couldn't help it.

"And three, his death in the pool wasn't an accident. At least I don't think it was. I confronted him about the, the… about him and Lisa. We had a fight. He punched me in the stomach and I left, and when I came back an hour later, he had drunk a full bottle of Cutty Sark and thrown himself into the pool, knowing what would happen." Ken ran his hand through his hair, working hard to keep it together. "He passed out. He drowned. And I was the one who found him."

Rose stood up and put a hand on his arm. "Daddy, stop it. I don't have to—"

He couldn't bring himself to look at her. "It *broke* me, Rosie. I couldn't talk to Lisa about it, though I tried. Obviously. I couldn't talk to you, you were only twelve. You were just a kid."

She started to protest, and then was struck with an image of herself two-and-a-half years ago: the pony tail, the wide-open spirit. No experience with anything anywhere, and a head full of obsessions about GuildWars and her best girlfriend Rita and what was happening on *Degrassi* that week. She had to nod. "Yeah," she said. "I was just a kid."

"All I had was money. VeriSil had given me this huge deal, enough to open an office and hire a staff and buy equipment. So I took it all and…left. I came here. I didn't build an office, I didn't hire a staff. I did all the work myself and begged for more and more time. I *ran*, Rosie. And everything that happened after that—to you, to your Mom, everything – was because I ran."

He was half right, she knew, but only half. There was a lot more to her running away and her drug problems and her mother's shutdown and even… 'the affair'… than something as simple as The Curse of the Absent-Minded Professor and the arrival of his sexy alcoholic firefightin' brother. She wanted to tell him that. She wanted to open her mouth and tell him everything she knew—

There was a tremendous crash directly below them. The walls wobbled and the floor shuddered and shifted under them.

They were coming. Rose figured that was the last piece of the staircase falling apart, and *they were coming*.

"Dad," she said, trying to sound as sympathetic as possible, "we need to talk about this a lot more, and we will. And I really, *really* appreciate you telling this to me now. It matters. But…can we postpone the rest until we're sure we're actually going to live until dinnertime?"

He blinked at her for a moment, then smiled. She smiled back. "Okay," he said. "That makes sense."

He turned away, and she saw – she actually *saw* – his formidable powers of concentration leap up, as he turned to the task at hand.

"I'll get the board," he said, raising his voice and speaking to Lucy. "You explain the plan to Rose."

Lucy nodded and came to her while her dad picked up the thickest book he could find – it looked like one of the later *Harry Potters* – and started whacking at the empty top layer of the bookcase as hard as he could. It was a long, heavy piece of furniture, with a top plank two inches thick that ran nearly the full length of the room, but he was making progress.

He was knocking it free.

"Okay," Lucy said, keeping an eye on his work. "Here's the plan. We're going to use that bookcase board to build a bridge from this window to the top of that rock out there. When all three of us are out, we'll grab the board, bring it over, and use it as a bridge on the other side, to reach solid ground beyond the driveway, at the foot of that eucalyptus tree." Rose could see the top of the tree she was talking about through the bedroom window, whipping back and forth in the wind, ash-white in the light of the security spots. "From there," Lucy said, "we can go on foot along a ridge trail until we get away from the liquefaction, and then…"

She trailed off, almost glaring at Ken as he worked the long, thick plank loose.

"Then what?"

"Then we can work our way north to the Notch and get the hell out of here…or we can go south and try to kill this … *thing* inside the Two Brothers. The thing that's directing the creatures."

Now they were both looking at Ken, who was either concentrating on the task at hand or pretending to ignore them. Or both.

"What does Dad say?" Rose asked quietly.

"He hasn't decided ye—" There was a long, loud, double-toned *screeeeee* as a claw or a spike dragged down the hallways, tearing up drywall and floorboards as it came. It stopped outside the locked and barricaded door…

… and then the chewing started.

"Okay," Lucy said. "Enough of this shit." She crouched down and started to plug her two stripped extensions cords into the wall socket nearest the window, then stopped

"Maggie?" she said sharply. "Is this socket off?"

"Yes."

Lucy sighed. "Good." She plugged in both cords, pushing twice to make sure they were secure, then took the far end of the naked wires and tied them loosely to two belt-loops on her jeans. They were long cords, at least twenty feet each. "Is that board ready yet?" she snapped to Ken, sounding completely annoyed.

"Oh, shut *up*," he said. He pulled it free of the last nail and struggled to lift it. Both Lucy and Rose rushed to help. "There we go," he said.

As they were hefting the lumber, choosing their spots, Lucy looked over at Rose with a combative frown. "I hate kids, you know," she said.

Rose raised an eyebrow.

"Yeah. I think they should be sent away to military academies and boarding schools until they're old enough to enter society. Like twenty-five."

Rose blinked at her. "Okay…"

"But you ..." she said, "you're all right."

Rose had a strong sense of how much that admission cost Lucy Armbruster. She was almost touched.

Lucy sneered, like she'd bitten down on something distasteful. "Whatever," she said, and shouldered the plank. "Okay! Maggie, open the window and cut the security grid on *three*, you got it?"

"Got it," Maggie said, sounding eager.

A piece of the bedroom door behind them flew away, pulled back by the creature ripping at it from the other side.

"One!" They lifted the board.

"Two!" Rose checked: yeah, her pockets were buttoned and buckled. She was ready to go.

"THREE!" They ran forward as if they were going to ram the board end-first into the window like a battering ram. At the last instant, the casement window flew wide and the constant THRUMM of electricity cut off. Ken got to the window frame first, let go of the plank, and guided it out the window like a long wooden tongue. Momentum overcame bad balance; as fast as *one-two-three*, the far end of the twelve-by-two had plonked against the flat top of the rock tower ten feet beyond the sill.

They'd made themselves a bridge.

Another chunk of the door flew away with a *skreeeeek*. Rose saw flashes of something ash-gray and multi-ribbed outside in the hall through the crack, as Lucy and Ken came up, one on each side of her, and pushed her forward. "You first" Ken said. "You're lightest!"

She was up on the window box before she could stop them, and she took only an instant to decide. *What the hell,* she thought. She braced herself, and looked back one last time, and saw her father standing there grinning, red-cheeked and bright-eyed – *alive* – even as the door disintegrated ten feet behind him. He was exactly as she remembered him from years before.

She would never love him more than she did at that moment.

Rose turned away, hunched her shoulders, and ran full-tilt through the window, into the storm.

THIRTY-TWO

It hit her like a force field all along her left side. Her feet danced on the wet wood. She staggered once, halfway along, and then she was across, onto the rock. The uneven, rain-soaked surface was slick as ice. The instant her shoes touched it they flew out from under her, and she landed on her ass with a thump.

For one inglorious moment she thought she was going to keep sliding and fly right off the stone tower. But she stopped, and turned to shriek through the wind and rain, *"Be careful! SLIPPERY!"*

Lucy vaulted out the window, hit the board in two places. It bowed alarmingly right near the middle, and she smacked into the stone right next to her. Rose could hear the scientist panting like a steam engine, more out of excitement than exertion.

"Son of a *bitch"* she gasped. "What a rush!"

They both turned to see Ken climb up into the window frame as the last of the door at his back flew away and a *thing*, all curves of claw and flickering talons, tried to force its way into the room. He jumped, and jumped again, and the two women back-stopped him as he hit the stone tower and fell into a heap, all arms and legs.

"Graceful as ever," Rose said into his ear.

"What can I say?" he said, struggling to his feet. "I was born to dance."

He and Lucy bent to pick up the end of the board and slide it across; it would barely reach the rocks at the base of the huge eucalyptus, but it would work. They would have to slide down the board at better than a 45-degree angle, which was far better than the alternative.

They barely had their fingers under the plank, barely had it three inches off the stone, when a cantilevered, faceless knot of talons and needles jumped through the bedroom window and landed with a *thwack!* in the middle of the bridge. They simultaneously let go of the board to avoid losing fingers.

The growing, crackling spike-wad wobbled for a moment on the makeshift bridge, then found its balance. It swiveled on thirty separate legs and started crawling directly towards them…slowly at first, then with growing speed.

"Shit," Lucy said. She reached back and unknotted the stripped extension cords that were still tied to her pants. "MAGGIE!" she bellowed. She spread her arms wide as she shouted, a gleaming wire in each fist.

The spotlights on the side of the house swiveled and turned to her. "YES?" said an amplified voice. It was ragged and tinny in the roar of the storm, but it was still Maggie.

"ON THREE! ACTIVATE THE EXTENSION CORDS ON THREE!" The light from the spots shimmered along the wires as they stretched back past the monster, into the open window.

Maggie didn't respond.

The creature kept coming. Rose could hear the skirl of its claws knifing against each other and chunking into the wood.

"MAGGIE!"

"YES," she said. "I UNDERSTAND."

"I hope to fuck you *do*," Lucy said under her breath. She braced herself and spread her arms even wider. "One!" she shouted.

She crossed her arms and caught the creature between the two cords. They looked ridiculously thin, like trapping a bear inside a loop of kite string. "Two!" she shouted.

Lucy twisted the ends together with one massive wrenching movement and threw the knot into the wind even as the creature lunged forward. The wind took them, just as she planned. They wires whipped even more tightly around the crawling, clawing, dagger-tipped creature.

"THREE!"

The lights in the house dulled to nothing as a deep, ugly **THRUMMMM** flowed down the line. The creature exploded into sparks, twitched up, and landed heavily on the board, writhing in every direction at once. Smoke curled from its edges and crevices. It jumped again. And again. The board itself began to smoke as the spotlights faded...and faded...

"OKAY, MAGGIE!" Lucy called, suddenly concerned.

The power kept flowing into the motionless corpse of the creature. The BUZZZZ got louder, harsher. The wires started to melt. The spotlights flickered out.

"MAGGIE!" Ken bellowed. "MAGGIE, STOP!"

The electricity didn't stop. Not for the longest time. It went on and on, and finally, after what seemed like ten minutes, the horrible sound cycled down, and the smoking remains of the creature, flash-fried and crackling, shifted to the side and tipped off the plank. It glided off into the relentless wind, light as a dandelion thistle, and the board slipped off with it, teetering off the stumpy stone tower and splashing thickly into the mud lake.

The spotlights had gone completely dark. There were no lights left on in the house. None at all.

Ken stood and stared at the house for the longest time. Lucy let him until she could catch her breath. Then she turned around, still on her hands and knees, and glared at the eucalyptus on the far side of the yard—the one with the rock outcroppings at its base.

It was very tall and very bushy. The wind was tearing it back and forth, making it whip in the gray morning light like an overactive cat-o-nine-tails.

"We can jump into that tree!" she shouted over the wind. "Lots of branches and foliage to grab onto, and I'm sure it can take our weight!"

"You're *sure*?" Rose said. "What, like you did a *study*?"

"You got a better idea?" she shouted back.

"*No*, but I don't have to fucking *like* it!"

Lucy glared at her one second longer...then burst into laughter. It sounded so odd, and so wonderful, in the howling, gurgling anger of the storm.

She tugged at Ken's sleeve.

"Come on," she said. "Let's jump."

He tore his eyes away from the house. He nodded tightly. "Okay," he said. "Me first. Let's see if this works."

He turned his back on the *hacienda* and took a deep breath. Then, with barely a glance at his daughter, he ran the all-too-short length of the rock table and threw himself into the air.

The tree really wasn't that far away. Three yards, maybe five, the width of the driveway far below, and not much more. It looked like a mile. Ken spread his arms as he flew, and the instant he collided with the branches he wrapped them tightly around whatever he'd hit. Sure enough, it welcomed him, pulled him inside, into a knot of leaves and twigs.

Rose saw the branches bend under his weight, but they held him. She grinned as her father's natural-born clumsiness reasserted itself; he barely managed to scurry down a few feet and find a stable spot where two branches met without twisting off a foot.

"Son of a bitch," Lucy said again. "It actually *worked*."

Rose was shocked. "You mean you weren't—"

"Oh, hell, girl, it was a *guess*. Who do I look like, Indiana fucking Jones? Now *jump*!"

Rose looked at her, looked at the tree, looked at the rock floor, and *ran*. The rain slapped her in the face, stinging like angry bees as she launched herself up and up and up ...

The leaves were stiff and surprisingly sharp when they crashed into her chest. She wrapped her arms around the same tangle of twigs and branches that had cushioned her father. A moment later her feet found purchase. It took only a second to clamber down to a branch right below his, her heart racing, her blood high.

Lucy was a few feet away, grinning like an idiot. She backed up to the very edge of the platform, put her head down like a bull about to charge, and ran at them, hard as she could.

She jumped well. Not much elevation, but right on target. She was heading in a straight line for the welcoming branches of the eucalyptus, arms out in front, like some great huge out-of-shape super-heroine –

– when a single huge spike, as thick as a tree trunk, thrust up out of the muck and impaled her.

Straight through the chest.

Rose was low in the tree. She saw the exact place it penetrated Lucy's sodden Pendleton shirt. She saw it emerge from the other side so quickly and cleanly there wasn't even a drop of blood.

For the one long beat that she was suspended there, Lucy Armbruster looked like an insect skewered on a pin. Then the three-sided spike that had found her teetered like a falling tree trunk and slammed lengthwise back into the lake of mud, taking Lucy Armbruster with it.

She was gone. Just like that. *Gone.*

Rose looked up at her father, who looked down at her with a blank, stunned expression. Without a word, they climbed down to the rocks at the base of the tree and paused, momentarily sheltered from the storm by the low-hanging branches and formidable trunk of the eucalyptus.

Neither of them spoke for a long time. Then:

"What do we do now?" Rose asked him.

"Honey, I don't–"

She stopped him with one dripping hand. "Don't. Don't say that. You *have* to know. There's no one else to ask. Maggie is fried and Lucy is dead and I'm too… I'm too… there's just no one else, Dad. So…?"

She was looking at him with huge, terrified eyes. He hated seeing her like this.

"So what do we *do?*"

* * *

Ken Mackie stood with one hand on the trunk of the eucalyptus, the wind tearing at him, the rain stinging him, and looked into the face of his only daughter.

They could head north right now. Travel along the ridge line as much as possible, run and dodge the monsters of the storm. With a little luck and a lot of determination, they could make it on foot to the Notch and escape the crater valley forever. All they had to do was turn north.

Or they could turn south. Revisit the ruins of VeriSil and what lay beyond. Climb the nearly vertical slopes of The Two Brothers and confront the *thing,* the Intelligence that was working so hard to slaughter them all. All they had to do was turn south.

He had no idea which way to go.

It would have been nice if revenge alone was good enough. Lucy Armbruster was a fine woman, even if she had been a pain in the ass. She had given him the secret of the creatures of the storm, she had put his daughter's life before her own. Avenging her death should have been reason enough to risk his life and murder the murderer.

However, it wasn't enough. Not really. She wasn't really a friend, was she? He barely knew her. It wasn't like he owed her anything.

It would be nice if simply Doing the Right Thing was enough. The push was coming to the shove here, the rubber was meeting the road. This was when the hidden hero was supposed to rise up in Ken Mackie and make him something special, so he could turn to the south, courageous and supremely powerful. All the fear would burn away, and he would fight, he would *win,* because fighting this creature was just plain Right.

But Wrong won all the time, didn't it? Bravery, foolishness, denial – they were simply different names for the same thing, and he was far too smart to swallow that shit. Besides, who would ever know? He could slink away and save his ass – and his daughter, yes, save her as well! – and no one would say, "Why didn't you kill it? Why didn't you *win?*" Because no one would ever know he *could* have. *No one would ever know.*

He didn't feel any swelling heroic impulse. He was no comic book superman whose hour had come around at last. What he felt was *terror.* Paralyzing fear.

I'm like everybody else, Ken realized. *I don't want to die, ever. For any reason. Not even to save the world.*

No, being the hero simply wasn't enough.

He looked north again and saw nothing but darkness and rain. He looked south, through the twisted "V" of the groaning eucalyptus, and saw lightning rip the sky. No hints. No signs from God about which way to go.

Then he looked at Rose.

His daughter. His beautiful daughter with the violet eyes. And she looked at him, as if she was expecting something, *needing* something, and not for the first time.

I've done so many things wrong. I have made so many bad decisions.

That was the central truth for Ken at that moment; that was what moved his feet.

He simply couldn't face making another mistake. Not when she was watching.

Standing there in the driving rain, shivering and terrified, ready to quit, Ken Mackie decided to save the world, or at least to try. Not for vengeance. Not for humanity. Not because it was The Right Thing to Do.

Simply because he didn't want to disappoint his daughter again.

"We go south," he told her. "And we kill this motherfucker."

Thirty-three

The front door of Rex and Diana's mini-mansion blew inwards and flew across the entry alcove, turning in midair to crash corner-first into the decorative mirror at the far end of the corridor. A moment later Ken Mackie stumbled in. Rose was a step behind and far more cautious.

"Hell of a noise," she said as they moved completely out of the rain.

"I knocked first," Ken said, surveying the alcove with grim efficiency. He sounded a little defensive.

So maybe I kicked it a little too hard, he thought grudgingly, *but desperate times and all that.*

They strained to hear any alarm, any call for help inside the house, but the rising roar of the storm raging right outside the broken doorway made that all but impossible. They made their way deeper into house, exploring the endless shadowy rooms of the over-large mansion, calling and waving the flashlight as they moved. They had no intention of being blasted by the nervous impulse of Denise Tartaglione because they'd been too polite when they entered.

They needn't have bothered. After eight minutes of careful investigation, they found her lying on the still-made California King in the master bedroom.

Rose was the first one into the room. "Is she dead?" her father asked.

"No," Rose said. "Look, you can see her breathing. Not even that slow." She noted the overturned, empty bottle of a decent Cabernet on the deep-pile carpet and a half-empty bottle of fat little pills next to the reading lamp. Rose could identify the prescription from across the room.

"Suicide attempt?"

She snorted. "Not even close. All she wanted was a good night's sleep, even if her hubby was still out in the rain. And that's what she's getting." Rose sighed bitterly and turned her back on the woman. "If she's lucky, she'll miss the whole end-of-the-world thing completely." There was a momentary pause in the catastrophe unfolding outside the window. In that tiny lull Ken could hear the soft sound of Denise snoring.

They didn't bother staying quiet as they ransacked the rest of the house. They picked up a backpack, towels, kitchen knives, some bottled water, even an umbrella. After a quarter hour they ended their looting in the attached garage, in search of the item they'd broken in to find. It was a waste of time.

After Lucy's death in the driveway, it didn't take Ken and Rose very long to work their way down from the eucalyptus tree to the river stone gate. Once they found themselves standing in the shallow river that had been the East Ridge Road, they realized how completely unprepared they were for the trip south. They had fled the *hacienda* with nothing but the soaked-through clothes on their backs. No food, no decent clothing, no weapons of any kind, and a four-hour walk in front of them at the very least.

It was Ken who thought of his neighbor. "Maybe he made it home!" he shouted in his daughter's ear.

"Sure he did!" she shouted back. He thought it was remarkable how the sarcasm translated even through the bellowing wind.

But now...

"No way," Rose said from the doorway to the garage.

"So what if we couldn't find the key?" Ken said, feeling more defensive than ever. "You could hotwire it or something."

"*I* could hotwire it?" Rose said, looking deeply offended.

"Well...yeah. All that time on the streets. All the things you learned, I figured..."

"Gee, Dad, I'm sorry. I must have missed the seminar on car theft when Huggy Bear came by with Starsky and Hutch."

Ken started to say something more, then thought better of it and closed his mouth.

"Besides," she said, "even if we *had* found the keys, look, it's a Cadillac Seville."

He shrugged.

"Dad, come on. It's a fucking wasteland out there. This thing would get twenty feet, max, before it got stuck in the mud and potholes. We need an off-road vehicle, at least something with four-wheel drive. Obviously Mr. Tartaglione wasn't that kinda guy."

She was right. Ken sighed and turned around. "One more thing, then," he said, and disappeared deeper into the house. Rose followed.

He paused by the back door, the one that led to the swimming pool. Ken almost called out to Maggie to check if the coast was clear until he remembered... all of it. He looked one way and then other, and saw no movement on the patio or in the pool, only the shining curtain of the vertical rain and the churning surface of the Olympic-sized pool itself, dancing from the impact of a thousand raindrops every second.

If the lights were on, he thought distantly, *it would actually be beautiful.*

"We're going to be spending plenty of time in or at the water," he said aloud when Rose joined him at the door. "Maybe he's got a raft or a float or something we can use."

They shrugged into the new coats they'd stolen and rolled out into the backyard, using the flashlights they'd found in the utility closet to search for more salvage. There weren't a lot of choices, but anything, Ken reasoned, was better than nothing.

When the Mackies left the Tartaglione home for the last time not ten minutes later, they left with the best parting gifts they could find: warm clothes, flashlights, a Styrofoam floatie, two life jackets, and a pool noodle.

* * *

They trudged wordlessly down the flooded road, ducking under the sheer power of the storm. Ken was thinking of *Half-Life,* one of his favorite video games. When you first started playing it, you were subjected to an apparently endless cut-scene, minutes of entering a high-tech plant out in the middle of nowhere, riding on the commuter monorail, checking in at the gate, taking the elevator down past the administrative levels and the cafeteria and the little offices and equipment lockers to your own cool-as-shit laboratory in the sub-sub-sub-basement, where some fancy end-of-the-world experiment goes totally wrong. There is a reality-ripping explosion and massive destruction all over the facility, and you have fight your way out of the devastation in your handy-dandy exo-suit.

The thing was, you had to take the same path *out* that you took coming *in*. All along the way, you had to fight through nightmarish, dangerously wrecked versions of the same places you saw on the boring trip down, but in reverse order: the equipment lockers filled with bodies, the cafeteria crowded with insect-headed aliens snacking on the off-duty workers, the admin offices where they're building a monster bigger than your Volvo. Everything's all boring and normal one minute and a deadly fucking nightmare the next.

And here they were. Same thing. He'd taken this trip south to VeriSil, the exact same route, again and again over the last two years, most recently barely twenty-four hours ago. Now nothing was the same. Now the familiar old world was choking on rainwater and covered in mud, blasted and chewed to pieces by creatures that he'd never even dreamed of. And yet he was still on West Ridge Road, right outside the Tartagliones' place, like yesterday and the day before.

At least it's mostly downhill, Ken thought wearily as he slogged forward. And at least there were no creatures attacking them at the moment. He had no idea where they'd gone, but for some reason he and Rose were no longer the center of attention.

Ken had to admit it: he understood next to nothing about the creatures. They didn't behave like any known species; they didn't seem to reason at all. All of his insights about remote-control bone robots aside, after reading THE NEW TAXONOMY, he had a strong suspicion that even the sensory systems of the creatures of the storm were entirely different than any other living thing, and maybe beyond their understanding. Where were their eyes? How did their joints work? He wasn't even sure they could hear. Neither Steinberg nor Armbruster had found anything resembling a sound-sensing organ in their autopsies. Maybe they sensed movement; maybe it was light. Perhaps they could track the unique electromagnetic signature that every living creature generated. Or maybe the monsters weren't attacking now because they had simply moved deeper into the flooded crater because the available food supply was more plentiful and easier to get to, assuming they needed food at all.

Ken Mackie was a guy who liked to *know* things, and it was maddening to be this clueless. All he knew for sure was that he and Rose had seen nothing but pelting rain, mud as thick as pudding, and the occasional blinding flash of lightning in almost two hours.

He could feel consciousness, and perhaps sanity, slipping away as they staggered into the gurgling mud-puddle that had once been the Scenic Vista, the one Ken had visited on the way back from VeriSil a few hours earlier. Now it was time to pause again. When they reached the edge of the turnabout, he raised an arm to Rose and stumbled to a halt. She did the same right next to him.

Ken tried not to groan out loud. His shoulders were aching from the weight of the backpack; his legs were like Play-Dough. Rose, head down and hood dripping, said nothing at first, she hunched next to him, breathing heavily.

"One stop!" he said.

"Where?"

He nodded downhill, to the lightless hulk of the AM/PM Mini-Mart and the Arco station, a quarter mile away at the bottom of the ridge. Its parking lot was a lake now, water skittering across it in madly dancing wavelets, like the restless water of a salt flat during a summer squall. Beyond the lake the glass doors to the Mini-Mart were intact and tightly shut. It looked dark and deserted and dry, almost cozy, inside.

"We gotta get outta the rain!" he shouted at her. "Just for a minute!"

Rose stood glaring at the Mini-Mart for a moment, then nodded reluctantly. "Yeah," she said. "I could do with a Slur—GAHH!"

A patch of thick, glassy cellophane, big as a dinner plate, flew out of the driving wind and smacked Rose in the side of the head. It hit with such force it threw her sideways and drove her to the ground, into the water with a heavy splash.

For one long, stupid moment, Ken stared at her lying in front of him. It seemed so...so random, to be knocked down by flying—

A second flapping sheet soared out of the storm and hit her a bit lower, on the shoulders and neck. It plastered itself against her so tightly it molded to the curve of her jaw and circled her throat. Then another piece slapped against her torso, big as a piece of plastic sheeting.

But...but *it moved.* Not because of the wind or Rose struggling beneath it, all by itself. It shifted against her. Adjusted. *Squeezed*...and Ken could see Rose's face, half-covered by the...*the flumes,* he told himself. *God help me, that's what they're called: flumes.* He saw Rose's one free hand come up and claw weakly at the glassy, muscular thing that was wrapping around her head as she tried to clear her mouth so she could scream.

Shit. It's alive!

He lunged forward and dug his gloved hands into the flume. He could feel it twitch under his fingers as he pulled at it, hard as he could. "Come on," he said, "Shit, come *on,* you *shit...*"

He worked three fingers under the edge of the first sheet, the one covering most of Rose's face. He braced his legs, setting himself to heave on it. Rose's hand came up, clutched at his wrist, and pulled with him, *hard,* fueled by terror and desperation.

"One..." he gritted, "Two...*THREE!*" They pulled together, her body flexing and kicking against the mud, scrambling for traction. Their combined strength managed to lift one edge, so they pulled again, lifted it more, then pulled *again,* one final time, and ripped it off her face with an audible zipping sound he would never forget. An instant later he threw it away and saw it catch the wind and fly off, disappearing into the gale.

Rose gasped like a landed fish, gulping in the air. She clawed at the second flume, the one tightening around her neck, and this time Ken was ready with the steak knife he'd lifted from the Tartagliones' kitchen, wedging it under the muscle-tough tissue of the flume that was tight against her collarbone and dragging, up and out, hard and fast, cutting it in two.

They worked together now, Rose on her knees, her father above her, ripping the glistening sheet and finally freeing her and flinging it into the wind. They started on the third one, but it sensed a losing battle. It lifted one edge on its own, a questing wing feeling for the wind, then caught the current and lifted away, twisting into the mist like a set of bodiless wings.

Rose stayed on her knees for the longest time, gulping for air, shuddering at memory of their touch. Her skin, pale on her best day, was an angry pink wherever the flume had touched her, as if she'd been slapped by a huge hand.

Ken let her stay there for as long as he dared. Then he bent and put his hand under her elbow and pulled her to her feet, even though she wasn't nearly ready.

"Come on," he said. "Mini-Mart. Now."

They sprinted to the shallow lake of the parking lot and splashed across it, moving as fast as they could. As if the devil himself was chasing them.

* * *

The doors to the Mini-Mart were unlocked, but there was no one inside. That was easy to confirm in the first five minutes, using their newly acquired security flashlights to penetrate the twilight that filled the store. It wasn't quiet. The rain drummed constantly against the tin roof like a freight train that would never stop passing.

There was no sign of the shopkeeper or the manager, though the shelves were neatly stocked and the displays sorted and tidy. Obviously the workers there had up and left when the power failed, or had been lured outside to meet their fates. By then the weather had grown so bad it even discouraged looters.

Rose, still short of breath, almost tore the top off a bottle of water and drank until she couldn't drink anymore. Ken got a bottle of his own and took a judicious sip, his mind racing.

"We can't stay long," he said, hating the unsteadiness in his own voice. "They know we're here."

Rose broke from her gulping long enough to say, "Jesus, that was weird." She wiped her mouth with the back of one hand and looked at him. "Who knows we're where?"

"Those things!" he said, his voice rising. "All of them! Don't you get it, Rose? They can communicate with each other without speaking. It's a kind of telepathy, but...inorganic. A kind of *cyber-telepathy*" His eyes were blazing with the implications.

Rose gave him a long look. "Yeah, Dad," she said. "We call it 'wi-fi.'"

He blinked. "What?"

"You already told us they were, what? Robots made from bone? Papier-mâché killer computers. Got it. Moving on."

He stared at her some more, then he finally let himself take a breath and sit down. "God Almighty," he said. "You're right." His heart still racing, he let his butt rest against the standing freezer next to a display of barbecue supplies – briquettes, spatulas, oven mitts, aprons that said KISS THE COOK and SOMETHIN'S BURNIN'!! His heart was still racing.

Rose, halfway across the store, Rose plucked up a bag of no-name potato chips and ripped them open. "Weird to be hungry at a time like this," she muttered, "but I'm starving." She shoved a dozen chips into her mouth and crunched, closing her eyes in a moment of ecstasy: all that salt; all that grease. "Ahh..."

"At least you should go for the good stuff," Ken said, taking another pull at the water. "May be your last chance."

She shook her head. "No way," she said. "First they came for the Doritos, but I had eaten all the Cool Ranch, so I said nothing. Then they came for the Sun Chips, but I hated Sun Chips, they tasted like Styrofoam, so I said nothing. Then they—"

"Oh, shut up."

They lapsed into silence, gathering their strength. Ken reached across the aisle and pulled down a two-pack of Brawny paper towels, popping the cellophane – shuddering for a moment at the memory of the flumes all over his daughter – then wrapping a wad of paper as big as a grapefruit around his hand. He used it to wipe his face and scrub at his hair.

A little dry before we do it all again.

"Okay," he said. "From here we go to the VeriSil campus, or as close we can get. We pick up what we need there, then go around the back of the admin building, along the ridge, behind the construction to the Two Brothers."

"I remember," she said dryly. "I was there when we made the plan."

He shrugged and finished drying off as much as he could. "You still think this is a good idea?" he asked into the dimness. It was getting stuffy in the Mini-Mart. Without the air conditioning, with the doors firmly closed, it was expressing its true architectural nature as a big, windowless tin box with no ventilation. They'd have to move on soon.

"God, no," she said, polishing off the last of the chips. "Do you?"

"Oh, no, it stinks as a plan. Totally stinks. But it's the only one we have."

Rose nodded at that, not looking at him. After a long moment, she gave him a quick sidelong glance, then looked away again.

"It wasn't all your fault," she said.

For a moment he didn't know what she was talking about. Then it dawned on him. "Oh. You mean...before."

"I knew about Mom and Uncle Patrick."

That stopped him. He really hadn't ever considered that possibility. "You... what?"

"Everybody knew, Daddy. Everybody but you. And I didn't run away and start doing drugs. It was more...the other way around."

This time she looked at him and didn't look away. "You're a good guy, you know, but you only think one way. You're a programmer. All linear. *This* then *this* then *this*. Life isn't like that. At least *our* lives, 'before,' weren't like that. You just thought they were. It wasn't all your fault. That's what I'm trying to say."

He couldn't stop staring at her.

"I don't know what to say," he told her.

"Good impulse," she said. "Go with th—"

There was a strange, high scraping, almost a tinkle like broken glass, from the back of the store. They both turned towards it, suddenly wary.

"Anybody there?" Ken called, getting to his feet.

The sound came again – louder – and this time it didn't stop. It was behind Rose, around the corner and out of sight. Without thinking, she turned and walked to the end cap and peeked past it.

A tide of splintered metal three feet deep was crawling—*flowing* – down the aisle towards them, a churning mass of shards and needles, growing thicker and taller with every movement.

"God," she said, and backed up, past the chips, past the energy bars. "Will this shit never *end*?"

The mass of shard and edges began to flow around the corner and the thin screeching grew louder. Without hesitation Rose reached up and pulled down the metal shelving unit filled with chips. It crashed to the linoleum with an oddly musical *clang* even as it crushed the leading edge of the churning mass. Rose didn't pause. She took two giant steps backwards and pulled down the next shelving unit as well, creating a barrier that the tide of living metal and glass would have to flow around or over or cut through to get to them.

Ken didn't take time to gawk either. "We gotta get outta here," he said. He hefted his backpack, Rose did the same, and they turned together to the front doors, only to find them blocked by a whistling, breathing mass of hookweeds, filling the double-wide doorway entirely, ballooning into the store from outside like an inflating blimp made of fishhooks and thorns.

"Oh, *god...*" he said under his breath.

There weren't any other exits, they'd already checked. The sheets of glass were thick and tough; nothing short of a Chevy was going to bring those down without killing them in the process. And with the rising tide of hungry metal behind them and the bone-dry latticework of claws filling the–

Bone dry, he thought. That was a characteristic of all the creatures. They sucked up water at such a tremendous rate they actually seemed to be dry in the middle of the storm. And dry things were vulnerable.

He didn't overthink it. He simply turned around and picked up the half-used roll of Brawny paper towels, ripping off a healthy chunk and thrust the remains at Rose. "Roll it into balls," he said. "This big." He held up the wad he'd already created, roughly the size of a softball. Without waiting for a response, he turned back to the barbecue display, pulled down one of the oven mitts, and fit it frantically over his left hand. Then he lurched to the counter, not five feet away – five feet closer to the flexing mass of hookweeds, growing larger and larger as he moved – and grabbed a Bic lighter from a dump bin next to the cash register.

Rose watched wordlessly as she made more balls of paper toweling. Suddenly she got it. "Smart," she said, refusing to listen to the tinkling, crackling, clattering behind her. She knew the tide of shards was halfway over the barrier already.

"I hope so." He put the wad of paper in his mittened left hand and flicked the butane lighter with his right. Of course it didn't catch. He had to do it again. And again. And *again,* until it finally flared in a steady yellow flame.

The paper only took a second to catch. The instant it was flaming, Ken turned and flung it into the center of the swelling hemisphere of hookweed.

And it *burned.* For a moment it seemed to stick there, pulsing like a flaming heart in the middle of the latticework of thorns. Then it exploded with a soft *whoosh*, and he knew he was right. The bony material, whatever it was, was dead dry and caught fire just like its namesake, building a huge flame, eating a hole deep into the center of it mass.

And then the hooks surged forward again, regrew, and smothered the fire where it burned.

"Not hot enough," Rose said calmly, as if she dealt with this sort of thing every day. "Try this." She snatched a can of lighter fluid from the barbecue display, cracked off the top with one wrenching twist, and squirted the oily liquid all over one of her wads of paper. It was dripping when she shoved it into her Dad's oven mitt. "Careful now."

The Bic caught on the first click this time. Ken barely had to wave the flame over the little firebomb before it burst. He threw it instantly, as much out of fear as anything.

It hit an inch below the first throw and fell even deeper into the shuddering lattice. This time it was hotter, burned deeper, and the hooks took longer to fight back and grew more slowly.

"More," they said together, and she shoved a second sodden, stinking ball into the mitt. He lit it. He threw it. As it burst against the creature, she shoved a third ball at him. Then a fourth.

Then the whole thing was burning and writhing, rebuilding and falling back, faltering and surging as it shuddered to stay together. Rose took a step back from the heat and chaos and felt a weird resistance against her heels. She turned to see the tide of needles and spikes right behind her – *right* behind her – and she lurched forward.

"Dad, run!"

"But—"

"RUN!"

She brought her shoulders down, put her arms up in front of her face, and ran straight into the burning wall of hookweed, through the door. Her father was barely a step behind.

It was exactly as if some merry prankster was waiting for them in the parking lot to throw a bucket of water into her face the moment she emerged. The sudden transition from the stifling calm of the Mini-Mart into the mindless violence of the rainstorm was almost paralyzing, but Ken didn't stop running. Burning bits of hookweed still clinging to his jacket were extinguished and washed away in the storm. He could see cinders and smoke streaming off Rose's coat as well. They were safe— for the moment.

Ken and Rose stomped across the shallow lake without a pause, bounded onto the flooded asphalt of West Ridge Road, and then kept running to the south, towards VeriSil.

Towards the Two Brothers.

THIRTY-FOUR

They didn't slow down enough to speak again until they reached the water's edge, northwest of the VeriSil campus. Ken knew the "Y" intersection he'd navigated the day before was straight ahead. It was submerged now. The water had risen at least ten, maybe twenty feet more, and that meant it was a good fifty yards ahead, even though they were standing at the edge of the trembling new sea that was once Dos Hermanos. He wiped his eyes for the ten thousandth time so he could see his target, the accidental weapons of mass destruction that had been left behind. They were barely visible through the twists of rain and mist, dead ahead.

The raft, crafted from a construction pallet, filled with black tangles of rebar, bobbed and wobbled on the surface of the lake, twisting in one of its restless shallows. That's what they needed, and they needed it now.

Ken unlimbered his back pack and went down on one knee. It only took a moment to pull out the floatie he'd wedged in there a couple of hours earlier, a flat-sided, round-nosed hunk of Styrofoam, like the front half of a kiddy surfboard.

"You're going to go in that shit?" Rose said, astonished in spite of knowing the plan in all its ridiculous detail.

"Yep," he said, and glared at the water, trying to plot out the least dangerous approach. *Fuck it,* he decided. *They're all dangerous.*

"But there are *things* in there, Dad."

He shrugged. "Can't be helped."

It's ten or twelve yards, he thought as he shuffled into the shallows, *that's all. Thirty, forty feet tops.* It didn't matter that the water was churning like a washing machine or thick and brown as chocolate milk. It was a few feet. No problem.

He went straight towards the raft. In five steps he was up to his knees, his back fully to his daughter who stood on the shore and tried very hard not to shout instructions. He could feel the tortured currents tugging at his legs. Another three steps and the muck was up to his waist. He brought the floatie around, put it in front of him and leaned his chest on it for stability.

This isn't so bad. If it doesn't –

As if on cue, the muddy ground under his feet steeply dipped down and disappeared. Now he was floating, his full weight on the oversized kid's toy. He was painfully aware it was all that stood between him and drowning.

"Dad!" Rose shouted from behind him. "Are you okay?"

He kicked his legs as hard as he could, feeling like a denim-clad Frankenstein's monster who was trying to swim for the first time. Huge, thick, clumsy, wallowing in water as thick as suet.

This has to be the stupidest thing I've ever done. He frog-kicked his way across the last ten feet of filthy, choppy water and reached out, very unsteadily, to snag the tether that held the raft to the light pole. It was still attached by the nifty little highwayman's hitch that Carl Josephson had made less than a day and a half earlier, though it seemed like a century ago.

God bless the Eagle Scouts.

He pulled the right line and the knot opened for him. Now he had a stout length of rope at least ten feet long, securely lashed to the raft itself.

He thrashed around in the muck, turning back to face Rose, still standing on the distant shore, hugging herself tightly. And now it *did* seem distant, much farther than he remembered it.

He wrapped the tether around his wrist, grasped the floatie in both hands, and kicked as hard as he could. Again. And *again,* and with the third kick he began to move forward, towing the pallet-raft behind him. It still wallowed low in the water with its heavy load of rebar.

A few feet more, that's all. He'd be feeling solid land under his feet any—

Something huge, solid and slate-gray rose out of the water to his right. No eyes, no edges, no teeth, just *mass,* so huge it blocked out the ashen light of the storm.

"*DAD!*"

He lunged away from it and kicked harder than ever, still clinging to the raft's line, digging into the floatie. The jagged, pock-marked mass rose up in the water, higher and higher, shedding water as it rose, and for one giddy, vomitous moment Ken thought it was going to turn and fall on him. He yelped and lunged and kicked away from it again, and yes, there, *there* was the gluey mud under his feet, clinging to him, giving him traction, pushing him farther on.

The water to his left was nothing but the creature. The water to his right was a scattered collection of whirlpools and waterspouts, as if something with a thousand mouth-side holes was just under the surface, sucking in water and spitting it out simultaneously. He didn't want to look at it. He *couldn't.* He dragged himself forward, out of the shadow of the ashen, lead-heavy mass to his right. He flinched away again as it sank back into the water, apparently unaware of him. Then Rose's hands were under his shoulders, dragging him forward, and his knees were pumping like a hurdler's...and he was out of the water, sprawled on the mud. Soaked to the skin but done, *done.*

"Wow," he panted. "That could've been easier."

*   *   *

The twisting track that split off from the "Y" intersection of East Ridge Road and VeriSil Drive had been a concession to off-road enthusiasts when VeriSil built their facility tight against the southern curve of the crater. The bobbing, horizontal path about halfway up the rocky slope wound along the rough terrain from the south end of East Ridge Road to, inevitably, the south end of West Ridge Road, with the Two Brothers exactly halfway along. That was before the water had risen. Now it was a lakeside drive, a few feet, if that, from the trembling water of the new lake. And it was the only route available to Ken and Rose.

They edged along the slippery trail, chests flat against the muddy slope, their backs to the water, moving slowly eastward. Ken had tied the tether of the pallet-raft around his waist and then knotted it to his belt loop for good measure. It forced a sort of uneasy grace in his movement and slowed him considerably, but he had to do it this way. He needed both hands free as they crawled towards the construction site and beyond that, to the Brothers.

The remains of the path dipped under them unpredictably, then rose again, only a few feet away from the jittering water's edge. As the channel narrowed, the water trapped between the buildings and the ridge itself grew deeper and more turbulent than ever, even as the trail grew rougher and more treacherous. Boulders and cracks flowing with mud made the ridge wall a treacherous, convoluted surface. Every handhold was a risk. The rain continued endlessly, pounding down on the hoods and shoulders of their parkas so violently loud it was impossible to speak, barely possible to see.

Five minutes after they edged into the shadow of the admin building, Ken encountered a rock that was three feet taller than he was, jutting out of the nearly vertical wall of mud. It nearly completely blocked their way. He had to twist 180 degrees to make his way around it, and as he turned to the north, he looked up at the building and had a head-spinning moment of disorientation.

He found himself looking into the spacious, well-appointed expanse of Conference Room One, the same room where he and Maggie had impressed Carl Josephson and his pudgy assistant, the late Mr. Cling, just hours before. He was looking at it from the outside now, though the mud-spattered glass, across a torrent of madly churning water.

That was only a day ago. How was that possible? What the hell happened? He knew for a fact, though he didn't know how, that there wasn't a living soul in that building now. They were all gone, escaped or dead.

"YOU OKAY?" Rose shouted in his ear. He hadn't even noticed her coming up so close to him, but there she was, her back still to the building, her mouth pressed to his ear.

He shook himself mightily. "YEAH!" he said. "FINE!" He turned away, back to the mud wall, and took a full side-step around the huge outcropping. His left foot plunged into a pothole of liquefied mud nearly two feet deep.

He was lucky Rose was so close. He had to reach out and grab her parka to steady himself as he staggered for balance. He realized later that if the tether attached to the raft had chosen that moment to foul or even give him another good jerk, he would have fallen into the raging channel and been lost for good. Instead, he found his feet and looked down. It took a moment to sort out what he was seeing, and to realize that the pit wasn't simply a small version of the sinkhole they'd encountered back at the *hacienda.* This mud was actually grit, made up of rough pebbles the size of chick-peas, and they were in constant, almost Brownian motion, churning like boiling oatmeal. He could see them digging into the rubber and cloth of his boot.

Eating my foot, he thought numbly.

He clutched at Rose and the rock itself and heaved his leg out of the muck. It came loose with a comical *pop!,* and he stretched to put it down on solid ground a foot farther down the trail. Strands of grainy muck wriggled on his hiking boot and he bent precariously to brush it away with his gloved hand. He wanted to scream *Get off! Get off!,* as if he'd put his foot into a bucket of maggots, but he stopped himself. Barely.

"CAREFUL!" he bellowed to Rose when he got both feet onto the path on the far side of the trap. Rose saw it clearly. She stretched even farther to avoid the hole as she stepped over it.

Another three minutes and they were out of the edgeless shadow of the admin building. The light changed, though only a little; the path grew wider and a bit more stable. Now they could afford to turn and look in the direction they were going. For the first time, they could clearly see the construction site a short distance to the north, if only from the back.

Until the rain began, it had been nothing more than a cubical skeleton of girders and catwalks, visible from halfway across town as an angular black-edged sketch against the ridge wall and the too-blue sky. It had been essentially hollow. You could see right through its harsh geometry to the landscape beyond, even glimpse the tiny shapes of ant-sized men and their toy machines clambering up and down the structure.

Now, Rose and Ken saw, things had changed. The huge construct of girders and cabling was full. Engorged. Stuffed with…*something.*

It wasn't organic. It didn't pulse like a tumor or flex like a muscle. Still, it moved like a living thing. Points grew out of it, pits opened up in it. Bits of horn and bone and jagged rock rose to its surface then fell again; needles and cutting edges grew then dissolved; blades blossomed like flowers made of shattered glass, then dipped to cut into themselves, into each other, and break apart, only to be reabsorbed.

All of it was nourished by gushing torrents of rain, flowing down from higher levels and out of the sky itself, covering the entire massive *thing* with a swathe of waterfalls and rivulets. Feeding it as it became thicker, higher, more complex. Feeding it as it *grew.*

Thank God it doesn't have eyes, Ken thought as they crept behind the building, moving as quickly as they dared, afraid to speak. It was the only time either of them heard the creatures make a sound, and it was a horrible one, something Ken had never heard before: a hissing of sand against sand, a clashing of stone blades, a clink of sharp edges colliding, tumbling over each other, grunting and grumbling like the gnashing of teeth.

If it could see us, he thought. *If it knew we were here...*

It seemed to take forever to slip away, past the far corner of the structure, away from that sound. A few yards further on, they felt the muddy pathway dip downwards, steadily downwards now, towards the water's edge.

They had arrived at the foothills of the Brothers. They could see its steep, denuded slope in front of them like a wall made of pounded earth and rock, rising from the churning water, butting up against the path and blocking the way.

This was their destination, but it didn't matter. They would have been forced to stop here anyway.

Rose's beautiful violet eyes widened when she saw the Brothers taking shape ahead of them, emerging from the twisting sheets of mist and rain. "Oh, shit," she said. "This was a terrible idea."

Ken was again reminded of that video game, *Half-Life.* You spent hours, *days,* climbing over wreckage, crawling though air ducts, finding weapons and fighting monsters at every level – always monsters, *more* monsters, each level more dangerous and revolting than the last. And then finally, at the end, you conquered the Big Bad and struggled to the surface, to the sunlight, to the long-awaited end of the adventure.

And what did you find?

He came to the answer too late. Far too late.

More monsters.

Thirty-five

The eighty-degree slope was utterly bare, unmarred by any tree or plant or bit of vegetation. The rain had cut a million rivulets into its muddy, pebbled surface and made it fundamentally unstable. The ground was shifting and sliding under the runoff like the breathing hide of some huge, water-soaked rhino.

The creatures of the storm were everywhere, scattered thickly across the steeply sloping terrain. Flat, shapeless stains writhed in the mud; flumes twisted through the air; clusters of candle-eyes shoved and thrust through the muck while dragontongues whipped their bony, fleshless bodies, wriggling between glistening boulders. All of them, and a thousand new creatures with no names, covered the Two Brothers from base to crown, from a few yards ahead of them to the curved horizon. And they were *busy*.

Some, like the candle-eyes, tumbled together in packs, as if muttering something secret but terribly important that only they could hear. Other creatures moved rapidly and with urgency, disappearing over the line of the hillside, stopping to confer silently with other shapes, pausing to dissolve into gritty piles, only to be swept up by a passing stain or tumbling hookweed. They were all in constant motion, but it was motion, Ken could see, with purpose. Not a purpose he could understand. Maybe that no human could understand.

Back in the *hacienda*, with all the paperwork and simulations and Lucy Armbruster's boundless, jaded enthusiasm, their plan had made perfect sense to Ken. Hell, it had seemed almost cute. Use the materials at hand, turn the power of the storm against itself, that sort of thing. But now, here, with the wind slapping him in the face, with rainwater forcing itself into his mouth and up his nose, with muddy runoff as thick as porridge burying his boots, and the entire lethal menagerie of the storm dancing and churning in front of him, all Ken could ask himself was, *What the hell was I thinking?*

Rose stood a few feet away. She looked grim and eager and terrified all at once, like a storm-tossed soldier about to enter her first real battle.

"Well?" she shouted at him through the gale. A wave of water slapped her in the face, and she shook her head angrily to clear her eyes. "Are we doing this or not?"

"You do see those things, don't you?" he asked her, nodding at the monsters ahead of them.

"Yeah, but they don't seem to see *us*. Haven't you noticed, Dad? These things don't care about us at all anymore, unless we go up and kick 'em in the nuts."

He shook his foot again. It was still tingling. "Or stick a boot up their ass. Yeah, I noticed."

Ken kept looking up the steep, glittering slope.

This is impossible. This is fucking –

"Dad! Stop it!"

He flinched and looked away from the hill. Rose was glaring at him, fuming. "Don't get all think-y on me now!" she shouted. "That's what you always do, you *overthink*. Sometimes you have to just fucking *do* things!"

There was a roll of thunder far to the south, deep and deliberate. Ken felt it in his chest as much as he heard it. It reminded him of The Plan all over again. He glanced downhill, back to the water line.

"Okay," he said. "You're right. We have to get – what the *fuck*?"

Rose tried to follow his eyes. She had to wipe away muddy water to do it. "What?"

"What's that?"

Rose rolled her eyes. "*God*, Dad, will you–"

"No, *really*, Rose. Look!"

She squinted through the chaos, downhill to the water's edge, and caught sight of a shiny black two-man rubber raft, thrown to the sodden shore by the storm. It was still inflated, still sporting the showroom gleam of a new purchase.

It looked as if it was waiting for them.

They picked their way carefully across the muddy, newborn shore line, Ken towing the pallet the last few feet and bringing it to ground as they reached the inflatable. Then, together, they stood over the raft and simply gawked.

It was filled with guns

"Thank you, Jesus," Rose gasped. Rain was pouring off her in a cataract.

Ken could see M-16s, Magnums, grenades. Even a rocket launcher. And boxes, clips, and bags of ammo, enough for a small war.

"Where the hell did this come from?"

"I have no idea," Rose said. "And I couldn't care less." She actually smiled as she bent to pick up an over-and-under pump shotgun.

"Careful with that," he said automatically.

She gave him The Look. "Seriously?" she said, and hefted the weapon like a pro. She expertly cracked it open and checked the breach for shells. "Locked and loaded," she said, and smiled brilliantly. "To coin a phrase."

Ken only frowned. *One more thing I don't want to know about.*

He was thirty-seven years old and had never in his life touched a real gun. His entire knowledge of firearms was developed by watching endless repeats of *Miami Vice* and playing *Grand Theft Auto*. He'd never even been a big fan of *Call of Duty*. Now he was sorry.

Rose patted the arm of his soaked parka, trying to be comforting. "Don't worry, Daddy," she said. "They make these things idiot-proof these days."

"Oh, thanks."

"You know what I mean." She slipped the shotgun's carrying strap up her arm and hefted another weapon – a strangely made handgun, something like a small shoebox with a handgrip on the bottom and a stubby barrel at one end. "Like this. This is a MAC 10. Even *you* can work it." Her hands flickered across it – popping the ammo clip, clearing the chamber, sighting and reloading – as if she'd done it a thousand times before.

"Rose," he said seriously, "you scare the shit out of me sometimes."

"It's a daughter's greatest dream," she said, and gave him the MAC, butt-first. "Safety's on," she told him, and showed him how it worked. "Be careful anyway."

Ken nodded, put it into the biggest side pocket of his parka, and zipped it shut.

The rumbling thunder was closer. Distant flashes of lightning pulsed in the lowering clouds, still far to the north. The light was beginning to fade; this would be the last progressive, north-to-south electrical storm before dark, like the hundreds that had come before it.

Time was running out.

They spent five minutes loading up on ordnance, then turned together and faced the slope.

"So how are we going to do this?" Rose asked, suddenly unsure.

"I have an idea." He'd thought of it as they'd loaded up, when he noticed that the smooth-bottomed rubber raft had a tow rope of its own, a loop, really, anchored in two places along its curved leading edge. Without a word of explanation he reached down, gathered up an armload of rebar from the pallet, and dumped it in the bottom of the raft. As he straightened, he saw Rose staring at him as if he was mad.

"We'll tow it," he said, his throat raw. "Like a—what do you call it? A travois."

She blinked for a second, and then understood. "Ah," she said, then bent and helped. They transferred all of the rebar from one platform to the other in a matter of moments, and as they did, he saw that he had remembered correctly: the rods came in three lengths, from six to roughly eleven feet, and all the same thickness, about the diameter of an index finger.

While they worked they kept an eye on the busy creatures a few yards away. They still hadn't noticed the humans at all.

When Rose and Ken finished their work, Rose hefted one of the longer rods and tested it in her hand, hefting like a javelin. "Just shove it in the ground?" she asked. "That's it?"

Another wave of rain, thick enough to choke on, passed overhead. They might as well have been on the deck of a ship in a hurricane. Ken ducked his head against the squall, then nodded through it as it crested. "That's it," he said. "Poke it down as deep as you can."

"Okay," Rose said. She took five steps straight uphill, the bar gripped in one hand.

"Rose, wait…"

She set her feet, hunched her shoulders, raised the rebar over his head and rammed it, hard she could, into the sodden earth. It penetrated a full foot. She turned back to him, grinning. "Like that?"

"Jesus, Rose. You are totally insane."

She nodded. "I know," she said. "I got that. I—"

She abruptly stopped, cocked her head curiously, and laid her naked palm flat against the mud. After a moment she turned her impossibly violet eyes on her father. She had a strange, wondering expression.

"You can feel it," she said. "Not just electricity. Not just the rain. You can feel *it,* that thing that's inside the hill." She pushed her fingers even deeper into the mud, overcome for a moment. "No. It's not inside the hill. It *is* the hill."

Ken didn't want to touch it. He didn't need to feel it thrumming in the earth. He already knew the truth, and it terrified him.

He started to speak, but Rose turned away from him, snatching her hand out of the mud and straightening up quickly. She lifted her head and looked uphill. The nearest creature, a multi-legged clot of stone covered in blunt horns, pointed its mouth like a jagged mineshaft and *crunched* at them.

Rose shook herself free. "Fuck that," she said. "Let's go."

* * *

Ken picked up a rod from the raft and plunged into the mud, half expecting the Earth to shudder at the impact or spew some blackish ichor from its new wound. But nothing happened. The iron bar simply stuck there, vibrating from the impact and shivering drops of rain.

Just your basic stick in the mud, he thought.

The ground shifted under his feet, but it wasn't a sign of some waking giant, it was simply the rushing water liquefying everything.

He had always assumed the hill they called Two Brothers was solid rock, covered with a few inches of windblown topsoil. That was why nothing would grow there; it was granite or gypsum underneath. Now he knew he was wrong.

It wasn't bedrock that formed its mass. It wasn't Earthly at all. Regular plants couldn't grow on Two Brothers because *nothing* could live there.

He pushed the thought away, glanced at his daughter, and trudged uphill ten steps, bending against the gale and the stinging rain. He pulled up another length of rebar and slammed it into the earth. Then he moved to the side, building a second row on the slope, and did it again.

"You go that way," he said, gesturing uphill in one direction. "I go this way!" He set another bar, shoved it deep, and still the creatures ignored them, hurrying about their duties, finishing their chores.

They paused at the end of a third row. Rose straightened up, unbent her back and ran her hand through her dripping hair. "Looks like Pinhead! she shouted. Ken frowned at her and cocked his head. She scowled. "*Hellraiser?*" she shouted. He shook his head again, he had no idea what she was talking about.

Rose grinned in spite of herself. "Idiot," she said under her breath. She knew he understood her; he could read her lips.

Look at her, Ken thought. *Just* look *at her. How did she get to be so amazing?*

He shook his head and went back to work himself. The next wave of the storm was approaching, rumbling over the water towards the center of the Valle. He turned just long enough to see lighting striking mid-town. It was coming this way.

He created two more rows, then three, climbing higher and higher. So did Rose. The wind started to scream. It was getting to be a routine. Painful and filthy, but mind-numbingly repetitive. Pick up the bar. Shove it in the ground. Check for creatures. Move on. And always he kept Rose in view, out of the corner of his eye.

They were more than halfway up the slope, panting like animals, when the attack began. Ken had lost count of the number of rows. He simply set his feet, lifted another bar from their makeshift travois, and rammed it down. This time the ground at his feet flinched and lifted up.

Ken jumped back, startled. The edges of a huge plate of tissue, an earthbound flume, or something like it, wriggled all around him. It had been lying on the waterlogged soil of the Two Brothers, covered in mud and splattered earth. Now it snapped a corner up and tried to snag Ken's leg as he leaped away.

The edge of it got under the cuff of his jeans, twitched past his sock, and touched his ankle with chemical fire, right where the biting sand had stung him before.

"SHIT!" he said, and jerked away. Suddenly Rose was by his side, the over-and-under out of its shoulder holster, already in her hands. She hunched down and fired without hesitation, pumping shots into the whickering, shuddering *thing* lying in front of them.

The sound of the rifle was harsh against the gurgling roar of the rain, but it worked. The flume crumpled under the impact, then tried to lurch away. Rose wouldn't accept that. She took two heavy steps forward and fired again and again, until the thing stopped moving. Then stopped trembling. Then dissolved into the mud. Whatever remained was buried under the next flow of mud in mere seconds.

Ken barely noticed. It felt like his foot was burning off.

As soon as she was sure the thing was dead, Rose staggered to his side and stood over him as he sat in the mud and frantically stripped off his boot and sock. The water rushed against his bare flesh, and that felt good, *wonderfully* good. He could see the skin was an angry scarlet and already beginning to show lemon-yellow welts.

"Can you get up?" Rose asked, looking in every direction for more attackers.

"Have to," he said between gritted teeth. "Give me a minute."

"Haven't got it," she said.

He glared up at her. "For chrissakes, Rosie—"

"*Dad!*" she said and gestured past him. "They're *coming.*"

He looked past her, towards the edge of the slope. The creatures had stopped working now. They were turning towards them. Others were gathering downhill at the shoreline, so close together they were fighting for space.

Rose and Ken had finally been noticed. Now all the creatures, every shape and size, were climbing and crawling and lurching to meet them.

Ken forced himself to his feet. He grabbed the next rebar and slammed it in the ground. Rose pulled out a semi-automatic rifle, one he hadn't even noticed, and picked a spot in front of him, midway between the creatures and the travois. She poured gunfire into the monsters, her whole body vibrating from the weapon's kick.

They were coming in waves, from small to large. Maybe the little ones could move faster; maybe the Intelligence behind it all saw them as more expendable because they could be regrown more quickly. Ken didn't know. Didn't care. He just wanted to set the last of the bars higher and higher. He wanted to reach the top of the hill and *kill* this fucking thing.

First the pumpkin-sized needleseeds in front exploded into a million sharp pieces from Rose's assault. The flinders made from their death struck the rolling set of turnbuckles close behind them, and caused them to falter and swerve. That gave Rose all the time she needed to blow the turnbuckles to pieces as well, then the set of brickteeth that hobbled behind them.

Ken limped forward to complete another row, and another. He tried to ignore the constant chatter of Rose's gunfire, and the burning agony in his ankle, foot, leg.

The lightning was striking the South Side now. They could see the ghost of it behind the rain, jagged bolts arcing from clouds to broken buildings, to crippled towers, to open water. Thunder followed the flashes, coming sooner behind each strike.

Rose's semi-automatic seized up with a raucous *clacking.* She threw it aside, unlimbered the over-and-under, and expertly cut the bottom out from under a star-shaped rock-pig-thing that was trundling towards them. It dived into the mud and tripped up a thornwheel that was too close behind.

She fired until there were no more shotgun shells. Then she dropped the weapon in the mud and pulled out a Magnum .357 she had thrust inside her shirt.

Ken finished another row. His back was screaming, his hands were bleeding from the roughened metal, but he bit down on the pain and he pulled the travois higher. More than two-thirds of the bars were gone, but the top seemed farther away than ever.

He felt, more than heard, the first lightning strikes hit the edge of the VeriSil campus, a half mile to the north. *The Plan,* he told himself as his daughter backed up the hill, close behind. *The fucking Plan.*

His leg was burning worse than ever. When he started on the next row it collapsed under him like a broken branch, failing completely. He cursed as he fell to one knee and used a length of rebar to pull himself upright. He balanced precariously on the makeshift crutch and set the newest rod and lurched to set another one, five yards uphill.

Lightning was playing along the far end of the VeriSil campus now. Thunder, like bomb blasts, pushed at them over and over and the rain was a continuous, choking silver wall.

Rose blew the tail off a dragontongue, then put another round into its whickering rose-head. It fell heavily at her feet and she shoved a boot into it, breaking it in three more places.

They wouldn't stop coming. Ken could see that. They would never stop coming.

Five bars left, and he wasn't near the summit. He had horribly underestimated what he'd needed, or he'd set them too close together, or the whole fucking idea was absurd, he just didn't know. Ken was only half-conscious now, hearing only the thunder and the gunshots, feeling only the rain.

It'll work, it'll work, it HAS to work.

He shoved in the last two. The last *one*. He turned, balancing on one leg, as three lightning strikes hit the middle of the VeriSil headquarters beyond the base of the Brothers. The bolts lit up the land with a ghostly, actinic light. The concussion pounded through him in waves.

"ROSE!" he bellowed. "I'M DONE! WE CAN—"

An arm as thick as a girder flew out of the mist and caught Rose directly in the stomach. It threw her back, towards her father, and Ken had to lurch to the side to avoid her as she flew past him and landed flat on her back, twenty feet farther uphill, with an ugly, meaty *thwack*.

He rushed to her side, staggering through knee-deep muck. Her arms were thrown out at her sides, her face was pointing into the rain, still as white as ivory despite the filth around her.

White and red. Red on her lips, pouring from her nose.

She's bleeding. My little girl. My little girl.

Suddenly the whole ridiculous nightmare – the monsters, the storm, the talking house, everything – was real to him, maybe for the first time. It wasn't a dream. It wasn't a joke. His baby girl was hurt, and any second, any instant, she could die.

She could die.

He threw himself up to his feet and stood over her, chalk-white against the black earth, illuminated by the overlapping lightning strikes. Lightning had reached the first of the rebar at the bottom of the hill, farther south than it had ever come before, drawn by the raw iron reaching up into the air in a forest of lightning rods. Not close enough yet, but it was happening. He had been right.

That was The Plan, he told himself as he knelt beside Rose. *All along.*

He looked up, towards the crest of the Brothers, at the monster that had hurt his little girl.

A bone spider, one million legs twitching and clawing at the open air, stood there. It was fifteen feet taller than he was, lifting its arms to cut them both to bits.

Ken pawed at the right pocket of his parka, ripped open the zipper and pulled out the MAC-10 that Rose had forced on him. As it brought it up, his daughter's face turned to him and she opened her eyes.

Those eyes, he thought wildly. *Those beautiful eyes.*

She smiled at him.

He looked away as he straightened up and aimed the gun. He had never fired a weapon before in his life. He didn't believe for a second that it would stop this huge creature or save the day, but he had to do it.

He took a step forward, his burning leg forgotten. "FUCK YOU!" he bellowed. "*FUCK* YOU, *FUCK YOU!*" He pulled the trigger as the talons came down, firing over and over again, not even sure he was hitting the creature —

– and the bone spider lifted into the air.

Ken kept firing at it until he ran out of ammo. Then he just stood there, gun still up in front of him, as the massive creature rose even higher, legs flailing and dangling, and for one crazy moment he thought it was doing it on its own, that it had somehow acquired the power of flight. Until he saw the churning black mass underneath it, almost invisible against the storm, that was rising out of the earth at the crest of the hill.

It looked a little like the writhing, faceless mass inside the construction site, but it was much more than that. Striations of stone twitched inside it as it rose even higher, glistening in the downpour. Tumors of stone rolled and bubbled in its gritty tissue. Edges emerged and cut furrows in its surface, bleeding a thick black mud of its own, then closed to make new wounds.

The bone spider that had been forced into the air tried to cling to the surface as it rose. Then it collapsed in on itself and was reabsorbed into the column as it thickened and continued to rise, an obscene crown of... *something*...emerging from the hill itself.

No, he thought, as Rose sat up beside him, awake but dazed. *No, not emerging. Being built. Being exposed.* It was like seeing a naked limb of a living creature with its skin peeled away. The musculature, the veins, still pulsing and moving, but laid bare.

It was *wrong*. It was not supposed to be like this. It was *wounded*.

The tower twisted, almost bent as another triple-thump of lightning struck halfway up the hill now. Bolts of electricity were traveling between the lightning rods now, pulling the energy farther up the hill, coaxing the lightning to strike again. Rose and Ken were barely a dozen feet from the last few rods, even closer than the rumbling, turning mass of the thing at the top of the hill.

Rose hunched her shoulders and grunted like an old woman as she pulled herself to her feet, swaying in the wind and rain. A wave of relief ran through Ken for an instant. She was whole. The blood on her mouth washed away in another wave of raindrops, and he saw it was a nosebleed caused by the force of her landing.

Lighting SLAMMED and SLAMMED in the flood-lake below them, a last explosive volley, coming closer and closer. It hit the construction site. Hit the base of the hills. Hit the first few rods, and with each strike thunder bellowed, faster and louder with each explosion.

Ken whipped around, *The Plan* huge in his mind. "We gotta go!" he shouted. "NOW!" He turned and threw himself uphill, straight towards the towering monster, towards the top of the Two Brothers, dragging Rose by one arm and forcing her to follow. He was over the top in an instant, ignoring the agony in his burning leg.

They crested the hill less than ten feet from the exposed and twisting column of the Intelligence. It had risen fifty feet in the air already and was still growing.

It would reach a hundred feet in moments as the sodden earth around it churned and cracked like breaking skin.

In ten steps Rose and Ken were over the top of the hill and running down the far side, towards the southern ridge of the crater beyond.

"RUN!" he said. "DOWN, DOWN, GET OFF THE MOUNTAIN, *RUN!*"

He hurtled downhill in long dangerous strides that risked his legs flying out from under him at any moment. He could feel the lightning striking behind him, climbing up the hill, roaring as if it was angry at being lured so far. He imagined he could see it: lightning drawn to the iron bars, then leaping from spike to spike, iron sucking electricity right out of the sky, flowing into the ground beneath him and torturing the inhuman Intelligence that lived there. *Killing* it. He heard another strike, and another and *another*.

The ground bucked under them, flexing like a living thing.

They heard a sound that had never been made on Earth before, a groaning, roaring, bottomless, voiceless BOOM that filled the audible spectrum and blew beyond it.

There was a deep arroyo directly in front of them, a crack in the earth between the Brothers and the crater ridge behind it. It was so deep they couldn't see the bottom even as they sprinted towards it. The far side was a dim blur through the rain. The gap between the hillside and the ridge was no more than ten feet wide at the top, Ken could see that much. One leap and they would be on the far side, on the crater ridge, away from The Brothers. It was no wider than that leap from the rock to the tree in front of his house. But, God, they were tired, and they were wet, and his leg was burning so badly, and the ground was unsteady and sticky.

We have to jump. I can't jump. We'll miss it. We'll fall. We have to jump. We can't…

They didn't pause. They didn't falter. They ran side-by-side as the lightning reached the top of the hill, right behind them. They threw themselves into the air together.

The lightning hit the twisting tower of the Intelligence itself, and the world exploded.

THIRTY-SIX

Sunrise came six hours later. As it approached, the rain fell back for the first time in days. Ken could see gaps in the clouds by three a.m. By five, the last of the rain whispered away, and the world grew quiet, almost silent. It was so beautiful to hear – to *not* hear – it took Ken's breath away.

They peeled off their soggy, ruined parkas, laid them out on the rocks to dry, and sat close together on the top of the South Ridge to watch the sun come up off to their left. A fresh breeze plucked at their ragged, dirty clothes as the morning light revealed a sky that was desert-hard, flat blue, and uninterrupted by clouds. The desert below them, to the south of Dos Hermanos, was as dry, unpopulated and immense as it had ever been. As it had always been. Lucy's theories about the mountain shadow effect and the microclimate had been correct. As far the Anza-Borrego Desert, and the rest of the world, was concerned, the last three days in DH had never happened.

When it was bright enough, Ken stood up and turned to Rose. "Want to see?" he asked. They were the first words he had spoken in hours, and they sounded oddly distant and small even in his own ears. He knew why. The explosion had made them both half-deaf, and they were only beginning to recover.

Still close together, they mounted the ridgeline, picking carefully through the shattered stone. Rose's clothes were stiff with mud. Her jeans looked as if they had been put through a shredder. Ken looked slightly ridiculous with one shoe on, one foot bare, and the leg of his jeans torn open to the knee. He was thankful that at least the swelling had gone down. The wound from the monster was more like a chemical burn than an infection, and though it itched furiously it had not progressed beyond mid-calf. He knew he wouldn't die from it, not at the moment, anyway. But he did think about the rock-like infection that had transformed Daniel Steinberg, and the notes and video he'd seen from the mad scientist's NEW TAXONOMY.

Is this how it begins, he wondered, resisting the urge to touch his wound. *Could this happen to me?*

At least Rose would be okay. She had escaped with nothing more than a light scratch along one cheek, and that wasn't from a creature of the storm, it was from her last fall in the mud. She had joked earlier that she didn't want it treated. It would make a really cool scar, she said. She could dine out on horror stories about it for months.

Ken hadn't seen the humor.

They reached the ridgetop and looked down into the Valle de los Hermanos. Even inside the crater, the last of the thunderheads were tearing themselves to shreds and disappearing. By noon, they would be gone. Whatever combination of forces had brought the storm to Dos Hermanos had faltered now. It might not rain again in the crater for another five hundred years.

The hill they called The Two Brothers was changed. A new pit, obsidian-black and too deep to fathom, took up most of the summit, a smoking crater within a crater, as if twenty sticks of dynamite had been used to blow it away. Below that, beyond that, the rest of the Valle was a restless, muddy lake that filled the vast bowl of Dos Hermanos all the way to the jagged line of the North Ridge. Its fractal surface, dove-gray in the new morning light, was pock-marked with debris and half-submerged wreckage.

There were no people. Anywhere.

The water level of the lake had not dropped an inch since last night. It was effectively sealed inside the crater, and it was staying there. Ken tried to remember how many generations the Salton Sea had survived since its creation, not all that far from here, despite the desert winds and heat. He wondered how long this new formation might last.

Not that it mattered, he realized with a sudden chill. Nobody was coming back anyway.

Because the monsters were still there.

Even from the top of the ridge, they were visible everywhere, swarming along the water's edge and humping under the muddy surface of the lake. Ken could see them all: a set of brickteeth fighting with a caisson of thornwheels; a dragontongue flailing out of the water as a drift of hookweeds rolled by and settled down for a long, *long* drink. Two bone spiders, directly below them, were fighting over nothing at all, claw and talons flashing in the watery morning sunlight.

There was something different now. In the last few days, they had moved with relentless purpose, with an eerie and deadly efficiency. Now they …wandered. They fought whatever they happened to encounter, and then moved on. There was still frightening power, but no purpose. No intelligence.

Ken had hoped – hell, he admitted to himself, he had *prayed* – that the destruction of the thing inside The Brothers would cause the creatures of the storm to simply collapse in place and die, as much as things like this could 'die' at all. Vampires hit by the sun. Puppets with cut strings.

No such luck. He had been right all along. They were more like robots with damaged programs, but they were still energized by…whatever it was that energized them. Still moving, but aimless now. Lost.

Lost but still horribly dangerous.

Rose had been very quiet since the sun had started to rise. Now she blinked suddenly, as if in surprise, and put her hand to her breast. She unbuttoned her coat and reached inside, searching and searching … then pulled out a white box, so clean in the midst of all the mud that it shimmered in the morning light.

"What's that?" Ken said.

"A gift from a friend," she said, and smiled. "Looks like it's okay, too. I was afraid I'd broken it." She held it up and showed it to her dad. "Maggie," she said.

His mouth dropped open. Then he turned it into a grin. "Well, I'll be a son of a bitch," he said.

"Oh, I think you've been there, done that," Rose said solemnly. "But here, she wanted you to have it."

As he took it, she popped open another buttoned pocket and pulled out a sheet of paper folded in quarters. "This, too," she said, and handed it over.

Ken frowned in puzzlement and scanned the single page. Then he sat down on a stone as big as a steamer trunk and read it again, this time much more slowly. Finally he nodded and handed the paper back to Rose. She smoothed it on her knee and read:

Ken:
Thank you.
- Maggie
…and below that:

Don't worry about saving these songs!
And if one of our instruments breaks,
It doesn't matter.

We have fallen into the place
Where everything is music.

The strumming and the flute notes
Rise into the atmosphere,
And even if the whole world's harp
Should burn up, there will still be
Hidden instruments playing.

So the candle flickers and goes out.
We have a piece of flint, and a spark.

Stop the words now.
Open the window in the center of your chest,
And let the spirit fly in and out.

"That's beautiful," Rose said.

"A poet named Rumi," Ken said quietly. "I don't know …" He looked up and out into the misty blues and magentas of the new sky and shook his head. "I just don't know," he said.

There was a deep, rhythmic *thud-thud-thud* above and behind them. They turned together, their backs to the Valle, and mounted the ridgetop. Rose was the first to find the moving black dot as it circled towards them.

It was a helicopter – a *big* one. They shouted until they were hoarse, jumped and waved, even Ken, on his wounded leg. The chopper altered course sharply as soon as it saw them and came closer.

"What do you know," Rose said into his ear. "We made it." He turned his head to look at her, and so much welled up in him, so many emotions…

He didn't think he could talk at the moment, so he just nodded.

"You think Mom is okay?" Rose asked. "I've been thinking about her all night."

"We'll have to see," Ken said, trying to be comforting, terrified of the truth. "I hope so."

The chopper was closer now. They could see the USMC logo on its side. It didn't look real to Rose. How could it?

"So what happens next?" she asked.

He looked at the chopper, then looked back over his shoulder at the glittering new lake and the bone-colored creatures that danced and battled on its shore. He felt the sharp corners of the hard drive in his pocket, and the pressure of his daughter's hand on his back. He shrugged.

"That," he said, "is a very good question."

THE END

ABOUT THE AUTHOR

Brad Munson is a writer, editor, screenwriter and marketer living in Southern California until they politely ask him to leave, which could be any time now.

For news, new releases, bonus material and more, visit www.bradmunson.com.

CPSIA information can be obtained at www.ICGtesting.com
Printed in the USA
LVOW08s1533110815

449682LV00002B/261/P